PRAISE FOR THE CAPTA

IMPURE BLOOD: U.S. Library Association's Pick of the Month

"Engrossing...An auspicious début" – Publishers Weekly

"Great plot, appealing hero, glorious setting plus taut writing – a real winner" – Martin Walker, bestselling author of the Bruno Courrèges novels

"Impressive... will delight fans of international crime" – Booklist

"A vibrant, satisfying read" – The Crime Review

FATAL MUSIC: One of *Strand Magazine's* Top 25 Books of 2017

"A thoroughly satisfying novel... Morfoot brilliantly captures the sights, smells and attitudes of southern France as well as giving us an engaging hero" – Mike Ripley, Shots eZine 5 Picks of 2017

"Pulls you along like an iron bar to a magnet. Crime and mystery readers will consume every last morsel of this book." – David Cranmer, Criminal Element Magazine

"Deftly interwoven plot lines... vividly captured Riviera setting... This strikingly well-written crime novel should appeal strongly to many." – Bruce Crowther, Jazz Journal

BOX OF BONES:

"An accomplished piece of crime fiction. Captain Paul Darac... has become, without doubt, my favourite foreign detective created by a Brit since the late Michael Dibdin gave us Aurelio Zen." – Mike Ripley – Shots eZine, 5 Picks of 2018

"The plot, filled with enough twists and turns for a corkscrew, is intriguing while never losing touch with either reality or humanity." – Crime Review

"Darac leads an engaging and distinctive team of officers, all of whom grow as the reader learns more about them. Not only are the good guys well drawn, but so too are the bad guys and the plot is intriguing and filled with many twists and turns." – Bruce Crowther, Jazz Journal

KNOCK 'EM DEAD:

"Pin sharp...A winner from page one"
– Dagger-winning author Jim Kelly

Peter Morfoot's policiers featuring jazz-loving Captain Paul Darac of Nice's Brigade Criminelle comprise one of the best crime series I have discovered in the last ten years. The fourth instalment, Knock 'Em Dead, is published by Galileo, and delivers on all fronts.
– Mike Ripley: *Shots Magazine.*

Captain Darac Mysteries

FATAL MUSIC

A Captain Darac Mystery

PETER MORFOOT

Galileo Publishers, Cambridge

Galileo Publishers
16 Woodlands Road
Great Shelford Cambridge
CB22 5LW UK

www.galileopublishing.co.uk

Distributed in the USA by:
SCB Distributors
15608 S. New Century Drive
Gardena, CA 90248-2129

ISBN 978-1-912916-69-6
First published in the UK by Titan Books 2017
This new Galileo Edition © 2022 Peter Morfoot

2nd print 2022

Printed in the EU

DARAC MYSTERY SERIES BY PETER MORFOOT
AUTHOR'S NOTE

When I began devising what became the Captain Darac Mystery series, I knew what I *didn't* want for my central character. To be authentic, any character needs flaws but I determined Darac would not be a slave to his. I determined he would not always make the right moves in an investigation; nor would he solve cases over a chat in a bar.

I conceived him as a strong-minded individual but, attesting to the essentially collaborative nature of police work, I needed him to be a whole-hearted team player, also; an interesting dynamic and one that gave me the pleasurable task of creating a permanent cast of supporting players for him. This led to Darac's genesis as a "*poète policier*," a term derived from a resonant assertion by award-winning writer and, to Anglicise his rank, chief superintendent of police, Philippe Pichon: "A poet can be a policeman and a policeman can be a poet." But which art form for Darac? I felt that jazz with its tension between structure and improvisation would give me the most relevant and interesting possibilities.

The setting for the series? With its vibrant light, the spectacular Alpe Maritime mountains at its back and that celebrated azure coastline at its feet, Nice is as beautiful as any Mediterranean resort. But it's also a multi-ethnic city of almost half a million souls. And are there serpents in this particular paradise? Ask Darac, Commissaire Agnès Dantier and the other officers of Nice's Brigade Criminelle.

A senior police officer who also plays jazz in a high-quality group, a significant player therefore in two different sorts of team, was someone I was looking forward to getting to putting through his paces on the page. Unlike some of his fictional counterparts, Darac is a character drawn to living not so much on the edge as on the borderline; a man who chooses to position himself at points of connection or collision with the world. And in the five novels of the Darac Mystery series thus far, he has encountered plenty of both.

CORE CHARACTER LIST

The Brigade Criminelle of Nice

Agnès Dantier: Commissaire
Paul Darac: Captain
Roland Granot: Lieutenant
Alejo 'Bonbon' Busquet: Lieutenant
Christian Malraux: Lieutenant Intern

Yvonne Flaco: Officer
Max Perand: Officer

Francine 'Frankie' Lejeune: Captain, Vice Squad.
Jean-Pierre 'Armani' Tardelli: Captain, Narcotics Squad

Forensics
Raul 'R.O.' Ormans: Senior Forensic Analyst
Erica Lamarthe: Principal Technician

Pathology
Deanna Bianchi: Chief Pathologist
Carl Barrau: Deputy Chief Pathologist
Djibril 'Map' Mpensa: Pathologist

Lami Toto: Technician
Patricia Lebrun: Technician

Other Officers
Jean-Jacques 'Lartou' Lartigue: Crime Scene Co-ordinator
Serge Paulin: Beat officer
Alain Charvet: Duty officer
Sabrina Fabre: Interview Recorder

Judiciary
Jules Frènes: Public Prosecutor
Albert Reboux: Examining Magistrate

At The Blue Devil Jazz Club
Eldridge 'Ridge' Clay: club owner
Pascal Malata: doorman
Khara Oliveira: waitress
Roger Oliveira: chef

The Didier Musso Quintet*
Didier Musso: piano and bandleader
Marco Portami: drums and director of JAMCA youth jazz
        orchestra
Rama N'Pata: deputising for Marco
Luc Gabron: bass
Paul Darac: guitar
Dave Blackstock: tenor sax
Trudi 'Charlie' Pachelberg: alto sax
Jacques Quille: trumpet

* It's something of a running gag at the club that Didier Musso's group of high-quality local musicians is always billed as the Didier Musso Quintet irrespective of the number of players on board at any particular time.

For Liz

1.

Jeanne Mesnel loved her hot tub. It was such a wondrous thing, it amused her to recall how sceptical she had been at first. Well, how could 'those jaunty, jet-propelled bubbles' soothe *and* invigorate? But when she tried it, Jeanne could no more have resisted the effect than a sugar cube resist hot coffee. The girl had been right about that.

And relaxing in roiling heat brought other pleasures.

She was beguiled by the way spindrifting steam transformed the look of things: blurring her bougainvillea into swathes of magenta silk; smudging the back wall of her villa into dabs of pink and blue. It was like sitting in the middle of an Impressionist sunset, especially on a cold day like today.

Nothing was perfect, of course. The thing did take up most of the lower patio. But if its looking out of place offended visitors, well, screw them.

Taking another sip of champagne spawned an idea. Why not throw a hot-tub party? It could seat four comfortably. Six at a squeeze. She smiled. Wouldn't Alain have loved this?

Jeanne no longer enjoyed the robust health she had once taken for granted. At times, she could hardly get her breath; the increasing stiffness of her joints was a nuisance; and most irritating of all, her hearing was starting to fail. But it wasn't all bad news. She had no liver spots, or that Roquefort-legged look she sometimes saw among her peers down on the beach. Hats off, anyway, to the varicose bathers of Beaulieu-sur-Mer. They were just as entitled to disport themselves in their dotage as they had been in their sleek and slinky youth.

She pressed the play button on the tub's built-in music console and closed her eyes. Swirling her legs in time with the languid beat of the music, it occurred to her that the only pity was that she hadn't acquired the hot tub years before. She disowned the thought instantly. What *should* have happened was irrelevant.

A voice called to her through the spindrift.

'Come and join me,' she called back. 'And bring a glass.'

2

In summer, you could fry crêpes on the pavement outside the Blue Devil Jazz Club. A cold Thursday night in early January was a different story. Sucking resentfully on a Gauloise, Pascal the doorman was trying to stamp some heat into his feet when a strongly built man carrying a guitar case appeared on his blindside.

'They always said smoking kills, Pas.'

'They were right. I could freeze to death out here.'

The men exchanged kisses of greeting.

'Much of a crowd in?'

'How many in the band?'

'Four, tonight.'

'They've got you outnumbered, anyway.'

Captain Paul Darac's broad-boned face broke into a grin. 'See you later.'

Pascal pulled the lapels of his jacket together. 'If I live that long.'

Darac headed down the steps, gingerly flexing his left hand. The culprit wasn't the cold; it was a brick wall. You weren't supposed to punch them, apparently. The hand was healing well but fingers slowed by stiffness and swelling wasn't what he needed tonight. Playing guitar in the Didier Musso Quintet was a challenge as it was.

Framed posters lined the walls flanking the steps. But on the lintel over the scruffy, red-painted entrance doors themselves, there was just one. Darac was in the habit of reaching up and touching it as he passed underneath. Tonight, he felt the need to linger.

The focal point of the poster was a photograph that captured the atmosphere of a live gig so completely, Darac could practically taste it. On the bandstand, the bass player: solemn, monumental, a solitary bead of sweat about to drop from his brow. Behind him, the drummer: an explosion of energy, sticks fanning blurred arcs around the kit. Facing the band, rows of spectators, nearly all of them smoking. And one woman in particular: strong, sloe-eyed, superb. And here was the master stroke: the photographer had captured the moment a plume of smoke from her nostrils dispersed as it met the onrush of air from the band's front line. Later captioned *Blown Away by the Brass Section*, the photo had been taken at the Blue Devil in 1963 and had set the tone for the place ever since. A snapshot of a different world.

Up top, Pascal gave a knowing smile. 'We're going to put a shelf under that poster,' he called out. 'Somewhere for the holy water.'

'You've got to believe in something, Pas.'

Darac's gaze settled on the sloe-eyed woman. As a young guitarist, he would often picture her as he played. Over time, she had become something of an absent muse but he knew she would never fully leave him. Reaching up, he ran a tender finger over the poster and continued into the lobby.

A handwritten card reading *Box Office* sat on a folding table just inside the doors. On it, a stack of CDs entitled *At The Blue Devil Again* by the Didier Musso Quintet vied for prominence with a reel of tickets and a biscuit tin for takings. The reel was plump; the takings thin. Behind the table, venerable club owner Eldridge Clay was doing his best to stay square on Pascal's usual perch, a skinny drum stool. The impression that he was squatting in mid-air at odds with the gravity of his mien, Ridge looked up from the newspaper he was reading, slipped off his glasses and clasped Darac's good hand.

'So we made 2010. What's this new decade going to bring, Garfield?' he said, using his pet name for Darac. The voice was deep; the accent six thousand kilometres from home. 'More of *this*?' Straightening the paper, Ridge put his glasses back on, their thin wire frames looking wrong on his large, statesmanlike head. 'Listen:

It's now two years almost to the day since the government saw fit to sanitise our cafés, bars, restaurants and clubs by imposing a ban on smoking. But in taking a scrubbing brush to the rich patina of French life – and especially to the musky underbelly of its demi-monde – politicians have done more than remove a layer of grime; they have removed a layer of our national identity. Our beloved Gauloises are now made exclusively in Spain. Other atrocities will follow. Indeed, I fear that soon, there will be little left in our country that is truly French.'

Ridge fixed Darac with the kind of look judges favoured when passing sentence. 'Well?'

'I've just been thinking about this sort of thing, myself.'

'Back home we say, "If it ain't broke, don't fix it." But if it is, I'm all for change. Look at my marriage. Or take you and Angeline. You wouldn't wind the clock back, right?'

Darac wouldn't wind it back to the end part. It was six months since she had left him. At times, he felt her loss as acutely as pain from an amputated limb.

'No,' he said.

'Exactly. I tell you, France is cleaner than Switzerland now.'

'It's wrong. Khara in the bar?'

Ridge went back to his paper. 'Kitchen.'

Darac found the club's Senegalese waitress scattering a white powder cordon around the food preparation table.

'How's it going?' he said, struck by the grace with which Khara performed even this most unglamorous of tasks.

'For me, fine. The rats? So-so.'

'You should just let them eat Roger's steak tartare.'

'This is cheaper.' She binned the canister and exchanged kisses with Darac. 'Let's look at your hand.' She examined his red, swollen knuckles. 'You have been using the lotion I gave you?'

'Yes.' He smiled, then winced slightly as he flexed his fingers.

'See?'

Khara narrowed her eyes, the look accentuating the diamond-cut angularity of her face. 'Have you?'

'No.'

'Darac!'

'But I've brought it with me.'

'Then go apply it.' She turned his shoulders in the direction of the open archway behind him. Darac had the build of a light-heavyweight boxer but under the pressure of Khara's fine, tapering fingers, his torso swivelled as freely as a weathervane.

'Do you push Roger around like this?'

'Yes!' boomed a voice from the cellar. 'And I heard that about my steak tartare.'

Darac shared a look with Khara and headed for the archway. A medley of sour smells assailed his nostrils as he climbed the stairs to the first floor: drains, damp plasterwork, and more subtly, an undernote of ink, a legacy of the club's former existence as a printing works. It was all balm to Darac. After the blood, sweat and tears of the past few weeks, he needed the release the gig would provide. But one step at a time. He wasn't certain he would make it through the opening number.

The quintet's pianist and bandleader, Didier Musso, swept on to the landing above. His boyish quiff nodding on the off-beat, he began descending the steps two at a time.

'If you were thinking of checking out the audience, Didi, there isn't one.'

'It'll pick up.' They exchanged greeting kisses. 'How's the hand?'

'No problem.'

'Excellent.' Didier's soft-featured face crumpled. 'Is it my imagination or is the drain stink worse than ever?'

'Careful, that's one of the "valuable layers of the patina of French life" you're talking about.'

'What am I thinking?' Didier continued on his way.

'Oh, Marco's sub is upstairs,' he called over his shoulder. 'Half man, half giant spider, he is. But wearing an orange dashiki.'

'If I'd known, I would've worn mine.'

Darac was looking forward to meeting Marco's latest protégé, one of hundreds of students the drummer had mentored through JAMCA, the region's young musicians programme. This one, though, Marco said, was special. Swishing through the streamer curtains that served as a doorway into the shabby, sparsely furnished dressing room, Darac found the starlet occupying the lowest perch in the room: the driver's seat from an old Citroën 2CV.

'Hey. I'm Darac.'

Beaming through beaded braids, the young man unpacked his impossibly long, stick-thin legs and stood. 'Rama N'Pata.' Skin dark as black bamboo and milk-white teeth combined to dazzling effect. They shook hands. 'I'm in for Marco for the next few gigs.'

The young man's appearance was so joyously extreme, it made Darac smile. 'Marco's told us about your work with JAMCA, though he doesn't call you Rama.'

'I'm Stretch to him. Most of the kids in the band call me Beanpole or Bones.' He grinned again. 'And they are the polite ones.'

'*That's* why you're so miserable.' Darac put down his case. 'This your first pro gig?'

'I can't believe it. Being paid to play? Wow!'

'Yeah, you'll be a millionaire after tonight.'

Despite the depth of Rama's voice, his laugh was a high-pitched *tee-hee*.

'How come Marco's never invited you to the club?'

'I only moved here a couple of months ago. Still settling in.'

'Ah.' Darac reached into his jacket and fished out a handwritten note headed *Set list, Jan 8*. 'So what's after JAMCA? The Conservatoire?' Darac's voice dropped to a monotone as he deciphered his scrawl. 'Quite a few of Marco's kids have made it on to the jazz course over the years.' He looked up. 'Including Didier, but don't be put off.'

More *tee-hee*ing. 'No, we talked about it but I decided I needed to get a job. It's cool.'

'OK.' Darac brandished the set list. 'Pretty challenging. Got it down?'

'Marco's been over and over the charts with me.'

The quintet's bass player, Luc Gabron, emerged from the toilet with a fat spliff sticking out of his bearded face.

'Just keep your eyes on Didier for the changes,' he said, blowing smoke. 'And on me for spiritual guidance.

A sign reading fire hazard – no smoking was nailed to the wall over the sink. Darac gave it a meaningful glance.

'I know, I know.' Luc took a deep toke. 'But you know what today is? More or less. It's the anniversary of the ban. Want a hit? For old times' sake?'

Darac flicked open the locks on his guitar case. 'Pass.'

Luc examined the guitarist's knuckles. 'Sure? For happy joints nothing beats a joint.'

Darac opened a compartment in the case and took out a small bottle. 'I've got this.'

Luc peered at the label. 'Witch... hazel. *Witch* – that's one of the better hazels, they tell me. Still useless.'

Drinking it all in, Rama was looking on like a star-struck fan.

Luc turned to him. 'How old are you, Stretch?'

'Eighteen. Just.'

'And are you as hot as Marco says?'

The young man's smile could have lit up a small town. 'It's down to him.' He declined a hit. 'From videos to Skype lessons and now in person, Marco's taught me everything I know about playing drums.'

'But has he taught you everything *he* knows?'

Luc bantered on with Rama as Darac released his guitar from its blue velvet cocoon and began his warm-up. Perversely for a player who loved to improvise, the routine never changed. Once in tune, he opened with a series of single note runs, followed that with a set pattern of chord changes, and then finished off with a chorus of 'Limehouse Blues' in the style of one of his heroes, Django Reinhardt.

The warm-up didn't go well. But Darac had touched the talisman poster for luck; he'd greeted Ridge and kissed Khara. What could possibly go wrong?

Didier Musso's band was billed as a quintet however many players were on board at any particular time. But whether going out as a trio or a big band, one thing remained constant: Thursday was their night at the Blue Devil and had been for the past six years. With players signing up on a gig-by-gig basis, the quality of the performances inevitably varied. But on its best nights, the DMQ was as compelling as any jazz group in France.

The audience had filled out considerably by the time the guys took the stand. Despite Darac's injured hand, a debutant drummer, and nostalgia for the old smoke-filled club uppermost in everyone's minds, the band hit its straps from the first downbeat, and continued hitting them. Running into the set break with the stampede in six-eight time that was Charlie Mingus's 'Better Git It In Your Soul' proved a joyous experience; all the more joyous for the drive and snap of Rama N'Pata's drumming. Marco hadn't exaggerated. The kid was a phenomenon.

A crate of their favourite Leffe Blonde beer was waiting for the band when they returned to the dressing room at the interval. Luc opened three bottles as Darac fished Khara's lotion out of his case and went to the sink.

From the unfavoured 2CV seat – genius or not, the youngster knew his place – Rama watched Darac massaging the fluid into his knuckles. 'You haven't got... what do they call it... tendonitis?' He began rippling his sticks on the sides of his boot heels in a series of perfect double paradiddles. 'Marco has had that.'

'My hand? No, it just got in the way of something. But here's a question for you, Stretch. Where were you living before?'

'Nantes. Why?'

'And are you here legally? In France, I mean.'

As if a switch had been thrown, the young man froze. 'Yes I am. *And* I pay my taxes.'

Darac turned, smiling. 'I'm glad.' He flexed his hand. 'Because we've lost good people to that shit before.'

'True.' Luc fired up a spliff. 'A couple of times.'

Rama's sticks resumed their utterly precise rhythm. 'Oh. Sorry I misunderstood, guys. But you know how it can be.'

'We know.' Darac joined Didier and Luc. The three of them raised their bottles. 'Rama, here's to you, man,' Didier said. 'In the years to come, you're going to win things in jazz. When you do, I hope you'll remember tonight.'

For a moment, it looked as if the boy might cry. 'I'll never forget it.'

As Rama raised his Evian bottle, Ridge swept massively into the room. 'Gabron, what does that sign say? Put it out! After you've hit me.' Luc took a long toke and passed on the joint. 'To jazz. And to France!' Ridge sucked the thing practically inside out before crushing the lit end. He turned to Rama. 'Stretch, you living at home?'

'By home, you mean?'

'With your parents.'

'My parents are gone but I live with my brother, Modibo.'

'Older brother?'

'Seven years older.'

'He do the cooking?'

'Mostly.'

'Well, he's not feeding you up. I've been watching those twiggy little arms of yours and I'm scared they're going to break clean off. You need to start—'

Khara's voice stole through the beaded curtain. 'Ridge? The drinks guy is here.'

'Now? Shit.' Turning on his heel, he lashed the curtain aside and headed off. 'Twenty minutes, you guys,' he called out, his footfalls shaking the floorboards. 'Garfield? No pissing in the sink. I got the toilet fixed yesterday.'

Rama turned to Darac. 'Why does Monsieur Clay call you Garfield?'

'Maybe he thinks I'm a cat.'

'Ah.'

A warm round of applause welcomed the quintet back to the stand. Nods and smiles from the guys first to the audience and then to each other; a moment to check tuning and they were ready. Fuelled by their interval beers, the quintet always opened the second set with a Thelonious Monk number. Leffe Blonde seemed to lend itself to skew-whiff scampers through the man's elusive, off-kilter melodies.

Cued by Didier to take the first solo, Darac flexed his sore hand a couple of times, upped the volume control on his instrument and prepared to take flight. Getting into an up-tempo Monk solo was like chasing a three-legged gazelle but after a few lunges in the thing's general direction, he began to home in on it. The goal wasn't to bring down the beast but to jump on its back and see where the mood took them. It took them far and wide, further and wider indeed than was sensible; that was the joy of it. The band played variations on the number's main themes as they waited to welcome the wanderer back into the fold. And then, just when it seemed Darac had gone so far that there could be no way back, a series of notes suggested itself to him that solved the problem; new material that formed the bottom rungs of an escape ladder out of the remote place he'd strayed into. The moment of discovery drew smiles from the band and then the audience. A few bars later, Darac came surfing out of the solo on a warm wave of applause.

The possibilities of the evening seemed endless to him now: the band was playing like some fabulous composite being powered by a single beating heart; his hand was coping with everything he asked of it; and his head felt freer than it had in weeks.

But as he relaxed back into the jinking groove that would carry the quintet on to the next solo, his heart sank. With no curtain of smoke to lessen the impact of the moment, the huge figure of Lieutenant Roland Granot of the Brigade Criminelle hove into view at the back of the room. A hot twinge ran across Darac's knuckles. Not now, surely? Couldn't it wait?

An exchange of looks across the floor confirmed that what Granot wanted was Darac. And he wanted him now.

3

Darac was thankful for his mask as he entered the exam tent. 'Professor Bianchi here, Lami?'

'No, she isn't.' The lab assistant's smile was a transparent attempt to appear upbeat. 'She assigned the case to Dr Barrau.'

'Right.' It sounded more professional than 'shit'.

'Careful where you're walking there, sir. We haven't examined that yet.'

Darac looked down. At his feet was an empty champagne bottle, lying forlornly on its side like a spent firework. 'Many at the party?'

'There was only one glass. That's about all we know at the moment.'

'OK.'

'It's not a pretty sight, Captain.'

Fifteen years of shootings, stabbings, beatings and stranglings had all but immunised Darac against the grotesque but a wave of nausea broke in his stomach when he looked into the hot tub. Hideously bloated, the corpse appeared to be made of patched green rubber. The left arm had been chewed off at the shoulder, the right at the elbow. But strangely, the tongue, protruding invitingly from the mouth like the end of a good *boudin noir*, had remained untouched. The dogs or foxes or rats of Chemin Leuze had missed a trick. Darac shook his head. Drowning and mutilation. What a coda to the evening.

'At least she didn't catch fire as well,' he said, to no one in particular. Although if she had, it would at least have taken care of some of the insect life. If the sight was bad, the smell might have been worse: a sweetish, rancid stench that before the introduction of forensic overalls would have stayed on his clothes for hours. He turned to the white-suited figure bent low over the mess. 'Barrau. Care to offer an opinion?'

The pathologist's long, lancet-thin fingers stopped moving all at once. Maintaining an imperious silence, he waited a moment before resuming his work.

'Thank you, Doctor.' It sounded more professional than 'arsehole'.

Senior crime scene analyst Raul Ormans was examining the hot tub itself. A man who usually took his time, his hands were moving like an assembly-line worker on piece rate.

'R.O. Anything?'

'The hot tub works.' He handed a stack of bagged-up CDs to an assistant. 'We'll run further tests on it in the lab tomorrow.' His gloves slapped the air as he pulled them off. 'Now I'm going home.' He marched away. 'And I do mean *now*.'

'Hey, nobody wants to be here.' Darac risked another glance at the bag of stinking green matter that was the corpse. 'Especially her.'

A young woman carrying a specimen box obliged Darac to take a step back.

'Look, I'm in the way here so I'll leave you to it, Doctor. Guys.'

Darac lurched out of the tent, picked his way around the rest of the forensic team's gear and then took the steps up to the villa. Pulling back the hood of his suit, he gave a tentative sniff. The Blue Devil's drains had nothing on this. He exhaled, his breath condensing into vapour in the chill night air. He met Granot coming the other way. 'The victim was seventy, you said?'

'Seventy-one according to her cleaner, one Alphonsine Loret.'

'She found the body?'

'Yes. She hadn't seen anything of Madame Mesnel for a few days so she called round to check on her. Flaco's talking to her now up in the house. Or trying to. The woman's hysterical, for some reason.'

'And Flaco herself. How's she coping?'

'OK for a youngster. Only threw up twice.'

'That's good.' Their shadows flickered as they passed under a faltering arc lamp and climbed the steps. 'You know what I'm wondering about all this?'

'What the hell are we doing here?'

Darac ducked under the tape that marked out the red zone, the hot-spot at the heart of a crime scene. He held it up for Granot. 'Exactly.'

'And why did it have to be tonight?' The big man negotiated the hazard with the touching grace of a circus elephant. 'My first night off in three weeks and *Le Gym* are live on telly. PSG away. Ten minutes to go, we're one-nil up. We win a corner. Never got to see it.'

Darac reflected that he'd missed out on some corners of his own. The quintet's take on Monk's 'Brilliant Corners' had been going spectacularly well until the interruption.

A fresh-faced woman wearing overalls stepped forward and offered Granot a clipboard. 'Autograph, if you wouldn't mind?'

'Come on, Patricia – I was only down there a minute.'

'You signed into the red zone, Lieutenant; you have to sign out.' She handed him a pen. 'And PSG equalised.'

'See?' Granot cast a filthy look at the hot tub as if the Nice side's concession of a late goal was all the corpse's fault. 'How did it happen?'

Penalty,' Patricia rolled her eyes. 'Ten seconds from the final whistle.'

Granot scrawled his name, signature and the time in the appropriate boxes. 'Idiots... Definite, was it?'

'Definite.' She gave Darac a look as he took the clipboard. 'Trust our boys, eh?'

A weak smile was all he could come up with. So 'our' team hadn't beaten 'theirs'. How could it possibly matter to anyone?

'Ah, looks as if I'm wanted.' Patricia indicated a figure summoning her to the exam tent. 'Just put the clipboard on the table, Captain. Sorry, I keep forgetting! *Commissaire*, I mean.'

'*Acting* commissaire,' Darac called to her retreating back. 'I'm still just a captain.' He turned to Granot. 'Thank God.'

'You took the words right out of my mouth.'

Darac ran an eye over the scene. 'Apart from Flaco, who's here from our lot?'

'Perand, and one, two... three uniforms. And Malraux's floating around somewhere.' Granot made a clicking sound with his tongue. 'So to speak.'

'What have we got so far?'

Possibly the last detective in France to wear a Film Noir-style trench-coat, Granot slipped a notebook from an inner breast pocket and angled it to catch the light. 'So... the deceased is one Jeanne Mesnel. Seventy-one years old. Seamstress. Widow. Lived alone. Health: poorish. The hot tub is brand new—'

'And works, according to R.O.,' Darac said. 'By which he means it didn't electrocute the poor woman, I guess.'

Granot gave a little grunt. 'An empty bottle of Bollinger was found next to the hot tub. There's no sign of a break-in or anything obviously missing. No suicide note. That's it.'

'And there's a suggestion Madame was alone when it happened. Whatever *it* was.'

Granot's signature hangdog expression hung even lower as he pocketed the notebook. 'It's got natural causes written all over it.'

'Yet in his usual whistle-stop tour, our beloved public prosecutor seems to have thought otherwise.'

Granot swept an arm across the scene. 'Look at all this. Ridiculous.'

The Cirque du Meurtre was in town, alright. On Public Prosecutor Frènes's say-so, it had rolled in and pitched its tent on Madame Mesnel's patio: nine police officers in total; a four-strong pathology team; two forensic analysts; and two trolley dollies from the morgue. Then there was the hardware: portable generator, lighting, cameras, laptops, recorders, cabling, cordon tape... The list was endless.

Darac keyed a number into his mobile.

'Chasing public prosecutors,' Granot said, spitting out the words. 'He should bloody well still be here.'

'Answerphone...' Darac waited for the tone. 'Monsieur Frènes, we're at the Mesnel house over in Beaulieu. Call me or Lieutenant Granot when you can.'

Granot gave Darac a nudge in the ribs. 'Hey, I'll bet this Jeanne Mesnel is somebody. Ex-mayor's wife or whatever. Hence all the brouhaha.'

'We don't really know anything yet, do we?'

Further thoughts were interrupted by an other-worldly sound. The men turned to see a little wisp of a woman hurrying toward them in a whirr of flailing arms and sobs. In pursuit was the short but strapping figure of Officer Yvonne Flaco. A blanket in lieu of a net, she looked like a butterfly collector chasing an evasive specimen.

'The corpse finder?' Darac said.

'Uh-huh.'

The two men braced themselves. The steps behind them were steep and the upper patio was slippery with dew.

'Whoa there, ladies!' Granot called out. 'You're going to have us all down. Steady!'

Skidding to a halt, Flaco netted her quarry only a centimetre or two from the precipice. Madame Loret's monologue continued without a pause.

'Captain! Thank God, I can't tell you how—'

'You've got the wrong one, madame,' Granot said. 'I am

Lieutenant Granot. This gentleman is in charge – Captain, indeed Acting *Commissaire*, Paul Darac.'

'Him?' Rearranging the drape of the blanket, Madame Loret seemed suddenly in possession of her faculties. 'He's far too young.'

Madame had a point. At thirty-one, Darac was young for the role. But his promotion was only a stop-gap measure while the squad's actual head, Commissaire Agnès Dantier, remained on extended leave.

'Let's not worry about any of our ages but you've had a shock madame and it's cold out here. We'll go inside, eh?'

'Very well.' The blanket rose from her sides. 'You may take an arm each, gentlemen.'

Delving blindly under the cloth, the pair took a moment or two home in on their joint objective and, concluding that a quail's wishbone would have had greater tensile strength, took care not to pull against one other as they slow-marched back to the house.

'I've known Madame for years. Worked for her for nearly two. Two years and now this! The stench of rotting flesh. My God.' She swallowed a sob. '*That* was my greeting here this evening. And when I saw… saw her poor—'

Short on patience when it came to children, old people and humanity in general, Granot grasped the nettle. 'Having seen her, can you confirm the deceased was indeed Madame Jeanne Mesnel? Just unofficially.'

'She was unrecognisable but I know it was her.'

'If she was unrecognisable—'

The wishbone gave a sharp tug. 'Who *else* could it be? It's Madame Mesnel. Definitely!'

Darac decided to spare Granot further pain. 'Go on ahead, would you, Lieutenant? Make a start upstairs.'

'If you insist, chief.'

Darac had seldom seen the man move so fast. 'Flak? In here, please.'

Madame Loret accepted the substitution of Flaco for Granot. Slowing with every stride, she was still talking away as they approached the back door of the villa.

'Madame, on second thoughts, I think we'll leave it there for now. Let's reconvene—'

'The sight of her poor swollen body, Captain. I'll never forget it. Never!' A graunch of gears suddenly shifted her into a happier place. 'She was still so slender, you know. Slender and quite, quite lovely.' Back with a jolt into first. 'And now here she was all... blown-up. And green as a frog!'

Flaco craned her neck around Loret's shaking head. 'Sir, may I assist the Lieutenant? Or anyone?'

'You can assist me by taking Madame Loret home.'

Madame was having none of it. 'Go home? No, no. I have more to tell you, Captain. A lot more!'

'You can tell me tomorrow morning. You'll feel better after a good night's sleep and your thoughts will be much more clear and concise.' He hoped. 'Alright?'

'Sleep? After this... horror?'

'You must try.' Darac gave Flaco an expectant look. 'Flak?'

'Just a moment.' Madame Loret raised a staying hand. 'Yes, perhaps tomorrow might be preferable. Oh, that smell—'

'Flak – take the lady home.'

'Yes sir. This way, madame.'

'I know which way it is, young lady. Haven't I been coming here every Friday for the past two years? And let me tell you this...'

As Flaco began to lead Madame Loret away, her full-on moue told Darac she knew she'd drawn the short straw. But that was the lot of the junior officer.

'Be sure to come, Captain!' Madame Loret took a closer look at the blanket she had been issued. 'I wouldn't give this to a dog. I'll keep it, nevertheless.'

As Darac watched them go, a wave of tiredness broke over

him. Just that morning he had concluded an investigation into the armed robbery of a security van in which two guards had been blinded and half a million euros stolen. After eight long months, the culprits had been caught and virtually all the cash recovered. *Chapeau* to Acting Commissaire Darac and Nice's Brigade Criminelle.

Ten hours later, it was as if it had never happened.

The combination of Allure mixed with formaldehyde signalled Patricia had come back. He turned to her. 'Let me ask you something.'

'If it's "Do you like jazz?" you already asked me.'

'This is one you won't get wrong.' He ran a hand through his hair. 'How long have you been with the pathology unit?'

'Ten… eleven years.'

'So – Madame Mesnel. What would you say was the most likely cause of death?'

Patricia's eyebrows disappearing into the hood of her white overalls gave her the look of an astonished nun. 'You want *my* opinion?'

'Yes.'

'I just check people in and out, you know.'

'You do a lot more than that.'

'We-ell—'

'Patricia, we've worked on hundreds of cases together, right? You've seen it all.'

'You *think* you've seen it all. Poor woman, being… chewed up like that.'

'I know.' Darac gave a sympathetic nod but he also felt a little ill-disposed toward Madame Mesnel. Taking alfresco dips in this weather? At her age? 'So?'

Patricia dropped her voice. 'How'd you like to know what *Barrau* thinks? I overheard him dictating into his recorder. He didn't realise I was there.'

'This is gold. Go on.'

She raised a latex-covered finger. 'You didn't hear this from me, right?'

'No, no.'

'What he's thinking is that the lady was in seriously failing health; that she died between three and ten days ago and...' Hearing voices below, Patricia glanced toward the tent. Barrau had finished his examination and was on his way toward them. 'And that all the visible injuries appear to have been caused post-mortem.'

'Thought so. Alright, one detail is odd here, I grant you, but when you add it all up, what does it look like to you?'

'Heart attack. Stroke, maybe.'

'And when you factor in the empty Bollinger bottle?'

'I didn't know about that. Maybe she drank too much and passed out.'

'And as a result?'

'Drowned accidentally.'

'Making all this a waste of?'

'Police time, money and effort?'

'Isn't it, though?'

To say nothing of the waste of a great evening's jazz, Darac thought.

As Dr Barrau arrived, Patricia turned in time to proffer the clipboard to with the expected decorum.

'So – what do you make of this Jeanne Mesnel woman, then, Doctor?' Darac said. 'Dead, is she?'

Stifling a grin, Patricia was suddenly fascinated by her clipboard. If Barrau had registered the dig, he didn't let it show. 'They can take her.'

Darac gave the trolley dollies a nod. 'Anything to add?'

'My preliminary report will be ready within an hour of returning to the lab,' Barrau went on, part of a litany Darac could recite verbatim. 'A full report will follow once the autopsy itself has taken place.'

'Email the preliminary to me as well as to the commissariat, will you?'

A request to perform one of the seven labours of Hercules would hardly have been greeted with less enthusiasm. 'Very well.'

Young Officer Max Perand loped lankily between them. 'We've just got an address for one Cristelle Daviot, the deceased's next of kin. Granddaughter.'

Barrau glanced at his watch. 'Local?'

'Wait a minute. Granddaughter? She's not a youngster, is she, Perand?'

'No – she's...' He checked the message. 'Thirty-one. And she lives over in Saint-Laurent-du-Var.'

Job done, Barrau was on his way. 'See if they can get her to the morgue by midnight.'

Darac followed him. 'Not everyone works nights like you, Barrau. Surely the ID could wait at least until the morning?'

Barrau kept walking. 'The sooner formal identification has taken place, the better.'

Darac caught the man's sinewy arm, halting him. 'In fact, do you need to drag her over to the morgue at all?'

Barrau's eyes slid to the hand that held him. Darac exhaled deeply but let go.

'Captain, I only consider waiving the personal identification procedure in the most extreme of circumstances.'

'What do you call *this*? And how do you expect even a close relative to positively ID a body in that condition?'

'Leave that to me.'

Casting scalpel-sharp shadows in all directions, Barrau strode away into the night.

'Thank you,' Darac called after him, adding, 'Shithead,' scarcely *sotto voce*. It sounded more professional than 'fuck off'. He turned to Patricia. 'One of these days, I tell you...' He gave her arm a comradely pat. 'I'll be in the house if anyone needs me.'

'The detail, Captain?'

'Pardon?'

'You mentioned one detail that seemed odd? About the death?'

'Ah yes. It's probably nothing but have you ever known a colder couple of weeks? Around here, I mean.'

As if prompted by the question, Patricia shivered suddenly. 'I don't suppose I have.'

In lieu of asking the question, Darac raised his eyebrows.

'Ah, I see what you mean. But perhaps that's all the more reason to take a nice bubbly hot tub.'

'I'm thinking of Madame Mesnel being naked.'

'Only her head would've been exposed to the air though.'

'Once she was in the thing, yes. But where's her robe? Where's her coat? Where are her sandals or flip-flops? There's no clothing at all next to the tub. She *could* have come out of the house with only a champagne bottle and a glass to keep her warm but at her age and in this weather? Seems unlikely, don't you think?'

'It *is* a good few metres. But that's what she must have done, I suppose.'

'It's nothing, I'm sure. Thanks, Patricia.'

He found Granot sorting through an old-fashioned drop-down cabinet in the kitchen.

'Sent Madame Loret home, then?'

'Seeing her there tomorrow morning.'

'Very wise.' Granot extracted a bottle. 'Mapin cognac, no less. And it's an XO.'

'Pricey.' Darac looked around. Apart from a new washing machine, nothing looked up to date. 'Modest.'

'Same story upstairs. Back garden's good though, isn't it? Spacious, split-level.'

'And furnished with a brand-new hot tub. In which Madame sipped Bollinger.' Darac's mobile rang. 'It's Frènes. I'll put it on speaker.'

'Apologies that I had to call you in, Captain. And apologies also that I had to cut away before you arrived. But we all— sacrifices.

Anyway, I've— your work for you— occasion. But what—?'

'Bear with me a moment, monsieur – you're breaking up.' Darac waved to Granot to follow him back onto the upper patio. 'Should be fine now. Continue, please.'

'I said, what have *you* discovered?'

'Monsieur Frènes, Lieutenant Granot and I have been here ten minutes. What can possibly be learned in that time?'

'A good deal if you know what to ask,' Frènes said. 'And of whom.'

An impromptu lecture on the theme of 'Best Practice on Arriving at a Crime Scene' proved too much for Granot and, mugging that the breeze was starting to penetrate his trench coat, he mouthed, 'Two minutes,' and set off in the direction of his car.

'Another issue, Captain. Have you located the next of kin, the granddaughter?'

'Yes.'

'Good. The Palais is looking for a quick wrap-up on this.'

'And just what is there to wrap up?'

'The murder of Madame Jeanne Mesnel, of course.'

'What evidence do you have to support that theory?'

'It is *not* merely a theory. I learned from a key witness that a neighbour threatened to kill Madame Mesnel and three weeks later, she finds her dead.'

'And that key witness is?' Darac asked, knowing the likely answer.

'The victim's cleaner, Madame Loret. She actually witnessed the threat being made.'

'The woman is hysterical and one could hardly blame her. Besides, I suspect she may not be the most reliable of witnesses at the best of times.'

'She witnessed the threat *and* she will repeat it in court.'

'What did she hear exactly?'

'She heard the suspect threaten to drown the victim in her hot tub.'

'Which, a few weeks later, he or she obligingly did. I see.'

'These things happen, do they not?'

'What motivated this threat?'

'The hot tub has a music console. Warnings about noise had been issued and ignored. Ignored once too often, it would seem.'

'Monsieur, this sounds at best—'

'I have the suspect's name for you, here…'

In the background, Darac heard a sleepy, Asian-sounding voice. Whoever the woman was, she wasn't Madame Frènes. Perhaps she was part of the 'heavy case load' the public prosecutor was always complaining about.

'It's Battail. Marcel Battail.' Frènes gave the address. 'They should have him over at Commissariat Joinel by now. The man has a record, by the way. Of violence.'

Darac heard Frènes's companion murmur something whose seductive undertow, even on the line, was obvious.

'Uh… Duty calls, Captain. Good evening.'

'Don't work *too* hard, monsieur.'

Granot reappeared. Producing a hip flask from one of the endless pockets in his trench coat, his eyes slid to a bench set against the rear wall of the house. 'Let's have a couple of snifters.'

'Good idea.'

'What did Frènes have for us, then?'

'The whole package.' Darac took one of the cups. 'Murder suspect, witness – the lot.'

'Don't make me laugh while I'm pouring… Who is the so-called suspect?'

'Guy by the name of Marcel Battail. A neighbour. *Santé.*'

'And the witness?'

'Madame Loret, who else?'

'She didn't say anything about witnessing a murder.'

'That's because she didn't. She witnessed the suspect *threaten* to murder the victim. Three or so weeks ago. Allegedly.'

'That doesn't mean anything. Odile threatens to kill me, regularly.'

'Just once will do, tell her.'

'Funny.'

The morgue boys appeared from the lower depths. As the laden trolley rolled by, Darac and Granot raised their cups in salute.

'Can't see this scenario appearing in one of those Mapin cognac ads, can you?' Granot mimicked the voiceover. ' "Mapin – for those special moments." '

'Nothing like the guy.' Darac took another sip. 'What are you on tomorrow?'

Granot shook his head. 'I can't be on this.'

'You won't need to be but as I'm pretending to be in charge, I'm supposed to know these things.'

'It's paperwork for me tomorrow. All day.'

'Bonbon will be back from lunchtime on. Any idea what he'll be picking up?'

'More paperwork, obviously.'

'Why did I even ask?' Darac handed back the cup.

'Much needed. Ready?'

'What, to go and interrogate this Marcel Battail? You don't think Frènes's come up with a live one, do you?'

'I doubt it but he thinks he has so the sooner we talk to Battail, the better. I suppose we'd better check the coffins before we go.'

'There'll be hardly anything in them.'

'Humour me.'

As well as the boxes for the path lab, there were three evidence cases still at the scene. One contained all the portable objects that were going back to Raul Ormans' crime lab for further analysis. A second contained tested items already cleared into the Brigade's custody. The third contained Madame Mesnel's personal documents taken from her bureau by Jean-Jacques 'Lartou' Lartigue, the crime-scene coordination officer.

The boxes were stacked on the upper patio. Darac glanced around for their keeper.

'Where's Lartou got to?'

'He's checking out the hot tub.'

'For what?'

'I think his missus wants one.'

'Lartou!' Darac called out. 'When you're ready.'

'Right away, chief,' came his voice from below.

Granot poured himself another one while they waited. 'What is it you're looking for?'

'Did you notice the tub has a built-in music console?'

'Quite the fun palace.'

'An eight-CD changer, no less. I just wanted to check what the discs were.'

Granot had no peer in performing what was known the world over as a Gallic shrug. 'So the old dear pegged out to the strains of Charles Trenet or Jean Sablon. So what?'

Lartou arrived on the scene. Burly and bald, the man from Ghana was wrapped up so completely against the cold he looked like a walking mummy. 'Sorry, chief.' He handed Darac a release form. 'It's a fine machine, that hot tub.'

'Good. You all finished?'

'Yes I am.'

'OK, shut the site down. Post just a couple of uniforms. They can alternate, maybe.'

Darac opened one of the cases and found an entry specified as 'Zone One: Disc A'. Seven separate discs were listed next, labelled 'B' to 'H'. He took Disc A out of its sealed poly bag. 'Well, well… I think we'll go and sweat this Marcel Battail, not just talk to him.' He handed it to Granot. 'Look at that.'

Featuring the Duke Ellington Orchestra in its brassy pomp, the album was a movie soundtrack entitled *Anatomy of a Murder*.

The big man mugged a look of astonished admiration. 'The word "murder" in the title? Yes! Madame Mesnel was trying to alert us.' He mimicked an old woman's voice. ' "Would you hang on a second, Monsieur Battail, while I put this incriminating CD into the console?" ' He shook his whiskery chops. 'Ridiculous.'

Darac checked the other discs from the player. 'I do realise it doesn't mean that.'

'Then why have you got so interested in this nonsense all of a sudden?'

Darac gave Granot an almost cheery look. 'Because we now know that that poor maggoty sack on her way to the morgue wasn't just any anonymous old lady. She had good taste in music.'

'Ye gods.'

'And anybody who threatens to drown an old lady for trying to turn the neighbourhood on to the Duke deserves a good kicking, don't you think? Let's go.'

Granot didn't move for the moment. 'Battail threatened to *drown* Madame Mesnel?'

'Allegedly.'

'Threatened to drown her if she didn't turn her music down – is that it?' Granot's eyebrows tramlined his forehead. 'It was obviously just an idle threat.'

'Madame Loret found what was left of her in the hot tub, didn't she?'

'Oh yes, she did.' Granot was still unconvinced. 'Absolutely.'

'You can carry the heavier case, I've got a damaged hand.'

'Use your other one.'

A crowd had gathered in the street, clustered against the dark night like a colony of bats. A few may have been there in solidarity with their departed neighbour. Most were rubberneckers. Although they couldn't see into the rear garden itself, there was still plenty to entertain them: police radios chattering away like electronic cicadas; uniforms and non-uniforms coming and going; the thought that esoteric forensic activity was going on *just over there*.

As always, the highlight of the show had been the Body Removal Sequence. Craning necks; gasps; signs of the cross. Darac had no time for it. Indeed, he sometimes felt more contempt for murder-scene groupies than he did for murderers themselves.

'Keep a lid on it, chief.'

'Yeah, yeah.'

Darac scanned some of their faces. He knew that for the less prurient ones, life on this gently winding cul-de-sac of small, pastel-washed houses would never be quite the same again. It would always be the place where *it* happened. Weird death left a taint on innocent walls.

More cicada chatter, this time from Granot's radio. 'Lieutenant?' The speaker's neutral Parisian accent identified him even through the electronic mush.

'Go ahead, Malraux.'

'I've taken statements from most of the neighbours. Nobody but Madame Loret saw or knows anything.'

'Surprise, surprise.'

'But the suspect Public Prosecutor Frènes ordered us to detain?'

'Marcel Battail. Yes?'

Granot turned the ignition, cutting out the radio for a second. '…wasn't there.'

'Who wasn't where, Malraux?'

'Battail wasn't at home. His woman suggested a couple of places he might be. He wasn't there either. And he's not in the house. We've looked everywhere.'

In the passenger seat, Darac turned to stare out of the side window, eyebrows raised, head shaking. Frènes had just assumed Battail would be at home? Or did the gibbering wreck that was Madame Loret assure him of the fact?

'We'll see what *we* can get out of her,' Granot said.

'You won't get any more than I did.'

Granot rolled his eyes. 'Find anything else, Malraux?'

'No.'

'Weapon?'

'He drowned the old dame, didn't he?'

'I was forgetting. You take shoes and clothes for forensics?'

'Of course I did.'

'Hey! Mind your manners.' The team's newest signing was a taste Granot hadn't yet acquired. 'Lieutenant *Intern*.'

'Anyone posted near the house?' Darac said.

Granot relayed the question to Malraux.

'Yes. He couldn't get back into the house unseen or even into Rue Balmette itself. And he isn't in the crowd where you are, either. I've checked.'

'Alright, that's it.' Granot turned to Darac. 'Home? Back to the club? Battail's?'

Darac checked his watch. 11.20. The band would still be playing. If Granot stepped on it, they could be back at the club in fifteen minutes. He ran a hand through the black wavy thicket that was his hair.

'Battail's.'

4

Closing her eyes, the woman rotated her pelvis and began sighing 'Yes!' in time with her partner's thrusts. A moment later, 'Yes!' gave way to a crescendo of squeals as she went into her default orgasm. During it, she held up her wrist behind the man's grunting head and glanced at her watch.

Forty-five minutes later, she was back in her apartment, enjoying a cigarette on the balcony. An al-fresco smoke was something she reserved for night time. By day, it just wasn't relaxing: planes blasting in and out of Nice airport; the ricocheting rattle of trains; and worst of all, traffic screaming along the highway right under her nose. It was like having a front-row seat at a never-ending parade of fumes and noise. It might kill you eventually, she believed. A sort of drip-feed, drive-by slaying.

She took a deep drag on her cigarette and peered through the sprawl toward the marina. A breeze was rippling the inky black water, scattering silver necklaces of light between the hard white shells of yachts tied up at their moorings.

'Would you like one of those boats?' Léo had said to her just after she had moved in. A penthouse in one of the quieter, swankier blocks nearby was what she really wanted; or a garden apartment at Villeneuve-Loubet further down the coast. In the meantime, somewhere without a stinking drag strip outside her window would do. At least she knew *that* was coming. And soon.

It had been a decent workday, although, for once, Full-on Freddie, the only client capable of giving her a genuine orgasm, had misfired badly. The evening had been given over to her favourite part of the job: escort work. Fixed-rate, one-shot-deal stuff. Tonight, the john had sprung for cocktails at Lapis in Juan-les-Pins, then on to dinner at Bleu in Antibes. After all that, he had managed less than two minutes on the job. She calculated how much she had made. On top of a free evening out, it came to eight hundred euros. Four for her, four for Léo.

Out in the marina, the breeze had stiffened, whipping rigging wires against their metal masts. It sounded like a round of applause.

5

The police database contained a lengthy entry for Marcel Battail. He lived in Rue Balmette, a winding lane that ran more or less parallel to Madame Mesnel's Chemin Leuze. As Granot pulled up outside a small, neglected-looking property, he glanced across at Darac's laptop screen. 'Is that a zip in his forehead?'

'Scar. I think.'

'Looks like a sweetie.' Granot climbed out of the car. 'Mind you, mug shots can be deceptive.'

'The camera adds seven convictions, they say.'

There seemed to be no one in the street.

'What's the lady friend's name?' Granot said.

'Brigitte Andreani, proprietor of a local hairstylist's. You open with her, I'll check out the back yard. It might share a boundary with the Mesnel villa, mightn't it?'

'Don't think Chemin Leuze goes quite this far.' Opening the yard gate triggered a night security light. Darac was grateful for it: the patio was littered with dog crap. Checking out possible entrances and exits supported Granot's feeling that there was no common boundary with Madame Mesnel's property. Her hot tub was probably no more than thirty metres away on the diagonal but high walls and dense greenery rendered it inaccessible. The upshot was that Battail couldn't have sneaked into her back garden from his own, unseen. He would have had to use her side entrance in Chemin Leuze. At the door, Darac was met by a fleshy peroxide blonde of about fifty. Heavily made-up and wearing a leopard-print halter-neck over tight white trousers, her appearance, tattoos and all, put him in mind of a drag queen he'd once known.

'I'm Brigitte.'

He followed her into the house; the dog house, by the smell of it. The beast in question, a Rottweiler, was stretched out on a sofa. In front of it was a low table strewn with beauty magazines and empty beer bottles. Each bore a lipstick smear around its throat. If anyone had been sharing them with Brigitte, it presumably wasn't Battail.

'You don't mind doggies?' she said, giving the detective some serious eye now she could see him in the light.

'No, I like them.' The baby-pink blush on her left cheek bore a raised, purplish hem, he noticed. 'As a rule.'

'There's no need to worry about Thierry. He's as harmless as a kitten.'

Harmless or not, Darac saw that Granot had taken the seat furthest from the animal.

'Fancy a beer? Your boss is having one.'

Amused at his battlefield promotion, Granot smiled graciously.

'Why not?' Darac looked around for a seat. 'Thanks.'

'Thierry, get off the sofa. Good boy. Now!' The Rottweiler yawned toxically and padded away into the kitchen. She followed it. 'I'll have one with you.' She returned with a couple of Peronis and sat next to Darac.

'So, Madame Andreani, where is your partner?'

'I'd tell you if I knew. We've got nothing to hide. He'll be back when he's ready. And before you say anything, I know he's got a temper. He can be rough. But I wouldn't have him any other way. Do you know what I mean?'

'What about the year he served for assault? Or the three for malicious wounding?'

She took a swig. 'That all happened before I knew him. Anyway, he told me they were scumbags who were trying to cheat him. Marcel doesn't take shit like that.'

'What would you call spending time behind bars?' Granot said. 'Taking the waters?'

'OK, you're right. But I swear on my mother's eyes that Marcel didn't do anything to poor old Madame Mesnel. He couldn't. Not to a defenceless old lady.'

Darac's gaze lowered to Brigitte's bruised cheek.

'I am not old, monsieur. And I'm not defenceless either.'

'When did you see him last?'

'Listen, do you think if he was going to drown her, he would have come out with it in front of that gas bag Loret?'

'When did you see him last?' Darac repeated.

'This morning, when he set off to the parlour.'

'Parlour?'

'Tattoo parlour. Blood Brothers in the Babazouk.'

'Ah, yes, Rue Jules Gilly. I've passed it.'

'This is Marcel's work.' She sported a shoulder all a-flutter with butterflies and lovebirds. 'And I've got others in more...' Raising her pencilled-on eyebrows, she gave Darac a look. '... interesting places.'

'Anybody work there with him?'

'Sometimes a guy helps him out at weekends: Dagger. Don't know his real name.'

'Could Marcel be spending the night with him?'

'I suppose he *could*. Never has before.'

'Do you know where Dagger lives?'

'Somewhere in Nice. I don't know.'

'How did he get the name of Dagger?'

'Big tattoo on his arm. Crossed daggers.'

'Uh-huh. Marcel have any relatives?'

'No.'

'And you've been together how long?'

'Just over a year. And I tell you this.' She lowered her voice. 'I've had more fun with Marcel in that time than I had with my husband in *fifteen* years of so-called marriage.'

'Any other friends?'

'Loads, sweetheart.'

'Marcel, I meant.'

'No. And I've said this already. To that nice young officer.'

Darac shared a look with Granot. Both thought Christian Malraux a potentially useful recruit to the Brigade. But 'nice' wasn't a quality usually attributed to former members of the Paris riot squad.

Brigitte collapsed her features into a masterpiece of sympathy. 'When did the old dear die, exactly? Because whenever it was, I was with Marcel. And I'll swear to it in court.'

Granot stared at her. 'You're admitting to perjury before you've even committed it.'

'I know.' She stared back, fierce as an old cat in her faded leopard-print top. 'So?'

Darac's beer bottle made a dull, sticky sound as he set it down on the table. 'Have you got a pen and paper somewhere, madame?'

'Somewhere. Why?'

'Get them.'

She returned with an A4 jotter. Darac handed her his pen. 'Write on that sheet everything you know about your boyfriend's movements for the past fourteen days. Be especially accurate about the times you have spent together.'

'Two whole weeks? Why should I?'

'The carte blanche alibi you're willing to give Marcel has no value. A blind alibi, one given before other timings are known, is far more likely to convince a jury.'

'We-ll.'

'You're certain he didn't kill Madame Mesnel?'

'Listen, if he went round there at all, it was just to get her to turn her music down. He's very sensitive, is Marcel.'

Granot snorted.

'Then if you want to help him,' Darac said, 'fill that in. And list your own whereabouts as well.'

Brigitte's thin lips curled cheekily at the corners. 'Alright.'

'If Marcel gets in touch, don't bother alerting him to what you've written. He is chief suspect in a murder case. Accordingly, the public prosecutor has already authorised the monitoring of your landline, mobiles, emails and post.'

'Tapping our phones and everything? *That's* nice.'

Brigitte looked as if she could spit but she began the task.

Granot found it almost painful to watch. 'You'll find it easier if you make a grid of squares for the different hours and days.'

Brigitte started again. 'You know where the fridge is.' At the end of the task, she sank back in her seat as if she had completed a final exam. Darac stood and brought her a beer.

'Thank you, darling.' She smiled, pulling back her shoulders to raise the puckered *Titanic* that was her bosom. 'Listen, if you ever feel like having your hair cut, my salon is just over the way. I have a room upstairs, as well. Your boss wouldn't mind you having a little time off now and again. Would you, sweetheart?'

'Actually, the captain here is *my* boss,' Granot said. 'And we must be going.'

'Thanks for the drinks and for this.' Darac brandished the sheet. 'We'll no doubt be seeing each other again.'

'Any time, as I say.' As they left the lounge, Thierry padded in from the kitchen and resumed his seat on the sofa. Brigitte took Darac's arm as she showed them out. She smiled, suddenly. 'Something's been nagging me about you ever since you came in. It's just come to me. You look like that old Hollywood actor. The strong but sensitive one. In that film – you know. The one about the postman always ringing twice. What's it called?'

'*The Postman Always Rings Twice?*'

'Yes – that's it. John … John… Garfield! Yes, you're his double, darling.'

'You're dating yourself.'

'It was on TV just last week.'

Brigitte pressed herself into Darac as she deliberated over opening the front door.

'Bye, madame,' he said, gently extricating himself. Once they were out of earshot, he swiped his mobile. 'Malraux? You've checked Brigitte Andreani's salon for Battail? There's a private bedroom above it.'

'I did that already. Anything else?'

Darac flexed his left hand. It was feeling easier. 'That's it.'

Granot let out a phlegm-rattling chortle. 'Brigitte must think our public prosecutor is quite the human dynamo. Five seconds' notice and he gets all those wiretaps in place.'

'Touching.'

'Just for argument's sake, let's say Battail did do it. They've probably concocted the story already. Before the body was even discovered.'

'You think Brigitte's that good an actress, Granot?'

'He could've done it without her knowing.'

'Well, we're yet to meet Marcel Battail in the flesh but… we'll see.'

Pausing at the car, Darac scanned the apparently empty street. 'Malraux's got his men well hidden, hasn't he? Or maybe they've all just gone home.'

Granot gave Darac a look. 'How about Brigitte referring to

Malraux as *nice*?'

'Says something about her day-to-day experiences of men.'

'Maybe the boy has hidden talents.' They got into the car. 'And while we're on this, I'm surprised you didn't take Brigitte up on her offer. Nobody's baked your baguette since Angeline... in months, I mean.'

Darac turned to him. 'Do you know what the key stages of the "grieving process" are supposed to be?'

'When my wives ditched me, it went cognac, wine, beer.'

'First comes denial, followed by anger, depression and, finally, acceptance.'

'If you say so.'

'But it's not until crass comments from members of your inner circle bounce harmlessly off that you realise you're finally over it.'

'Glad I could help.'

Another key stage for Darac had been the blues. Somewhere along the line between depression and acceptance, he'd taken a guitar out on to his roof terrace and played until the button-hard calluses on his fingertips, eighteen years in the making, had split apart and bled. They were healed now. Another layer had grown over them.

'So home, then, chief?'

'Yeah. I can look through Madame Mesnel's papers while I'm waiting for Barrau's preliminary.' His broad brow lowered. 'Got a favour to ask.'

'Ye-es?'

'I was thinking about Madame Mesnel's granddaughter having to ID the corpse. After you've dropped me off, you'll be passing the morgue.'

'Oh, no, you don't.'

'You've got a big shoulder, there. And your trench coat's shower-proof.'

'I'm a chaperone now?' Granot pulled away. 'As well as everything else?'

Something moving in Brigitte's back garden triggered her night security light.

'Hold it, Granot. This could be…'

In sharp silhouette, they saw Thierry pad out on the patio and squat.

'Drive on.'

6

The doorbell rang. And rang again. Léo had a key and no john knew the address. Stubbing out her cigarette, she went to the door and peered through the spy hole. It was a policeman. Uniformed, the safer kind. And in a hurry by the look of it. She took a moment to compose herself and then opened the door sharply to the limit of its chain.

'Yes?'

'Mademoiselle Daviot?'

'Who wants to know?'

'Mademoiselle Cristelle Marie Daviot?'

Granot arrived at the morgue just in time to oversee the ID process. He and Darac had decided to tell Cristelle only that her grandmother had drowned in her hot tub. On seeing the look in the young woman's eyes, it was the correct decision.

'You don't have to do this, mademoiselle.' Sod Dr Carl Sodding Barrau. 'We could get dental records.'

'It's alright.'

'You sure?'

She set her jaw. 'Yes.'

'This way, please.'

He led her into a small room containing only a TV monitor. The screen was blank.

'May I smoke?'

'Sorry.' Granot reached up and removed the battery from the smoke alarm. 'It's not permitted.'

Cristelle lit up, offered him one – he declined – and sucked in a lungful of familiarity.

'Are you ready?'

A nod.

Granot turned on the TV. He had to admit that in such a short time, Barrau had done a remarkable job on the right-hand half of the drowned woman's face. And with the mutilated and missing parts of her skull hidden by cloths arranged to mimic bedclothes, the effect was as natural as could be imagined.

'Mademoiselle, do you recognise your grandmother, Jeanne Honorine Mesnel?'

Shaking, Cristelle blew smoke, whispered that she did and then lost her cordon-bleu evening all over the floor.

'Léo.' She groped around in her handbag. 'I need Léo. I have to call.'

'What's his number? I'll ring him.' Granot steadied her as she found a tissue. 'There's a bathroom across the hall if you want to use it.'

'No, no.' She closed her bag. 'I'll ring later, it's alright. Across the hall?'

'Hang on to my arm, I'll take you.'

'You're very kind, Lieutenant.'

Cristelle's stomach had settled by the time the police driver returned her to her apartment. She went to bed wondering how long she would have to wait. How long before she could enjoy stretching out in the sun? How long before gazing at the sea through a curtain of fumes would be a thing of the past? Not long, presumably. A smile giving way to a smirk, she lit a cigarette. 'Thank you, Grand-mère,' she said aloud. 'Thank you, at last.'

7

It felt warmer as Darac closed the heavy black door of his apartment building and stepped out into the glorified courtyard that was Place Saint-Sépulcre. As often seemed to happen when he set off to work, he met his neighbour Suzanne returning home. A bright, auburn-haired woman in her mid-thirties, she was a nurse at the nearby Saint-Roch hospital.

'Hey, Paul.'

They exchanged greeting kisses.

'Still working nights then, Suzanne?'

'I can see why they made you acting commissaire.' She made a pillow of her hands, closed her eyes and laid her head momentarily upon them. 'This will be me for the next eight hours. I hope.'

'Me too, probably.'

He left the Place through a locked gate and followed a narrow, doglegged passageway into the broader Rue Neuve. The oyster shuckers were already at work at their stand outside the café at the end of the street but as a swish new tram whirred across the elegant Place Garibaldi beyond, Darac turned back into the tangle of alleyways that made up the old town, a quarter known to cognoscenti as the Babazouk. Living on the cusp of the old and the new Nice suited Darac. It offered the best of both worlds, didn't it? It was a view not shared by everyone. Granot and his other trusted lieutenant, Alejo 'Bonbon' Busquet, had more than once warned him about the potential dangers of the Babazouk, especially at night. Replete with hiding places, it was, they believed, an ideal location to carry out a quick, quiet hit. Darac's feeling was that if he was going to wind up with a knife in his back, it could just as easily happen outside the Negresco in broad daylight.

Maybe.

A zigzag route brought Darac to Bar Cantron. A bustling shoebox of a place adjoining the fish market, it had become his regular breakfast stop since the break-up with Angeline. The *viennoiseries* were not to the standard of their beloved Pâtisserie Fantin but the coffee was among the best around. Calling '*Bunjou!*' – *bonjour* in the local Nissart – Darac headed for a perch at the bar. Carrying a tray of croissants in from the kitchen, owner Jean Cantron bellowed his reply. Announcing comings and goings at top volume was part of the swagger and machismo of the quarter.

Without having to ask, Darac was presented with a *pain aux raisins* and a double espresso, a combination for which he hadn't paid a cent since Jean had discovered that the boy from nearby Vence was also a *flic*. 'What do you make of all these immigrants?' Jean had once asked him. Darac hadn't paid him the compliment of telling him what he really thought. One day, the cover might prove useful.

There was only one topic of conversation in the bar this morning: the Nice–Paris Saint-Germain football disaster of the previous evening. Easily shutting out the debate, Darac began mulling over Barrau's preliminary report on Jeanne Mesnel. Like all homicide detectives, Darac first turned to the page citing the cause of death. Expecting a tick in the 'Natural causes' box, he'd been disappointed to find 'Awaiting further tests' written at the head of the page. As he read on, there seemed little doubt about the eventual verdict, though, especially as 'Consistent with natural causes' appeared in most of the detailed entries, just as Darac had judged.

Barrau had noted that 'entomological analysis' – studying the insect population that had colonised the corpse – would play a major role in establishing the time of death. For now, sometime between twelve noon and 6 pm on the preceding Saturday afternoon was as close as he could estimate, five days before the body had been found.

Barrau assessed Jeanne Mesnel's health at the time of her death as not untypical for a woman her age. She had been on the lean side for her height, but the musculature of her legs and trunk was sound. Her bones were dense and the arthritis in her joints moderate.

Organically, he found she had been in far worse shape. Her cardiac and respiratory systems were weak. It seemed it wouldn't have taken much to have stopped her furred-up lungs and arrhythmic heart for ever. All visible signs of external trauma, including the mutilation of her arms, were caused post-mortem. Dogs were responsible for the latter.

The question Darac had entertained at the scene – why no discarded clothing had been found near the tub – wasn't accounted for in Barrau's report but it ruled out one possibility. The degree of respiratory haemorrhaging in the body and other factors indicated that the woman had been alive when she'd entered the tub. So she could not have been killed elsewhere, stripped, carried outside and then dumped in the water. There were other possible scenarios but it seemed she had indeed walked the twelve or so metres from the house to the tub in the nude.

The immediate cause of death was cited as myocardial infarction followed by hypoxia through submersion in water. In other words, the woman suffered a heart attack and then drowned. Darac knew that the most efficient method of drowning someone was not to push the head under water and then try to hold it there; it was to grasp the body by the ankles and then pull them clear of the water. It wasn't a perfect method, however: it tended to leave tell-tale finger marks on the victim. No such marks were found on Madame Mesnel. Correlatively, particles of the victim's skin could sometimes be found subungually – under the nails – of the perpetrator. Unless they had worn gloves.

Victims of deliberate domestic drowning tended to thrash against the sides of baths, acquiring characteristic contusions on their forearms and hands. Barrau, therefore, found it 'regrettable' that Madame Mesnel's arms were 'unavailable' for examination. And it meant she had nothing subungual to offer.

In practice, DNA evidence was not the go-to-jail card the general public believed but Barrau had collected examples that might ultimately yield something. Hairs in the filters and other clues suggested someone had shared the tub with Madame Mesnel at some point, possibly three others. One of the hairs was natural blond. Matching techniques might find these people but proving that one or more of them deliberately drowned their hostess would be a different matter. Dog hairs were also found in the filter.

Darac drained his espresso, called out, '*Vivà!*' – the Nissart *au revoir* – and took his leave. His car was parked beneath the Théâtre Esplanade, one of a series of promenades laid over the course of the old River Paillon. Crossing a busy Boulevard Jean Jaurès, he swiped his mobile and called a number at the Brigade's temporary new home, Commissariat Joinel.

'Granot, I'm on my way to the Mesnel villa. Any news?'

'Young Erica had an RTA last night. Some idiot ran up her arse on the A8. She's alright but her Smart car's not so smart any more. Nor is some of the IT stuff that was in the boot. She wasn't even scratched, though.'

'Thank God.'

'You know, for a guy who doesn't believe in God, you refer to Him quite a bit.'

' "Thank Django" doesn't work, somehow. You had a look at Barrau's report, yet?'

'Doesn't exactly shout "homicide".'

'Quite.'

'There are a couple of funny things. Well, not *things* as such but what about that blond hair found in the filter? Brigitte Andreani is blond and her boyfriend Marcel Battail *did* threaten to drown Madame Mesnel. Not compelling evidence but it's suggestive.'

'The filter hair was *natural* blond. Brigitte's golden locks have brown roots, if you noticed.'

'I didn't get close enough to tell.'

'The second thing?'

'This mutilation business. You realise that if he thinks about it, Frènes might want us to round up all the local dogs? He might reason that if one of them hasn't got around to chewing Madame Mesnel's fingers off yet, particles of the killer's skin might be found under her nails.'

'What did you have in mind, a line-up? "Dog number three: show us your fangs. Well, look at that, we've got ourselves a biter." '

'I was more concerned about having to dig up half of Beaulieu-sur-Mer looking for chewed-up bits of flesh.'

'The sooner Barrau comes up with a natural causes verdict, the better. What about the stake-out? Anything from that nice Officer Malraux?'

'Only that he was lucky to survive the night. Good old Brigitte practically suffocated him between her enormous breasts. Or so he says.'

Darac paused by the down ramp into the car park – any further and the mobile signal was prone to die. 'He waited for Battail in his own bed?'

'It was quite funny the way Malraux told it. Seems he might be loosening up at last.'

'Screwing witnesses? Loose enough for me. I'll have a word with him.'

A familiar figure appeared on the boulevard. Rim shots and cymbal crashes went off in Darac's head as, beaded braids flying, drummer Rama N'Pata came rollerblading past the rearmost carriage of a tram and overtook its entire length in a few flashing cuts. Victory flags waved with every stride: the young man was clad in a kitchen porter's black-and-white checks. A couple of seconds later, he was out of sight, a day of drudgery in some restaurant or hotel ahead of him. But it wouldn't be forever. Darac was sure Rama had a big future in jazz.

'Still there, chief?'

'Sorry, yeah.'

'Find anything in Madame Mesnel's papers?'

'Her most recent bank statement shows a credit of a couple of hundred thousand. Must have just come into it, I guess. Hence the purchase of the hot tub and assorted goodies.'

'I might check on where that came from later. Just for interest.'

'There's one other thing: she left no will.'

'That's unusual for someone of her generation.'

'That's what I thought. What will happen to the estate?'

'Cristelle Daviot will cop everything. As the granddaughter, she wasn't just Madame Mesnel's next of kin – she was the *only* kin she had.'

'Lucky girl. How did she cope at the morgue, by the way?'

'Pretty well, considering. And credit where it's due, Doctor Frankenstein did a good job of preparing the corpse for the ID.'

'That's something. So is Cristelle the type to drown her grandmother to speed up the inheritance process? A pleasant villa in Beaulieu-sur-Mer is quite an incentive.'

'I didn't get *that* feeling. I think there might be a pimp in the background, though. Guy called Léo. She wanted to call him, then didn't. Such a thought isn't beyond that type.'

'What makes you think she's a working girl?'

'In an unguarded moment, she opened her handbag in front of me. There was a hell of a lot of Viagra and condoms in it if she isn't.'

'She known?'

'I rang Vice. Frankie has never heard of her. And there's nothing on the database so she's no pavement artist, this girl.'

'An appointments-only type?'

'I would say so, yes. What used to be cheerfully termed a high-class prostitute.'

'And this Léo?'

'Again, Frankie doesn't know a Léo, locally. But I guess she can't know everyone.'

'Couldn't he be just a brother or a boyfriend?'

'I didn't sense any feeling of warmth toward him. More like… dependency. "I need Léo," she said, groping around for her phone.

When I offered to call him, it seemed to bring her to her senses and she changed her mind immediately. Alarmed at the prospect of giving his ID to a *flic*, I think.'

'It's suggestive, Granot. We'll pencil in an interview with the guy.'

'Just in case you're thinking of asking me to get back to Cristelle, I should respectfully point out that I've still got shitloads of paperwork to get through.'

Even in the age of electronic information gathering, every police case still generated mountains of paper. Darac recognised that mainly because of his size, Granot had his limitations as a detective. But he had one priceless asset: he was as indomitable and skilful a paper mountaineer as there was in the force.

'No, no need to get back to Cristelle. I'll go and see her in a day or two.'

'Good. And hey, you may get your end away at last.'

'Let's make a deal, Granot. You forget about my sexual well-being and I'll forget yours.'

'Since when have you cared about mine?'

'See, we're halfway there already.'

8

In daylight, the layout of Jeanne Mesnel's home patch was easier to take in. Chemin Leuze was one of a peloton of narrow lanes and cul-de-sacs sandwiched between the steeply raked terraces of the Grande Corniche to the north, and the embankment of the Nice to Ventimiglia rail line to the south. Connected to Beaulieu's eastern fringe by the long, winding Rue Slave, the area had a self-contained, almost cut-off air.

Pink-washed with sky-blue shutters, Chez Mesnel was a picture-perfect crime scene. A uniform saluted Darac as he ducked under the cordon tape and made his way into the bereaved silence of the back yard. The hot tub had already been taken back to the lab and, without it, the high bougainvillea-clad walls gave the lower patio a somewhat hemmed-in feel.

A check revealed that there was no access to any of the neighbouring gardens, not just Battail's, and no windows but Madame Mesnel's own overlooked her lower patio. Or rather, they usually did; Lartigue's crew had boarded them up, blinding the house.

Something Darac hadn't spotted the previous night was a rash of small black scuff marks outside the footprint of the hot tub. What had made them? Maybe something up in the house held the answer. He made his way up the steps to the back door and let himself in.

The case might not have been of much criminal interest to Darac but as he moved from room to room, his interest in Jeanne Mesnel the person grew exponentially. He'd already discovered her penchant for good music. It soon became clear she was something of an art lover as well. Her walls were alive with modern art prints, reproductions and a few original oils.

'No!'

The source of the surprise was a print he knew well. An abstract piece in which six radiating black lines were superimposed on fluid blues, yellows and reds, Kandinsky's *Improvisation 26 (Rowing)* was meant to evoke the coordinated exertion of taking the oars. For Darac, those taut black strokes were not oars but guitar strings playing something fabulously vibrant. A jazz solo realised in paint. He had the very same print hanging on his own living-room wall.

The connection he was beginning to feel with the dead woman intensified as he checked out her collection of LPs, CDs and cassette tapes. In other circumstances, he could have spent a happy day working through it all. There must have been four hundred vinyl LPs alone, including really avant-garde stuff: Cecil Taylor, Ornette Coleman, John Zorn. Darac had known only one of his grandmothers. At seventy-one, her idea of a challenging art form had been needlepoint.

He smiled as he handled the sleeves of records he'd seen only in CD format before. Bearing coffee cup rings, red wine splotches and a couple of scorch marks, Sun Ra's *Jazz in Silhouette,* purchased, he noticed, in the States, was so richly patinated it looked almost worthy of excavation.

The woman had had no hang-ups about the newer technology, it seemed. She had almost as many CDs as LPs and she must have acquired these herself; or at least, her husband hadn't. The death certificate for Alain Mesnel that Lartou Lartigue had removed from the bureau was dated 3 February 1965.

'Where's...?' Darac found the disc he was looking for and fired it up. 'OK, you owe me this one, Jeanne.'

With its tiptoeing gait and portentous vibrato, the opening statement of 'Brilliant Corners' conjured the image of a pantomime ghost stalking an oblivious victim. He stood listening to the upbeat chase-like section that followed, remembering the thrilling way the quintet had interpreted it just the night before.

But there was work to do. The number acting as an almost comic accompaniment, he mounted the stairs and began exploring the upper floor.

A new-looking bed sat under the window in the largest bedroom, its duvet pulled back at one corner. A sense of futility and waste washed over Darac suddenly but then he remembered the old lady had gone to her maker drinking champagne and listening to Duke Ellington. He should be so lucky when the time came. A well-thumbed copy of *Candide* sat on her bedside table. A bookmark depicting an oddly prosaic Alpine scene indicated she had been well on the way to finishing it. For the hundredth time, possibly.

There was no sign of discarded clothes in the room but on the floor by the door he found a pair of pink, fluffy mules. The soles were of a hard, black rubber compound. The source of the scuff marks on the patio? Slipping them into his jacket pockets, he resolved to test the theory later.

There were only a few framed photos in Jeanne's bedroom. Unusually for a widow, none was of her wedding day. In fact, there was none of her and Alain together at all, or of the young Jeanne, either. The only shot of her Darac had seen was a passport photo taken eighteen months ago. On the wall over the bed head were three photos of a younger woman. In the most recent, she was nursing a baby. An inscription on the back read: *Sarah and Cristelle, March 1980.* Darac knew from a second death certificate that Sarah, Jeanne and Alain Mesnel's only child, had pre-deceased her mother by sixteen years. If the photo was representative, Sarah made an attractive but sad Madonna. The bright optimism conveyed in the two earlier photos had gone. The detached way she was holding baby Cristelle almost made Darac wince. On her birth certificate, Cristelle's father's occupation was listed as 'Shaman'. Detached mother; fruitcake father. Not the most helpful start in life.

A shot of a lively-looking man in his thirties stood on the dresser. Taken on the lower patio, a dated inscription identified him as Jeanne's husband, Alain. He looked as if he were just about to tell the photographer a funny story.

As Darac left the bedroom, he caught sight of himself in a full-length mirror. A pink mule sticking out of each pocket, he looked like the campest gunslinger in town. Resisting the temptation to draw and fire, he continued on to the landing. There proved to be nothing else of note in the upstairs rooms but in an airing cupboard he found what were probably Jeanne's discarded clothes from her fatal trip to the hot tub. Uppermost on the pile was a pair of cotton briefs. Under those were a pair of thick black leggings, a knee-length tweed skirt, a long-sleeved cotton vest, and finally, a heavy roll-neck pullover. It was a complete outfit for a cool day, stacked in the order she had taken them off. He checked the central heating timer.

It was due to come on once a day at four o'clock and go off

again at eight. He thought back to Barrau's report. He had given a pro-tem time of death as Saturday between noon and six o'clock. It seemed that Jeanne may have intended putting her clothes back on ready-warmed after braving the cold walk back from the tub. He thought about sending the garments over to the lab but left them on the shelf. He could always send them later if need be.

Darac headed off down the stairs but as he reached the turn he stopped dead. Attached to the newly revealed wall space was a framed copy of the same *Blown Away by the Brass Section* poster that hung over the entrance to the Blue Devil. In the lounge, Monk's band hit a rising crescendo: *Dah! Dah!! Dah!!! Dah!!!!* Darac stood for a moment, then reached out and touched the poster before passing underneath it.

He went to the bureau next. Lartou always removed the important documents but the inconsequential stuff left behind occasionally proved revealing. Not this time, it seemed: the compartmentalised upper section contained nothing of interest.

Darac turned to the two drawers beneath. The upper one stuck in its runners and he had to give it several to-and-fro tugs before it opened, the final effort yanking it free of the cabinet altogether. It was then that he saw a crumpled cardboard file nestling in the space between the bottom drawer and the carcass of the cabinet. A label on the spine read: *Will etc.* Darac exhaled deeply. Why hadn't Lartou seen this? He wondered if the file had ended up behind the drawer accidentally or if Madame Mesnel had placed it there deliberately, a rough-and-ready hiding place against prying eyes or thieving hands. He took it out.

The cardboard was bent around a deep crease that ran across the width of the file. Perhaps at some stage it had slid over the rear edge of the top drawer, then, pivoting around that edge, had become pinned against the back of the cabinet when the drawer was closed. When it was next opened, the file simply slid out of sight. However it ended up where it did, Lartou was due a bollocking for missing it.

According to a note, the will had recently been re-written. The 'etc.' referred to a house sale document dated just a few weeks before.

'Well, well...'

The sale in question was Madame Mesnel's own villa. The buyer was one Taylor Walters-Halberg, not a multinational company but an individual living on nearby Cap Ferrat. The address made him raise an eyebrow. Villa Rose was a spectacular belle époque mansion visited by thousands of tourists and art lovers every year. Darac powered up his laptop and began a search. Taylor proved to be thirty, single, female and an American citizen.

The Mesnel house had been sold '*en viager*,' a scheme in which an individual seeking to buy a property for future occupation secures it by making a relatively modest down payment – the 'bouquet' – and thereafter pays monthly instalments to the vendor who continues to live on in the sold property until their death. Darac totted things up. Now the vendor had died, the American had purchased her little piece of France for €180,000 plus three lots of €1,500. Not bad for a property valued at €650,000. Once everything had been sorted out, the house would be the American's to do with as she wished. Furniture and appliances were excluded from the sale but carpets, curtains, Madame Mesnel's collection of paintings and, perhaps oddly, a rather tarnished-looking carriage clock were all included.

'Unlucky, Cristelle.'

It got worse for her as Darac began ploughing through the labyrinth of technicalities that complicated the will. The bulk of the rest of her grandmother's estate, basically the initial 'bouquet' payment from the house purchase, had been bequeathed to 'my dearest friend', a Madame Anne Corot. Darac read through it all again. The notary had done a bang-up job, it seemed. In essence, Madame Mesnel had disinherited her direct heir, Cristelle; a very difficult thing to achieve in French law.

Darac performed a double-take as he turned to the lesser bequests. Among them was the name of one Eldridge Barton

Peters Clay.

'What?' Darac said aloud.

In "recognition of his great contribution to the local jazz scene", Madame Mesnel club had bequeathed club owner Ridge her entire collection of jazz records, CDs and tapes. Darac smiled and glanced at his watch. It was still too early to ring a night owl like Ridge with the news, so he continued reading the will. There, finally, was an entry for Cristelle. Her grandmother had bequeathed her just one item: "the jazz poster on the stairs".

Why had Jeanne Mesnel disinherited Cristelle? Had she discovered how she earned a living? A woman with a wide-ranging love of jazz, literature and art, Jeanne was unlikely to have been a judgemental prude. But prostitution was a desperate business.

Darac picked up his bag and fished out Brigitte's account of Marcel Battail's movements. He turned to Saturday. Between noon and six o'clock, Barrau's initial estimate of the time of death, Battail was supposed to have been at work in his tattoo parlour in Nice. He had no alibi from Brigitte until he got home after seven. She, herself, was in the clear. Her sister's family, all six of them, had been visiting her at the house until then. As Monk went into 'Ba-Lue Bolivar Ba-lues-Are', Darac swiped his mobile. The signal in the house had been weak the previous night. Now, there was none at all. He went outside.

'Malraux? Have you climbed off Brigitte long enough to find her boyfriend yet?'

'Oh you heard about that, eh?'

The self-regard in his voice was evident even on a weak signal. But bragging about sleeping with Brigitte? A woman old enough to be his mother? Darac felt sorry for him.

'Listen Malraux, this is not the kind of undercover operation we sanction, alright? When the case is over, you can screw each other's arses off for all I care but until then, better keep things professional.'

'He's still lying low somewhere.'

'What?'

'You asked me if I knew where Battail was.'

Malraux had caught the reprimand, alright. No stranger to insubordination himself, Darac decided to leave it there. 'If he's got any sense, he'll show up for work as normal. If he doesn't, this guy Dagger might. Know about him?'

'Yeah. Brigitte says he works one weekend in about every four. He hasn't been for a few weeks so he could be due. I've got a uniform keeping tabs. Once every hour.'

'Do you know when the place opens?'

'Around lunchtime.'

'Alright, get down there for noon.'

'I'm over in Saint-André — the Buchon case.'

'There's nothing in that for you, surely?'

'Public Prosecutor Frènes thought so. Me and Lartigue were both called in.' Malraux's voice had lost its familiar strut. 'It's an all-day job. As the Mesnel drowning isn't even—'

'We don't know for certain what it is yet. I want you there if Battail shows.'

'But—'

'Just do it. I'll square it with Frènes if necessary. You say Lartigue is with you?'

'Yes. Sir.'

'Put him on.'

As he waited, Darac's eye fell once more on the Kandinsky print, a work he'd never seen on anyone else's wall but his own.

'Chief?'

'Lartou? Bone to pick. I'm at Chemin Leuze. I know it's not like you but you missed a lot of vital stuff in Madame Mesnel's bureau last night. There's a will here, for a start.'

'Sorry. It was all so rushed.'

'Partly, I gather, because you couldn't wait to check out the woman's hot tub. If you want to go window-shopping, do it after work, will you?'

'Another thing was that it's such an obvious natural-causes case—'

'But that doesn't mean we can just do what the hell we like, does it?'

'No. Commissaire.'

'Hey! Bullshit, Lartou. You stuffed up, that's all there is to it. Don't do it again.'

Darac rang off. 'Commissaire?' Where did Lartou get off with that? Everyone knew Darac had never given a stuff about rank. If a brash newcomer like Malraux couldn't stand him, so what? It was mutual. But Lartou? That was different. Before he got hung up on questions of rotten apples in barrels, Darac told himself to forget it and move on. He had a date on the lower patio.

The concrete felt cold as he knelt down and looked again at the scuff marks. Sitting on his haunches, he took Madame Mesnel's mules out of his pockets and slid his gloved hands inside them. A voice called out from above.

'I think you're supposed to put them on your feet?' The voice belonged to a tall young blond woman.

'I was misinformed.' He remained kneeling. 'You OK after your excitement, Erica?'

'I'm fine.' She gave a little shimmy to prove it. 'No whiplash. Not even a headache.'

'Excellent.'

Darac slipped the mules off his hands and stood as Erica made her way down to him.

'I hope you're not here to check out the deceased's computers or anything. The only IT is a landline phone and even I know how to chase up those records.'

'No, I was picking up a courtesy car from down the road so I thought I'd call in. Granot told me you were here.' Erica's fine hair fell away from her neck as she ducked easily under the cordon tape. 'What are you up to? I thought everything pointed to it being accidental.'

'Or natural causes. A few interesting things are emerging, though. I was just about to check out those black scuff marks.' He indicated them with a nod. 'But as you're here, you can lend me a hand. Or rather your feet.' He held out the mules. 'Got time?'

'I've got a couple of minutes.' The mules were not to her taste. '*Lovely.* So what do you want me to do? See if I can produce marks to match those others?'

'Exactly. Let's do it over in the corner, there.' Taking a marker out of his pocket, Darac drew a rough circle on the concrete and captioned it: *Test – PD & EL 9 Jan.*

Erica took off her shoes. 'My heels will probably hang off the back.'

'Doesn't matter.'

She slipped on the mules. 'And my motivation in this scene is…?'

'To not try too hard. Just do it naturally, as if you were putting them on after getting out of the hot tub. Remember you're seventy-one and have a weakish heart.'

'Still gorgeous though, I hope?'

Darac remembered the way Jeanne had looked the night before. 'Of course.'

'Good. Right… Here I go.'

Erica began the performance. With each take, the mules left the requisite marks. 'They're the cause, alright.' She kept them on for the moment. 'Why is it significant?'

'The deceased, Madame Jeanne Mesnel, obviously made a practice of wearing these mules to the hot tub. Yet it seems she didn't do that last Saturday when it was so cold.'

'How do you know she didn't wear them?'

'I found them back in the house along with her clothes.'

'Hmm. On the other hand, I've heard you say a thousand times that there's no predicting what people will do.'

'It's probably nothing,' he said, studying the ground again. Something caught his eye. He stared harder. Look there. Some of these marks are not the same. Something stubbier has made them.'

'Oh yes… A walking stick with a rubber end?'

'Maybe.' He took a couple of paces back. 'No, they're grouped in a pattern. See?' She shook her head. 'It's like finding a hidden design in a puzzle. Once your eye is in, you can't *not* see it.'

Shielding her eyes, she stood on tiptoe. 'I've got it. Triangles.'

'Yes. Tripod foot marks? Looks as if it was set down roughly, then jagged into position. Three… four times altogether.'

'Tripod marks on a patio.' She drew down the corners of her mouth. 'If it's evidence, what's it evidence of?' She looked at her watch. The minute hand had reached Tintin's quiff. 'Ah.' She handed him the mules. 'Got to go.'

'OK.'

'Now I have to break it to those nice people at Commissariat Foch that two laptops and some other gear were totalled in the accident.' Balancing flamingo-like, she slipped on one shoe, then the other. 'They've charged the other driver, by the way.'

'Good.'

'Dead drunk, he was. Apparently his football team conceded a last-minute penalty and it sent him loopy.'

'Strange people, football fans.'

They exchanged parting kisses. 'Thanks, Erica.' He held on to her shoulders. 'I'm glad you're alright.'

'I'm tougher than I look. See you later.'

Darac played around for another five minutes, then took the mules back to the bedroom and prepared to lock up the house. Turning off the sound system gave him pause.

Why had the old lady never visited the Blue Devil? Or at least, he had never seen her there and he'd been a regular for fourteen years. Everyone would have made a fuss of her, especially Ridge, who was as soft as a ripe Camembert under the carapace.

Taking one last look at what had been a whole world of jazz, literature and art, Darac closed the door and walked away.

Madame Alphonsine Loret lived in a small villa just around the corner from her former employer. Recalling her scattergun monologues of the previous evening, Darac rang the bell with some misgivings. But then he noticed the layout of her front garden. If the slide-rule symmetry of her flower beds was anything to go by, the woman was possessed of an obsessively ordered mind and that was a useful quality in a witness.

The door opened.

'Captain, you came. Good. The garden is lovely, isn't it?' She stepped aside. 'My son does it. Go through to the back. Oh, the hideousness of last night…'

In the kitchen, the grass-and-urine scent of camomile tea hung in the air like a cloud. A folded white cloth, soaking in a bowl on the table, was immediately pressed into service.

'This cold compress is the only relief I've had.'

'I'm glad you're feeling better, Madame Loret. Now if we can—'

'Better? Hardly. Sit down. No, not there, *there*.' She pointed blindly to an upholstered chair in the corner of the room. 'It's more comfortable. I sit and read my magazine there when there's time. But of course that's—'

Concluding that herding cats would have been easier than keeping Madame Loret to the point, Darac decided to take a tighter rein. 'Madame Loret, I have some questions for you which I want you to answer fully but concisely, Understood?'

'Coffee?'

'No coffee, thanks.'

'Or tea? I have camomile. It's *so* calming.'

Calming as speed, by the look of it.

'No, no camomile—'

'The smell, Captain. The smell that greeted me when I went— "Madame Loret!' At last, he had her attention. 'Thank you. Did you touch or move anything during your visit?'

'Certainly not. What was I going to touch?'

'I was interested that no clothes or footwear were found near the hot tub. I wondered if you might have taken them back into the house.'

'I did no such thing.'

'So you believe Madame Mesnel may have ventured out to the hot tub—'

'Stark naked? Yes, she did that sometimes. Good for her! *Joie de vivre?* Madame had that in spades. And just because one reaches a certain—'

'Thank you. To your knowledge, has a tripod ever been set up near the tub? Perhaps with surveying equipment mounted on it? Or a camera?'

'No? Why on earth…'

The interview went on far longer than Darac had planned but on the few occasions he managed to dam the woman's stream of consciousness, he gathered some useful information. Jeanne Mesnel, 'a lovely woman, odd in some ways but lovely nevertheless', had suffered a dip in her health during the last few months of her life. Instead of giving in, it had made her all the more determined to enjoy herself. She had loved the hot tub from the word go.

A question about Jeanne's granddaughter, Cristelle, brought a sneer. It seemed Madame Mesnel had had no contact with her since she was eighteen.

'Until six months ago. All those years without even a card and she turns up.'

As far as Loret knew, there had been no further visits. She believed Cristelle was responsible for the gift of the hot tub and for the other household improvements.

'She was just feathering her own nest, of course, Captain.'

Darac didn't challenge the assumption. 'Did Madame Mesnel know what Cristelle does for a living? Did she ever talk to you about it?'

'I didn't need her to tell me. I know what the little monkey does.'

'How?'

'I've seen her at work.' She reapplied the compress as if

providing an antidote to the thought. 'Several times.'

Darac doubted it but odder things had happened. 'Where have you seen her working?'

'Palais Masséna. Cosmetics floor. Surly. Very surly with the customers. Now I think about it, I haven't seen her for a year or two. There must have been complaints and the management got rid of her, I suppose. I said to—'

'I see. Who else visited Madame Mesnel? Regular visitors, I mean?'

It seemed Jeanne had suffered a premature version of one of the curses of the elderly; only two of her close friends were still living. The first, the will beneficiary Anne Corot, lived in Théoule-sur-Mer, a small coastal resort to the west of Cannes. Until recently, the women had taken it more or less in turn to visit one another every couple of weeks. The other, a Monsieur Gaston Cartin, had moved to Paris to be near his daughter the previous year and hadn't visited for some months.

In terms of casual visitors, the only regular was Berthe Lepic's boy Henri who 'ran the occasional errand' but hadn't been running anywhere since last Friday. He'd broken his leg, skateboarding.

On the whole, Madame Mesnel had been on cordial terms with her neighbours; especially those for whom she had made or altered clothes. But 'that big animal' Marcel Battail was not the only one to have been irritated by her new habit of playing 'that jigaboo music' outdoors.

Darac began to take down the names of all those who had expressed anti-jazz-playing sentiments. He couldn't resist a smile – the Brigade Criminelle had spawned a new division, the SS of Swing. However, only Battail, Loret insisted, had remonstrated with Madame Mesnel about it. 'Like I told Monsieur Frènes, I heard everything that animal said and I'll repeat it in court!'

'Can you remember what Battail said, word for word?'

'Oh yes.' The old lady did her best to transform her fine-boned face into a replica of Battail's battle-scarred mug. 'He said: "If you don't turn that… effing music down, I'll drown you, you effing old bitch." '

Darac looked up from his notebook. 'That's quite a—'

' "*And*" ' Madame hadn't finished. '…"nobody will ever know it wasn't an effing accident." '

'That is quite a threat.'

'Of course, Captain, he didn't actually say "effing". He said "fucking". There! To that lovely woman he said that!'

Darac found himself taking a shine to Madame Loret. Whatever else she was, she was a game old bird. Ten minutes later, he took his leave having established one further point: Loret herself was in the clear. She cleaned Madame Mesnel's place on Friday afternoons and the old lady had been on good form when she'd left her. On the day of her neighbour's death, Loret was performing one of her 'many acts of charity' – volunteer hospital visiting. Between midday and six, she had been cruising for victims on the wards at the Clinique Pasteur in Saint-Pons. A string of witnesses could swear to it.

Before leaving the neighbourhood, Darac went to pay a follow-up call on Brigitte Andreani. His knock unanswered, he went into the back yard to find the patio freshly hosed but no sign of Brigitte. He got back in his Peugeot and after a quick phone call, set off on the short drive to Cap Ferrat and the person to whom an ill wind had just blown a great deal of good: Ms Taylor Walters-Halberg.

9

Rue Jules Gilly ran along the lower eastern edge of the Babazouk, a quarter suffused with the savoury scents of every tourist's favourite snacks: the hot chickpea pancakes called *socca*, and *pissaladière*, pizza-like pastry bases topped with olive, anchovy and onion. There were few tourists milling around the cafés and carts today but there was still a feeling of hustle and bustle in the tightly winding streets.

Blood Brothers had a discreet frontage for a tattoo parlour, especially one run by a three-time loser like Marcel Battail. The exception was the design painted on its front door: crossed tattoo needles spelling out the shop's name in blood-red droplets. Blinds drawn across the windows hid the interior from the street.

Lieutenant Intern Christian Malraux was sitting at a café table opposite, his lashless eyes trained on the parlour's front door.

'That'll be two euros.'

He tossed the waitress the till receipt. 'I already paid.'

'Not for the coffee.' She indicated the teaspoon he'd been playing with for the past twenty minutes. 'For *that.*'

Straightening it back into a roughly spoon-like shape, he dropped it into his empty cup. 'Good as new. Now get me another latte.'

'*Pffft!*'

The waitress disappeared as a tall, spike-haired young woman walked up to the door of Blood Brothers and unclipped a bunch of keys from her belt. She was wearing the kind of outfit Malraux's riot squad mates dubbed 'guerrilla goth'. Above: short-sleeved black leather jacket over a layered selection of skinny black tops, the letters *NA* and *ENT* visible on the uppermost layer. Below: studded leather belt, leggings into Doc Martens.

Malraux watched the woman set about opening the front door. It had three locks: cylinder deadbolts top and bottom and a central mortise. He moved in before she could lock the door behind her. 'Hello, princess.' He put his boot between the door and the frame. 'What's up?'

Adèle Voska saw the boot first. 'Come back in an hour.' Her eyes slid up to the man's face. 'Now shift...' His oddly porcine physiognomy halted her. 'Shift your fucking foot.'

Before she could stop him, he reached in and, opening the lapels of her jacket, read the full legend on her T-shirt. 'So you're

"Anally Retentive", are you?'

Making fists, she batted his hands aside and gave his shoulders a hard shove. He stumbled back over the threshold but he came again, fending off the door as she tried to slam it in his face. She was several centimetres taller than her attacker but she could do nothing against his barrel-chested strength. Clamping her arms to her sides, he pinned her back against the counter and flicked the door shut with his foot.

'This is police business, Rambo.' He held his denim jacket open. 'See this?' Held by tags to the lining was something that looked like a cosh.

'So?'

'It's a cut-down riot baton. Little souvenir of my days with the CRS. If you don't answer my questions, we'll find out just how anally retentive you are.'

The threat was so over the top, she almost laughed. But then she looked into the man's eyes. The lack of expression in them made her blood run cold. 'Take your hands... off me and I'll talk.'

The man squeezed, compressing her spine and sending a shock wave through her belly. Already tender with first day period pain, she felt as if she might burst.

'You'll talk anyway, bitch. Marcel Battail. Where is he?'

Pulling her head back as far as she could, she looked away. 'He'll be here soon.' Her words emerged in a constricted gasp. 'Let go.'

Out of the corner of her eye, she saw one of Battail's tattoo machines sitting on the counter behind her. Its needle had been left in the grip.

'You've heard from him, then?'

'It's when he always comes.' She was sure the *flic* couldn't see the machine. 'Will he be alone?'

She tried to get one hand free. 'Yes.'

'Who is Dagger?'

'He works here... sometimes.'

'I know that. What's his real name? Where's he live?'

'I don't know.' More compression. More pain. 'I don't know! I swear.'

She eyed the tattoo machine. Centimetres away, a kilometre: it didn't matter. She couldn't move.

'And who are *you*, sweetheart?'

'Voska.'

'What kind of a name is that?'

'Adèle...' Another spasm, this one keener. 'Voska.'

'Thank you.' He gave her a final gratuitous squeeze. 'Was that so hard?'

Adèle collapsed on to the counter, her heaving torso shielding the tattoo machine from the policeman. She grabbed the handle. Jabbing the needle into his little pig eyes and then turning the power on. That was what she wanted to do. Her stomach turned over at the thought. His hands, then. Or neck. Yes, neck. Her finger found the switch. But feeling his taut bulk flex against her back, she began to think better of it. A creasing pain in her belly acted as the final deterrent. She let the machine slip quietly back on to the counter.

'If you'd been nice at the start, Adèle, we could have avoided that little spat.'

Feeling doubly violated by his use of her given name, she slowly righted herself. 'Get out.' She felt dizzy, suddenly. 'Out.'

'Slow learner, aren't you? That's all behind us. We're friends now. So we are going to wait for dear old Marcel together.' He indicated a leather sofa. 'Shall we?'

His words echoing from far away, Adèle took a few faltering steps, stumbled and fainted into her attacker's arms. Carrying her to the sofa, Malraux dumped her on it and sat down side-saddle on its arm. Like all policemen, he was a trained first-aider so he knew what his next move should be: raise the girl's legs and then loosen her clothing. Ignoring the first requirement, he slid his hand under the waistband of her leggings and kept going. As he reached her groin, he withdrew it in one sharp movement. 'You filthy…' He looked around. There was a white porcelain sink in the corner. He hurried to it as if to delay might prove fatal. Believing with the certainty of the righteous or the psychotic that, even in her unconscious state, the girl had somehow been responsible for violating *him*, he began scrubbing his hand.

He turned as Adèle stirred into consciousness and tried to sit up. And then, in a cloud of booze and cheap after-shave, a tattooed man appeared massively in the doorway.

'Who the fuck are you?' he said.

10

Villa Rose stood high up on the verdant crest of Cap Ferrat, commanding sea views to the south, east and west. As Darac followed the lane that wound its way up to the entrance, he caught occasional glimpses of a cornice or a window but it wasn't until the final curve paid out that the building came fully into view, revealing itself in all its pink deliciousness like an iced cake turning on a stand. That the villa and its gardens had once been a private residence was remarkable. That its original owner, the late Baroness Rose de Sainte-Caranville, had owned two even grander palaces on the Riviera beggared belief.

Visiting such places tended to bring out Darac's proletarian instincts. Yet he had a personal reason for forgiving, even for being grateful to, the baroness. Quite simply, without her, he would never have existed.

In the late 1930s, the dying baroness bequeathed the house and its entire contents to the Académie des Beaux-Arts. Among the conditions she laid down was that the property be opened to the public at a rate 'any Jacques or Jacqueline could afford'. Some forty years later it was in Villa Rose's English Tea Room, a vaulted salon overlooking the glittering waters of the Rade de

Villefranche, that trainee parfumier Martin Darac met a young maths teacher named Sandrine Martigny. They fell to talking and carried on talking as they made a tour of the gardens. They met again later that night and hardly talked at all.

Smiling at his parents' raciness those thirty-three years ago, Darac left his car and set off on the broad curving footpath to the front entrance of the villa. The romantic atmosphere didn't last long; his mobile rang almost immediately.

'Darac, I know you are a stranger to politeness, patience and any sort of protocol—'

'Afternoon, Monsieur Frènes.'

'But hear this, never under any circumstances take one of *my* people off *my* case again without clearing it with *me* first.'

'Malraux, you mean? I thought he was my man. Nevertheless, I apologise. Unreservedly. I'm going into a tunnel now. Bye.'

A banner announcing a forthcoming Matisse exhibition was hanging over Villa Rose's main entrance. Darac made a mental note of the dates, entered the foyer and identified himself at the desk to a man whose face was so smooth it looked ironed.

'Where might I find Ms Taylor Walters-Halberg?'

Directions duly received, Darac walked through the colonnaded space of the atrium and took the curving marble staircase up to the first floor. On the landing, an armed guard from a security firm was standing with his back to a huge picture window. Darac took up position next to him and gazed out toward the low rocky outcrop at the cape's southern tip. Only a couple of kilometres away, it was out of sight even from such an elevated position. This, combined with the narrowness of the terrain, created a magical effect: the long flat plane of the parterre garden laid out in front of him appeared to project over the sea like the foredeck of some fabulous liner.

Ms Walters-Halberg's office was accessible from the Louis XVI salon, one of a series of sumptuously decorated rooms displaying the fine art works, furniture and *objets d'art* the baroness had acquired in a lifetime of collecting. Darac glanced at his watch. Having a little time to kill before the interview, he decided to take a spin around the exhibition. A series of lithographs caught his eye: strong, menacing works that were somehow still decorative. Jean Cocteau, perhaps? He leaned forward to check the wall label. Behind him, a young guide walked in, trailing a loose caboose of tourists in her train. Tall, slender and spectacularly braided, the guide could have been drummer Rama N'Pata's twin, except that she was white.

'It is thought', she announced, 'that this Derain seascape was painted in return for meals taken at the Restaurant des Chevaliers in Collioure in 1905. It originally hung next to the toilet door in that establishment. I think it looks better here, don't you?'

The group chortled. For his part, Darac thought swags and festoons in cream and gilt a *non-sympa* backdrop to the artist's vibrant studies of the Vermilion Coast. But what did he know? He returned to the lithographs, wondering which would be easiest to conceal under his jacket. After a further glance at his watch, he abandoned the idea and crossed behind the group toward a short corridor marked private.

'Sir? There's no way through there,' Rama's long-lost twin said, smiling.

'I have an appointment with Ms Walters-Halberg.'

'I beg your pardon.' She resumed her routine. 'This second seascape…'

Darac knocked at the door and waited. Now he'd been put in mind of Rama, he couldn't help wondering how the young man's workday was shaping up. Having to wash pots and scrub floors for a while wouldn't do him any harm. Many of Darac's heroes had had menial jobs before they made it: night-watchman, cotton picker, slaughterman…

The door was opened by a young woman wearing a well-cut grey trouser suit over a blouse of rose pink silk. She was blue-eyed and blond and a smile played on her lips, which were wide and glistening and matched the colour of her blouse.

'Ms Taylor Walters-Halberg?'

'I'm happier with *mademoiselle*, Captain... Darac?'

'Forgive me.'

Darac recognised in her the particular air of assurance that stunningly good-looking people so often possess. High on health and gloss but low on mystique, it was a look he himself didn't find particularly captivating.

'Listen,' she said, 'I have to meet some press people shortly but I'll be free from two o'clock for at least an hour if that would be preferable.'

'No, no. Now would be fine.'

'Then please come in.'

The American woman's French was word-perfect but the rapid nasal monotone in which she spoke was extraordinary. An upward inflection had so far turned every statement into a question.

He followed her through a vestibule into a plainly decorated space, smaller than he had pictured from the outside, but one rendered light and airy by a double *porte-fenêtre* that gave on to a terrace overlooking the Rade de Villefranche. A portable CD player sat on top of a bank of filing cabinets, some fitted with ranks of shallow trays. A notepad and a couple of art books lay open on her desk, behind which were a water cooler and a door that led, presumably, to the rest of the apartment.

'Shall we talk in here or...?'

'Wherever you would feel most comfortable.'

She smiled and showed him out on to the terrace.

'Your French is impeccable but you're from the United States?'

'Thank you. Yes, I'm from Santa Cruz, California. Do you know it?'

'Afraid not.'

A couple of cane chairs were drawn up at a small wrought-iron table.

'Let's sit there.'

'So what brought you all the way from California to Villa Rose?'

'A degree in Art History and French, number one. From the University of London.' Pausing at the table, she invited Darac to take in the scene. 'Stunning, isn't it?'

The view across the shimmering azure of the Rade de Villefranche was sensational.

'It's almost too beautiful,' he said, turning to her. 'Shall we?' They sat down.

'And back to something like our usual temperatures today. Some water, coffee?'

'Nothing, thanks. Your role here at Villa Rose is what, exactly, mademoiselle?'

'I'm assistant curator.'

'Assistant to Monsieur Philippe de Lambert?'

'I have that privilege.'

The aristocratic old man was an internationally regarded scholar, or had been at one time, and was still something of a local celebrity, a throwback to a different world.

'I find it remarkable that someone so young could have risen to such a position.'

'Thank you.'

'You have other senior staff?'

'There are three of us in the gallery management team. And of course, there are security, catering, gardening and various other people. But anyway, Captain, to business. I'm afraid I know why you're here.'

How? Nothing had been released to anyone concerning Madame Mesnel's death.

'I didn't mean to do it.' She lowered her eyes. 'Well, I did but I know I shouldn't.'

'You didn't mean to do what, mademoiselle?'

'Punch that man on the jaw.'

'Ah yes?'

The knuckles of her right hand were almost a mirror of his own, he noticed. But he was a *flic*, not assistant curator of one of the most prestigious collections of paintings and *objets d'art* on the Côte d'Azur.

'Look, I know you French don't think like we Americans do, and when in Rome and all that... but the man was torturing that poor donkey.' She sat forward in her chair, ready to fight her corner. '*Torturing* it.'

'Refresh my memory.' Darac took out his notebook. 'When did this happen?'

'Last Sunday, in one of the lanes up near Tende. I don't think it has a name.'

'What were you doing up there?'

'Power hiking. I told the man politely, to begin with, that a donkey was not designed to carry that kind of load. He should have used a...' She searched for the French term. '...a pick-up or a tractor or something. He took no notice.'

'And the load was?'

'Stone.'

'Stone shot through with greenish streaks?'

'Ah, you know the area –yes. There looked to be tons of the stuff on the poor thing's back.'

'Now this man—'

'Has brought charges. I was hoping he was too much of a peasant to realise he could.'

Speaking so candidly was a peculiarly American trait, Darac believed. He found it refreshing. 'But you admit you punched him?'

'Yes, and then before he came round, I unloaded as many of the rocks as I could and shooed the donkey away. Or tried to. It wouldn't move.'

Darac couldn't help grinning. 'You knocked this man out cold?'

'It didn't take much, believe me. He was practically falling over with drink as it was. But I'm afraid I did punch him out, yes. No, actually, I'm not afraid. I'd do it again.'

Darac met her steady cornflower-blue gaze. He suspected the woman hadn't the slightest sense of what the life of a French 'peasant', not a pejorative term to him, was all about; nor its donkeys, come to that, but he liked her defiant spirit. '*Chapeau!*'

'Oh. But…?'

'Perhaps I should come clean, mademoiselle. I am not here in connection with the Tende Donkey Torture Scandal.'

'I don't think it's funny, Captain.'

'I'm sorry. But the fact remains I'm here on an unrelated matter. I believe you have recently purchased a property, locally. *En viager.*'

'Yes?' She scrunched her forehead. 'In Beaulieu, around the other side of the bay.'

'This splendid apartment is yours also?'

'No, it goes with the post. What's all this about, Captain?'

'Just bear with me a moment. Are you planning to leave your position here?'

'Not at all, but one must be realistic. Philippe de Lambert is the godson of the late Baroness Rose de Sainte-Caranville, as you possibly know. When he passes, Villa Rose and everything in it will revert to the Académie des Beaux-Arts. I may lose more than an esteemed colleague and mentor that day; I may lose my job and my apartment, also.'

That American frankness again. Darac knew it would have taken far longer to have elicited such a revealing answer from a French person in her position. 'On Monsieur de Lambert's death, might you not retain your post and therefore your apartment?'

'I would hope to but, Captain, I believe I have borne with you long enough.'

'Agreed. Well, mademoiselle, I have to inform you that you have made your last monthly payment on number seventeen Chemin Leuze, Beaulieu-sur-Mer.'

'I imagine the last payment has gone through, yes. I don't understand.'

'I meant that you have made your last payment *ever*. The vendor of the house, Madame Jeanne Mesnel, has died.'

'Madame Mesnel is... dead?'

'Well, she was seventy-one and in poor health latterly.'

'I know. I suppose I... should be happy, in a way. After all, making as few monthly payments as possible is what *en viager* is all about for the buyer.' Her eyes misting, she gazed out over the Rade de Villefranche. 'But that lady was a sweetheart and so full of life for a woman of her age. What happened?'

'She drowned in her hot tub.'

Taylor blanched and for a moment it looked as if she might be sick.

'I'll get some water.' When Darac returned, she was looking a little stronger. He handed her the glass. 'Are you alright?'

'No, uh... you see, the hot tub... was my idea. I bought it for her as a thank-you for selling me the house.'

'Mademoiselle, we can postpone this.'

'No, I'd rather...' Setting her shoulders, she took a breath. 'Please go on.'

'You're sure?' She nodded. 'Alright. Your thank-you gift was remarkably generous.'

'I paid for a ten-year care contract, too.' She shook her head. 'We joked about it.'

'The sale agreement included curtains and carpets, I noticed. And some other odds and ends. Paintings, lamps, a clock?'

'The paintings.' She gave a sad little smile. 'Local scenes. I think she had done them herself. Because I'm an art historian, she wanted me to have them.'

'The clock?' Darac said, lightly.

'The one in the kitchen?'

'No, the one on the mantelpiece in the living room. The carriage clock.'

'Oh, is that part of the sale?'

Darac nodded.

'I'd forgotten. I probably admired it in passing once, or something. Sweet, sweet lady. I can't believe she's gone.' The sun sank further into the horizon of her sadness. 'You say she drowned? She slipped or—'

'We're not quite sure what happened yet. Nor when exactly.'

'If I hadn't been so insistent that she have it...'

'But I hear she loved the hot tub.'

'Yes, she did.'

Remembering that the hot tub's filter had yielded a strand of natural blond hair, Darac looked again at Taylor's own. It was so perfectly blond, he had assumed it was dyed. But in the daylight of the terrace, he could see the colour was her own. It begged a question. He smiled, keeping the mood light. 'Did you ever go in the hot tub with her?'

'Yes. It was wonderful. Forty years between us but we were like kids.'

'More than once?'

'Three or four times. It was such fun. Her errand boy, Henri, caught us playing tickle toes once. I think he thought we'd lost the plot completely.'

If Darac knew teenage boys, bemusement may not have been Henri's only reaction.

'We were both wearing swimsuits, Captain.'

'I'm obviously not the brilliant poker player I thought I was, mademoiselle. When was the last time you bathed with Madame?'

'It was a Saturday...'

Darac gave nothing away. 'Uh-huh?'

'Two, no three weeks ago tomorrow. The... 20th.' Dabbing her eyes, she froze for a moment. 'I've just remembered what your ID specified, Captain.'

'We are obliged to investigate any unexplained death.' He flipped open his notebook once more. 'It's strictly a matter of routine.'

'But you are with the Police Judiciaire, right?'

'The Brigade Criminelle of the Police Judiciaire, to be exact.'

'So you don't think the death unexplained so much as suspicious.'

'Potentially.'

'But you can't think anyone would want to kill Madame Mesnel?'

'It seems unlikely, I agree, but these things happen.'

'Don't you have… what's the term? Medical examiners here?'

'Not proper ones, of course. But I think we have a couple of test tubes and some litmus paper lying around somewhere.'

'I'm sorry. Of course you have medical examiners.'

'In fact, forensic science is more or less a French invention. Something we gave to the world along with wine, cheese and the art of living. So they tell me.'

She ignored the wider claim. 'In that case, won't your lab people be able to come up with a definitive analysis of what happened?'

'In a few days, perhaps, but we still have to ask pertinent questions in the meantime.'

'Of course.'

In lieu of asking the most pertinent question, Darac raised his eyebrows and smiled.

'Yes, I suppose you need to know where I was when poor Madame Mesnel died.'

Darac had once trapped a suspect into incriminating herself in a murder investigation when she had produced an alibi for the exact time of the victim's death before he'd informed her of when it had happened. Ever since, it had become part of his technique never to volunteer such information prematurely. 'Just for the record.'

'When did it happen?'

'Some time last Saturday.'

'Saturday, the 2nd?' Taylor tilted her gaze upwards as if her itinerary for the day were written in mid-air. Scrunching her forehead formed a perfect trident-shaped crease on the bridge of her nose, Darac noticed – a devilish mark indeed for the face of an angel. 'I got up at seven o'clock and then, as I do every morning, went for my jog down to the beach at Passable and back. Breakfast at 8.15. From 8.30 I worked for an hour here in my office, before driving over to Cannes. I went shopping, then I had lunch with Philippe and some people who want to use the villa in an advertising campaign.'

'Lunched here?'

'No, in Cannes: Hotel Martinez. That was from one until two o'clock. Afterwards, Philippe and I came back here and worked until eight. We should have finished at seven but we've an important exhibition coming up. I then had only half an hour to change before I went with Maggie – that's Margaret de Lambert, Philippe's wife – to La Rascasse down in Saint-Jean for dinner. We do that sometimes; two Yankee gals together.'

'Is Madame younger than Monsieur de Lambert?'

'Maggie's seventy; Philippe's seventy-five. It's a mid-to late-December situation.'Darac grinned. Taylor was witty, sensitive and, even in these moments of stress, everything about her seemed to shine. But it wasn't just her laser beam of a voice that sounded an off-key note. There was something else he couldn't put his finger on.

She resumed the search of her airborne itinerary: 'Then, let's see, I was back here by 10.30 and went to bed.' Finally shifting her gaze back to him, she looked flustered, suddenly. 'Oh, I bet you didn't believe a word of that. I didn't look you in the eyes once.'

Darac's customary half-smile widened a little. Liars always looked into the eyes of the lied-to. Unconscious tells were the real giveaway. 'So what can you buy in Cannes that you can't in Nice, mademoiselle?'

'Clothes made by Julie Suche for one thing. She has a little place on Rue des Serbes.' She smoothed her jacket lapels. 'I've worn it three times since. I'm such a child.'

Darac smiled. 'Use a credit card?'

'Yes.'

'And if you still had the transaction receipt, the time on it would be?'

'I do and it would be about 12.30. I bought some shoes at Carla in Rue Macé about an hour earlier.' She stood. 'I'm sure I have that receipt as well.'

'Don't worry, I can check with the credit-card company.'

'No trouble at all.'

A moment later, she returned with her handbag. The receipts tallied with her story.

'Thank you. Again, just for the record, did you and Monsieur de Lambert drive back together from Cannes to Villa Rose?'

'I drove him, to be precise. Philippe's eyesight isn't what it was.'

'And that took?'

'An hour and a quarter. My old VW isn't what it was, either.'

'And you didn't disappear for even, say, half an hour during the work session?'

Fingering a pearl earring, Taylor stared blindly into space. 'I can't believe it.' She shook her head. 'I'm a suspect in a possible murder case.'

'No, no. As I said, it's just a matter of routine. My team is putting these same questions to half the residents in the area.'

She seemed to regain her focus. 'Of course. Uh, the answer to your question is yes. No, I mean. I didn't disappear, that's what I'm trying to say. Philippe will vouch that I was with him, apart from the odd minute or two, that whole time.'

As far as Taylor's possible involvement in Jeanne Mesnel's death was concerned, if everything checked out, she was basically in the clear. Alibis provided by everyone from celebrated couturier Julie Suche to the aristocratic art historian Philippe de Lambert were about as good as they got.

'Mademoiselle, there may still be some things to discuss but you have your meeting to attend and I think you could use a few minutes to clear your head.'

Letting go of her earring, she rose and extended her hand. 'That's kind. Thank you.'

Taking care not to squeeze the bruised knuckles, he shook her hand. 'Thank *you* for your co-operation.' He jotted down a number on a page in his notebook and tore it off. 'Here's my mobile number if you want to talk to me in the meantime.'

'I'll give you mine.'

'Should anything come through from the Gendarmerie Regionale about that other matter, I'll make sure it goes no further.'

'That is so kind.' She gave him her business card.

'Thank you again.'

Actually, he had no such authority but he knew nothing would materialise. No peasant from the Mercantour, especially one who had obviously been nicking lumps of *schiste verte* from the quarry at Tende, would admit to being KO'd by a slender young woman. 'Finally, do you know if a tripod was set up on Madame Mesnel's patio recently?'

'A tripod? No. Sorry.'

They said their goodbyes and Darac walked back into the gallery, tempted to take an early lunch. But the English Tea Room's legendary *salade de saumon fumé* would have to wait. First, he needed to interview the Villa Rose's head man, Philippe de Lambert. Catching an elderly room attendant's eye, Darac flashed his ID and asked the way. Delighted at having a reason to break his vow of silence, the man explained that Monsieur's study was part of the Lamberts' private wing at the far end of the building.

'It's on the next floor up but you can't get to it through the galleries.'

The official route involved taking the stairs back down into the atrium, exiting the building and, now two floors beneath the objective, re-entering it around the side where Darac would then have to check in with a security guard. However, as Darac was a senior police officer, the attendant was sure nobody would mind if he advised him of a quicker, 'secret' route, a disused service corridor that cut straight across the building.

'You'll need a torch. It's a bit on the dark and damp side.' Darac showed the man his penlight. It got the nod. 'Right, go through into that storeroom.' He indicated a door marked CLEANERS. 'You'll find what looks like a cupboard door in the corner. Open it and you're in an old scullery. Go through the door at the back and you're in the corridor. Just keep going and you'll come out by their terrace. Monsieur's study's off that. If he's not in, he'll probably be in their apartment upstairs.'

In the corridor, Darac's torch beam played ahead of him as he followed puddled paving toward a door rimmed in daylight. It soon became clear it hadn't been opened in some time but he managed to drag it free of the jamb. As the dank air gave way to the salt breath of the sea, he emerged on to a corner of a broad, sun-flooded terrace lined with classical statuary.

Access to Philippe de Lambert's study appeared to be via a vaulted porch built on to the far end of the terrace but for the moment, it was the view along the coast toward Monaco that drew Darac's attention. Immediately below, the lane that wound up to the villa's main entrance was all but hidden under a canopy of pines and palms. Beyond, the landscape appeared as if it belonged in an oriental artwork, the various land masses beyond the Baie des Fourmis receding in hazy overlapping planes to a horizon formed by the black inky ridges of the Alpes-Maritimes. In the foreground, the resort of Beaulieu-sur-Mer, blanched by the *contre-jour* lighting, seemed to fasten the sea to the land like an intricate ivory clasp. Trying to pinpoint Jeanne Mesnel's home street, Chemin Leuze, Darac picked out the railway tracks and followed them. He couldn't find it. Too much in the way.

He turned and hadn't taken more than a few steps when, through an open window, he caught sight of the man he'd come to interview. Sitting with his chin resting on raised index fingers, Philippe de Lambert was gazing into a part of the room hidden from the terrace. Whatever he was studying, it held his full attention. Standing just five metres away, Darac felt he could have jumped up and down singing the 'Marseillaise' and remained unnoticed.

Tanned, lean and with his silvery-grey hair brushed back in a leonine wave, Lambert was a refined, impressive-looking figure. By Taylor Walters-Halberg's account, he was all of seventy-five but even at repose, the man exuded a quality of sleek vitality. His clothes were a co-ordinated emblem of his class: a navy-blue blazer worn over an open-necked cream shirt, both hand-made, no doubt, the combination enlivened by a burgundy cravat.

Darac felt an urge to stick his head through the window and announce himself with a Babazouk-style bellow but he thought better of it. Continuing to the porch, he turned under an archway and entered a stone-vaulted foyer. Ahead, glass doors gave on to a wood-panelled landing between flights of ascending and descending steps. The study door was to his right. He knocked twice before he noticed a bell set into the wall off to the side. He rang it. After a moment, the door was opened by the tall, upright figure of Philippe de Lambert himself.

'Monsieur.' Darac flashed his ID. 'Please forgive this intrusion.' Noticing Lambert watching his lips, Darac resolved to raise his voice. 'I have some questions concerning your assistant, Mademoiselle Walters-Halberg.'

'Taylor? There hasn't been an accident?'

The voice was weaker than Darac had imagined. 'No, monsieur. It's a routine matter. Is this convenient?'

'Of course. Come in, Captain.'

The room was furnished less sumptuously than Villa Rose's public salons. On a desk, stacks of papers, bookmarked tomes and trays of slides denoted it was a study in more than just name. Lambert invited Darac to sit in one of a pair of armchairs set by an open fireplace. 'I realise you're on duty, Captain, but a drink perhaps?'

A tantalus containing three decanters was set on a chiffonier away to his left. Around the neck of one of them, a pewter tag read *Mapin XO*, Darac noticed, the same exclusive cognac Granot had found in Madame Mesnel's kitchen cupboard. Perhaps that, too, had been a gift from Taylor Walters-Halberg.

'Is that the house cognac, monsieur, the Mapin?'

'They do send me the occasional case. Would you take a glass?'

'It's too early for me.'

'Thank goodness. I would have to have joined you. An espresso, perhaps? I was just about to have one.'

'Perfect.'

'I'll just be a moment.' He strode easily toward a door in the far corner of the room. For a man who had enjoyed a reputation as a hard-drinking hedonist well into his fifties, Lambert was a remarkably fit-looking individual.

Naturally, signs of ageing were evident up close: broken veins around his eyes and nose; liver spots on his hands; and the flesh under his strong jawline hung in a stringy sack above the gathered silk of his cravat. But this was all superficial; the man looked as fit as a fiddle.

An enquiring mind was a useful attribute for a police officer. So was plain nosiness. Wondering what had so captivated Lambert, Darac went to his chair and looked straight ahead. There was only one candidate: a wall-mounted cabinet about forty centimetres deep and the size of a large flat-screen TV. Darac moved toward it and, glancing over his shoulder, couldn't resist trying the doors. Locked. The old man must have done it before answering the bell. Then Darac spotted a shallow box leaning against the desk. Less than half the depth of the cabinet, it was just the size and shape to fit tightly inside it. Metal catches were set flush into its upper rear edges, he noticed. Darac had come across similar box-within-a-box arrangements before, the slightly smaller one often serving as a false bottom or back. Whatever Lambert's object of fascination was, it seemed he didn't want to keep it merely shut away: the cabinet's doors would have achieved that. Perhaps he wanted to keep its very existence a secret.

As the cabinet was the size of a TV, perhaps a TV was what it housed. Darac loved the thought that the aristocratic art historian's secret pleasure might be watching telly. Perhaps football or all-in wrestling. Darac glanced around for a remote as he returned to his chair. He couldn't see one. The door opened.

'Here we are.'

Lambert set down the tray and after a brief exchange of pleasantries, the interview began. Asked about his movements the previous Saturday, he corroborated Taylor's account, substantiating it with relevant entries in his diary. With nothing of interest emerging, Darac soon drew the meeting to a close and Lambert showed him to the door with the same graciousness with which he'd admitted him.

'The wall cabinet,' Darac said, in passing. 'Elegant. Eighteenth century, like the chiffonier and the other pieces?'

Lambert's smile was somewhere between sympathy and condescension. 'I'm cheered you think so, Captain. It's twentieth-century repro.'

'I'm afraid I'm on safari when it comes to the arts. Is it a TV cabinet or something?'

Lambert lowered his voice. 'It hides my safe. Quite effectively, it would seem.'

'Quite. But on the issue of security, monsieur, I note there is no CCTV outside. And I didn't notice a burglar alarm, either. Is that wise?'

'Forgive me, but do such measures guarantee immunity from burglary? Naturally, every object in the galleries is protected by a state-of-the-art system: pressure pads, daily-changing door codes, et cetera. And upstairs, my wife and I have had a modified version installed in our apartment.'

'But you haven't followed suit with your study?'

'My den, I call it. No, and I'm glad I haven't. Modified it may be, but between us, Captain, the system is such a pain to live with, my wife and I have it turned off most of the time. Besides, there's nothing valuable in the den safe. Just papers.'

Darac didn't buy it. 'I see. Thank you for your time, monsieur. And the coffee.' An exchange of smiles, a firm handshake, and Darac was on his way.

In the English Tea Room, he fell to talking with a tall, unprepossessing young German who proved to be the third member of the gallery's management team. Lean and hungry-looking with a wide grin, Dr Ivo Selmek bore a curious resemblance to a wolfhound.

By the time Selmek took his leave, Darac had gained some interesting insights into life at Villa Rose. Or at least Selmek's wry take on it. Referring to Taylor as everything from 'the Beautiful One', to 'Little Miss Prim and Proper', the whiff of sour grapes seemed to hang over his account of the young American's rise to prominence under the Lamberts. Darac was still considering how much credence to attach to it when his mobile groaned in his pocket. He stepped out on to the terrace and took the call.

'Boss?' The voice was Malraux's, for once observing the formalities. 'Marcel Battail? I've got him.'

11

Adèle Voska had expected big Marcel Battail to have slowly taken apart her pig-faced assailant but the contest had ended before it began. Flogging Battail in the kidneys with his baton, the *flic* had him cuffed and away in ten seconds flat. On the short walk from the parlour back to her car, she began to take some comfort in the thought that her own ordeal could have been worse.

Once out of the city, she made for the Grande Corniche, the highest of the three coast roads that wound east from Nice toward the Italian border. She felt like driving for hours but her destination, a campsite tucked away on the slopes of Mont Bastide, was only a few minutes away. Perhaps it was just as well. The spin she was trying to put on the events of the day was becoming less positive with each turn of the wheel.

As she crossed the bridge under Mont Fourche, the weather along the corniches seemed to be worsening. But then, as if by the hand of an invisible waiter, the cloche of mist covering the cone of rock above her lifted and the spectacular *village perché* of Eze was revealed all at once.

It was a place Adèle knew well. As a child, she used to fantasise that she would one day be married in its pretty, apricot-washed church. The groom would be a handsome man in uniform. Possibly someone in the Foreign Legion, as her father had been.

Now she wanted to kill him. She rehearsed a few thoughts. *'You said there would be no problem. But there was a big, fucking massive problem, papa. The part I was conscious for. You arsehole!'* But she knew she wouldn't say anything.

Strolling side by side, a couple of backpackers emerged from the narrow track to the campsite, unconcerned that Adèle was waiting to turn in. In one glance, she had the pair worked out. They were snooty little gap-year girlies, the sort who believed the world belonged to them. Jagging hard on the wheel, she blasted gravel and dust all over them as she powered past and set off down the track. The recreational vehicle area was at the far end of the site. She found the one she was looking for and parked close in. No one came. She got out and knocked on the RV's door. Still no one came.

'No fucking way!' She kicked the door as hard as she could. What now? She wanted to turn around and get out of there but it wasn't an option. 'Shit!'

The sour-faced woman behind the desk in the site office reported she had not seen Monsieur Voska all day. Maybe he'd gone for a walk, she said.

Adèle checked the toilets and shower block, then made a tour of the rows of tents pitched among the scrub beyond. Her father was still nowhere to be seen. She returned to the car and settled down to wait. After a long half-hour, he appeared, seemingly out of thin air. A powerfully built man with a bullet-hard, hollow-eyed skull, Voska opened the door to the RV but remained outside.

'Did you bring the stuff?'

Saying nothing, Adèle took two holdalls out of her car and tossed them past him into the vehicle. One landed softly, the other with a thump.

'Did the *flics* come?'

'One did.'

'And Marcel?'

'He turned up as normal. The *flic* arrested him.'

'And led him away immediately?' Voska scratched the dagger insignia tattooed on his right forearm. 'He didn't look around?'

'No.' Her stomach turned over. 'He had his hands full.' Wearing the cocksure expression of a man who was used to being proved right, Voska pressed his lips together and nodded. 'You had no trouble at all?'

She handed the keys back to him. Now she could say something. 'No, papa.'

'You did well.' He pinned the medal of a kiss on to each cheek. 'Keep it up.'

Twice rewarded, Adèle got into the car and executed a rapid three-point turn. Heading up the track, she waited until the RV had safely disappeared from her rear-view mirror before she braked hard and skidded to a stop. Dust billowing around the car like thin smoke, she lowered her head into her hands and broke into heavy, jolting sobs.

Something hit the windscreen. Adèle looked up.

'Hey, you in the car!' The girl's friend threw another stone. 'You almost ran us over, you bitch!'

Adèle floored the pedal and almost ran over the girls again as she drove away.

12

Darac had something of a love–hate relationship with the Brigade's permanent HQ, the Caserne Auvare. But he could live with it. Love–hate relationships were the French way. If such a thing as the French way still existed.

The Caserne had witnessed some grim events in its history and its rows of stark, barrack-like buildings could conjure them all too easily if you let them. But even on an everyday level, many found the place depressing. Offices tended to be cramped and shabby; the place needed numerous functional upgrades; and Darac was not alone in judging its contracted-out catering abysmal.

But for him, the Caserne had one enormous plus. Occupying a sprawling site off Rue de Roquebillière, it was situated close to home and to the Blue Devil. Darac could walk to work if he felt like it; drop into the club after work; and nip to any number of nearby bars, cafés and restaurants. His lieutenants, Granot and Bonbon Busquet, felt similarly. They had no use for the jazz club, but they lived even nearer to work than he did.

And so it was with considerable irritation that while their section of the Caserne embarked on a programme of general refurbishment, the Brigade had had to decamp all the way over to the gravelly mouth of the Var river on the far western edge of the city. The brand new Commissariat Joinel was different in every way from the Caserne. One of its missions was to present a far more appealing face to the public.

Angeline had once observed that in flying the national flag from a pole, official buildings were expressing the 'phallocentricism of state power'. There was no prominent pole at Joinel. The *tricolore* appeared as a pastel-toned suffusion in the building's glass frontage.

So there the public had it: non-macho and literally transparent, Commissariat Joinel promised a new era of policing. Although their takes on many things were different, neither Darac, Granot nor Bonbon had much time for such style-over-substance thinking. And as for the seemingly inexorable rise of sound bites and buzzwords, some expressed in the increasingly invasive English language, the trio thought the world was better off without them. 'Up to speed'? What was wrong with *au fait*, now? And it was faster to say.

It was three o'clock before Darac arrived back in his office from Villa Rose. The room still smelled of paint. He didn't like its bland, drawing-board purity, and his first glance at the coffee machine installed in his absence inspired little confidence. The Koffeemat, a rectangular box on feet, looked as if it could have dispensed anything at all. Where were the filter holders? Where was the frothing nozzle? But at least Darac had a bolthole he could call his own and despite his gripes, he was grateful for it. The rest of his team had been allocated space on the vast open-plan Police Judiciaire floor outside.

He called Granot's number. Waiting for the pick-up, he leaned back in his chair and through force of habit, reached up to open his window. The catch was that there was no catch. His hand made a series of dull pinging sounds as it patted the pane.

'Yes?'

'Non-opening windows, Granot. I tell you, we're not just disconnected from the city over here. We're sealed off from the outside world altogether.'

'You rang to tell me that?'

'No. Battail will be here shortly. Bring Bonbon in and I'll update you.'

'Might it include trying out the new coffee machine?'

'I daren't.'

'We'll be right there.'

His eyes glued suspiciously on the Koffeemat, Granot plodded in with his fellow lieutenant, Alejo 'Bonbon' Busquet. A thin, frisky individual with a frizz of copper hair, Bonbon seemed equally unimpressed. '*That* is what I call a crime scene,' he said.

'Krime with a K.' Darac rolled his eyes. 'Check out the brand name.'

Granot grunted. 'You'll just have to bring your Gaggia in.'

'They won't let me.'

Twinkled-eyed as a young fox, Bonbon could portray gravity when needed. 'Fascist bastards!'

'Absolutely.'

Granot lowered himself incrementally into a chair. 'So what else is new?'

Darac began by taking a cat out of the bag and throwing it right in among the pigeons. 'I know you're both snowed under but this Mesnel case… I'm getting a feeling about it.'

'Oh-oh.'

Bonbon proffered a striped paper bag to Granot. 'Cherry cup? Think blood sugar.'

Granot took one.

'Yes, guys, I know.' Darac ran a hand through his hair.

'But bear with me a second.' He flipped open his notebook. 'The first thing is that Madame Mesnel *did* leave a will. There was a copy in the house.'

Granot performed his impression of a perplexed walrus. 'Lartou said there wasn't one.'

'Well, it was easily missed. The cleaner, Madame Loret, reports that after years without contact, the granddaughter Cristelle, the obvious beneficiary of Jeanne Mesnel's estate, called in to see her six months ago. So thrilled was the ailing old lady by the visit, she promptly sells *en viager* the €650,000 villa Cristelle naturally assumed was coming to her, and bequeaths the rest of the estate, quite legally it seems, to someone else. "Never mind," says classy call-girl Cristelle. "Absolutely," says her dodgy mate Léo, alias Monsieur 60-40, or more probably, 80-20. "We're better off without it." '

Bonbon snorted. 'Don't leave out the bit about the dish running away with the spoon.'

A suit, a shirt and a pair of loafers walked into the room.

Wearing them was a man with the looks and bearing of an Italian film idol. As vice squad head Frankie Lejeune had once said, Captain 'Armani' Tardelli was such a cliché, she wouldn't have believed him in a novel.

'Want to pitch a few to Clorent, Darac? We could do with a fresh line of attack.'

'Who's Clorent? The coke guy?'

'*The* coke guy, yes. Take five minutes to fill you in. Certainly no more than ten. Fifteen at the outside.'

'Sorry, Armani, we've got a guy of our own coming in shortly.'

'What, it's going to take all three of you?'

'I'm not sitting in on the interview,' Bonbon said. Armani flashed him a smile. 'Come on over.'

'Impossible. Chasing paper for the rest of the day.'

'OK. Alright.' Saying a pleasant 'fuck you' to each of them in turn, Armani turned on his heel and left. 'It was never like this under Agnès.'

'You're not doing too badly, chief,' Bonbon said. 'For a jazz musician.'

'Well, thanks.' Darac glanced at his notes. 'OK, Cristelle and her possible pimp Léo we've mentioned. We also have the new *en viager* owner of the Mesnel villa, one Taylor Walters-Halberg. The mademoiselle winds up paying next to nothing for the property when the old lady ups and dies while the ink is still drying on the sale agreement.'

'People have killed for less.' Granot nodded. 'Who is this Halberg? Any previous?'

'No, no. She's the assistant curator at Villa Rose. It's always possible, of course, but having met her, if she turns out to be a murderer, I'll eat my guitars.'

'All of them?' Bonbon said.

'Maybe not the D'Aquisto. Besides she has an alibi for the time of death, mostly involving none other than Monsieur Philippe de Lambert.'

'The aristocrat? The old art expert? I thought he died years ago.' Granot's eyes slid to the Koffeemat machine. Unable to resist its dubious appeal any longer, he got to his feet.

'Quite a gent, Lambert.' Darac sat back. 'He misled me, though, on one point.'

Granot paused in front of the machine's selector panel. 'Not over the alibi?'

'No, that all checks out. But through a window, I saw him gazing at something in his study. Rapt, he was. It proved to be a cabinet he'd locked by the time he let me in. I thought it might be hiding a TV but when I asked him about it, he said it was his safe.'

Granot warily pressed a button. 'So?'

'The man was fascinated. He wasn't looking at a *safe*, was he?'

'Lovely crishp stacksh of eurosh?' A second cherry cup was turning Bonbon's words into a sibilant mush. 'Could be a turn-on.'

'There were only papers in it, he said. Besides, he's used to money, this guy.' Darac swatted the thought away. 'Back to the principals. On top of those already mentioned, we've got a Madame Anne Corot. She is set to cop a couple of hundred thousand from her old friend's death.'

Granot removed a steaming cardboard cup from the machine's delivery hatch. '*She* hasn't got form, I suppose?'

'Yes, she has. Threw a bunch of grapes at a Front National leader a couple of years ago. Black ones.'

Bonbon nodded, sagely. 'Symbolic.'

'Indeed. She missed, unfortunately. Still got an official caution for her pains. I'll go and see her later. So that leaves us where we came in: natural causes. And finally, there's Malraux's mate on his way up here, Marcel Battail.'

'So what's your—?' Granot screwed up his eyes as he took his first sip of coffee. 'Ai, ai...So what's your feeling?'

'We'll see, but I don't like wife-beaters and all-round bullies like Battail. And we do have something on him.' He tossed Granot his notebook. 'Penultimate page. That's the threat he made in front of Madame Loret.'

Granot read it and then handed the notebook on to Bonbon. 'How do you want to play the interrogation?'

Darac tapped the top of his desk with a loosely clenched fist. 'It's tricky.'

Granot produced a phlegm-rattling chortle. 'Alright, Battail was cute enough to show up for work as if nothing had happened but I doubt if he's a grande école boy, this one.'

'I'm talking about the drowning aspect.'

Bonbon nodded. 'We could knock the whole force out trying to place this Battail at the scene but even then, forensics would struggle to prove he drowned Madame Mesnel. Not without an eyewitness.'

'Exactly.' Darac ran a hand through his hair. 'I think we've got to go for a confession or we may as well forget it.'

'What are we talking?' Granot said.

'A bit of ginger up the backside. If Battail did it, he may just squeal. But, Granot, ginger not dynamite, alright?'

The big man essayed an innocent look. 'The very idea.'

Darac gave the desk a concluding rap. 'But first, I need coffee.'

Bonbon uncoiled his wiry frame from his chair and stood. 'I'll leave you to it, boys.'

'Think you can find the way back to your desk?'

'If I get lost, I'll ask a policeman.'

As Bonbon took his leave, Granot winced and with a sharp intake of breath, made a show of flexing his hands.

'Chief, this interview. Can we have Madame Fabre in to pen the statement as we go?'

Darac was weighing the various options on the Koffeemat's kontrol panel. 'I'd rather you wrote it up afterwards as usual.'

'I've got mountains of paperwork to get through and my hands are aching like hell already. Carpal tunnel syndrome's no fun, you know.'

'I know it isn't but you haven't got it.'

'It feels like it. Can't we have Fabre? She's good and never gets in the way.'

'She doesn't do *that*, I'll grant you.' Darac hit the button for a single espresso. 'Witch hazel lotion's what you want. I'll bring it in.'

'You said it didn't work.'

'Oh... Alright, give the woman a ring.' A cloud of vapour escaped from the serving hatch. 'God, this stuff smells like three-day-old fish.'

Granot picked up the phone. 'Wait until you taste it.'

'OK, our lives have lost vibrancy and meaning but we've got basement parking now so that makes up for it.' Darac risked a sip. 'This is espresso?'

As Granot got on with his call, Darac's mobile buzzed. A text from Didier: *Free for a quick word?* Darac rang him.

'I've got a couple of minutes, Didi.'

'Excellent. For the first time in a while, we've got the entire brass section signed up for next week's gig.'

'The DMQ big band? Fantastic.'

'I'm putting the rehearsal list together. Apart from the usual suspects, do you fancy tackling some super-slow swing?'

'We've done "Idle Moments". Grant Green. That's not exactly a gallop.'

'We were only a four-piece that night.'

'True. What are you thinking?'

' 'Lil' Darlin' from *The Atomic Mr Basie* album.'

'Beautiful thing,' Darac said. 'Slow as molasses on Mogadon yet still swings.'

'It'll be a stretch for young Stretch – think he'll be able to handle it?'

'He'll get super slow super fast. You can bet on it.'

'That's all I needed to hear.'

Noises off. Visitors were approaching.

'Got to go now, Didi, but yes, let's give the Basie a go.'

'In here, you.'

The uniform leading in Marcel Battail had the air of a handler parading a prize bull. As the necessary paperwork was exchanged, Assistant Police Officer Sabrina Fabre slipped quietly into the room behind them. Darac gave her a nod as he reacquainted himself with the various documents in the suspect's file.

Granot eyeballed the uniform. 'Hands behind his back, then cuff him.'

Darac gave Battail the once-over. The man could have played 'Heavy Number One' in any number of gangster movies: brawny build; scarred skull; cold, heavily lidded eyes. Tattoos on various parts of him proclaimed allegiances to everyone from 'Mother' to 'Psycho' – the same person, possibly.

The interrogation began in the formation Darac and Granot adopted when intimidation was the aim: Granot sitting opposite the suspect asking the questions; Darac standing behind the suspect, silent. It was against official guidelines but then so was murder.

Are you comfortable, Marcel?' Granot said, using the familiar *tu* form.

Battail kept his eyes solely on Granot. 'No.'

'The sooner you tell us the truth, the sooner you'll be able to go back to your cell. You know why you have been brought here?'

'No.'

'No?'

'You've got ears, haven't you?'

Battail would have been best advised to curb his tongue. Docile as a fat old Labrador most of the time, Granot wasn't averse to giving a low life like Battail a slap or two.

'You have been placed in custody to answer questions concerning the death of your neighbour, Madame Jeanne Mesnel. She drowned in her hot tub last Saturday.'

'So?'

'What were you doing at the time?'

'Why?'

Granot banged the desk hard. 'Answer the question!'

The suddenness of it made Battail start. Sitting no more than a couple of paces away, Sabrina Fabre didn't bat an eyelid.

'Saturday I was out all day.'

'We have a witness who'll swear in court you threatened to drown Madame Mesnel.' Battail shrugged. 'You said: "If you don't turn that fucking music down, I'll drown you, you fucking old bitch and nobody will ever know it wasn't a fucking accident." Expert in drowning people, are you?'

Perhaps feeling trapped, or perhaps in some primitive urge to get at Madame Loret, Battail tried to stand. Darac brought his hands down on the man's shoulders.

Sabrina Fabre wrote: *On hearing the alleged murder threat, Battail attempted to bolt*. No mention was made of the handcuffs manacling him to his chair.

'Well, Battail?'

'It's a bunch of crap. And it's hearsay. Hearsay!'

Darac remaining silent, Granot continued the questioning. 'It's not hearsay. I repeat: what were you doing between noon and six o'clock on Saturday, 2 January? Six days ago, in other words. Tell the truth!'

Darac could see Battail's neck muscles tightening into ropes and sweat was beginning to run in the deep crease between his shoulder blades.

'Trade was shit the week before so I didn't open the parlour. I spent the day with my girlfriend, Brigitte Andreani. Between the hours you said, we were in Nice. Shopping.'

'Beautifully recited, Marcel. Unfortunately, we've got her written statement that she didn't see you until seven o'clock.'

'What? Bitch!'

With Battail reacting as before, Darac had to reprise his restraining act. This time, it proved more difficult. Brigitte was in for a pasting when she and Marcel met up, he suspected. And

Darac recognised Madame Loret's vulnerability in the situation, as well.

'You lied about where you were because you were at Chemin Leuze carrying out your threat to kill Madame Mesnel. Admit it!'

'That's crap.'

'Then why did you lie about where you were?'

Battail considered the question. Levelling with the police was clearly anathema to him but he seemed to conclude that on this occasion it was his best option. 'I did go to work but I only had a few customers all day.'

'So there was ample opportunity for you to bunk off.'

'But I didn't.'

'Names of the clients you worked on? Quickly, we haven't got all day!'

'I don't know who they were, do I?'

'You hadn't worked on them before?'

'No.'

'And your esteemed colleague Dagger wasn't helping you that day?'

'No.'

'So nobody can vouch for your whereabouts between the hours stated, can they?'

'About two o'clock, I went to Bar Karl in Rue Benoit Bunico.'

'Why there? There are several bars nearer to the parlour.'

'They do Staropramen in there now. I had a couple. Or six.'

'You a regular? Anybody likely to remember you?'

'Only the second time I'd been there. Been in since, mind you.'

'Talk to anyone?'

Battail shrugged. 'And then after that, I went to another bar. Had a few brandies.'

'Which one?'

'Can't remember.'

'Your mate Dagger. What's his real name? Where does he live?'

'No idea. He just comes and goes. I don't ask questions.'

'You don't answer them, either.'

'Listen, I admit I went into the old bag's back yard that time and gave her a warning. Loret was there, right? And I might've put a fingerprint on the side of that stupid fucking bath where I leant on it. But that's all I did.'

'But she didn't turn her music down, did she? She gave you the finger over your warning and carried on as before. You're a man, Marcel. And you have a hot temper. You didn't like it. Did you! You drowned the woman. Tell us the truth!'

The interview continued in the same vein for another half-hour. To each previously asked question, however reformulated, Battail offered the same answers. To each new line, he issued flat rebuttals. Threats that officers would turn his house upside down looking for 'clues', and that they would bring in Brigitte for questioning had no effect on him.

'I don't care. Do what you like. I'm innocent.'

'Where were you hiding last night?' Granot said.

'I got tanked up at the Karl. And then another place, I can't remember where.'

'After that.'

'I left but then I passed out. Spent the night in a doorway at the end of some alley.'

Battail certainly looked and smelled as if he'd slept rough. And he'd had a half-empty bottle of brandy in his pocket when he'd been brought in.

'Which doorway? Which alley?'

'I don't know, do I? Somewhere in the Babazouk.'

Granot's hand crashed down hard on the desk. Fully acclimatised, Battail didn't so much as blink. The time had come to change things. Still standing directly above and behind the suspect, Darac spoke for the first time.

'Know anything about marks left by something with rubber feet, probably a tripod, on Madame Mesnel's lower patio, Marcel?'

Battail's shoulders twitched as if he'd been prodded.

But he still didn't turn around. 'No.'

'You didn't notice them when you were drowning Madame Mesnel?'

'I didn't do it.'

Darac took the rap sheet out of his inside jacket pocket. 'Let's see, you've served... three terms of imprisonment altogether? Two for aggravated assault; one for... what was it?'

'I want a lawyer. Here. Now.'

'You'll get half an hour with one later on.'

Battail shrugged. It had been worth a shot.

'Answer my question. What was the third term for?'

'Malicious wounding.'

'You're a tough guy?'

'He deserved it.'

'He? I thought you could only handle women. That's your level, isn't it? You're a waste of skin, Battail. A great big fucking waste of skin.'

'Whatever.'

Time to rack it up a notch. Darac gave Sabrina Fabre a dismissing nod. Acting like the only non-speaking extra in a movie scene, she remained silent as she stowed away her things and left. Once she had gone, Granot beckoned Darac to the doorway, took off his jacket and slowly rolled up his sleeves. 'They're in my desk. I'm going to get them.'

'Don't think you should,' Darac said. 'I mean it.' Granot pushed the younger man aside. 'Out of the way.' He barrelled through the door. 'I've had it with this scum.'

Darac turned to Battail. 'OK, it's obvious I don't like you, Battail, but here's a piece of advice: admit what you did before he gets back.'

'Got a fag?' Here was another casualty of the ban, Darac thought to himself. It made bartering smokes for info more difficult. 'No, but that's the least of your worries. Think my mate's all talk? You're wrong. Tell me what happened.'

Battail wasn't buying it.

Granot returned with the biggest set of knuckle dusters ever seized in a local raid. He put them on, brushing their raised brass ridges against Battail's cheekbone. He looked him in the eye. 'OK, Marcel. Admit what you did, and there's a chance you'll be able to walk out of here in one piece.'

'You fuckers don't frighten me.'

'One more chance.'

Battail didn't flinch. 'Even if you were going to beat me up, you wouldn't be doing it with them knucks.' He grinned, revealing a row of surprisingly small teeth. 'Would you?'

'Admit you drowned Madame Mesnel or I'll turn your face into raw meat.'

Darac looked uneasy. More uneasy than Battail. The suspect said nothing.

Yvonne Flaco appeared in the doorway. 'Captain? Lieutenant? Monsieur Frènes wants to see you both. Immediately.'

Darac put a hand on Granot's shoulder. 'OK, we'll stop here.'

The big man stood his ground. Darac gave him a shove. 'Now, I said.'

'Bullshit.' Battail shook his head. 'Bull-fucking-shit!'

In the doorway, Darac turned to Flaco. A wink told her she'd played her part well. 'Get custodial. It's back to the cells for the suspect.'

'Yes, Captain.'

'Let's go and cool down, Lieutenant.' They left the office. Used to the demarcated confinement of the Caserne Auvare, Darac felt almost agoraphobic as he led Granot out on to Commissariat Joinel's open-plan floor. 'Which route do you favour to your desk?'

'The scenic route around the outside and then cut in at the end. With my size, it's quicker than picking your way through all the desks.'

Like an aircraft taxiing to its gate, the pair began a lengthy circumambulation of the field. 'So that went well.'

'The bastard didn't buy the routine for a second, did he?'

'No.' Darac gave him a look. 'You scared the shit out of me, though.'

'Yes?' Mister Punch himself had never looked so pleased. 'I could have been an actor, you know. Still could. Got a sort of Jean Gabin quality, don't you think?' Granot essayed a look of electrifying intensity. 'Well?'

'You've got the trench coat for it, at least.'

'Pure jealousy. So what was that stuff about the tripod marks on the patio?'

'Erica and I saw them this morning. Just curious about what caused them, that's all.'

'We all know what "curious" means. Six weeks' hard slog coming up for some poor, overworked slob and that slob may be me and it'll all be for nothing in the end, anyway.' He performed the Look once more. 'Gabin wouldn't have stood for it.'

'Neither you nor Gabin need worry. *I'm* going to shoulder the heavy lifting on this one. As much as I can, anyway.'

'What's brought this on?'

'As I'm standing in for Agnès, I should at least try to act like her.'

'Easy, boy.'

'How does she keep it up, Granot? Year after year?'

'Dunno, but God bless her for it.' They began their final approach. 'I tell you what I *do* know. I can't wait to get back to the Caserne.'

'Neither can I.'

Sabrina Fabre was waiting for them.

'What say she's typed up Battail's statement already, chief?'

'Here's the interrogation statement, Lieutenant.'

'That was quick.' He gave Darac a look. 'Thanks. Wait until the custodial officer returns and get Battail to sign it then, if you don't mind.'

'I will. Don't hesitate to call on me again.' She picked up her things. 'Captain.'

'Sabrina.'

Darac pulled up a chair. 'So, what do you think, Granot?'

'One thing I think is that you don't think a great deal of our Sabrina Fabre.'

The observation caught him unawares. 'I've got nothing against her. It's just… that look. That bland inscrutability. Whatever's said or happens, nothing disturbs it.'

'You're saying she's too impassive?'

'Compared to her, the sphinx is a raving hysteric.'

'She's not *supposed* to react, is she? She's perfect, I think.'

'Alright, I'm being unfair. Let's get back to Battail. Did he commit this alleged murder?'

'It's possible. Remember… What was his name?' Like a spiritualist attempting to contact the other side, Granot rapped ponderously on his desk. 'Kowiak, that's it. The Czech fellow who strangled those poor nurses.'

'I remember him, alright. One of the victims worked with my mate, Suzanne.'

'Battail's got that same look, don't you think?'

Darac pursed his lips. 'To an extent, but I think Marcel has less submerged malice. The threat he poses is more obvious. He is capable of murder, no doubt. But culpable for this one? I still doubt it, somehow.'

'You called it murder. No "alleged" or "maybe".'

'I did, didn't I?' An odd feeling came over him. 'You know, it's strange. The music that meant so much to Jeanne Mesnel, and for which, if Battail does prove to be the culprit, she may even have died – that same music means a huge amount to me, right? And she had prints and posters on her walls that, again, are the kinds of things I have on my walls. I feel a connection with the woman. I would like to have known her. And yet, somehow I'm sitting here wishing that she *had* been murdered. A part of me wants that fascinating, very *sympa* old lady to have suffered a violent death so I can nail the person who did it. Explain that to me.'

'I can't. So what next?'

'Granot, are you aware we French are supposed to be a nation of philosophers?'

'Call me a logical positivist if it makes you any happier. What next?'

Giving a clearing shake of the head, Darac got to his feet. 'First, I'm going to check Battail's alibis, such as they are. Then, I'm going off to Théoule to see the day's big winner, Madame Corot; and finally, the loser, Cristelle.'

'Got two hundred euros in your wallet for her?'

'Now that *is* funny.'

13

Taylor steered Maggie de Lambert toward her favourite armchair and, with a practised hand, eased her carefully into it. Not a single swag had escaped the arabesque helmet that was the old chatelaine's hairdo; and her face, pretty and obdurate as a china doll, betrayed few signs of distress. But after the climb up to the second floor of Villa Rose, Maggie was breathing like an antique steam locomotive.

At the door, carrier bags from their shopping trip to Monaco stood stiffly to attention like soldiers awaiting further orders. 'I'll unpack the stuff in a minute,' Taylor said, in English.

'The French have strung cable cars…' Maggie took a breath. '…all over the Alps. But install one lousy elevator in the… private apartments of a palace? No. No can do!'

'Remember what the doctors said?'

'Before or after I signed the cheques?'

'Providing you take it nice and easy, walking is good for you. *Good*, right?'

'Yes, yes.' Bang to rights, Maggie gave a half-rueful laugh. 'I know.'

'If you promise to behave, I'll make you some tea.'

'Taylor, what would we do without you?'

'Oh yes, without me, you and Philippe would be nothing.'

Darjeeling leaf tea prepared in a warmed porcelain pot was Maggie's preference. Taylor dealt with the shopping while it brewed for the requisite four minutes. By the time it was ready, the old lady's breathing had returned to something less industrial.

'Now, anything else for the madame?'

Maggie took a long sip and shook her head. 'Nuh-uh. This is perfect.'

'Then I'll get back to work.'

'Just a moment.' Setting down her cup, she took both Taylor's hands in her own. 'What about you, honey? Are you alright?'

'I suppose I should be glad but I'm sad about it, actually.'

'Give it time. But I wasn't talking about the Beaulieu property. I was talking about your ordeal with that policeman.'

'Ordeal? No. It was a little strange but it was fine.'

'Will he need to see you again?'

'Possibly.'

'Be careful. The French police can be animals, you know. Philippe was in Paris in '68. They clubbed him. He was just standing there watching the riot and they clubbed him. Philippe de Lambert!'

'I know. It was terrible. But I don't think Captain Darac is going to start clubbing me.'

'I saw him when he was here, from afar, admittedly. He looks a bruiser.'

'His build, you mean?'

'And his face. A boxer's. Like Marcel Cerdan. If you know who he was.'

'Piaf's lover? He's much more sensitive-looking than that, especially when he smiles. Which he seems to do a lot. And he's got the loveliest soft brown eyes…'

Maggie gave her young friend a long, quizzical look.

'Well now.'

'Well *nothing*.' Taylor coloured slightly. 'Listen, I really have to get going or your husband will be on my case.'

'You leave him to me if he gives you any trouble.'

Knowing that trouble from Philippe was the last thing she had to worry about, Taylor smiled and exchanged kisses with Maggie. 'Later.'

'You bet.'

As Taylor let herself out, the older woman finished her tea and went looking for her husband. It was pointless calling out to him; he had been going progressively deaf for the past ten years. Unable to find him, she picked up the house phone. 'Philippe?'

'Speaking.'

'This is Maggie, your wife of the last thirty years, you ninny.'

'My darling, I am so sorry.'

'I'm coming down.'

'Might it be easier if I came up?'

'Stay there. Each one of those steps is supposed to put a penny in my health bank.'

In the study, Philippe was in the middle of writing an important planning document but he always observed the dictum that everything stopped for a lady. Adjusting his silk cravat, he stood, and intercepted Maggie at the door.

'Philippe,' she said, steaming slowly in, 'I must insist you give Taylor a few days off.'

'With the exhibition imminent, it would be rather inconvenient.' Maggie's gaze was unwavering, her stubby little jaw set. 'Of course, if something is amiss—'

'She went through a police grilling this morning. Is that amiss enough for you?'

'Grilling? I'm sure not. I saw the officer in question, myself. He was charming.'

Maggie's perfectly applied blusher took on a less subtle hue. 'You, too? Look, however charming this doe-eyed ruffian pretends to be, the girl needs a break after what she's been through. She was really fond of the dead woman.'

'Yes, I know.' Philippe essayed his famously disarming smile. 'I'll talk to her.'

'Good.' Maggie performed a miniature three-point turn. 'See you do.'

Philippe moved to escort her but she raised a hand. 'Taylor should never have felt she needed to buy in the first place!'

'Margaret,' Philippe sighed, 'I feel we have exhausted that subject. And consider that whatever happens in the end, Taylor's investment has returned a fine dividend already.'

' "In the end"? I may go *here and now*.'

'My darling, as you know, my most fervent wish is that *I* pre-decease *you*.'

She gave him a look, took a breath and began the ascent. Philippe still had work to do but his rhythm had been broken by the interruption. He poured himself a cognac and repaired to an armchair instead. After a moment, his eyes slid to his cabinet of delights. Now? Why not? Unlocking its double doors, he reached into the corners of the inner box and flicked open a pair of catches. He lifted it out, exposing a second set of doors. He paused and then pulled them open in the manner of a priest exposing the wings of a devotional triptych.

In a way, that's exactly what it was.

14

Gilles Voska had spent most of the day doctoring a set of chess pieces. Hollowed out, they could hold a surprising amount.

He was applying a second coat of varnish to the king when he heard someone approaching outside. The RV shook as the visitor mounted the step and knocked. Voska set his brush down and went to the door. A thick-set black man in his late twenties smiled at him as he opened it.

'May I come in?'

The man's voice was pitter-patter soft but Voska knew he would put up a good fight if it came to it. It might last all of thirty seconds. 'How did you know where to find me?'

'I asked if I might come in,' the man said, still smiling. 'I am anxious to know if you met with your contact.'

'Yes.'

'Then, as everything has been done, I want you to hand over what we agreed.'

'I won't have it all until tomorrow.'

The black man's smile faded as he returned Voska's stare. 'In that case, give me what you do have.'

'You think I'd keep something like that in the vehicle?'

'Then where?'

Voska's eyes slid toward a stand of trees.

'Get it, please.'

'In daylight? Come back after dark tomorrow and you can have it all.'

'When?'

'It's usually dead around here by eleven. Make it midnight.'

'Dagger, if you are not here or you try to cheat us, it will become a matter of much regret for you,' the black man said, softly.

'Midnight tomorrow.'

Voska closed the door with no further word.

The man made his way back to his Fiat 500, nursing an uneasy feeling that after everything he'd done, something might yet go wrong. But he tried to banish the thought as he got within sight of the car. His passenger, sitting with his knees pressed hard against the glove box, was a perceptive soul.

'Well?' Rama N'Pata said. 'Did you get it?'

'Tomorrow, he says.'

Their eyes met.

'Do you trust him, Modibo?'

He smiled and gave Rama's knee a squeeze. 'Ask me after tomorrow.'

Modibo was still looking cheerful as he pulled away. Inside, he was already preparing for the fight he suspected would come and reflecting that of all the bad cards he'd been dealt in his life, the one bearing the mark of the dagger might just have been the worst.

15

As stake-out spots went, the window table at Maison Branco in Saint-Laurent-du-Var was one of the best Darac had experienced in a while. Their *bourride* paired well with Pouilly-Fumé and the clear sight line across to the Résidence Floride meant its night man would easily be able to signal him when the time came.

Earlier, Darac had not found Jeanne Mesnel's oldest friend, Madame Corot, at home. A neighbour volunteered that she had flown to Montreal three weeks ago to visit her sister and wasn't due back for a day or two. Montreal in winter? A hardy soul, obviously. More importantly, one who hadn't been around at the time of her friend's death.

Darac lingered long over a perfect *tarte au citron*. As he savoured the final forkful, there was still no sign of Cristelle Daviot. More waiting. It wasn't until the staff began to close up the place around him that Darac decamped to his car, but first, he needed to update the night man.

Wearing the sour, put-upon expression of the traditional fleabag concierge, the old boy seemed out of place in the clean-lined setting of the Résidence. His smart uniform only added to the effect.

'OK, we move to plan B, monsieur.' Darac pointed toward a line of vehicles. 'See the grey Peugeot?'

'A white Cadillac I might see. A Peugeot? Grey?'

'I haven't finished. The grey Peugeot parked next to the green plumber's van.'

The night man shrugged.

'Same drill as before but now I'll be in that car if you see anything.'

'I am not stupid.'

Darac repaired to his car and slid Monk's *Brilliant Corners* album into the CD player. He listened to the title track and then phoned Ridge with the news.

'Garfield, you kidding me?'

'No. It's all yours, Monsieur Eldridge *Barton Peters* Clay.'

'Ever heard of Peters? Preacher. Good man.'

'Pleased to hear it. And Madame Mesnel – old friend?'

'No, she wasn't.'

'And I thought you knew all the jazz cats around here.'

'Yes. Me too.'

'Including the vinyl LPs and the tapes the bequest might amount to seven or eight hundred albums.'

A woman emerged from the parking area opposite and headed for the apartment block. Darac couldn't see her face but she was young, well dressed, slim. A candidate.

'I'm stoked, man. Stoked and choked.'

Translated literally, the American terms Ridge used often didn't make sense in French but Darac had come to understand most of them.

'I would be stoked too, if someone had left me all that.'

Ridge's voice took on a more sober tone. 'What happened to her?'

'She had an accident. Drowned.'

'Drowned? Well, there's no good way to die, I guess.'

The night man appeared in the doorway and cursorily made the signal.

'Got to go, Ridge.'

Darac paused at the desk just long enough to stuff a ten-euro note into the old man's breast pocket. The lift Cristelle had taken still hadn't returned so Darac pushed through a door at the rear of the lobby and took the service stairs. He rang the bell of apartment 312 and, almost immediately, the door jagged open on its chain.

'Yes?'

He wasn't prepared for the impact seeing the woman in the flesh had upon him. 'Mademoiselle Cristelle Daviot?' He omitted to produce his ID. 'Darac. Police.'

'At this time of night again? My, I am lucky.'

She closed the door to release the chain and then re-opened it, doubling the thrill of the reveal. A simple navy-blue jersey dress showed off her slim but athletic build, and she had glossy, shoulder-length, dark-brown hair. Her nose and chin were probably too prominent to be considered classically beautiful but taken with her almost black, almond-shaped eyes, the overall effect was sensational. Darac felt a curious urge to touch her as she let him into the apartment.

'Drink?'

'Uh… yes.'

Darac couldn't fathom the depth of his reaction.

'What would you like?'

The word 'beer' came out of his mouth.

He sat down on the sofa and stood up again as she went to get the drinks. What was going on here? And then it hit him. Cristelle Daviot wasn't just a strikingly attractive woman. She looked like *the* woman, the smoking sloe-eyed beauty in the Blue Devil club poster. A crazy thought struck him. But no, no, it couldn't be. Could it? *Think, man.* He considered the time element. The woman in the poster looked to be in her early twenties and the photo had been taken in 1963. So that meant she would be about seventy if she were still alive. Jesus Christ... But slow down, slow down – that's just one factor. What about relatives? He ruled them out: Cristelle's grandmother had had no sisters and her one female cousin had been at least twenty years older. Yes, it was at least possible.

He weighed the extraordinary resemblance between Cristelle and his poster girl; the sort of resemblance that often skips a generation. And then he considered Jeanne's jazz record collection and her own copy of the poster, bequeathed to Ridge and Cristelle, respectively. Darac shook his head but he knew everything pointed to the most incredible conclusion. The woman in the poster, the enduring emblem of the world he loved, *that* woman was Jeanne Mesnel. In a strange but real sense, he had been in love with Jeanne, or at least her image, all his adult life.

An ambulance raced by below, the pitch of its siren falling as it headed west. A very different image of the woman came back to him.

'Take it, then.'

Cristelle was standing in front of him holding an opened bottle of San Miguel. He took it and followed her out on to the balcony as if in a dream. A low, blond wood table was set down next to her sun lounger. On it was a packet of Gitanes.

'You don't mind?' She took one and lit up. 'I've been looking forward to it.'

Mind? No, smoke your gorgeous head off. 'Not at all.'

She lay back in the sun lounger and, folding her legs under her, blew out a long column of smoke. Fade in the club, the bass player, the drummer, the brass section...'There's a director's chair in the corner.' He didn't react. 'If you want to sit.'

'Ah.'

He brought the chair and unfolded it. Cradled in canvas, he felt even more at a loss, somehow. He needed to make a start but how? Cristelle had a powerful sexual charisma of her own but it was the sense that he was in the miraculous presence of the young Jeanne, a living reincarnation of his muse, that overwhelmed him. His original plan for the interview spooling off on to the floor like a torn reel-to-reel tape, he dragged his gaze away. 'Mademoiselle—'

Another snorted plume of smoke. 'Cristelle.' She began absently stroking the side of her bare foot. She might as well have been stroking his manhood. 'Please.'

'Cristelle... Obviously, I'm here in connection with your grandmother's death.'

'Would you like to spend the night with me?'

Darac closed his eyes and exhaled deeply. Picture the hot tub. Picture the mess of flesh. Picture the morgue trolley. 'That would clearly be a bad idea.'

'Why? Because you know or have guessed that I'm a prostitute?'

'No, no. Not at all.'

'I don't want your money, if that's what you're thinking. I want us to fuck purely for the pleasure of it. I have needs, as well, you see.'

Sweet Lord... 'That isn't the reason, either.'

'Why then?'

Because I'm struggling to separate your identity from a woman I've been half in love with all my life and you're a potential suspect in her murder. That good enough for you? 'Cristelle, I am with the Brigade Criminelle.' He showed her his ID.

'Captain Paul Darac.' Her eyebrows rose. '*Captain?* You must be good at your job.' She blew smoke, holding the pout that went with it a little too long. '*Very* good.'

'You certainly look as if you're working.'

'Don't you recognise real flirting when you see it?'

He needed to get into gear now or there would be no way back. 'Whether real or not, I have to ask you some questions.'

It was with a sense that the seduction was merely on hold that she stopped stroking her foot and started paying a different kind of attention to him. 'Questions? Why?'

'You don't have to answer them now but I hope you will.'

'No, it's fine, I suppose.'

'Thank you. First, I'd like to know what kind of a person your grandmother was.'

The question seemed to surprise, even discomfit her. 'Why do you want to know that?'

Because the Canadian winter might kill off Madame Corot before I get the chance to talk to her. And when I get to the heavy stuff later, you might be in no mood for casual reminiscence. 'Just for background.' Darac smiled. 'If you wouldn't mind?'

'Alright.' Her head tilted back as she took a nourishing suck on her cigarette. 'For what it's worth, I thought she was a remarkable woman. Very bright. Interesting. She wasn't really like other grandmothers. Or other mothers, come to that.'

'Go on.'

Cristelle's eyes narrowed. 'You haven't touched your beer.'

Darac hadn't registered that he'd been given one. 'I don't really want it. Mothers?'

'Mothers, yes. Mine died of cancer when she was only thirty-five. I was fifteen. I fell apart. I wanted *grand-mère* to fall apart with me but she didn't.'

'She didn't grieve?'

'Oh yes, she did. Briefly. My own pain wasn't so easily relieved.'

'Maybe her response was—'

'Healthy?' More smoke. 'No doubt.'

'I was going to say perhaps she got through it quickly so she could be strong for you.'

'You're that type, are you?'

'What type is that?'

'The type that looks for a silver lining.' She made a dismissive sound in her throat. ' 'Look for a Silver Lining.' She used to sing that to me. Stupid song.'

'I think it's quite a good song. Especially when Chet Baker sings it.'

Cristelle shrugged.

'Was she religious, mademoiselle?'

'No. If she had been, perhaps she wouldn't have been such a self-centred person.'

Darac remembered the photo of Cristelle's mother nursing her as a baby. 'Did she pass those selfish qualities on to your mother?'

'No. My mother always put me first. Always.' The flame that danced in her beautiful sloe eyes had been lit way down. 'Now, suppose you tell me why you really want to know these things. That oh-so-winning smile won't do it for you a second time.'

'Alright. We're not absolutely certain that your grandmother died accidentally.'

Cristelle sat up. 'What?'

'It could be that someone, or some people, drowned her deliberately.'

He watched her as she came to terms with the news. If she wasn't genuinely shocked, it was some performance.

'I... would be lying if I said I haven't been waiting for my grandmother to die, Captain. But that was alright. I knew I wouldn't have to wait *much* longer for what's coming to me.'

'And what's coming is?'

'The house, obviously. I don't think there'll be much else.'

'There may be other treasures. I was very taken by the jazz club poster on the stairs, for instance.'

Cristelle filled her lungs and held in the smoke for what seemed an age before exhaling. 'It's not worth anything.'

'You don't think it's remarkable? Especially as the woman featured in the shot—'

'Is my grandmother, I know.'

Hearing her granddaughter confirm his suspicions sent a thrill like an electric shock down his spine.

'OK, enough.' Cristelle emphatically stubbed out her cigarette. 'They said she died last Saturday, right? When exactly?'

Darac gave only a vague indication.

'I'll get my diary.'

It felt like a reward when she returned. Riffling pages, she leaned in close, strands of her soft hair tickling his cheek. It was only the initial sortie in an attack on his senses whose power was heightened by her scent: a subtle medley of wild herbs and flowers floating over a heavier base of sweat and tobacco. 'I think these entries account for my, what do you call them?' Again, the pout. 'Movements? My first client was in Fréjus. See there.'

Darac read the entries: Gassin, Sainte-Maxime, three in Saint-Tropez. 'And these people would testify in court?' It seemed like a dumb question but he had to ask it. 'That they were with you, I mean?'

She ran a perfectly manicured nail across each name. 'Not him. Or him. Possibly her. And yes, actually, I think those two would love to broadcast the fact.' She smiled at Darac. 'You see, I'm very good at my job, also.'

It had been some time since Darac had had sex and he hadn't intended doing anything much about it until someone significant came along. But here was the sight, the sound and the scent... He kicked back his chair and stood. Cristelle's lips were already on his as he pulled the soft jersey material of her dress over her buttocks. Without feeling her weight, he lifted her off her feet and wrapped her legs around his waist.

It was morning before he told her she wouldn't be inheriting the villa after all.

16

Philippe de Lambert usually left the hanging of temporary exhibitions at Villa Rose to Taylor and her assistant, Ivo Selmek. But Henri Matisse: Figure, Face and Form was different. A lover of the artist's work, Philippe had taken personal charge of the operation from initial conception to final execution. The most important show in Villa Rose's history, it boasted fifty-three easel paintings and paper cut-outs garnered from museums, galleries and private collections from around the world.

The final piece to be hung, an arabesque in vibrant blues, magentas and greens, was of special significance to Philippe. Lent by Washington's National Gallery of Art, *Souk at Asilah* was one of a series of works inspired by Matisse's visits to Morocco. Philippe had loved *Souk* and a companion piece, *Woman at Asilah*, all his life. But *Woman*, on permanent display in Nice's Musée Matisse, could be enjoyed anytime. It had been almost two years since he'd been in the presence of *Souk*.

The honour of easing the modestly sized work into position was given to Villa Rose's senior shifters, Mario and Claire. The assembled throng of gallery employees looked on expectantly.

'*Voilà!*'

Applauding along with everyone else, the pair withdrew a little, leaving Philippe standing directly in front of the work. Shaking his leonine head, tears began to roll freely down his cheeks.

'At this moment, my heart is too full to express the gratitude I feel to you all. Perhaps my tears will do that for me.' At that, Maggie slipped the silk handkerchief from the breast pocket of his blazer. Philippe took it, kissed Maggie, then Taylor, and turned back to the picture. 'On one level, this work conveys a simple truth. It reminds us that whatever else it may suggest, a painting is first and foremost an arrangement of shapes and colours on a flat surface. Actually, this work does not merely *remind* us of that truth, does it? It celebrates it in the most vibrant way imaginable. And yet, the painting conveys a sense of its familiar-world subject more palpably than any photograph. As a young man…'

As Philippe warmed to his task, Ivo Selmek's eyes were elsewhere. Although he was gratified at the status of the works the team had attracted to Villa Rose, as far as he was concerned, nothing of true aesthetic beauty had been created since the late seventeenth century. Nothing, that was, except the masterpiece that was Taylor Walters-Halberg.

Warm applause greeted the conclusion to Philippe's impromptu speech. As the gathering broke into informal groups, Maggie took Ivo's arm and steered him toward *Souk at Asilah*. 'Well, now. Even you must admit it looks wonderful in here.'

Ivo had made his feelings clear that the temporary exhibition wing, decorated in Villa Rose's ubiquitous belle-époque style, was unsuitable for displaying 'modern' works. Creating appropriate display spaces would be one of his priorities if he ever got the chance to run things. He flashed his wolfish grin. 'It looks as wonderful here as it would anywhere else in the villa. And it's not as effectively hung as it would have been had we approached the Musée Matisse for its companion, *Woman at Asilah*. But for those who respond to this kind of garishness, it's outstanding.'

Maggie could have said something equally rude, especially about Ivo's perpetually dandruff-flecked collar, and the strands of saliva that tended to net the corners of his mouth. But she confined herself to a loud harrumph as she returned to Taylor and Philippe.

'You know,' Taylor was saying, 'it's not too late to display quotations from Matisse's own writings next to selected works.'

'My dear, forgive me, but I feel that these works should be allowed to speak for themselves.'

'And of course they do. Richly. But for those who don't buy a catalogue, being able to read key points from *Point, Line and Plane* would enhance their viewing experience.'

Ivo gave Taylor a look. 'You mean key points from *Notes of a Painter*, don't you? *Point and Line to Plane* was written by Kandinsky. If you recall.'

'Of course – *Notes of a Painter*.' She made a pistol out of her hand and shot herself in the temple. 'Taylor Walters-Halberg, what have you got in your head?'

'It's Figure, Face and Form all day for God knows how long that's discombobulated you.' Her eyes lighting up her otherwise inexpressive face, Maggie turned to Philippe. 'And that's not all.'

'Yes, I think we've all been working too hard,' Philippe said, adding the benison of a smile to the combination of firmness and apology in his tone. 'But, Taylor, I really would prefer all secondary material to remain solely in the catalogue.'

'As you wish.'

'I tell you what *I* wish.' Maggie took Taylor's arm. 'I wish to sip a couple of margaritas down in Saint-Jean.'

Taylor shook her head. 'No can do at the moment but I'll scoop you up later?'

'Deal.' Maggie took Taylor to one side. 'That Ivo!'

'He means well. At least, I hope so.'

'He'd better. Listen, I've been meaning to ask when we can see your beautiful villa?'

'Not for a while. The property is still a...' Taylor lowered her voice. '... crime scene.'

'Understood.'

'Maggie, I'm sorry but I really must—'

'I know, chatting with me won't buy the baby a new bonnet.'

Maggie felt tearful as she watched Taylor walk away. Too many tears in the air, she told herself. But she knew that there was more to it. There was so much she wanted to do for Taylor. And she would, too, if against all the odds she managed to outlive Philippe.

Philippe had an empty cognac glass in his hand when the study doorbell woke him. Coming to, he lurched out of his chair and was halfway across the floor before he realised he was still holding the glass. He set it down on a side table, straightened his cravat and took several deep breaths. Satisfied he was finally in a fit state to receive his visitor, he went to the door.

'Taylor?' He glanced at his watch. It was too early for her to have returned from her evening out with Maggie. 'But—'

'Everything's fine, Philippe. Maggie was feeling a little tired, that's all.'

'Better to err on the side of caution where health is concerned.'

Philippe offered Taylor a seat in the finer of the two Louis XVI chairs in the room, facing the wall cabinet. 'A drink, my dear?'

'No thank you. May I get you one?'

'Best not. Continuing on that theme, your own health is a concern at the moment.'

'I'm fine.' The look in her eyes told a different story. 'Honestly.'

'I feel some time off might be in order. We are on schedule. Ahead, in fact.'

'So Maggie managed to persuade you, did she?'

'You know how much we care about you.'

'I do.' Taylor's eyes slid to the floor. 'But I don't need a break.'

Giving a start, Philippe suddenly realised what he'd done, or rather not done. In the corner of the room behind him, his cabinet of curiosity had been left wide open, its guilty secret sitting there in plain sight. His heart almost stopped. And although Taylor tended to look people in the eyes when speaking to them, from where she was sitting all she had to do was shift her gaze a centimetre or two off line and she would see everything. There was no escaping it. The moment Philippe de Lambert had dreaded for years was no more than a stray glance away. 'Well, if that's uh… how you feel. I must say I'm… I'm delighted.' He realised he could not get up to close the cabinet without drawing her eye to it. 'Delighted because even a day without you here is like a week without sun.'

'If I were Maggie, I would say "stuff and nonsense" to that. But thank you, Philippe.'

'Now my dear, if you would excuse me. I myself am feeling tired and—'

'Tired? You have boundless energy.'

'Normally, yes. But planning the exhibition has been a draining experience.' He stood. Perhaps he could usher her to the door, using his body as a shield. 'And therefore—'

'Philippe, I've had something on my mind so long, I don't

quite know how to raise it.'

'This is clearly important so I feel we must set aside more time.' He moved in close. Behind him, he felt his treasure shining out like a searchlight. 'Tomorrow, perhaps.'

Taylor remained seated. 'I think it has to be now, Philippe.'

'Oh?'

'It's about what will happen to me after…' She gave a sad little shrug. 'After.'

'Darling, I'm sure you remember the terms of Rose's will.' Though he knew it must have looked inappropriate, he had no option but to remain standing. 'In the event of my death, the Académie des Beaux-Arts will take over the running of the villa.'

'Indeed, and I realised some time ago that I ought to set up a fall-back position. My continuing here is by no means a given.'

'Taking steps to safeguard your future, such as buying the villa in Beaulieu, was very sensible. And although it has caused you some sadness, it has worked out brilliantly.'

Taylor stared off. 'Sadness is not the only thing it's caused me.'

Not clearly hearing the remark, Philippe ploughed on. 'So were I to shuffle off this mortal coil at this precise second, I could do so with a clear conscience.' He extended his arm toward the doorway. 'Now, perhaps—'

'So your conscience is clear, is it?'

The pressure of the air between them rose. 'Well, I—'

'Philippe, please rest your legs. I know what you're hiding in your secret little place there. I've known for some time.'

He froze and then, wearing the expression of a man who had been shot by someone to whom he'd handed the gun, fell back heavily into his chair.

Taylor stood. 'I think we will have that drink after all.'

'How long…' The words emerged as if from underground. '…How long have you known?'

'Some months.'

'How did—'

'I was curious about the cabinet ever since I started here. One day, I saw a key I didn't recognise on your desk and put two and two together. I couldn't resist a peek. Sorry.' Philippe felt the blood drain from his face. Taylor handed him a glass of cognac and kept one for herself. 'It's not so awful. Drink this.'

He compliantly raised the glass. 'You've known for months and you haven't told anyone?'

'Did I tell anyone you tried to bed me on my first day here? Did I tell anyone when I found out how much money you throw away gambling? Did I tell anyone when when—'

'It's not particularly kind of you to remind me of my sins, Taylor.' Suddenly aware of the glass, he downed his cognac in one. 'I feel deeply ashamed of them.'

'I'm sorry you find *me* unkind.' Her head twitched sharply. 'I have told no one.'

He looked at her in a way he hadn't allowed himself in some time. Taylor, the most captivating flesh-and-blood woman he had ever seen, looked all the more beautiful to him when her colour was up. It was the regret of his life that he had never experienced it in bed. But he hadn't entirely given up hope. On Maggie's death, which, despite his own little health problem, he assumed would precede his by some years, he intended to invite Taylor to share the Lambert apartment with him. Anything could be possible, then. But that might be months down the line. What was happening *now*? Taylor had discovered his guilty secret and said nothing. It seemed extraordinary but it must have been true or he would certainly have been brought to book. She had kept it to herself as she had kept quiet about his other, lesser peccadilloes. Thank God, he thought, his heart returning to something like normal.

'My dear, ever since I plucked you from obs— Ever since you arrived here, I think that when all things are considered, our relationship has been one of mutual benefit.'

She nodded, as if taking the remark as a compliment.

'However, with this...' He wasn't sure how to characterise it. '... development, the balance has shifted somewhat. I shall be forever in your debt.' He produced his most gracious smile. 'One I could never repay.'

'Don't think of it like that, Philippe.' She closed the cabinet doors and turned to face him. 'But there a couple of things you *could* help me with.'

17

Members of the criminal demi-monde were a useful source of information for the Police Judiciaire. But for Christian Malraux, the best stuff often came from amateur informants. Although his understanding of the historical context was limited, he had intuited early on that the whistle-blowing spirit of the Revolution, and later of Vichy, was alive and kicking in twenty-first-century France. In almost every street, he was able to find an upright citizen prepared to spy on a neighbour and then report back to him. Some snitched in return for a few euros or a quashed parking fine. Most did it for free.

Malraux was sitting in his car eating breakfast when he took a call from one Albert Luget, owner of the property opposite Marcel Battail's.

'Morning, Lieutenant.'

'Albert,' he replied, without hesitation. Malraux made everyone feel special in one way or another. 'What's new?'

'Madame Sleazebag's just left the house.'

'Brigitte?' He took another spoonful of yoghurt. 'What's she up to?'

'She's up to *something*. To begin with, she's not dressed in her usual tart gear. She looks smart. And she kept looking around. *Real* nervous.'

'I think we'd better get on her arse. Where did she go?'

'The lock-up garages at the end. You're going to follow her?'

'Operation Albert, we'll call it. She on the road yet?' Still trying to close the roller door. Usually takes her a couple of minutes.'

'And it's the red 205 we're talking about?'

'That's the one. Operation Albert, eh?'

'You've earned it. Keep in touch.'

'Will do. Over and out.'

Malraux rang off. 'Prick.' He set up the tail. With Mobile Control calling the shots, it was easy tracking Brigitte's progress toward the city. He took over from the lead vehicle as she dropped down into the old port and stayed with her until she parked.

Away from the surveillance hot spot that was Beaulieu-sur-Mer, Brigitte's guard was down and Malraux found her an easy subject to shadow on foot. Her first call was a dry-cleaner's in Rue Fodere, the opposite direction to the tattoo parlour. He waited for her to emerge and slid quickly into the shop behind her. He showed his ID to the middle-aged woman behind the counter. 'The customer who just left. I need to know the time and date she brought in the clothes she just collected.'

'*Bonjour*,' the woman said, reminding him of his manners.

'Yes, yes, *bonjour*. The time?'

Her records showed it had been three whole weeks ago.

Dead end.

Malraux caught up with Brigitte at the far end of the street. Peering at a window display, she straightened, hesitated for a moment and then strode confidently inside. Malraux followed on a few moments later. In flowing copperplate script, the sign on the door read: BERCY FRÈRES, MONTRES, BIJOUTERIE, OBJETS PRÉCIEUX, ACHAT ET VENTE. Inside the shop, Brigitte opened her handbag and took out just such a precious object.

18

As Résidence Floride was only a few kilometres from Commissariat Joinel, Darac decided not to go home before going in to work. The day man performed Disdainful Look Number Seven from the Concierge's Handbook as Darac emerged from the lift. A hearty '*Bonjour!*' brought no more than a curt nod. Darac enjoyed such exchanges. The day when every coming and going was marked with a beaming 'You have a nice day, now,' would be another sad one for France.

He pushed through the door into a grey, dampish morning, phoned Granot and asked him to meet him in his office in fifteen minutes.

What a night it had been; one whose narrative was unlike any Darac had experienced before. With the payload of blurred identities Cristelle carried for him, it could hardly have been otherwise. But by dawn, things had changed. The image of the woman he needed to touch every time he went to the Blue Devil had all but faded away, as had part of his sexual interest in Cristelle. It had made it easier to talk to her later. And it had certainly made it easier to give himself a hard time over his actions. As passionate and cathartic as the encounter had been, he knew it was something of a low point to have had sex with a woman not entirely for what she was in herself, but for what she represented.

As further food for thought, he couldn't shake the feeling that although it was six months since the break-up with Angeline, he'd somehow betrayed their trust. He imagined that part of it was a consequence of four years of monogamy. But he realised it was also a sign that in some imagined continuum, he needed Angeline still to think well of him.

It mattered less but there were policing issues, also. Darac had criticised Malraux for sleeping with Brigitte because she was a witness in a murder case. Darac had gone one better: he'd slept with a suspect. Technically a suspect, anyway. He had no feeling Cristelle was actually involved. Nevertheless.

At first, she had been furious about news of the house sale. The second bombshell that almost nothing of Jeanne's estate was coming her way did nothing to improve her mood. But by the time he left, she seemed to feel a sense of release about it. 'Now I can forget about the old cow for good,' she'd said.

Maybe.

Once on the move, Darac began picking over the fabric of the case so far, looking for threads, loose ends, holes. Rain was falling as he crossed the Var, obscuring the view of the airport beyond but accentuating the red glow of the runway lights. Out in the grey distance, they appeared to merge. It was an illusion, of course.

'Here comes Stud Boy,' Granot said as Darac entered his office. 'You look as if you got about five thousand euros' worth last night.'

It was routine banter. The words jarred, nevertheless. Darac made straight for the coffee machine. 'Want some hot brown liquid?'

'I'll get some in a minute. So what did you find out – apart from the fact that Mademoiselle Daviot is the hottest thing this side of—'

'Let's get on with it, shall we?'

'Wait just one minute. Don't tell me you *did* go to bed with her? Darac's silence speaking volumes, Granot's face fell. 'You did, didn't you! Are you insane?'

'Probably.'

'She's really got to you, I can see.'

'Not sufficiently, actually. There are feelings flying around – flying high. But they are mainly to do with Madame Jeanne Mesnel. You will never guess who *she* is. *Was*, I mean.'

The story seemed neither to move nor even surprise Granot.

'Alright, Acting Commissaire Compromised, let's get to the nitty gritty. Did Cristelle know she had been disinherited before

Saturday last?'

'I strongly suspect she didn't.'

'Did Léo know?'

'Again, Cristelle says no. You were right, by the way. Léo is her pimp. I'm going to see him later.'

'On a "talk or I'll arrest you" basis?'

'Under the circumstances, no.'

'Ai, ai, ai... Cristelle have an alibi for the time of death?'

'Yes and no.'

'Johns?'

Darac gestured that he'd got it in one.

'If you can get them to testify,' Granot said, rising. 'Johns make damn good alibis.,'

'I've asked Saint-Tropez to question them. She was based there on the day.'

Granot prowled over to the coffee machine and like a laboratory chimp performing a cognition experiment, jabbed buttons in sequence. He brought his reward back to his seat as Darac took a call on his desk phone.

'Go ahead, Malraux.' As he listened, Darac gave Granot an encouraged look. 'Interesting. Any inscription on it?' He picked up a pen. 'OK, get it over to forensics and bring her in. And Malraux? Good work.'

He hung up.

'Not a breakthrough?' Granot said.

'Certainly sounds like one.'

19

A hiding place, a cross-country course, a gym: the woods around the campsite of L'Ancienne Bastide had served Gilles Voska well in the ten months he'd been holed up there. A couple of collapsed outbuildings alone had provided enough material to keep him happy. He was irritated at having to leave the place sooner than planned but he was well prepared for what was to come.

He picked up the movie camera's remote release and staring into the lens, pressed the record button. In front of him were two columns of bricks, a metre high and forty centimetres apart. Bridging the gap on top was a V-shaped roofer's ridge tile. Voska took a pace back. Breaking flats by hand was nothing to an ex-commando. A ridge tile was a different proposition, yet the thought that what he was about to attempt was impossible never crossed his mind. Breathing deeply, his eyes bored into its rolled top.

He screamed, the flexed power of his torso releasing in one cataclysmic explosion. He felt no pain as his forehead hit the target. Pain was a state of mind. The tile fell between his bare feet, snapped in half like a breadstick.

He stopped the recording.

'Alright, Messieurs Modibo and Rama,' he said aloud. 'I'm ready for you.'

20

Smiling pleasantly, Brigitte Andreani took off her coat and sat down opposite Darac as if she'd just dropped in for a chat. Court shoes, a dressy navy-blue skirt and, showing off the lovebirds tattooed on her upper arm to advantage, a sleeveless seersucker top completed her outfit. A sisterly nod toward Sabrina Fabre, sitting pen at the ready in the corner, went unreciprocated. But Brigitte wasn't deterred. More *sympa* spirits were present. 'Lieutenant Granot,' she smiled. 'Oh, and hello, Captain. Nice to see *you* again.'

Amused, Darac almost replied 'me too' but he began conventionally. 'Madame Andreani, you were apprehended at Bercy, the jewellers on Rue Fodere trying to sell a ring. How did you acquire it?'

Brigitte's expression hardened like quick-drying cement. 'That's the way it's going to be, is it? An interrogation!' A wispy black bra strap slid down her arm, a blindfold for the lovebirds. 'And how young Christian could have strong-armed me in here like that, I do not know. Especially as I haven't done anything.' She pulled the bra strap back over her shoulder. The lovebirds would just have to take it. 'Not one thing.'

Granot gave her an irritated stare. 'You struck Lieutenant Intern Malraux during the execution of his duty, madame. That in itself is an offence.'

'Struck? It was just a slap. And so would you have slapped him if you'd got up to what we did the other night.' She dropped her voice to a conspiratorial whisper. 'I thought we'd got something going, you know? But if I'd known what sort he'd turn out to be, I would have bitten that thing of his right off.'

Despite the situation, Darac laughed out loud. Suddenly delighted with herself, Brigitte smiled as if she had intended her remark to be funny.

Granot was a far tougher audience. 'How did you come by the ring?'

'It was my mother's.'

'Your mother is dead?'

Making the sign of the cross occasioned further adjustment of her bra strap. 'God rest her soul.'

'She is not dead, madame.'

'Well, not technically, no.'

The ring in question, as Darac had learned when Malraux had called, bore a faint but legible inscription on its inner surface: *On this our wedding day, 7 May 1958.* 'When is your parents' wedding anniversary?' he said.

'September 22nd.'

'And they married in what year?'

'Nineteen six... nineteen seventy-one.'

Granot made Brigitte jump as he brought his hand down on

the desk. 'Cut the crap!'

Darac laid a calming hand on Granot's forearm. It looked like classic good cop–bad cop shtick but the sentiment was genuine enough. 'Brigitte,' he said, 'the wedding ring belonged to Madame Mesnel. An inscription proves it.'

Her pulpy cheeks flushed. 'I want to see a lawyer.'

'You're not entitled to one yet. Answer the question.

How did this ring come into your possession?' She tugged the crucifix at her throat first one way, then the other. 'I found it.'

'Where? On Madame Mesnel's dead body? After your boyfriend drowned her?'

Darac was no longer her favourite. 'He didn't drown no one.'

'Look, he's got form. He'll go down for fifteen to twenty years over this. And you, an accessory, will also do time.'

Brigitte set her jaw, crossed her arms and, picking a spot on the side wall, stared resolutely at it as the questions penetrated deeper, the penalties for not co-operating made more explicit. In exasperation, Granot finally reached for her chin.

'Look at me.'

She allowed him to guide her head back into line but then immediately turned back to the wall.

'Enough.' Darac got to his feet. 'Book her.'

'About bloody time. Brigitte Maria Andreani, I am arresting—'

'No, wait a minute! I'll tell you the truth.' She composed herself. 'I did find the ring just as I told you.'

'Where?'

'On my patio.'

Granot threw up his arms. 'Ridiculous.'

At that moment, Flaco brought in a note and handed it to Darac.

Brigitte smiled at the newcomer. 'Nice cornrows, darling.' She looked a little closer. 'Quite nice.' Slight concern now. 'Do them yourself?'

'No, I don't. Why?'

'No reason. Bye, dear.' As Flaco took her leave, Brigitte's smile faded. She leaned across to Granot and shook her head. 'Not trained, whoever did them. Three years I did. Apprenticeship.'

'If you've quite finished? You've been brought in for questioning. Remember?'

Brigitte sat back, put out all over again.

'So there you are, sunning yourself on the patio when out of nowhere, you notice a twenty-four-carat gold ring glinting between all the piles of shit? Pull the other one.'

'Actually, madame,' Darac said, passing Flaco's note to Granot, 'you didn't so much find the ring between the shit as *in* it, true? In a sample excreted by your dog.'

For the first time, Brigitte looked vulnerable. It offered Darac a way forward. 'Do you ever allow Thierry to roam the streets unsupervised?'

'Never. He is always on the lead. Always!'

'So who was walking him when he bit Madame Mesnel's finger off? You or Marcel?'

Brigitte shook her hands in front of her as if rubbing out the words she'd uttered. 'No, I didn't mean to say that. He has got out once or twice. Ask the neighbours! And any dog coming across... well, a piece of meat, will help itself, won't it?'

Granot could see where Darac was going. 'Yes, but a Rottweiler can turn live flesh into dead meat all by itself. That is what happened to Madame Mesnel.'

'No! Thierry is as gentle as a kitten. You've seen him!'

'In light of this...' Granot stared hard into her eyes. 'I must tell you that Thierry will have to be put down.'

'Put down? No!'

'Your dog bit Madame Mesnel's hand off in the attack and the proof wound up on your patio. Dogs have DNA as well as humans and their teeth leave characteristic bite marks. And we have hair samples. We can prove it was Thierry.'

'No, it wasn't.' The words spluttered out as Brigitte's tears began to flow. 'It wasn't!'

Darac passed her a tissue. She clutched it, absently. 'Where is the dog now?' Granot said.

'You're not taking Thierry.' She shook her head determinedly. 'You are *not* taking him.'

'We-ll, there just might be a way of saving his life.'

'What? Tell me!'

'If it was Marcel who *set* the dog on the old lady, Thierry won't have to be put down.'

Brigitte wiped her eyes.

'I repeat: we won't have to take Thierry if you tell us the truth about Marcel. Effectively, it was he who killed Madame Mesnel, wasn't it?'

Brigitte was thinking about it. Granot shared a look with Darac.

'We-ell he did…' she began, the words bubbling through her tears. 'He did once teach Thierry to…' But the magnitude of the moment got to her and she went no further.

'Teach Thierry to do what?' Darac said. 'Attack on command?'

Brigitte ran her tongue over her lips.

'Would you like some water?' She shook her head. 'Marcel did do that, didn't he? Train Thierry to attack when he said a certain word or phrase?'

She stared into space, defeated. 'I shouldn't have tried to sell the ring. I couldn't see it had an inscription. Marcel would have done but he was stuck in here.'

'But he did train the dog as I said?'

' "Pulling Thierry's trigger," he calls it. He's tried to show me loads of times but I don't want to see.'

'Has he shown anyone else?'

'He said he showed Dagger.' She gave a sour little laugh. 'As if *that* would make me change my mind.' She looked into Darac's eyes. 'Thierry's been trained. But he could be untrained, couldn't he?'

It was as heartfelt a plea as he had witnessed in an interrogation.

135

'Of course he could,' Granot said. 'And he wouldn't have to be put down if you come clean about Marcel. He didn't just threaten to kill Madame Mesnel, did he? He went to Chemin Leuze and did it.'

Brigitte lowered her eyes. Granot lowered his voice.

'I can see your difficulty. And what's a dog's life matter, anyway? If you're worrying about it, Thierry wouldn't feel any pain. He wouldn't feel the injection. It would be just a jab like any other. Some dogs even wag their tails before the poison—'

'Shut up!' Sobs now. 'Shut up!'

'But you can save him. All you have to do is—'

'Alright. Alright. He… did it.'

'Who did?' Granot said.

'Marcel, you dick. Who do you think?'

'Marcel Battail murdered Jeanne Mesnel last Saturday, 2 January?'

Brigitte lowered her eyes and kept them there. 'Yes. It was Marcel.'

Granot turned to Darac wearing the sort of expression conjurers favour after pulling off a deft sleight of hand.

'So Marcel told you what he'd done?' Darac said. 'Yes.'

'How did he do it, exactly?'

'Uh… Using Thierry, like you said.'

'Where did the dog bite her?'

'Where? Well, the hand.' She fingered her own wedding ring. 'The left hand.'

'And the attack words. What were they?'

'I don't know. I swear.'

'Excuse us a moment. Officer Fabre will pour you a coffee if you'd like one.'

Darac led Granot out of the office and closed the door. They began a slow-motion taxi around the floor. 'Promising start but we've strayed off into the realms of fantasy. Or even into the Theatre of the Absurd.'

'Good old Brigitte has just fingered her boyfriend for the

murder. We've got a result.'

'The bite marks on the exposed arm stumps were caused post-mortem, remember?'

'The exposed marks, yes. But what's to say the dog hadn't bitten off the old woman's lower arm and hand days before that? Between noon and 6 pm last Saturday, to be more exact. She's told us Marcel trained him to attack on a trigger word.'

'Yes, Battail is the sort of fuckwit who would think it clever to teach a dog to attack on command; but you're forgetting the COD. Madame Mesnel didn't bleed to death, she drowned. It's obvious Brigitte hasn't the faintest idea how she died. She didn't give Marcel an alibi when she had the chance. And she's only saying he did it now because she would rather lose her boyfriend than her dog. You can hardly blame her.'

Granot looked for a hole in Darac's argument and couldn't find one. 'I still think he did it and Brigitte will testify to it. With his record and with Madame Loret's testimony against him as well, he'll likely be convicted even without the lab's corroboration. Everyone's a winner. Frènes will be happy his initial suspicions were proved correct. Now you're acting commissaire, you should be happy your figures for the ministry will get a boost. The only loser is a wife-beating arsehole named Marcel Battail.'

They turned the corner at the end of the first leg of the circuit.

'It's tenuous.'

'People have been convicted on less.'

'Tenuous and untrue, at least in the way you outlined it to Brigitte...' Darac put his hands on his hips and kept his eyes on the carpet as he walked.

'What are you thinking?'

'I forgot the immediate cause of death, myself. She drowned, yes. But she suffered a heart attack first, didn't she? Is it possible Battail could have used the dog to frighten her to death? It is the biggest bloody hound you've ever seen in your life.'

'So it happened like I said except he didn't free the dog once he'd said the word.'

'Madame Mesnel *did* have severe cardiac problems,' he conceded. 'An experience like that might trigger a heart attack.'

'The bastard probably laughed as he watched the poor old dear go under.'

Darac gave Granot a look. 'You're not talking to Brigitte now. "Wag their tails?" '

'It worked. That's all that matters.'

'It's an unlikely way to kill someone. If she did die that way, Marcel possibly didn't intend it. He was just giving teeth, real ones, to the threat he made before: "Turn the music down or next time I'll let him off the lead." Now *that* scenario I can picture.'

'It might downgrade it to manslaughter,' Granot said. 'We can do better. I'm looking forward to my next chat with Battail. Even though he'll have seen a lawyer by then.'

'Having his rights pointed out to him won't help him much.'

'What now, then?'

'We release Brigitte. No charges. Alright, the property she was trying to sell was technically stolen but the word I don't like there is "technically".'

'Like her mother wasn't "technically" dead?' Granot shook his grizzled head. 'We could give her real grief over that ring. This wouldn't have happened in the old days.'

'This isn't the old days and we can always come back to it. And for her own safety, advise her to move out for a while. If Frènes doesn't grant us an extension on Battail's custody, he could be home tomorrow so tell her to do it straight away.'

'We're not social workers. Except where her dog is concerned, that woman is as hard as nails. And you, my friend, are as soft as a pile of its shit.'

'I'm in good company.'

'What do you mean?'

'I hear you let Cristelle smoke in the morgue.'

'I thought she might knock a few euros off for me later.' Darac let that go. 'Alright, the next thing we do is ask Raul Ormans to send a forensic team to Battail's. The dog may have buried Madame Mesnel's hand there, somewhere. We should have done it before, really.'

Granot shrugged. 'We couldn't dig up the whole of Beaulieu-sur-Mer, could we? Thanks to Brigitte, at least we've narrowed it down.'

'If Thierry frightened Madame Mesnel to death, there'll be no exchange evidence to examine. But if he did bite off her dead hand and we can dig up even a fingernail, there may just be some skin particles from the perpetrator.'

'So is it Frènes time for you now?'

Darac looked at his watch. 'Still got a couple of hours, but I have other stuff to do first. Clear on everything?'

'With this old brain of mine, I don't know.'

'Have another koffee,' Darac said, as he took his leave. 'That'll sharpen you up.'

21

Through Cristelle, Darac had arranged to meet Léo at Café Avanti in Boulevard Risso, a favoured spot before the Brigade's temporary move to Commissariat Joinel.

A couple of regulars acknowledged him as he entered but the owner, Sandro, signalled his delight at the return of the native by blanking him even more comprehensively than he used to. Darac ordered what was probably the best *pan bagnat* in town, paired it with a half-bottle of Banyuls Rosé, and took them to a back corner banquette. If Léo was in the house, he wasn't showing himself for the moment.

Darac had spent the previous hour with Frènes at the Palais de Justice. The meeting followed its usual pattern, Darac acting as a reluctant vein to the prosecutor's phlebotomist's needle. His rationale was simple. The less Frènes knew about a case at the start, the less he was able to hinder the investigation thereafter. It was an approach that irritated the Palais and Darac knew it wouldn't be tolerated if the results stopped coming.

A chunk of tuna escaped his sandwich, smearing oil over his shirt cuff en route to the floor. Changing his shirt was no problem. It was only a short walk to Place Saint-Sépulcre.

Using a napkin to pick up the mess reminded him of Thierry's contribution to the case. *Had* Battail taken the mutt along to Chemin Leuze? Granot had already rung with a report on his second interview. Battail denied everything, including training Thierry to attack on command. 'Produce anyone who has seen the dog do that,' he'd said. Darac unscrewed the metal closure on the wine bottle – what was wrong with cork? – and poured himself a glass. He savoured a mouthful, staring into space as he considered why Battail hadn't even thought of citing his helper Dagger as an alibi. It suggested he was neither a close friend nor someone he could pressure. It made Dagger potentially useful to the investigation: if he had witnessed Marcel performing his party trick with Thierry, there was nothing stopping him spilling the beans about it. The only problem was that, his eponymous tattoo aside, nobody seemed to know anything about the man. Granot concluded the call with an update on Brigitte. He'd released her and dutifully advised her of Darac's concerns for her safety if she remained at Battail's place. Later, a local beat officer confirmed that she had returned only long enough to pack a couple of cases and leave.

Darac scanned the café. Still no sign of Léo, there was time to make a call. 'Patricia? Darac. Listen, has R.O.'s team collated the evidence from the Battail garden search yet?'

'I'm just about to email it to you.'

'Anything I need to know?'

'There were no significant finds.'

'Shit.'

'Plenty of that. But not much else.'

'I was hoping for a hand, a finger, even just a nail.'

At a nearby table, a man gave Darac a stare as he got up to leave.

'We've done a particulate analysis. Nothing.'

'OK. Thanks for that, Patricia.'

As if she had been waiting for him to finish the call, a bright-eyed, studious-looking woman of about forty slid on to the seat opposite him. Dissolving a cube of sugar into her *noisette*, she fixed him with a business-like smile.

'You're Darac?'

Her manner was assured, the voice refined.

'Yes?'

'In that case, you owe me.'

He looked blank.

'But as Cristelle tells me she'd signed off for the evening, I'll waive the fee this time.'

'You're Léo?'

'Léonie Salle. Your new bed partner mentioned you wanted to see me.'

'Sorry for being slow on the uptake but I've never met a female pimp before. Do you mind if I finish this?'

'Go ahead. Pimp? I think of myself more as a mobile madam. A care-in-the-community thing.'

'That's original.'

And so was admitting to living off immoral earnings. But as Léo had implied, Darac was hardly in a position to pressure her over it.

'You've already wondered what led a nice girl like Cristelle to sell her pussy for a living. Now you're struggling to picture someone like me running the cattery.'

'You do look more like a lecturer in postmodern critical theory than a sex-industry boss.'

'How many lecturers in postmodern critical theory do you know?'

Angeline, for one. But it was a colleague of hers that Léo brought to mind; a cheerfully dismissive soul who had once referred to his love of playing jazz as 'drastic overcompensation'. For what, he couldn't remember.

'Running the cattery. What's the story there?'

'That story is none of your business.'

'If this were a cheap movie, I might say, "I could make it my business." ' She gave him a disappointed look. 'Yes, alright. But I would like answers to some questions. If you wouldn't mind.'

'Well, since you ask so nicely... First, it's important you understand that mine is a strictly boutique operation. Cristelle and my other three girls are not streetwalkers turning fifty tricks a day. They're specialists, selective. When they choose to work, they have time actually to enjoy it. And they *do* enjoy it, Captain.' She smiled. 'As you partly know.'

Darac ignored the point. 'Her grandmother's house in Beaulieu. You know it's no longer going to Cristelle?'

'Yes, she told me the old cow had sold it *en viager*.'

'And there's nothing for her in the will.'

'Apparently not. So much for our ironclad inheritance laws.'

Darac had imagined asking these questions of some male sociopath; the kind of slimeball who might very well kill an old woman for being 'cheated' out of what he thought was coming to him. Léonie Salle was in a different league altogether.

'Cristelle has told me where she was last Saturday. Officers are interviewing the clients in question as we speak.'

'She gave names?' Léo's eyes hardened to flint. 'She really shouldn't have done that.'

'Now you sound like a pimp.'

'Oh, there'll be no recriminations, don't worry. Although a thorough tongue-lashing is called for.' She raised one eyebrow and smiled. 'Don't you think?'

Her act – for that, he was sure, was what it was – reminded him of Cristelle. He was already wishing she would drop it. 'I have to ask what *you* were doing last Saturday.'

'From about 8 am until well into the evening, I was digging up Roman potsherds in Fréjus. We use lights now.'

She had dropped it, alright. Darac knew of a sex-club owner who restored vintage cars; but archaeology? 'You… were on a dig?'

'What should madams do in their spare time? Design bondage gear? Make dildos?' She took a sip of her *noisette*. 'Do you know what garum is, Captain?'

'No.'

'It's a sort of fish paste – a staple of the Roman world. You know what an amphora is?'

'Yes.'

'The Fréjus site is particularly rich in garum amphorae. None whole, unfortunately.'

'The site manager—'

'Site director.'

'The site *director* will verify you were there between those hours?'

'I'll ask her. "Were you there, Léo?" "Yes, I was." '

Darac let out an involuntary breath. 'It gets better. So I take it several people could vouch for you.'

'At least ten.'

'Uh-huh.' He thought about it for a second. 'Just out of interest, this dig: where did the funding come from?'

'Ah.' She nodded, approvingly. 'You're more astute than I thought. Funding? *Very* difficult to come by these days.'

'And it's been like that for how long?'

'In other words, when did I start up my lucrative little side line?' She pursed her lips while she thought about it. 'Alright, you've earned an answer. Two years ago.'

After the meeting, Darac went home to change, wondering how a woman like Léonie Salle had had the balls to carve out an entrepreneurial niche in the sex industry, albeit a small one. He enjoyed the symmetry of it, though: using profits from the oldest profession to fund the finding of antiquities.

He swiped his mobile and keyed in the Head of Vice's new number at the commissariat. A silk-soft voice answered.

'Paul, how's it going?'

'It's going, Frankie, that's the main thing. You?'

'So-so.'

'Listen, I've got some info to give and a favour to ask.'

He knew favours were no problem. Before her move to Vice, he and Frankie had worked side by side for three years. It had been a perfect partnership.

'If you're shouting up next Thursday at the Blue Devil, I'm busy. Sorry.'

'It's not about the gig.' For a second, the musician in Darac got the better of the *flic*. 'But you should give the DMQ another try, you know. You and Christophe.'

'I've tried, Lord knows.'

'Ah, well… Listen, you're *au fait* with the Jeanne Mesnel case?'

'To an extent.'

'In working on it, I've come across a…' Léo Salle's term came back to him. '…little boutique sex operation.' He told Frankie about it. 'Two years it's been going.'

'My God, she's been careful, Paul. If the boys who run most of the pay and lay action around here had got a sniff of it, they would have muscled in. And I do mean muscled. There would have been no warnings: her business and all its assets would have defaulted to them on the spot. And that would have included your friend Cristelle.'

'Frankie, she's not my friend.'

'Is she not?'

Darac gave her the story from the beginning.

'Whoa, whoa. Let me get this straight. The murder victim, Madame Mesnel, was the star of the poster you love? Your muse, I think you called her, once.'

'That's right. Amazing, isn't it?'

'Absolutely. But, oh, you need to go carefully here, Paul. With Cristelle, I mean. There's an element of fantasy in most relationships at the start, true? But *this* one?'

Darac ran a hand through his hair. 'Frankie, there *is* no relationship.'

'If you say so.'

He needed to move on. 'What do you think of Léo Salle's chances of keeping her business a secret?'

'Well, you've just blown it, haven't you?'

'Here's the favour: I'd like you to keep this under your hat. At least for now.'

'Let sleeping pros lie?'

'Well if Cristelle and Salle are to be believed, there's no huge criminality here. The thing runs on very discreet lines. There's no real touting or pimping going on; there's no culture of coercion or punishment of the girls; and they assure me that none of them is in it to feed a drug habit.'

'No assurances needed. People in desperate need make desperate mistakes and that would have delivered the operation into the hands of the boys quicker than anything.'

'Right. So what about it, Frankie? Will you turn a blind eye?'

'Yes. After all, in two years, I haven't heard anything about it until now. But if you do find out that things aren't quite as buttercups and roses as they seem, it'll be open season on Madame Potsherds. Clear?'

'Thanks, Frankie. And by the way…?'

'Yes?'

'Are you *really* doing something on Thursday evening?'

'You know me too well.'

The call over, Darac picked up his lounge guitar and began strumming chords to nothing in particular. *Chang, chang, chang, chang…* Jeanne Mesnel the poster girl came strutting into his head. The superb confidence; the life in those eyes; the lips blowing smoke; the interaction with the band. Cristelle's verbal portrait of her grandmother had been aggressively critical. Was it accurate? Would it change anything for him if it were?

Darac's phone rang. It was the duty officer at Joinel.

'I have Madame Anne Corot on the line for you, Captain.'

'Really?' Uncanny. 'Thanks, Béatrice… Madame Corot? Paul Darac. I imagine Théoule is warmer than Montreal. You found your sister well?'

'Quite well,' she said, as if it were natural that the minutiae of her life were constantly in the thoughts of others. 'Thank you.'

'You've obviously heard the news. It must have come as a shock to you.'

'You can't imagine, Captain. Jeanne and I were friends for twenty-five years.'

'I would like to come and see you, if I may. Today, if possible.'

'Certainly. Do you tango, Captain?'

'Uh, not as such. Or at all, in fact.'

'Then you'd better get over here shortly. I intend going to my lesson later and we usually go on to make an evening of it.'

'I admire your spirit, madame. I'll drive over immediately.'

'I don't feel like going out at all, to be honest, but Jeanne would have been disappointed in me if I didn't go. I can't let her down.'

Tango lessons in her seventies? Darac could imagine Jeanne Mesnel having a friend like Anne Corot. The thought made him smile as he set off for Théoule-sur-Mer, a quiet little resort just beyond Cannes. He was keenly looking forward to the meeting. Apart from its relevance to the case, he was going to interview someone who had known Jeanne Mesnel intimately and would want to talk about her. If Madame Corot couldn't answer questions about his jazz muse, nobody could.

22

With its graffiti-daubed landings hung with washing, the N'Patas' home apartment block in Nice's northern quarter of L'Ariane wouldn't have looked out of place in the outer *banlieues* of Paris; the kind of building in which some of Malraux's former mates in the riot police would have enjoyed being let loose.

In a corner apartment on the building's twelfth floor, Modibo N'Pata was still wearing the commis chef's duds he'd had on since 6 am. At least he was working in his own kitchen now. The fish stew he was preparing was going to feature a less than perfect red snapper he'd brought from the hotel. A line chef had told him to reserve the choicer parts for the bouillabaisse pan but Modibo had ignored the demand. For such a big man, he had a deft touch with a knife.

In his bedroom, Rama was making music on cymbals damped with pieces of cardboard and drum heads covered with practice pads. He was playing along with 'Milestones', one of the numbers Didier Musso had told him to work on for the next band practice.

He'd spent all day at the beck and call of the shift manager and the various chefs at the same hotel in which Modibo worked, the huge Grande Scarabée on Promenade des Anglais. Once again, he'd done his best to honour his mother's observation, 'no menial task demeans', by lugging and scrubbing with smiling good grace. But here, behind the drums, he had no need for homilies designed to preserve self-esteem, or perhaps to get more work out of him. Here, Rama N'Pata was king. Every component of the elaborate pattern of beats he was playing was articulated perfectly. He couldn't wait to play the piece on Marco's top-of-the-range kit at the Blue Devil.

Thursday night's gig had been the highlight of his life. He'd got on well with the band and, musically, it had gone better than he could've dreamed. He'd been especially intrigued by Darac. His playing was freer than the others, almost loose at times. But the way he'd shaped a couple of solos had been thrilling. To Rama's ears, the band had really missed the guitar after Darac had had to leave the stand. And then the others had told him what the man did for a living. It had sent a shiver down his spine.

A poster of drum god Elvin Jones presided over Rama's bedroom. CD racks and a single bed roll was all the furniture it contained. His kit was a rudimentary set-up but it still meant the door into the living room would open only half way. As Rama manufactured an end-stopping cadence over the fade-out to the Miles number, the door opened a crack. Modibo put his big head into the space, releasing a waft of sweet and savoury scents into the room. 'Dinner is served,' he said with mock hauteur.

The cooking smells hadn't lied: the meal was a triumph. At their small formica-topped kitchen table, Rama was the first to finish his plate.

'Any left?' he said, licking his fingers. 'Monsieur Clay says I need to eat more.'

'More?' Modibo wiped his mouth. 'Tell him you eat enough for two people now. And who is this Monsieur Clay?'

'The owner of the Blue Devil Club. He's from New York. Really cool guy.'

Modibo used a spoon to transfer a couple of heaps off his own plate on to Rama's.

'No, I can't,' the boy said. The token protest didn't last long. 'Oh, that's good! The meeting with Dagger is midnight, right? Pick me up at the club. I'll wait outside.'

Modibo got to his feet. 'I'm going alone.'

'No way. If it gets dangerous, you'll need me.'

Modibo laughed and gave Rama's biceps a squeeze. 'Oh yes, he'll be scared of you!'

Rama jerked his arm away. 'I'm coming. What do we do if Dagger doesn't deliver what he promised?'

'He'd better deliver,' Modibo said.

23

Arriving in Théoule to the sublime lilt of Django's *Nuages*, Darac parked in a street of small villas painted in the burnt orange tones of the surrounding Esterel mountains.

Every centimetre of wall space in Anne Corot's place appeared to be lined with books. She was an impressive-looking old lady, wide-set cheekbones and frank, hazel eyes lending her an intelligent beauty. She and Jeanne Mesnel must have cut a dash together.

Giving her even an edited version of what he knew of her friend's death proved a difficult experience for them both but, after her tears had dried, Madame Corot rallied sufficiently to provide coffee and cognac. Refusing help, she soon returned with a couple of Moka pot espressos and a bottle of Couzin VSOP. They toasted 'my dear Jeanne' and sat in silence for some moments.

'So,' Darac said, taking another sip of the Couzin. 'The tango?'

'My resolve to go has waned since we spoke, Captain. Jeanne would be so cross.'

'I'm sure not. You've always enjoyed dancing?'

'No, not really. I do it mainly for the exercise and for the social aspect.'

'But you shared Madame Mesnel's love of jazz?'

'No, alas.' She gave a sad shake of the head. 'Every so often Jeanne would play me something but I've always been rather tone deaf, I'm afraid.'

'So what did you share as friends? If you don't mind me asking.'

'I welcome it. Jeanne was a free spirit and I think she saw something similar in me. We didn't always succeed in seizing the day but we tried.'

'Apart from you and the gentleman now living in Paris, Monsieur Gaston Cartin, Madame Mesnel didn't seem to have any friends.'

'Have any friends *left*, you mean. Have you spoken to Gaston?'

'One of my lieutenants has.'

'Quite a character.' She took another sip of cognac. 'As, I dare say, am I.'

Darac smiled at her. 'You knew Monsieur Mesnel – Alain?'

'No, no. He'd died over fifteen years before I got to know Jeanne but she told me all about him. A charmer. Something of a rogue but a very lovable one.'

'A rogue?'

'Get-rich-quick schemes. Sudden crazes that were dropped and never taken up again. You know the sort. Exhausting but fun, Jeanne said.'

'He died relatively young. That must have been difficult for her.'

'Of course. But, as I hinted, Jeanne aspired to a Zen approach to life and it helped. Some misunderstood that in her, I think; people who couldn't see that there was a very complex, sensitive woman underneath.'

'She never remarried.'

'There were lovers, of course, but none ever matched up to Alain.'

'Anyone in particular?'

'They were rather brief affairs, I think. Quite insignificant.'

'And recently?'

'I can't think of anyone at all over the past ten years or so.'

'I see. How did you meet Madame Mesnel?'

'I lived in Beaulieu – I was a school teacher there – and one day took some skirts to her to alter. She was the finest seamstress in the area, you know. Supported herself solely by it after Alain died, just working at home. Anyway, I noticed she was reading James Baldwin's *Another Country* and we got talking about it. She said she'd got it because the central character is a jazz musician. A drummer. Are you familiar with the novel?'

'No, but I'd be interested to read it, though. I'm a jazz fan, myself.'

'Then it is a pity you never knew Jeanne.'

'You know, in a sense, I did know her. You recall the jazz club poster on her stairs? The one based on a photo taken in the early sixties? I've loved it most of my life.'

'Alain took that photograph.'

Darac's jaw dropped. 'He did?'

'Photography was one of his enduring passions. It endured for a few months, anyway. Then painting was the new thing.'

'Those local scenes in the living room were done by him? I was under the impression Madame Mesnel had painted them.'

'Oh no, they're his. Rather accomplished, aren't they? In their way.'

'I didn't really look at them closely. But are there any other examples of his photography anywhere? Not snaps, I mean, proper work?'

'I shouldn't think so. That image only exists because he managed to sell it to the woman who owned the club and she had it made into a poster.'

Darac shook his head. 'I think it's among the greatest jazz photos ever taken.'

'That's wonderful! But I can hear Jeanne laughing about it.' She rose. 'Whilst I remember.' With some difficulty, she extracted a volume from one of the bookcases. 'The Bs are rather crammed in, I'm afraid; mainly Monsieur Balzac's fault.' She handed him the Baldwin novel in an old hardback edition. 'This is what started it all.'

He opened the fly leaf. The elegantly inscription read: *To dearest Anne. Perhaps this will get you hooked at last!*

'I'll lend it to you on the proviso that you discuss it with me sometime.'

'It's a date. Although I'm not sure when that will be.'

'Just phone when you're ready.'

Darac slipped the book into his bag. 'I understand that Madame Mesnel's daughter was a deeply unhappy person.'

'When I think of Sarah, I always think of Ford's *The Good Soldier*.' She raised her eyebrows. He shook his head.

'It begins: *This is the saddest story I have ever heard.*'

'Ah.'

'A troubled young woman, unpredictable, difficult. She was already married when I got to know her. Not that I ever saw the husband – Daviot. Another charmer, by all accounts. Not so lovable as Alain. Not lovable at all, in fact. A charlatan. Do you know about Cristelle?'

'Yes I do,' Darac said, taking a sip of his cognac.

'When Sarah fell pregnant, Jeanne urged her to have an abortion, as I would have if I had known her then. That shocks you?'

'Not at all.'

Madame Corot nodded approvingly. 'She didn't want the child but Daviot somehow managed to put the fear of God into her about it. She went ahead. He left immediately the baby was born and Sarah went gradually downhill. Never to recover.'

'Ultimately, she died of cancer, didn't she?'

'That's what they called it, yes.'

'I see. Daviot?'

'He was blown to pieces in an explosion shortly after he left her. Somewhere in Italy.'

'One of the terrorist bombs?'

'Terrorists or freedom fighters.'

Madame Corot's caution for hurling grapes at Front National leaders suddenly came to Darac. Despite her frailty, he bet they had flown with some force.

Yes, Captain, he was just standing there when the thing went off. Unlucky, wasn't it? I felt like cheering when Jeanne told me. *That* shocks you?'

'I am a policeman, madame. I am frequently appalled but never shocked.'

She smiled and raised her glass to him. 'Please have another,

Captain. I will join you.'

He poured refills. 'The hot tub. Did you try it?'

'The day after it was installed. I enjoyed it so much, Jeanne…'
A catch in her voice swallowed her friend's name. 'Forgive me.'

'Please take your time.'

'Yes, I so enjoyed the experience that Jeanne said she would
buy *me* one. Can you imagine? But I really had nowhere to put it.'

'Generous of her.'

'Jeanne was the most generous person in the world, Captain.
Besides, she said, she hadn't paid a *sou* for hers.'

'Courtesy of Mademoiselle Walters-Halberg. An extraordinary
gift, don't you think? It must have cost what, a couple of thousand
euros?'

Madame Corot's eyebrows rose conspiratorially. 'Nearer
three.'

'Uh-huh. Did Madame Mesnel discuss the house sale with
you?'

'Of course.'

'It's a wonderful little place.'

'The times we've had there.'

'I imagine it wasn't on the market long.'

'The house was never on the market.'

'I don't understand.'

'I can give you chapter and verse on that. One morning,
sometime last August I suppose it was, Jeanne was resting by her
gate after returning home with a few bits of shopping – it had
begun to take a lot out of her – when this athletic young woman
appeared and jogged past. They smiled at one another. By the time
she jogged back a minute or two later, Jeanne still hadn't gone into
the house. The girl stopped to ask if she was alright. They shared
a joke about marathons, getting one's breath back and so on and
then Jeanne noticed that the bottle of water the girl was carrying
was empty. She offered to refill it. Speaking of which…?'Darac
obliged with another shot of cognac.

'They went into the house, got on famously, one thing led to another and before you could say spit, the girl had made the offer.'

'I see.' Darac nodded as if such a thing were an everyday occurrence. 'How was the value arrived at?'

'Jeanne had the house valued, naturally. Then a solicitor worked out the *en viager* side of it. The mademoiselle didn't bargain. It was all done beautifully.'

'Some of the contents were included, I notice.'

'Just the carpets, I think. Oh, and the curtains.'

'And the paintings and the carriage clock from the living room.'

'The clock?' Madame Corot looked put out, suddenly. Or at least surprised. 'And the paintings? I didn't realise.'

'They weren't part of the original valuation, then?'

'No. Well, perhaps they were. I don't know.'

The clock... First Walters-Halberg and now Madame Corot seemed anxious to deny any interest in it.

'Selling the house *en viager*: had Madame Mesnel ever considered the idea before?'

'Never. Cristelle was going to get everything. And but for the way she conducted herself when, quite out of the blue, she turned up at the villa one day, she *would* have.'

'So you would corroborate what I've heard about that visit from another source?'

'Which was?'

'That after years of neglect, Cristelle showed up to check her inheritance was still earmarked for her and not the Jazz Musicians Benevolent Association or whatever.'

'Quite so. But it wasn't simply a case of the girl mentally rearranging the furniture, Captain. She was so mercenary and uncaring, it upset Jeanne deeply. It changed everything. And gave her, if not a problem, at least some organising to do and new decisions to make.'

'You know that one of those was to include your name on the

list of beneficiaries?'

'No. Really?'

To the tune of just shy of €180,000. But Darac believed Madame Corot had had enough to deal with for one day. 'I think there might be a little cheque for you.'

Twenty-five years of friendship shone through her eyes. 'Jeanne, you sweetheart.'

'But I interrupted you. Madame Mesnel had decisions to make?'

'Yes indeed. But then almost immediately, in one of those happy accidents that misguided people tend to interpret as instances of divine intervention, up pops Mademoiselle Walters-Halberg and everything was solved.'

The interview concluded with questions about Battail and Brigitte's dog, the marks on the patio, and so on. Madame Corot could shed no light on any of them.

As Darac took the A8 road back to Nice, he began to entertain doubts about Taylor's purchase of the Mesnel villa. He didn't need the example of his parents' first encounter to recognise that serendipitous meetings happened in life. And so did oddly timed coincidences. On his first jazz trip to New York, he found he was staying in the same hotel as a man who had just landed the identical position in a Grasse perfumery that his father had once held. It was extraordinary but, as the saying goes, 'Everybody's got to be somewhere.' The Taylor property-buying saga was different. Who had ever put in an offer on a house, one that its vendor-to-be hadn't even put on the market, while out jogging? Taylor's supposed reason for buying, that she might be homeless following Philippe de Lambert's death, made good long-term sense but why the urgency? The man seemed sound enough. And then there was the issue of the jogging route. Taylor had told Darac she 'always' jogged down to the beach at Passable and back. But Jeanne Mesnel's villa in Beaulieu was in precisely the opposite direction.

Ivo Selmek had insinuated that Taylor's rise at Villa Rose had been due more to her puppy-like devotion to the Lamberts than to her talents as an art historian. He'd practically said she'd wormed her way into their affections for the purpose. Had she done the same with Madame Mesnel? If so, why?

Darac had doubts about the hot tub, also. Was it the post-facto 'thank-you gift' Taylor said or had it been offered prior to the sale as an inducement? A €3,000 gift was quite some thank-you. Darac intended putting these questions to Taylor directly but, in preparation, he resolved to start looking further into her life.

Losing himself in one of his favourite discs, *Shelly Manne at the Blackhawk Volume 3*, Darac didn't surface again until he'd followed the A8 past Cannes and turned toward the Baie des Anges at Château de Vaugrenier. The ziggurat complex at Villeneuve-Loubet was directly ahead now, rising from the shoreline like a theme-park rollercoaster. The sight demanded a flamboyant fanfare from Shelly's men. Instead, 'Whisper Not' floated from the speakers like a feather rising in a current of warm summer air.

'Tay-*lor*... Wal-*ters*... Hal-*berg*...' Darac sang absently in time with the melody's two-beat pulse. He swiped his mobile. 'Bonbon? Know anything about carriage clocks?'

'Enough not to miss a bargain. And I have books. Why?'

'Get them, meet me at the Mesnel villa shortly, and I'll show you.'

'How shortly?'

'I'm calling in at the commissariat en route... Say about an hour?'

'Just a second.' Darac heard Bonbon exchange a few words with someone. 'An hour, it is, chief.'

The call ended, Darac's thoughts soon returned to Taylor Walters-Halberg. What a name that was; one, he reflected, that seemed just made to precede the words 'I arrest you on a charge of...' Of course, he would need slightly more than that to proceed.

Once back at Joinel, he called Granot into his office. 'Koffee with a k?'

The big man sat down like a walrus flopping on to a rock. 'Why not?'

'Ever go for a walk and wind up buying something on impulse, Granot?'

'Once or twice, I suppose.'

'Anything big and expensive?'

'Does Odile count?'

Darac pressed on. 'Ever put in an offer on a house while out jogging? Just imagine that you do jog, for a moment. And I'm talking about an on-the-spot offer for a place that isn't even for sale.'

'No, that's… What are you getting at?'

Darac handed over the machine's take on a double espresso. 'Mademoiselle Walters-Halberg did just that.'

'How do you know?'

'Not from the mademoiselle herself, interestingly.'

Granot weighed the information. 'Strange… But it probably doesn't mean anything.'

'Well, it means *something*, doesn't it?' Darac ran his hand into his hair. 'The more I think about it, the more I don't like it.' He outlined his uneasiness about the clock. 'And that's just one thought.'

'Or maybe she realises the house is sitting on a disused goldmine and the tripod marks are where she set up her theodolite to check.'

'Yes, alright. But there's something odd about this house purchase and that, my old friend, is where you come in.'

Granot's grin faded. 'I've got nothing else to do, of course.'

'I know you have.'

'And what happened to "shouldering the heavy lifting"?'

' "As much as I can," I said. I've just applied for a raft of stuff on Walters-Halberg, which I'll go through. I want you to look at the vendor's side. Find out all you can about Jeanne Mesnel, Alain her husband, and anything that relates to the property before the Mesnels had it. I'll owe you one.'

'What you can owe me is next Wednesday evening. We've got the Shits at home.'

'Your sister's family?'

'Olympique Marseille.'

'Done.'

24

A vehicle Darac didn't recognise was parked outside the Mesnel villa. He blinked as its headlights flicked on, cutting a blue-white swathe through the murk toward him. Wiper blades made a single pass of the windscreen. The driver's door opened.

'Oh it's you, sir.'

They faced away from the wind and the rain as they talked.

'Martino, isn't it? How's it going?'

'I had a look around ten minutes ago. No problems.'

'Good. Better get out of the weather.'

Entering Jeanne's living room gave Darac a feeling he had experienced many times before. By some sort of anthropomorphic extension, it was as if the room itself were dead. And he knew that with each day that passed, the effect would only increase. Music was needed. Early Armstrong. It was presumptuous, but he felt Jeanne would have approved.

Silvery and sassy, the sound of the master breathed life into the place at a stroke. Perhaps disturbed by the displacement of air, a moth fluttered into the open and landed on the frame of one of Alain Mesnel's oil paintings. On his previous visit, Darac had paid more attention to the prints than the paintings but now that he looked at them he saw what Madame Corot had meant: in their way, they were quite impressive. Each was a study of a local landmark: the re-created ancient Greek palace, the Villa Kérylos;

the lighthouse at Pointe Malalongue; the house and gardens of Villa Rose. Each successfully evoked its subject; and each, whether she had any use for them or not, would soon be the property of Taylor Walters-Halberg.

The kitchen door flew open. His shock of red hair plastered to his head, Bonbon blew in with all the composure of a shipwreck. 'I've gone for wet and windswept.'

'You nailed it.'

'I'll dry off in here and I'll be right with you.'

When the moment came, Armstrong struck up a jaunty 'Heebie Jeebies' in welcome. Darac pointed to the carriage clock on the mantelpiece. 'There it is, Bonbon. I've already looked for hallmarks. Couldn't see any. There's a maker's name, though.'

'It's a start.' Bonbon eyed the speakers. 'Can we adjust the volume? Say, to nothing?'

'Phili-bloody-stine. I'm turning it down; no more.'

'That's something.' Bonbon took a couple of books out of his bag. 'I'm going in.'

Another stormy blast from the kitchen and Yvonne Flaco appeared, her braided head looking barely damp. Greetings exchanged, she gave Darac an enquiring look.

'Yes, Flak?'

'I've got a couple of questions.'

He set his weight against the back of the sofa. 'Go for it.'

Lowering her brow into her familiar scowl, she took a notebook out of her windcheater. 'First, I'm not sure why you are so interested in the details of Walters-Halberg's purchase of this place. You can't suspect her of being Madame Mesnel's killer?'

'I don't, although it's not impossible, of course.'

'But she has a watertight alibi for the time of the murder. You checked it yourself.'

'I was satisfied with it but *watertight*? Be careful with that.'

'How could she have faked buying clothes at Atelier Suche? She has a timed receipt.'

Darac glanced at Bonbon. Reference books open, he was passing a magnifying lupe over the clock's movement.

'I'll be a little while yet,' Bonbon said, anticipating the question.

'OK.' Darac turned to Flaco. 'How could she have a timed receipt? Simple: she sent an accomplice. Armed with Taylor's credit card, the woman buys the garment. No forgery skills are needed with chip and pin. Meanwhile Taylor was drowning Madame Mesnel to acquire her villa at a bargain price.'

'But Walters-Halberg is well known at the *atelier*.'

'Julie Suche herself may be the accomplice.'

Flaco pressed her lips together. 'Alright, what about lunch at Hotel Martinez? Several people saw Walters-Halberg there.'

'Again, she could have sent a ringer. None of them had met her before, remember.'

'What about Philippe de Lambert?'

'What's to say *they* aren't in it together?'

'For what reason?'

'Numerous possibilities. Madame Mesnel and Lambert had been lovers for years. He wants to drop her for a newer model so she threatens to tell all to his wife unless he comes up with a few thousand euros. Despite his noble status, he's broke – a lot of aristos are – so he and Taylor hatch a plot that takes care of everything and gives the young woman a nest egg into the bargain. Providing her with a seemingly watertight alibi is part of the deal. Or…' He gave a quizzical shrug. 'Shall I go on?'

'Yes.'

Darac loved Flaco's directness. 'Or more probably, the murder has nothing to do with Lambert and he was confused about the times he and Taylor were together that day. He's old, deaf and his head's in the stratosphere. Taylor simply tells him when they were together and he's grateful to be reminded. Once again, Taylor gains an alibi. Or…?'

'These scenarios are very unlikely, Captain.'

'They are and I'm obviously playing devil's advocate here but, as strange as they may sound, I've encountered variations on all of them on the job.'

'So even if a suspect's alibi seems sound, never rule that person out completely?'

'In an ideal world, it would be safer not to. How are you doing, Bonbon?'

'I'll have an answer in a second.'

He turned back to Flaco. 'You had another question?'

'Walters-Halberg's offer: do you suspect that as an art expert, she recognised the clock was valuable, bet that Madame didn't, then tried to con her out of it as part of the sale?'

'If the clock *is* valuable, perhaps. As to conning, I've only got her assistant, Ivo Selmek's, word for it, but it could be that Walters-Halberg's status at Villa Rose is down to her talents as a manipulator of people rather than as a scholar. And there may be something in that. I've discovered that she hasn't got a single publication or article to her name. Selmek has several.'

'Interesting,' Bonbon said, turning. 'It seems that behind every captain, there's a more talented lieutenant.'

Darac grinned. 'No argument here. So what's the verdict?'

'The clock is enamelled brass. The maker is Dötzel of Nuremberg and the serial number denotes it was made in 1917.'

'Brass.' Darac ran a hand through his hair. 'So probably not valuable?'

'The melt-down price is only part of the value of a metal object. This clock, though, is worth about €150. Twice that if it's restored, but it's probably not worth doing. Of course, there is the provenance angle to consider. If it formerly belonged to De Gaulle or Hitler or Coco Chanel or somebody, its value would be a different matter altogether.'

'Same thing with guitars. If it can be shown that the likes of Django or Wes Montgomery owned an instrument, it adds exponentially to the value.'

'It would be relatively easy to check an instrument's

provenance. A domestic clock?'

Darac shrugged. 'This marks the end of my little clock theory. But don't worry, there'll be another one along in a minute.'

Abandoning its perch on the picture frame, the moth flew between them. Its wings fluttering like a miniature fan, it headed toward the speakers as if drawn to the flame of Armstrong's playing. It prompted a different thought.

'What do you make of the paintings, Bonbon?'

'As a job lot? Worth less than the clock, probably.'

'I imagine so. I meant do you like them?'

'Uh… That one's fun.' He indicated a pastel-toned depiction of Promenade des Anglais, a frothy melange of palm trees, parasols, and pepper-pot domes realised in quick, sketchy strokes. 'Who painted it?'

'Alain Mesnel, husband of Jeanne. He painted all of them.'

'And no two alike,' Bonbon grinned. 'What do you think, Flak?'

'Art's not my thing.'

Bonbon looked more closely at an oil study of the nearby Église Saint-Michel, its subject emerging from a ground of dabbed lozenges of jewel-like colour. 'This one appeals to me. Quite Cézanne-like, isn't it?'

'Yes, now you say it. So you think Alain showed some talent as a painter?'

'In a Sunday-driver sort of way.'

'Follow me, both of you.'

Armstrong went into 'When You're Smiling' as the trio headed for the stairs and the work that was the one towering masterpiece of Alain Mesnel.

Bonbon's eyebrows rose. 'The poster from the club?'

'A copy of it, yes. Alain took the photograph in the early 60s. Good as it gets, no?'

Bonbon nodded. 'It's terrific.'

'Was it part of the sale also?' Flaco said. 'An original poster could be valuable.'

'No, and it's not a rare poster, anyway. And who's ever heard of the photographer?'

Bonbon slipped a blackcurrant pastille into his mouth. 'No justice in this world. Notice that?'

'The interest doesn't end there.' Darac pointed to a figure in the front row of the audience. 'See that young woman, smoking? Guess who she is.'

* * *

Back in the city, Modibo N'Pata was preparing for his meeting with the man he knew only as Dagger. Faced with such a challenge, many of his friends back in Mali would have sought guidance from divine, extra-sensory or even supernatural sources. Modibo put his faith in resources closer to home: his own power and wits, and the unstinting loyalty of Rama. Even when the kid had employed every argument he could muster to prevent Modibo aligning himself, however reluctantly, with Dagger, Rama's support had not waned. Now the relationship with the thug looked to be heading for a possible showdown, he'd offered his scrawny frame as extra muscle.

Rama clearly wasn't as feeble as he looked; he could beat all heaven out of the drums for hours at a time, after all. But the point was an academic one. There was no way Modibo was going to take him along to a midnight rendezvous with someone like Dagger. Instead, Modibo was taking a box cutter. Slipping it into his trouser pocket, he picked up his car keys and headed for the door. Under his full-length agbada, it didn't look as if he was carrying a weapon. The element of surprise was always a good one.

25

Despite showing Jeanne Mesnel's own copy of *Blown Away by the Brass Section* to Bonbon and Flaco only an hour or so earlier, Darac felt the need to commune with the poster in what seemed its proper setting.

'Jeanne,' he said aloud, reaching out to her. 'What happened to you?'

Pascal pushed through the lobby doors beneath, releasing the warm breath of 'Cantaloupe Island' into the chill night air.

'Look at that baby smoking.' Easing a glossy white packet out of his coat pocket, he fired up a Disque Bleu as he joined Darac on the steps. 'I tell you, I was born at the wrong time, man.'

'So was I. See you later, Pas.'

At the pay table, a card leaning against a coin-filled brandy bottle read: *Tonite: The Joao Pinsa Sextet.*

'Garfield, kick anybody's ass today?'

'Not today, Ridge.' As they slapped hands, Darac cocked an ear toward the sultry sounds drifting in from the concert room. 'Sounds good on a cold night.'

The number faded out under a swell of applause.

'Joao and the boys will take you anywhere you want to go. So long as it's hot.'

Speaking too close to his mike, the bandleader's voice carried easily into the lobby.

'Thanks, everyone. We're going to continue with the tropical theme...'

'They're calling your flight, man.'

At the bar, Darac shared greeting kisses with Khara. 'I've got a present for you.' She disappeared under the counter and emerged with a bottle of Courvoisier VSOP. A tag in Ridge's handwriting read: *Thanks for the notification, Garfield.* Darac smiled at the indirect way he had passed on the gift.

'What notification?' she said.

'Oh, just some good news I gave him.'

'Need a glass?'

Darac scanned the room. Didier and several other members of the quintet were in.

'Make that six.'

After pouring snifters for bassist Luc, trumpeter Jacques Quille and English tenor sax man Dave Blackstock, Darac repaired to a table shared by Didier and alto sax player Trudi 'Charlie' Pachelberg. He sat and poured out three good slugs.

As always, Didier assessment of the band began with the pianist. 'Great left hand, this guy.' He raised his glass. 'To genius.'

A tall, skinny figure appeared at the back of the room. 'Speaking of genius.'

Didier leaned into Charlie. 'This is Rama N'Pata. Even his name has rhythm.'

Charlie narrowed her heavily made-up eyes. '*Him*?'

Didier nodded. 'He can do it all. Put him on the stool tonight and he'd fit right in.'

'The white dashiki and pink trousers might clash with the tuxedos,' Darac said. 'Apart from that, he'd walk it.'

'Can't wait to play with him.' Charlie's Berlin-accented French sounded lascivious whatever the situation. 'On the stand, I mean.'

Darac dapped knuckles with Rama as he arrived at the table. 'How's it going, Sticks?'

'Sticks?' The young man produced a retina-frying grin. 'That's new. I like it. *Sticks* – yeah!'

'Charlie Pachelberg, alto.' She took Rama's hand. 'I'm holding on to this. Some of that talent might rub off.'

'You're embarrassing me. May I join you?'

'Sure.' Didier indicated the cognac. 'Have one.'

'Thanks, I'll just have water.'

'Water?' Darac considered the idea. 'Maybe that's where I've been going wrong.' He performed a mime toward the bar. 'Khara will bring you some next time she passes.'

'Khara is her name?' Rama's eyes were wide as he began tapping on the table in counter time with the quartet. 'Khar-issima!'

Didier gave him a look. 'Her husband Roger thinks so, too.'

'She's too old for you, anyway,' Darac said.

Perhaps out of deference to Charlie, Rama smiled awkwardly and for a moment he lost the beat. The kid was human, after all.

'So what about the band, Sticks?' Didier said, after a couple of further numbers.

'I like it.'

'The drummer?'

He made a 'so-so' gesture with his hand.

Charlie narrowed her eyes. 'Why so?'

Rama's basso register gave his verdict a definitive ring.

'The rudiments are in the bank, as Marco would say. His metre is metronome perfect. But he's showing no invention. Every fill and every accent is predictable.'

The young man's assessment was so cool and free of flannel, it made Darac smile. 'You don't know anyone named Yvonne Flaco, do you?'

'No.'

'Pity. You'd get on.'

As the evening progressed, beers took over from the wine that took over from the cognac, and as the second set reached the halfway stage, Didier was performing a passable impression of a drunk. Ridge joined the party just as Rama got up to leave.

'Something I said?'

'No, no, Monsieur Clay. I've stayed too long already. I'm meeting someone.'

Didier came to, his words emerging in a slurred burst. 'See you at the practice, Sticks.'

'I'll be on time.'

' 'Milestones' and the other numbers coming along?'

'They're all down, Didier. Bye everyone.'

The four of them couldn't take their eyes off Rama as he picked his way to the exit. Flamingos on speed have that effect.

Ridge nodded his sage old head. 'Hear that? He called me *Monsieur* Clay. Respect – that's another thing that's disappearing in our Brave New France. And Didi?'

'*Monsieur* Clay?'

'You're wasted, baby. And that's not French, either.'

'Shit! I forgot to tell him about 'Lil' Darlin'.'

'There's time, Didi.' Darac took another sip of beer.

'So what do you think, Charlie?'

'About Sticks? He'll do.' For what, she didn't specify. Ridge had a final thought. 'He's meeting someone? Let's hope they go eat.'

After the band had finally samba-ed off into the sunset and everyone else had gone home, Darac and Ridge repaired to a banquette for one of their periodic fat-chewing sessions. There was something about the atmosphere of an after-hours jazz club that lent itself to searching souls. Bill Evans's *You Must Believe In Spring* album playing quietly in the background only deepened the mood.

Once the band's performance had been picked over, Ridge continued with his theme of the moment. Without a trace of irony, he cited his homeland as a major contributor to the decline of the Frenchness of French life.

'Remember when seeing a McDonald's over here was weird? Now it's Le Macdo. And we got Budweiser now. I tell you, France Lite is where we're heading.'

Darac gave him a look. 'Uh… Louis Armstrong, Josephine Baker, Woody Allen—'

Ridge shook his head. 'No. Not the same thing.'

They talked that one through and then the big man turned to a question he'd been clearly meaning to broach for years. 'You know, you're a unique guy, Darac. You play guitar and you're a cop. How'd that happen?'

'Are the two things so incompatible?'

'Well how many others could claim that?'

'You'd be surprised. There are officers who are writers, sculptors – all kinds of things. One homicide detective I know does rap in his spare time. They've even dreamed up a term for us: *poètes policiers*.'

'No shit?'

'No shit.'

Ridge gave a shrugging nod, a mannerism that was as South Bronx as it was French. 'For you it's not just downtime, though, right? You ever think of turning pro?'

'At least once a day.' Darac drained his glass. 'Funny thing. I never feel more like playing than when I'm working on a case. If I didn't have that in my life… I don't know.'

'Another Leffe?' Ridge disappeared behind the bar without waiting for the reply. 'What pushed your buttons about becoming a cop in the first place?'

Darac shook his head. 'It's too corny.'

'Where I come from, we eat corn every day. Try me.'

Darac just couldn't say out loud that ever since he was a small child, he'd hated injustice and felt a strong need to fight it. Truth, Justice and the French Way – Paul Darac: Gallic Superman! He had other reasons. 'I like solving problems.'

'You could've taught math like Didier. Or become a systems analyst like Luc.'

'Too dry. I've also got an insatiable curiosity about people and the way things work.'

'You could've become a researcher or a journalist.'

'Alright, I'll tell you. It's the uniform. And the popularity.'

It never lasted long, but Ridge's seismic laugh was one of the great sounds of the world. It took a chorus of Bill Evans's 'Sometime Ago' to ease the mood back down.

'The lady you mentioned,' Ridge said. 'The one who left me the CDs and things?'

'Yes?'

'How's everything coming on?'

Darac made a point of never discussing open cases with his friends. When it was finished, he intended to tell Ridge all about Jeanne Mesnel, the woman who had been blown away by the brass section all those years ago. For the time being, talking about anything but the bequest would have to wait until the case was over.

'Case?' Ridge poured himself another drink. 'I thought she died in an accident?'

'I meant when the matter is over.'

'Right.' Ridge downed his Scotch. 'So you're never going to turn in your badge?'

'Unless they kick me off the force, which they've threatened to do a few times, I think I'll stay with it. Despite everything, it's the role I'm most comfortable with.'

'Being a cop? That's some comfort zone, baby.' Another Scotch hit Ridge's glass. Screwing the top back on the bottle, he eyeballed Darac with a look of such gravity, it sent a chill down his spine. 'Hope it don't get you killed.'

26

Darac's off-duty Sunday had begun in the way most had since he'd been acting commissaire: getting up early to tackle the paperwork he hadn't had time for in the week.

Remarking on the number of French terms in common usage around the world: *chic*, *tête-à-tête*, *panache*, and so on, Ridge had once asked Darac which word or phrase he thought most accurately evoked France. The detective didn't have to search for an answer. '*Dossier*,' he'd said. The national obsession with written records would be, he was sure, the one tradition of French life the forces of globalisation would never overcome.

As if it had been waiting for him to finish, his mobile rang just as he was completing the final report. The number was unfamiliar.

'This is Lieutenant Armand Gras from Foch. Sorry to disturb you, Captain, but I've got something of interest to the Brigade.'

There was a first for everything. 'Ah, yes?'

'I'm investigating a potential dangerous driving case at L'Ancienne Bastide, the campsite up by Col d'Eze. A couple of less-than-happy campers want us to nail the driver of a car who nearly flattened them on her way into the site on Friday. The evidence on the ground here seems to bear out their story.'

'How is this of interest?'

'The vehicle the woman was driving is registered to one Adèle Voska.'

Darac's ears pricked up. 'Go on.'

'The site manager has just confirmed she was here at the stated time, looking for her father, Gilles. He's got an interesting tattoo on his arm, this guy. Crossed daggers.'

'I'll be with you as soon as I can.'

'Hold it, Captain. After ten months of continuous occupancy, Gilles Voska, aka Dagger, paid up and pulled out yesterday evening.'

'*Did* he now?' His laptop still on, Darac clicked on the database: Voska scarpering the day after his mate Battail had been taken into custody was obviously suspicious.

'How did he leave?'

'In his RV.' The lieutenant supplied a description and the registration.

'Top work, Gras. If you ever consider trying out for the Brigade, come and see me.'

'Thanks, Captain, but I hear you lot in *La Crim'* do even more paperwork than us.'

Voska's mug shot came up on the screen. With the usual provisos about the photographic context, and the notoriously unreliable nature of physiognomy itself, Voska's hollow-eyed skull conveyed the purest image of evil Darac had ever seen.

He brought up his bio. As a younger man, Voska had served

for twelve years in the Foreign Legion, finishing as an officer in a commando unit. His adjustment to civilian life had not gone well. He had spent thirteen years in prison altogether. Drug pushing, extortion, publishing obscene materials, aggravated assault, rape. He had also been arrested for manslaughter but released due to lack of evidence.

'Somebody screwed up,' Darac murmured as he read the details. All in all, Voska was a versatile offender, one whose record dwarfed Battail's. Looking for a connection, Darac juxtaposed their prison records. There it was. So much for Battail stating that he knew nothing about Voska. The two of them had served in La Santé, their terms overlapping by six months – ample time to become acquainted. Yet under questioning, Battail had not cited Voska as an alibi. Instead, he'd offered 'I went to a couple of bars.' That didn't ring true. Providing one another with alibis was written into the charter of the Old Lags Club. It was an obligation.

But then Darac saw it. In not citing Voska, Battail *had* done his bit for the club. It was a delaying tactic. While officers were out combing bars for anyone who had seen Battail, Voska was taking his leave without having to account to anyone for anything.

Hoping it wasn't too late, Darac sent out an APB: Voska was to be sought and detained. He ran Adèle Voska's name through the database: no known offences. With her background, it meant she was either clever or lucky. Or a law-abiding citizen, of course. He rang Bonbon, updated him and outlined his unoffered alibi theory.

'I'm sure you're right, chief. When's the release or charge deadline on Battail?'

'Tomorrow afternoon, now. In light of Brigitte's accusation, Frènes extended it a day.'

'OK.' Darac glanced at his watch. 'I'm going to try another route in the meantime, Bonbon. Keep in touch.' He rang the path lab. 'Patricia, Barrau still there?'

'He's on his way out of the building.'

'Stop him.'

It was a pointless instruction, he knew. Once on course, Barrau never turned back. It wasn't long before Patricia returned. 'He's coming, Captain.'

'What? How did you—?'

'I told him I thought Frènes was calling. Quick! Here he comes.'

Jules?' Barrau said. 'For goodness sake, I was on my—'

'Jules has just been called away, Carl. Paul here.' He could almost feel Barrau's indignation pouring out of the phone. 'Any progress on the Mesnel autopsy?'

'The completed report has been faxed to your office.'

A clunk. Followed by silence.

'He really has gone this time, Captain.'

'You did brilliantly. Listen, can you route the fax to my laptop?'

'Sure.'

Having printed it off, Darac turned first to the cause-of-death page. Seeing it there in black-and-white caused an eruption of anger so sudden, he threw the pages across the room. Had Jeanne Mesnel's killer appeared in front of him at that moment, half the wild horses of the Camargue could not have dragged Darac away.

'The bastard.'

Snatching up the pages, Darac took some moments to gain the composure necessary to begin reading systematically through the report. Initially, entries showed only minor revisions from the original. However, the time of death had been narrowed down to somewhere between 3 and 5 pm. Then the hideous stuff kicked in. Traces of semen had been found in Jeanne Mesnel's vagina. Tearing and other factors indicated sex had not been consensual. Conclusion: she had been raped, suffered a heart attack and left to drown in the hot tub. There was no DNA match for the perpetrator as yet but it was not Battail.

Jeanne Mesnel raped. Raped to death. And convicted rapist

Gilles Voska was away and gone. Ridge was right, wasn't he? Being a cop was some comfort zone. Darac knew he had to start thinking of this as just another case. Agnès Dantier's words to new recruits came back to him: *Engage with facts; keep your distance from people.* Fifteen years into the job, he knew it was a bridge too far, this time. He tried to imagine the mind of a man who could traumatise a frail old lady to death in such a way.

Darac went out on to his terrace. Taking deep breaths, he looked out across the terracotta canopy of the Babazouk. It was glowing brazier red. He gazed beyond it to the mountains. No succour there, either. And then he remembered that a part of him had *wanted* the enquiry to become a fully fledged murder case. His stomach turning over, he went back inside and drank a glass of water.

He'd calmed down by the time he returned to the study. But a fire had been lit within him and he knew it would not be extinguished until everything had been settled. Tapping the arm of his chair more percussively than usual, he rang the duty officer at Joinel. 'Charvet?'

'It's Béatrice, Captain.'

'Bé, set up a squad meeting, will you?' He looked at his watch. 'Eleven o'clock.'

That gave him an hour and a half. His first move was to revise his earlier APB. Phone teams and slog squads added to the mix, the search for Voska and his RV was now a concerted, full-scale effort. He'd prime Interpol next. But before ringing Frènes to authorise it, Darac decided to pay a call on someone who might just give them a steer.

Flanking the delta of tracks draining Nice Ville station, the Emerald Apartments building did not conjure the precious jewel its name signified. Behind its shabby, green-tinted glass frontage was a shabbier interior. Entering the lobby was like stepping into an abandoned aquarium tank. Darac took one look at the lift and opted for the stairs.

As he made his way along the second-floor corridor, a train heading out of the station put the building's foundations to the test and everything around him shook. Checking that the safety on his SIG automatic was off, Darac found number 167 and knocked. The door was opened by a tall, broad-shouldered young woman wearing jeans and a sleeveless leather jacket. Her face, bare of make-up except for a gash of blood-red lipstick, was as strongly featured as a monumental bust: something to be admired from afar. But it was her coiffure that really caught Darac's eye. Sculpted into jet-black pyramids, it was a goth Valley of the Kings.

Darac showed her his ID. 'Adèle Voska?'

'I already made a statement. Those little hoity-toities were jay walking. Go grill *them*.'

'I'm not here in connection with that. May I come in?'

'I'm going out.'

'Nevertheless.'

Tucking a hand casually into a pocket, she shrugged and let him into a living space that belonged in a much classier building. Three doors gave off the room. Two were wide open and led to the bathroom and kitchen. Nowhere for Gilles Voska to hide in there. Darac indicated the third. 'Your bedroom? May I?'

'Got a warrant?'

'Yes I have.' He slipped a document out of his pocket and held it up, momentarily. Headed 'Palais de Justice', it was a warrant actually relating to a different case.

'Then what are you asking me for?'

Darac's hand slipped inside his jacket as he threw open the door. The bed was a divan and the wardrobe was an open rack on castors. No balcony. Unless Gilles Voska had the power of invisibility, he was elsewhere. Darac turned to Adèle. 'My notes say you're a design student.' One who liked to keep a hand in a pocket, it seemed. He indicated the décor. 'You do this?'

'So?'

'It's good.'

'It's condemned. In a couple of months, I'm out of this shithole.'

That meant Adèle was eligible for rehousing – in theory, at least. 'Housing crisis?' He grinned. 'What housing crisis?'

'What do you want, *flic*?'

'First, I'd like you to take your hand out of your pocket.'

'This is my apartment, my hand, my pocket. I'll keep it there.'

He couldn't allow it. As a young officer, Darac had gone to a restaurant in Cagnes-sur-Mer to question its chef about some minor misdemeanour. The interview ended when the man's 'little helper', his seemingly docile eleven-year-old daughter, stabbed the detective in the thigh with a paring knife, missing his femoral artery by millimetres. The incident had left an indelible mark. 'You can put your hand where you like but my problem is—'

A lunge, a grab and he'd relieved her of her weapon: a Mace spray. Her chest heaving, she tottered back against the door.

'Do you always go to the door with this for company?' Adèle was shaking. Darac could hardly credit it but he suspected if he made the wrong move, she might fall apart in front of him. 'Are you alright?'

'Don't come near me.'

'I won't, don't worry.' He kept his eyes on her as he picked up the canister, backed slowly to the window and set it down on the sill. Returning to the centre of the room, he lowered himself into a cross-legged position on the floor. 'There. Harmless.'

'You've got a gun, arsehole. Stamped property of the state just like you are.'

The observation took him aback. In what had been an uncharacteristically barbed exchange, Angeline had once hit him with the same accusation.

'I'll unload it.' Holding the barrel, he removed the magazine and tossed it over his shoulder. It went some way to calming the girl but it was a couple of minutes before her shaking stilled and the skin around her eyes and mouth lost its pallor. The way her lovingly prepared coiffure retained its perfect geometry throughout touched Darac, somehow. 'Shall I call a doctor, Adèle – if I may call you that?'

'No. In both cases.'

'Alright, but are you sure about the doctor? What's wrong?'

'A man attacked me the other day and I'm still edgy. Is that OK?'

'Did you report it to the police?'

She made a dismissive sound in her throat.

'You still could.' He gave her a couple of good reasons why. 'No?'

Once again, the building shuddered alarmingly.

'What do you want?'

'Alright. I want to know where Dagger is, the man you claimed not to know and who turns out to be your father.'

'My father's name isn't Dagger. It's Gilles.'

'Don't be cute, mademoiselle. Where is he?'

She recited the Ancienne Bastide address.

'Where is he *now*, I mean. He left the campsite last night, as I'm sure you know.'

'Did he? Uh-huh.'

'One last time. Do you know where he might have gone?'

'I don't know and I don't care.' Adèle's reply appeared to carry real conviction.

'May I stand?' he asked. 'My left leg's going to sleep.'

She shrugged.

'It doesn't surprise you that we're looking for him?'

'Nothing surprises me about anything.'

'Why did you go and see him at the campsite?'

She switched her weight on to her other foot. 'To tell him to fuck off.'

'Why? What's he done?'

Another shrug.

'You opened the tattoo parlour up on Friday. Why?'

'I often do it. En route from home, Battail stops off to see some stupid woman. When he gets in, I go.'

'Do you know the name of this woman?'

She gave him a withering stare.

'Address, then? Or anything at all?'

'The only thing I know is that she can't get enough of Battail. According to him.'

'Back to your father…'

Darac persisted for another ten minutes but he made no progress. Glad to be back out on the street, he swiped his phone and called mobile control.

'I need a tail on one Adèle Voska.' He gave the details. 'Anyone nearby?'

'About two minutes away, Captain.'

'You know what to do.'

He waited until he was back in his car before he rang Frènes. He kept his eye on the entrance to Adèle's building as he talked.

'So why do you want this man, Darac?'

He gave a recap of the thoughts he'd shared with Bonbon. Frènes was unimpressed.

'Was the semen Voska's?'

'We don't know yet. But it wasn't Battail's.'

'Until we do know, I suggest we—'

'Give him even more time to make good his escape? The man's a convicted rapist. Why do you think he skipped when he did? And consider the other details.'

There was action at the apartment building. Darac watched as Adèle Voska emerged and headed across the street toward a cluster of cars huddled on a patch of rough ground.

'The lack of an alibi, Captain? And a departure from a campsite in a vehicle designed for a mobile lifestyle? Unconvincing. Especially for a Sunday morning.'

'Sorry about the intrusion but we've been farting around.

Now we need action.'

'To ensure a swift resolution, I gave you action on Day One.'

'Yes, and I know it's inconvenient but your tip-off, Marcel Battail, didn't do it.'

'He may still be an accessory.'

'I'm sure he is but Voska is the main player in this, Monsieur Frènes. Trust me.'

Adèle's car turned into the street. Where was the tail?

Darac readied himself, in case.

'Escalating the case to these proportions—'

'You wanted this thing to be a quickie, monsieur. It still could be if you act now.'

'The Gendarmerie is one thing but Interpol? Do you know what the unit cost will be?'

Down the street, a grey Ford Focus pulled slowly away from the kerb.

'And for what?' Frènes went on. 'The murder of an old woman who according to Dr Barrau might have been dead within a year anyway?'

'Her murder will still count as a full tick in the "solved" column, monsieur.'

The Focus rolled past, its driver exchanging the slightest of nods with Darac. On the phone, a pregnant pause went to full term before Frènes finally delivered. Darac thanked him, rang off and made another call.

* * *

The day man blew a sour mouthful of air in Darac's direction as he admitted him to Résidence Floride.

'I've missed you, too.'

Cristelle opened the door on its chain. Once again, Jeanne Mesnel was alive for a moment; alive in a white towelling dressing gown, smelling of lime and cinnamon.

'May I come in?'

'That depends.'

'I've got some news of the investigation into your grandmother's murder.'

'So it was murder, then?' she said, keeping the door fettered.

'And we have an idea who may have been responsible.' Darac reached into the inside pocket of his leather jacket and took out the Voska photograph. Cristelle's eyes stayed on Darac's as he held it up.

'Is that really why you've come? Or have you come to see me?'

'Please look at the photo, Cristelle.'

Limes, cinnamon and silence.

'I'm not going until you look at it.'

She did as she was asked and shook her head.

'Never seen him?'

'No,' she said, softly, lowering her gaze. Her eyes settled on her bathrobe belt. She fingered the knot absently, then half-undoing it, slid her eyes up to meet his. The invitation was clear. He didn't move. Very slowly, Cristelle closed the door and unhooked the chain. When she opened it, the robe lay at her feet. And Darac was gone.

27

Telling himself to keep it professional, Darac walked into the briefing room and set up his stall front and centre. Behind him, flip charts, whiteboards and screens were arrayed like a display at a police-college open day.

'Flak and Perand, thanks for coming in. I'll re-jig your shifts.'

Perand gave Flaco a look that said he would believe that when it happened.

'Failing that, I'll owe you both one.' He took a sheaf of reports out of his bag and handed them out. 'This is Barrau's second autopsy report on Madame Mesnel. If you turn to page two, you'll see that a trace of motile sperm was detected in the victim's vagina.'

'Swimmers in the canal, eh? Bet the old girl hadn't seen any of that action for—'

'Malraux.'

Darac hadn't raised his voice but his eyes were burning.

'Yes, sir?'

'Shut up.'

'Seconded,' Flaco said, not quite under her breath.

Malraux spoke to the back of her head. 'I outrank you, sweetheart. Show respect.'

Flaco turned and fixed him with a look that showed all the respect she had for him.

Darac's eyes were still on Malraux. 'Let's continue.'

Granot stirred uncomfortably in his seat. 'How come we've had to wait so long for this? Surely Barrau should have found it in his preliminary exam?'

'I've just had a word with Deanna. The semen was no more than a micro-trace, apparently. Some might not have found it at all.'

Granot looked queasy, suddenly. 'I'm hoping it wasn't canine.'

Bonbon stopped sucking his sweet.

'It was human,' Darac said, as neutrally as he could. 'And as you see, slight tearing in the vagina and other factors indicate sex was not consensual. So we are now dealing with a case of rape and manslaughter at the very least.'

'Question, Captain?'

'Flak?'

'I don't understand. Isn't this a case of necrophilia?'

'The victim was alive when it happened.'

'I thought sperm only lived for a matter of hours outside the testes.'

'If the woman is alive, yes. In a corpse, it can live for up to ten days.'

'Ten?' She made the note. 'Thank you.'

'If you turn to the final paragraph, Barrau concludes that the victim succumbed to a fatal heart attack and drowned as a result of being raped in the hot tub.'

Granot turned back a couple of pages. 'The semen was the only exchange evidence?'

'What about pubic hair?' Perand said. 'They found one of the perp's snagged in the victim's in a case I was following in Biarritz a few months ago, even though the body had been tossed into a swimming pool afterwards.'

'No pubic hair,' Darac said. 'If you turn to page six, you'll see there were human and dog hairs found in the hot tub's filter. One of the human specimens still had its DNA-bearing follicle intact and it matches the semen. Accordingly, swabs are being taken from every male neighbour, and those we know were connected with the victim, including her friend Monsieur Gaston Cartin, who's now living in Paris. I've just been through Madame Mesnel's landline phone log. She received a call from Cartin a couple of days before her death and that's the only one of any significance. It turns out he has a solid-looking alibi for the day in question but the 14th Arrondissement is rechecking it.'

If Malraux felt nostalgic at the reference to his home city, he showed no sign of it. 'The 14th? Good luck with that. When is Battail's custody period up?'

'Tomorrow afternoon. One thing we know for certain is that the semen is not his. We're sure he's an accessory, though, so we will be interrogating him again.' He shared a look with Bonbon. 'Right after this?'

'I'm in. Voska's DNA details are obviously on file.'

'Yes, they were working on it but there's been some foul-up. Once it's cleared, it's their first priority.'

'Right.'

Checking the screen was set square on to the projector, Darac nodded to a uniform at the back of the room and joined the others. The hard, hollow-eyed face of Gilles Voska whirred into focus. The man looked threatening in a 15 by 10 centimetre mug shot. Projected five times larger than life, the effect was truly disturbing. 'So this is who we're dealing with,' Darac said, over a swell of voices. He turned to Voska's rap sheet. 'And this is why.'

* * *

Battail's interrogation began as expected. He claimed to have no idea where Voska had gone and his reason for not citing him as an alibi was the least believable answer he had given to date: 'I couldn't say I was with him because I wasn't. It'd be a lie.'

'You didn't name him because you wanted to slow us down. It worked. He got away.'

'Bollocks.'

'Adèle Voska told me earlier you visit a girlfriend on your way to work every day.'

Bonbon snorted. 'On his way *to* work?'

'He's quite a man, is Marcel. Who is this woman?'

'Nobody. She... doesn't exist.'

'Then why tell Adèle she did?'

Battail shrugged.

Bonbon exhaled deeply. 'So what *do* you do after leaving home and before you get to Rue Jules Gilly?'

'Walk around, relax, get some air.'

Bonbon grinned. 'Perhaps a jog along the Promenade?' He killed the look. 'Come on!'

'If you'd been shagging Brigitte all night, you'd need some R and R, believe me.'

At last, Battail had volunteered something that rang true. And looking into the man's eyes, Darac could see another truth. 'I bet you're missing her, though. Right? Gagging for her. Now we're talking man to man, Marcel—'

'Are we shit.'

Battail's shutters went down and this time, they stayed down. As the session ended, Darac dispensed a triple espresso from the machine and set off on a head-clearing walk with Bonbon. 'It seems Battail's already forgiven Brigitte, or his libido has, so I reckon she could move back in, don't you?'

'Definitely. I bet they've been through this countless times. But then what?'

'We put a wire on her. Or whatever.'

Bonbon slipped a striped paper bag out of his pocket. 'Honey trumpet?'

'Pass.'

Bonbon stuffed one into his mouth. 'Why would Brigitte want to help us?'

'I think she could be appealed to in all sorts of ways.' Darac's mobile rang.

'Captain? It's Taylor.' Her voice sounded softer on the line. 'Taylor Walters-Halberg.'

He put the phone on speaker. 'Mademoiselle?'

'Two reasons for ringing. I was wondering if there had been any developments in the, well, *case* I suppose is the word.'

'Case is very definitely the word, I'm afraid. In fact, I'm glad you rang. I have a couple of questions I need to put. And a photograph to show you.'

'Obviously, we can't do that over the phone,' she said.

'Why not?' mouthed Bonbon.

'And that leads me nicely to my second reason. I have some time off this afternoon. I was wondering if you would like to meet for a chat. Have you eaten yet?'

Bonbon gave Darac a look.

'No, I haven't.'

'Perhaps we could have a late lunch.'

'Did you have anywhere in mind, mademoiselle?'

'Yes, I have, but please call me Taylor. And may I call you Pierre?'

Bonbon involuntarily swallowed his sweet.

'You can call me Pierre but it's not my name.'

'I'm sorry! It's... Paul, isn't it? Start again. May I call you Paul?'

'Why not call me Darac? Most people do.'

'Al-right.'

Arrangements were made and the call ended.

'Château Park, eh?' Bonbon said, his eyes twinkling. 'Romantic.'

'Bonbon, this is the first warm day in a while and the park's roughly halfway between us.'

'Only if she knows where Commissariat Joinel is. Mate, she made a date with you.'

'She couldn't even remember my name. And I wanted to talk to her, anyway.'

'She didn't know that when she rang. The woman will be *tu toy*-ing you before you've chosen a table.'

'She *could* be mounting a charm offensive, I suppose.'

Darac drained his espresso and crushed the cup. 'Perhaps to keep her abreast of progress on the case.'

'Why might she need to do that? Think she's hiding something?'

'I sense she is, actually. Nothing murderous, I'm sure. But something.'

'So is this Walters-Halberg woman attractive?'

'Attractive, no. A blue-eyed, blond goddess, yes.'

A goddess with the mark of the devil between her eyes.

★ ★ ★

Darac was on the way to lunch when a chorus of horn blasts went up all around him. He'd run a red light. It was only then that he realised he was gripping the steering wheel hard enough to crush it. He couldn't get Jeanne Mesnel out of his head; nor what he wanted to do to her killer. Relaxing his grip, he told himself to go to another thought. Taylor? Bonbon was right to think that she had effectively made a date with him but lunch didn't carry the romantic connotations of dinner; its rules of engagement were of a lesser order altogether. In any case, Darac had resolved never to allow sex to get in the way of an investigation again. Maintaining a critical distance from Taylor, he felt, should not prove insuperable. For all her beauty, she held no real attraction for him. Cristelle exuded an overpowering whiff of pheromones from every pore. Taylor couldn't be more different. As perfect, or perfected, as a living Barbie doll, it was as if she had taken on the unformed sexuality of her plastic counterpart.

He swiped his mobile. 'Patricia, anything on the Voska DNA match yet?'

'Still waiting, Captain.'

Next, he called Joinel and checked on the search. Despite the number of officers deployed, there had been no sighting or lead on Voska or his RV. Darac began to crush the steering wheel all over again.

In bright sunshine, he met Taylor at the viewpoint on the crown of Château Park, the gardens laid out on the wooded promontory that rose between the port and the old town. She was wearing a pink pashmina over a grey woollen dress, the simplicity of the outfit serving only to accentuate her figure. They shook hands and made for the throng of sightseers lining the balustrade. Claiming the one free space against the rail, Darac took a half-step back. 'Please.'

Her hip gently nudged his as she slipped in front of him. 'Sorry,' she said and smiled. Her hair cascading over her shoulder like a shining waterfall of gold, she turned her back on him and gazed out over the view. 'Doesn't it just look wonderful?' Her voice, no more than a whisper, segued into a sigh. 'The city… The bay…'

Beneath them, the spice-toned streets of the Babazouk wound in a terracotta-topped swirl. Beyond, the modern city opened out into a paler patchwork that stretched between the fabulous azure arc of the Baie des Anges and the rocky *baous* and rounder peaks of the surrounding Alpes-Maritimes.

'Or do you see it as a collection of crime scenes?'

He smiled. 'I suppose I do see the serpent as well as the paradise.'

'Interesting.' She returned to the view. 'You've checked out *my* palace, Captain. I think it only fair you point out yours.'

He felt a rough indication would do no harm. 'The tops of

these trees get in the way but we can see it from over there. More or less.' He led her to the inland-facing balustrade. 'See the little cemetery chapel?'

'Yes.'

'The cupola is your sight line.' Over her shoulder, he moved his pointing finger until it was in line with the Tête Carrée, the cube-shaped library building perched on what looked like a human neck. 'Now look midway between the cupola and the Tête. That open space is Place Garibaldi. My place is in the tangle of streets just this side of it.'

Her sweet, floral perfume filling his nostrils, she adjusted her weight back against him.

'The streets in the old city have such romantic-sounding names. Which is yours?'

'Sorry to be stuffy but police officers aren't supposed to give out their addresses.'

She turned to him. 'Do you always do what you're supposed to?'

For the first time, he noticed that one of her canine teeth was slightly crooked. It improved her, he thought. 'Definitely.'

'Paul—'

He opened his mouth to correct her but Taylor beat him to it. 'Listen, I'm not going to call you Darac. It sounds like some sort of… cleaning product. *Blocked drains? Use Darac!*'

He laughed. 'Paul it is. Let's go to lunch.'

They descended a flight of steps and, emerging on to a broad stone apron, strolled in the lee of the wall around to the café. On such a perfect day, there seemed no need for the 'inside or out?' debate and the pair sauntered toward a group of tables offering the best view over the old town.

'You know, Paul, the first time I visited the café, I ate inside but I had to leave.'

'Oh?'

'Smokers at the next table. Four of them. Thank God for the ban.'

'God had nothing to do with it.'

'You're a smoker?'

She couldn't have uttered 'You're a kitten strangler?' with any greater distress.

'No, no. Shall we continue?'

'Surely.' The question was still exercising her. 'You gave up recently or…?'

'Never smoked a cigarette in my life. But tell me I'm not permitted to do something and, like most French people, I want to do it immediately.'

'That is *so* French.'

She smiled at him so knowingly, he didn't know whether he found it charming or irritating. He was clear on one point: it was easy to see how such an accomplished, beautiful and amusing young woman came to be valued by the Lamberts. How genuine it all was remained to be seen.

Taking their seats, they looked out across the tessellated roofscape of the Babazouk.

'It looks as continuous as a pavement.' Taylor shook her head in wonder. 'I feel I could step off this wall and walk around on it. Or at least play…' She searched for the French '…"hopscotch" we call it in English.'

'Upscuts?'

'I *love* "upscuts"!'

An obstacle course for his tongue, Darac felt he'd taken a pretty good stab at it. 'What is that, exactly?'

'A kids' game. You hop from square to square in sequence? One foot, two feet?'

'Ah yes. *Marelles*, we call it.'

'*Marelles*, I must remember that.'

A couple of laminated menus sat on the table. Darac recommended the *tarte aux courgettes, tomates et basilic* and the conversation rambled pleasantly along until the food arrived.

'On a different note,' Taylor said, cutting up her tart into bite-size pieces. 'Maggie de Lambert tried to persuade me not to meet you.'

'Because I'm a Frenchman or because I'm a policeman?'

'Mainly the latter. She's convinced you're going to treat me to a beating with your baton or your night stick or whatever you people use.'

'I was thinking of just giving you a light singe with my flamethrower.'

As if to stay laughter, she gave him a shocked look. 'That's not funny!'

'I thought it was. But then we French aren't perhaps in the first rank when it comes to comedy.'

'Nonsense. Jacques Tati, Louis de Funès, Ambroise Paillaud? They're wonderful.'

'True, but they're the exception, I think.'

Taylor still hadn't made her point, it seemed. Scrunching her forehead brought out the perfect trident-shaped crease at the bridge of her nose. On any other face, Darac reflected, he might not have noticed it.

'You're going to answer, "What are policemen supposed to be like?" to this but I have to say it anyway… It's difficult to believe you're a policeman.'

'What are policemen supposed to be like?'

'I walked into that one. But hasn't Maggie a point? I read more about… well, police brutality here than I did when I lived in England, for instance.'

'They're all brutes except me.'

'Seriously, Paul.'

Seriously merely brought a slightly less dazzling smile. Darac wondered if her cheeks ever cramped up.

'My second-in-command, Lieutenant Granot, divides all police officers into seven categories. Want to hear what they are?'

'Absolutely.'

'Category One is for moral paragons: officers who eschew all forms of intimidatory tactics. A Category One would never resort to physical or verbal violence, even if the officer knew for certain the suspect had committed the most hideous murder imaginable.' He shrugged. 'I suppose there may be such a detective somewhere. Category Two is for officers who might resort to violence if they knew the suspect were guilty of a brutal crime and there was no other way of securing a conviction. Three is for those who would always use violence in similar circumstances. Four brings down the level of certainty of guilt. Five brings down the level of brutality of the crime. Six is for officers who sometimes just can't help themselves. Seven is for sadists. And your next question is?'

'I bet I know the answer. You're Category Two.'

'That information is classified as well,' he said, smiling.

'So, brutality aside, are you a great detective?'

'Naturally.'

'Actually, is there such a thing? In real life?'

'No one is infallible, obviously. But if you wanted to call my mentor, Commissaire Dantier, a great detective, I wouldn't argue with you.'

'Oh? What singles him out?'

'*Him?* Shame on you.'

Taylor seemed genuinely astonished. 'A woman?'

'We do have them here, you know. And we let some of them vote and drive cars.'

'Let's not get started on that. But I repeat: what puts her above her peers?'

'Razor-sharp logic. Yet her intuition is unerring. It's a formidable combination.'

For a moment, Darac's thoughts strayed to the events of the previous summer. He wasn't going to share it with Taylor, but it was Agnès's courage that put her not just above her peers but above anyone he'd ever met.

'And she's a Category Two, also? Uh... Paul?'

'Sorry?'

'I said: "And she's a Category Two, also?" The same as you, in other words.'

'If that's your idea of finessing a witness—'

'You'd advise me to stick to art history.'

'Indeed.'

It was time to steer things toward business. 'Did I mention that your French is superb?'

'Thank you, yes. It's being here for three years. I was no more than average in my French studies at university.'

'I'm sure not. And afterwards, did everything immediately fall into place for you?'

The idea amused her. 'No! I owe it all to persistence and luck. Philippe has been incredibly kind. And Maggie's like a second mother to me.'

'Your own parents must be proud of all you've achieved.'

'Oh, sure.' The thought brought the widest smile of the day. 'I've been very fortunate.'

Darac could picture Mom and Dad thrilling to each new accomplishment of their little princess. Taylor just had to have been the most popular girl in school and all that went with it. 'What do they make of Villa Rose? It must be wonderful saying, "Welcome to my world," to one's parents in what is literally a palace.'

'They love it,' she beamed, tugging a pearl earring. 'What American wouldn't?

'And now, as you hinted, you have found a second family in the Lamberts.'

'Happily, I have.'

'Your assistant, Dr Ivo Selmek, is part of that family also?'

She let out an involuntary breath. 'In a sense.'

'He's envious of your position, isn't he?'

'It's normal. I'm a few years younger than he is. You've spoken to him, then?'

'He referred to that family closeness you mentioned –between you and the Lamberts.'

Taylor's smile persisted but the look in her blue eyes turned a degree or two cooler. 'You two *did* have a good chat.'

'They've come to rely on you personally for everything from going shopping to balancing their household accounts, he said.'

Her smile finally faded. 'In what spirit did he say that?'

'Forgive me but I wonder if he thinks you're something of a goody-goody.'

Taylor cut the few remaining morsels on her plate into even smaller pieces. 'That's because Ivo doesn't do friendship. He doesn't understand it.'

'There are other things Dr Selmek doesn't understand, I gather.'

'Oh?'

'The big Matisse exhibition Villa Rose is putting on. He disagrees with several decisions that Monsieur de Lambert has made regarding it, apparently.'

'Such as?'

'The principal one was to do with a work called *Souk at... somewhere* from one of the American galleries. He couldn't understand why, having acquired it, Lambert didn't approach a gallery nearer home for its companion picture, *Woman at... somewhere*. Especially as both you and Selmek listed it as a must-have on your initial plan.'

'Really, Ivo!' Taylor clanged her fork down on her plate. 'Sorry about that but we at Villa Rose have our classified information, also. Ivo shouldn't be discussing our business with outsiders.'

'Would you tell me why Lambert opposed his team's ideas? I'm interested in group dynamics, decision-making and so on.' Darac hoped capping the request with a smile might relax Taylor's professional scruples for a moment.

'Alright, I'll tell you. *Woman at Asilah* hangs in the Musée Matisse here in Nice. Our exhibition has far more scope than showing works one can see locally. "If people want to see *Woman*, they need only hop on a bus or take a cab," Philippe pointed out. And he was right.'

'I see,' Darac said, but he felt that Selmek had a point. Surely, displaying companion pictures side by side made more sense? Especially if they hadn't been exhibited together in years. 'So, by the same token, you didn't approach the Musée for any other works?'

'No.'

'Uh-huh. Shall we order coffee or something?'

'I'd prefer a something.'

When the drinks arrived, the young waiter was so distracted by Taylor, he almost missed the table with the tray. She seemed scarcely to notice as she took her lemon tea and handed Darac his espresso. 'You said you had a couple of questions and a photograph to show me?'

Despite everything that was exercising him about Voska, there were other issues he wanted to raise first. 'May we go back to your purchase of the Beaulieu house?'

'Uh... if necessary. Why?'

Darac had become a skilled liar over the years. 'Just to put everything together in my mind. I'm wondering where you first saw the advertisement for the sale.'

'Well, as a matter of fact...'

Taylor went on to tell the story more or less as Madame Corot had outlined it.

'I thought you always jogged to Passable and back in the mornings? It's in the opposite direction from Villa Rose, is it not?'

'Indeed, but they were digging up the lane down to the beach at that time. A whole week. It was a, what do you call it? — water main repair.'

It would be easy enough to check that and he would.

'It seems serendipitous that a would-be house buyer happened to be invited into the home of a would-be vendor; and then five minutes later, an agreement is struck to the satisfaction of both parties.'

'It was more like an hour, actually. Serendipitous things do happen in life, Paul.'

'Who first broached the question about the sale?'

'I did. No, Jeanne did. What does it matter?'

'While chatting, she suddenly said: "How would you like to buy my house?"'

'Yes she did! Virtually.'

'Go on.'

'I was telling her how lovely I thought the house was and quite out of the blue she said, "You wouldn't like to buy it, would you?" Just – like – that.'

He'd hoped she'd have come up with something better. If she'd been lying, though, she probably would have. 'The gift of the hot tub: when did that idea occur to you?'

'I can't remember *exactly*. Paul—?'

'Answer the question, please.'

Colour began to stain Taylor's cheeks like ink soaking into paper. It seemed this wasn't what she had had in mind for their lunch.

'It certainly wasn't a loss leader allowed for in the bid. It occurred to me *after* we agreed the sale, a gift pure and simple. Nor was it a… an inducement.'

'Had you any prior knowledge of Jeanne Mesnel, her husband Alain, the house or anything related to it before you met her that day and put in the offer?'

Taylor tugged so hard on her earring, an inflamed circlet of skin formed around the post. 'Did I have some sort of ulterior motive for buying the house, in other words?'

'Yes.'

She shook her head. 'No. I did not.'

'Thank you, Taylor.'

It was clear that if such a motive existed, Darac would have to discover it himself. He picked up his espresso and took a contemplative sip. Taylor followed suit with her tea. Gradually, the tension eased.

'Taylor, in your rooms, we referred to the unthinkable prospect that someone may have killed Madame Mesnel. I'm afraid that is what happened.'

As if it might contain a counter to the assertion, she searched the air around her. 'I don't believe it! Well, as *you* say it I do, but it *seems* unbelievable.'

Darac ran a hand through his hair. 'This isn't going to be pleasant.' Taylor was shocked by his account of Jeanne's death and for quite some moments, she wasn't able to speak. At length, Darac reached into a pocket and took out a photograph. 'Have you ever seen this man?'

Taylor drew her pashmina to her throat. 'This is the perpetrator? No, thank God.'

'His name is Gilles Voska, a convicted rapist.'

Taylor stiffened as Darac set the photograph on the table between them. 'Just a minute. Knowing all this, why did you persist in questioning me about the house? What relevance could it have? You can't possibly think I could be associated with this… pig.'

'I'm sure you know the film director Jean Renoir, son of Auguste, the artist—'

'Don't patronise me. I know better than you who he was.'

'Then you'll know one of his axioms was, "Everyone has their reasons." Given sufficient reason, anyone is capable of murder, Taylor. Anyone.'

'Me? Murder an old lady so I could save a few euros on a house purchase?'

'Murder has been committed for far less.'

Taylor's voice was really buzzing now. 'But I told you where I was at the time.'

'And as far as it goes, the alibis check out. But it wouldn't matter where you were at the time if, say…' Darac brought his index finger down on Voska's photo. '…this man proves to have been your accomplice.'

Taylor recoiled as if Château Park's midday maroon had just

been fired. 'You can't possibly believe that!'

Darac didn't believe it. He was forming a wholly different picture of what had happened that afternoon at the hot tub. But somewhere along the line, the ground rules of his relationship with Taylor had become blurred and it was time to redraw them. 'What you have to understand, Taylor, is that, as a policeman, I can't just believe the probable. I have to embrace the possible. Every avenue must be explored. Surely you see that?'

Taylor stared off over the Babazouk, its tessellated roofscape no longer inviting games of aerial *upscuts*. At length, she exhaled deeply. 'I can, yes. Now could you put the photo away, please? Those huge staring eyes make my blood run cold.'

Darac and Taylor went their separate ways shortly afterwards. Maybe he'd been hard on her but at least she now knew where they stood. He shared her reaction to Voska's eyes, though. It was as if evil were pouring out of them into the atmosphere. Yet he couldn't wait to see that face in the flesh. And he had a couple of ideas about how to bring the moment closer.

28

Darac took the stairs down into the dreary Rue Belgique and disappeared into the garrulous gloom of Hannigan's Irish bar. Stepping through decorative scatterings of sawdust, he found a familiar figure sitting alone in a corner banquette. 'Hello, Brigitte.'

She smiled, perhaps out of habit, perhaps remembering her first impressions of him. But then her face fell.

'May I sit down?'

She shrugged, giving herself a foam moustache as she took down a mouthful of stout. A finger flicked it away like a red-tipped wiper blade. 'I am still pissed off at you, *flic*.'

'How's Thierry?'

'He's fine.' She eyeballed him. 'And he's where you can't get him!'

'No need to worry.' He smiled sympathetically. 'He's off our list of suspects.'

A crack appeared in the ice. 'I want that on a piece of paper. Signed.'

He nodded. 'As soon as I get back to the office.'

A cloud of alcohol enveloped Darac.

'He bothering you, sweetheart?'

Darac turned. The speaker was a ruddy-faced hulk of a man.

'Piss off back to your seat.' Brigitte smiled as an afterthought. 'But thanks, darling.'

The hulk drifted away.

'Protecting me.' She pulled up a bra strap. 'Then I was mean to him. Bad Brigitte.'

'We're releasing Marcel tomorrow afternoon.'

She pulled up the other strap. 'But he's guilty of murder.'

'We both know he isn't.'

She put her hand on Darac's thigh. 'Does that matter?'

'I need to find out who really did it.' He put her hand back in her lap. She held on to it. 'And I think he knows who that person is.'

'What's that to do with me?'

'Maybe you could find out.'

She threw his hand away. 'Snitch? Me?'

'Brigitte, you were trying to get the man sent down.'

'Only to save Thierry.'

'Marcel's dying to see you, you know. *Dying* to, if you catch me?'

'Of course he is. But he might not be when he realises I've moved out again.'

'Still got your key?'

'Maybe.'

'Move back in before he finds out.'

More stout. Another sweep of the wiper blade.

'Brigitte, I want you to answer a question. Truthfully. Promise?'

'You can be really sweet, you know? And masterful.'

Darac pressed on. 'I think Marcel's shelved any plans to play it rough with you but if I'm wrong, could you handle it?'

Brigitte looked affronted. 'Of course! But if I do help you, what'd be in it for me?'

'Got anything outstanding?'

'Only my bust, darling,' she fsaid, delighted at her wit.

'Fines? Minor offences?'

'No. I've always been a good girl.'

'Uh-huh.' He thought about it. 'Alright. I'll tell you what you'll get out of it. The knowledge that you did the right thing when it was a lot easier to do nothing.'

For a moment, the concept evaded her. 'Well, that's all lovely. But—'

'Brigitte, someone raped Madame Mesnel and that's basically what killed her.'

There was an eruption of laughter at the bar. Brigitte said nothing until the aftershocks had ceased. 'That's terrible,' she said, staring into space.

'We're almost certain the man you know as Dagger was responsible.'

Tears began to puddle her eyes and then an even thicker cloud of alcohol enveloped the pair. Brigitte's knight errant had brought reinforcements. 'You're sure you're alright, sweetheart?'

'Yes! Bugger off the three of you!'

They stood their ground. Darac looked expectantly into their eyes. Waiting for the light of comprehension to dawn in them was like watching a row of fruit-machine wheels spinning incrementally to a stop. 'You heard the lady.'

Pledging their support with an elaborate dumb show of gestures, the three lemons slowly repaired to the bar.

'Look Brigitte, I wouldn't ask you to tap Marcel if I didn't think it was important.'

'Even if I did find out something, it won't bring Madame

Mesnel back, will it?'

'No. But it might stop it happening to some other old lady.'

'Old lady…' Brigitte's eyes closed. 'The bastard!'

'Look—'

'Alright! I'll do it.'

'You will?' Darac hid his surprise by squeezing her hand. 'Thank you.'

It took Brigitte some moments to recover. 'There's a problem, though. He never tells me anything.'

'Tell him we mistreated you, and all to protect him. He owes it to you to spill.'

'Don't think that would work.'

'Alright, tell him he can't have any… Can't *have* any unless he does.'

'*That* would.' She smiled weakly, then gave a forlorn shrug. 'I don't know. Me, a police informer. My father would have killed himself if he was still alive. God rest him.'

'You're doing the right thing.'

'I'm not wearing a wire or anything like that.'

'We have some very discreet gear.'

'Suppose I'm in the nuddy when I get him to talk? Where do you suggest I put it then? Think about it.'

He preferred not to. 'Just find out what you can and then ring us.'

'I'm not talking to that fucking Christian.'

'Malraux? OK, not him. But there are plenty of others you can talk to. We've got a very sympathetic female officer, Captain Francine Lejeune.'

'I only want you.'

'Alright.'

The barman appeared, grazing for empties. 'Just a second,' Darac said. 'Bring me a whiskey. And for you, Brigitte?'

Suddenly, all was well in her world. 'Yes, let's have a drink together. Bushmills, please, Michael. Doubles.'

The barman sighed and trudged off.

'And what happens after all this? To me, I mean.'

'What will happen?' Darac looked into her eyes. 'I can't promise you a new life in Paris or anything. A lot will depend on where it leads.'

She put her hand on his. 'You won't let anything bad happen to me, will you darling?'

'I'll do my best. Promise.'

'Come home with me.'

'I... I don't think my boyfriend would like that.'

Brigitte's brows went in search of her hairline. 'You're a bender?'

Darac raised his hands palms outwards. 'Sorry.'

When the whiskeys arrived, they sipped them in silence.

Thinking the venue might appeal to her, Darac had arranged to meet Adèle Voska in one of the hottest new spots in town, Bar Stendhal in Rue Verdi. A hit with fashionistas of all persuasions, the place was all planar surfaces, primary colours and black lacquer. In its way, Darac found it as depressing as Hannigan's. It was like entering a children's nursery or a 3-D Mondrian painting: *Rue Verdi Boogie Woogie*.

More than a few heads turned as Adèle walked in, including Darac's. Her face, a pale matte mask surmounted by a crown of black radiating spikes, had been rebuilt since their earlier meeting. Exit the Valley of The Kings; enter the Statue of Liberty. And there appeared to be a more subtle variation in play.

'Don't worry, *flic*. The Mace is in here.'

The bag was buckled in four places, he noticed. Safe enough, it seemed.

'OK. Thanks for coming.'

She declined his handshake. 'Did I have a choice?'

'Of course.'

A slow tango-like tune overlaid with spoken Spanish was fading out as a greeter showed them to the only free pair of seats in the house: stools attached to a small round table on the mezzanine.

'You could be arrested for walking around with that stuff, you know, unless you've got a permit. How did you come by it, anyway?'

'Got it in Barcelona. Just over the counter.'

'You've been there recently?'

'It's where I smuggled my father off to after you left. Disguised as a human being.'

The tail had confirmed she'd had no direct contact with Gilles Voska all day. Darac was happy she'd joked about it, though; a sign she was loosening up, perhaps. 'Look, it's clear you don't get on with your dear papa.'

An involuntary laugh cracking her make-up, she looked seventy years old, suddenly. 'We have the same surname, we're left-handed and we hate *flics*. That's *all* we share.'

'In that case—'

'I hate him but I'm also frightened of him.'

The ambience disc rolled on to the next track.

'Isn't that all the more—Oh, no.' Darac shook his head. 'This is Sonny Rollins. From *Saxophone Colossus*.'

'The music?'

'Music, exactly. Not muzak. Have they no shame, these people?'

'You look the sort of wanker who goes for jazz.'

He stared at her. 'To business. Do you know what I think your father has done?'

'No.'

A young waitress approached at the gallop. 'Ready to order, guys?'

'Have something to eat by all means. It's on me.'

'The... seared scallops, clams and Iberian ham.'

'On?' the waitress said, a bead of sweat dropping off her nose on to her keypad.

'Black.'

'Monsieur?'

Like most detectives, Darac didn't know when he might next eat. 'The same.'

'Any drinks with that?'

'A Martini Picasso for me. With ice.'

'Same, monsieur?'

'Beer. Leffe, if you have it.' She nodded. 'And turn this music off, would you?'

She gave him a withering look. 'That's against our—'

'Forget it.'

The waitress grabbed the menus, stowed the keypad in her tabard pocket and disappeared quicker than you could say 'difficult customer'.

'What exactly was the "on black" I just ordered?'

'Are you blind? Red and black plates: this is Bar Stendhal? Yeah?'

'Ok, but what does Stendhal have to do with Sonny Rollins or absurdly named cocktails?'

'This place was your idea, remember?'

Darac mounted a concerted charm offensive while they waited for their meals. It didn't take. At least the seared scallops proved to be excellent. 'Adèle,' he said, 'I know you're scared of your father. Help us and we could make sure he—'

'You're wasting your breath.'

'Until he's found, we'll be watching you, anyway. You may as well help.'

She said nothing.

'Let's return to what I believe your father did. He raped an old lady to death.'

At last, Adèle seemed discomfited. Slipping a mirror out of her bag, she formed a point with the corner of her napkin and with a surgeon's precision, dabbed at a droplet of sauce on her chin. In their earlier meeting, the care with which she had prepared her look had rather touched Darac. Now, it was irritating the hell out of him.

'He raped an old lady to death, Adèle.'

'You said. Get me another cocktail. A Martini Christo this time.'

Darac took a moment but then hailed the waitress. The order proved to be Adèle's little joke. There was no such drink on the menu. 'Same as before, then.'

The waitress scurried away.

'*You* were attacked recently, you say?'

'I don't say. I was.'

'And you remember how frightened you were?'

She stabbed a clam with her fork.

'Imagine what it was like for your father's victim. Jeanne Mesnel was her name. Seventy-one years old.'

The clam disappeared.

'Your father is a sadist. He's done this kind of thing before and he'll—' He suddenly saw an awful possibility. 'Was it your father? Was it he who attacked you?'

She turned to him. 'No, it wasn't, Captain Paul Darac of the Brigade Criminelle.'

He couldn't interpret the strange emphasis of her response but he knew his question had been a mistake; the rhythm he was trying to establish had been broken.

'Alright, it wasn't him. But there's more to your father's crimes than the hands-on stuff, isn't there? You know why he served his last term of imprisonment?'

Adèle ignored the question. 'I'll tell you—'

'Martini Picasso,' announced the waitress, setting it down on the run. Adèle took it as if she hadn't a care in the world.

Realising he was wasting his time, Darac screwed up his napkin and threw it on the table. 'Liberty doesn't give a stuff about the huddled masses. Does she?'

'At last you understand, you stupid fucking man.'

Darac got to his feet. Taking a hundred-euro note out of his wallet, he attempted to spike it on her diadem of hair. It wasn't as sharp as it looked.

She grabbed the note off the table. 'Go fuck yourself.'

'If you feel like rejoining the human race, give me a call.' The air smelled better outside. Darac slid Rollins's *Newk's Time* album into the CD player as soon as he got back into his car. 'Tune Up' went some way to restoring his spirits. Perhaps he shouldn't give up on Adèle just yet.

★ ★ ★

The last notes of the album were dying away as he pulled up behind a patrol car on Chemin Leuze. The young officer on crime-scene protection duty was asleep at the wheel as Darac rapped on her window. 'Six o'clock's a bit early for a kip, isn't it?'

'Mind your — Shit. Sorry sir. Yes. I assure you, this is the first time I've fallen—'

'It's forgotten – but try to stay awake. I'm off to interview the neighbours.'

Darac hoped to discover more than the uniforms he'd sent into action the day before. Starting at the far end of Rue Balmette, he knocked at a well-kept villa that stood a couple of doors along from Battail's. A harassed-looking woman holding a tea towel opened the door. A loud bass-heavy rap followed her out on to the step.

Darac flashed his ID. 'Madame Berthe Lepic?'

'Not again, surely?' She turned to the stairs briefly. 'Henri, turn that racket down! Captain, we've given a short statement to an officer about this *and* a longer one to that young lieutenant. And may I remind you it's Sunday.'

'Your co-operation in the matter is appreciated, madame.'

'I'm busy. Can't this wait?'

'No. Sorry.'

'Come in, then. The lounge is through the door at the end.' She paused at the foot of the stairs. 'Henri, turn it down! Now!'

The lounge was not the oasis of calm Darac had expected. The boy's bedroom, it seemed, was directly above. Darac proffered the Voska photo. 'Have you seen this man?'

Madame Lepic took it but her eyes couldn't seem to focus. 'Excuse me.'

'If you'd just—'

'One moment.'

As she hurried away, Darac glanced around the room. Antiseptically clean and tidy, its one point of interest was an alcove given over to model warplanes. Some sitting on glass shelves, others suspended on cotton threads, each was meticulously detailed. On the other side of the chimney breast, a matching alcove contained a framed Madonna and child.

The noise from upstairs ceased. Looking no less harassed, Madame Lepic appeared moments later.

'Impressive.' Darac indicated one of the models. 'Young Henri makes them?'

'Yes, he does.'

Darac showed her the photo once more. She no more than glanced at it.

'No, so if you don't mind—'

'You're absolutely sure?'

'Yes. I have never seen that man. Now if—'

She edged toward the hall with one arm raised as if shepherding a stray into a pen. Darac didn't move. 'On the day of the murder, the Saturday—'

'Murder? But the other officers and the papers said it was an accident.'

'The papers said it was an accident because I told them to say that.'

'Oh.' At last, Darac had her full attention. 'Poor Madame Mesnel. But why would—?'

'Would you look at the photo again?'

She took it. 'No. Still no, I'm afraid.'

'Alright. Now think carefully. I know you've already stated you didn't see any strangers around here that Saturday. Does that still hold now you know it's murder?'

'I didn't see anyone but I was home with Henri. He'd fractured his leg the day before.'

'Skateboarding, I know. You didn't go out at all?'

'No.'

'Your husband…' Darac consulted his notes. 'Adam. He was not at home on Saturday, 2 January?'

'He was in Geneva for his firm all weekend.' She gave the details. 'You can check.'

'We are doing so. If there proves to be a discrepancy in the timing, we'll need a DNA sample from him.'

She reddened. 'What discrepancy could there possibly be, Captain?'

'I don't know.' He made a note to chase the Geneva authorities. Maybe Adam Lepic's alibi was shakier than his wife had suggested. 'I'd like to have a word with Henri, now.'

It seemed Madame Lepic had used up her daily ration of co-operation. 'Impossible.'

'He ran errands for the late Madame Mesnel, did he not?'

'Yes?'

'Children often see things that—'

'Well he wasn't even ambulant on Saturday.'

'I'd still like to talk to him.'

Madame Lepic seemed even more discomfited, suddenly. 'He's doing his homework.'

'A minute ago it sounded as if he was throwing a party.'

'Things have changed since our day, monsieur. Henri could sit exams in a disco.'

Darac's unfading smile underlined his resolve to talk to the boy. 'Very well.' She followed him into the hall. 'What a nuisance.'

Darac paused at the foot of the stairs. 'Better if you stay here, madame. I'll just be a minute or two.'

'I insist on being present.'

'In that case, we should decamp to the commissariat. I've got a patrol car waiting around the corner in Chemin Leuze.'

'My Henri taken away in front of the whole—?'

'Aren't you more concerned that it might be a strain on his leg? He does have crutches, does he?'

She appeared chastened. 'Uh… yes. Since just yesterday but… Alright, then.'

Darac started up the stairs. Madame Lepic was still in tow.

'At least let me tell him you're here.'

'I'm sure you already have. I can find my own way.' Photos of ancient warplanes lined the landing walls.

Darac found the one closed door and knocked. No acknowledgement coming, he pushed it open. Except for a pair of crutches, the room was the typical multi-postered, gadget-festooned space of the modern thirteen-year-old. Henri was sitting up in bed, his plaster cocoon covered in signatures and graffiti. Wearing a basketball jersey and baggy shorts, he was an Everyboy who would have looked just as at home in LA as he did in Beaulieu-sur-Mer.

Darac touched his shoulder.

'Maman!' Henri pulled out his earphones. 'Oh. Sorry.'

'No problem. I'm sorry too.' Darac handed him his ID.

'But you'll be able to tell your friends you were rousted by the cops. Cool, eh?'

'Yes.'

The boy set his homework aside.

'What are you working on, Henri?'

'Maths. Calculus. Integration.'

Darac felt reassured, somehow. 'I know all about calculus.

Something to do with x, isn't it?'

The boy managed a grin.

'Love your planes, by the way. They must take you hours.'

'They're not mine. Papa makes them.'

'Does he?' Darac smiled, wondering why Madame Lepic had tried to conceal the fact. He pointed to a pile of skateboarding magazines stacked on the floor. 'You're more into that, I guess. May I?'

The boy brightened. 'Yes.'

Darac sat on the end of the bed and began flicking through a copy of *Wheelz!* 'Wow.' He showed Henri a photo spread. 'No cotton threads keeping him airborne, are there?'

'That's Troy Pinto. American. He's the Half Pipe world champion.'

Darac tapped the kid's cast. 'Is that how you did this?'

'Yes. Well, kind of.'

'How, then? May I add my name to all these other signatures?'

'Sure. I was high jumping. Over a cane? I got over but hit the edge of the board when I landed. I totally wiped out.'

'That sounds bad. When is it coming off?'

'Five weeks and four days.'

'But who's counting? Bet it itches.'

'Yeah.'

Darac gave the crutches a sideways nod. 'How's that going?'

'Don't know yet. Only had them a day.'

'You'll get the hang of it. Anyway, Henri, you know I'm not a member of the Skateboarding Accident Victims Visiting Squad, right? I'm in charge of the investigation into Madame Mesnel's death.'

Henri stared at the rug.

Darac continued flicking through the magazine. 'You ran errands and things for her, I know. You liked her?'

'She was alright.'

'Pay you much?'

'No. Well, it wasn't bad.'

'When was the last time you worked?'

'The weekend before she…'

'Died?'

'Yes.'

Darac turned to the next magazine in the stack. 'And what did you do for her?'

'Just went to get her baguette, jam and stuff like that.'

'Why did she ask you to do these things?' He turned the magazine through ninety degrees and allowed the folded centre pages to fall open. 'And not, say, Madame Loret?'

'Dunno.'

'No! Skateboarding across railings? This isn't a real photo.'

'Yes, it is. Totally. And look at the next page.'

Darac turned over. 'That's just ridiculous.' Smiling, he closed the magazine and took the Voska photograph out of his pocket. 'Ever seen this man, Henri?'

'No, monsieur.'

Like mother, like son. 'You didn't look.'

Henri took the photo and looked hard at it. 'No. I've never seen him.'

'Uh-huh.'

The interview continued in similar vein and after another five minutes or so, Darac got up to leave. 'Look after that leg, Henri. And good luck with your assignment.'

'Thanks, monsieur.'

Her arm extended toward the front door, Madame Lepic was waiting for Darac at the foot of the stairs. 'And did you learn anything from my son, Captain?'

'Only that one Troy Pinto is a very dubious role model.'

'What?'

'And that it's your husband who makes the toy planes.' Madame Lepic's face hardened. 'He can do what he likes in his spare time, can't he? He has precious little of it. I don't know what we're coming to in this country. Time off at the weekend? An hour for a decent lunch? Some may still enjoy what we once all took for granted but neither I nor my husband is one of them.'

'He's not expected home shortly, by any chance?'

She stared into space, shaking her head. In the alcove behind her, aircraft dangling in the altar to her husband's hobby seemed to align all at once. 'Is there no end to this?'

'Is your husband expected—?'

'It's another working weekend for him. Frankfurt.'

'I see.'

'It's bound to be some deadbeat, you realise? That's where you should be looking.' Darac turned on his heel. The woman virtually ran after him. 'Not among decent, hardworking—'

'Goodbye, madame. For now.'

★ ★ ★

As Darac took his leave, Madame Lepic hurried to the living-room window. Once he was out of sight, she closed her eyes, bringing her fingertips to her temples as if preventing any further worries from entering. She stood like that for some moments.

'Maman?'

'What is it now, Henri?'

'I didn't say anything, Maman. Honestly.'

'I know you didn't, Henri. I know you didn't.'

Two dozen further house calls. Two dozen shakes of the head. Only one more possibility remained. 'Good evening, madame. Allow me to show you a photo.'

'Captain! Come in. I've just made some tea.' Madame Loret turned and headed off to the kitchen. 'I was saying to—'

'Stop! I just want you to look at a photograph.'

She marched back to the door, snatched the photo, glanced at it and handed it back.

'I don't suppose you've ever seen the man, have you?'

'Yes,' she said, flatly.

'You have?' He could have hugged her. 'When?'

'About a month ago.'

'And?'

'And what?'

'Where did you see him?'

'At Madame Mesnel's.'

'For God's sake, why didn't you…' He took a breath. 'What was he doing there?'

She shrugged and saying nothing further, went to close the door.

Darac realised he'd screwed up. At first incapable of stemming Madame Loret's logorrhoea, he was now having difficulty getting her to say anything. 'Madame, I'm parched and as you can see, overwrought. A cup — or two — of camomile tea is just what I need. May I come in?'

'You're certainly in need of something! Come in, then. I remember that man coming distinctly because it was a warm afternoon and I was upstairs…'

The tea ceremony that followed ground on interminably before Loret would comment further on the photo. But when she did, it was worth the wait. 'It would be a Friday, obviously. December… the 18th. I don't remember Madame Mesnel mentioning his name afterwards… Yes I do, it was Max… Bernard. Max Bernard, that's right. He was wearing spectacles, a moustache and a cap, then. But it's definitely him. He was from the spa bath people. The firm that sold it to that scheming Cristelle…'

As Madame Loret's monologue continued, a whole series of scenarios auditioned in Darac's head. By the time he thanked her for her contribution and left, only one remained. Once outside, he rang Frankie Lejeune and ran his thoughts by her.

'It's feasible, Paul.'

'I'll call a squad meeting. Would you lead it with me?'

'Certainly.'

'How soon could we get relevant material from the evidence vault?'

'Tomorrow morning if you request it now.'

He rang them.

'Ten o'clock suit you, Captain?'

'Could you make it any earlier?'

'No.'

'Tell you what, then. Let's make it ten.'

29

'No darling, we're not going walkies at this time of night. You silly boy! Now lie down. No! Lie down, you bugger!'

It seemed Thierry was in the mood for chasing his little stump of a tail but he finally chased it into his basket.

'Good boy. Now stop your noise. Shhh! What's the matter? Is it because you're worried about me? I bet it is. Don't. I can handle Marcel. Yes I can.' She rubbed Thierry's ears. 'Look at your little lugs! That's better. You're the only one who really loves me, aren't you, darling? Yes you are.'

It took another ten minutes to settle Thierry but Brigitte didn't mind. The dog was a godsend at times like this. She went to prepare for bed reflecting that today had been the blackest of her life. How could the world be such a cruel place, she wondered. How?

'An old lady… Old lady!'

A hot soapy shower is what she needed. After just a few moments, the cubicle's glass sides were fogged with steam and she began to feel a little better. It was only then that the bathroom door opened.

30

Darac's day off was about to conclude as it had started: sitting at the desk in his study, working through reports. But there, he imagined, the similarities would end. Taylor Walters-Halberg's back story was something he'd been looking forward to reading.

He began with the information from London. Taylor hadn't claimed to be a stellar student but he was surprised to see she had graduated in Art History and French with lower second-class honours, not, he imagined, a typical degree class for someone destined to land a top job. With disarming frankness, she'd claimed that 'persistence and luck' had propelled her into the rarefied orbit of Philippe de Lambert and that thereafter, she had benefited from his 'incredible' kindness. In a more conventional institution, it seemed unlikely that Taylor would have risen higher than someone with Dr Ivo Selmek's track record. But the set-up at Villa Rose wasn't conventional and if she had been over-promoted, who was really to blame?

A quick spin around other areas of Taylor's recent past revealed no surprises. Everything from her credit rating to her driving record was blemish-free. Widening the net brought in more interesting finds. Records showed that with the exception of Taylor herself, no one bearing the surname Walters-Halberg had entered France within the past five years, yet the impression Darac had was that her parents had visited Villa Rose at least once. Seeking answers, he turned to the information from the USA.

Although shorter on dry detail than its French equivalent would have been, the documentation was systematic and resonant. The question of why no one bearing the name Walters-Halberg had visited Taylor was simply answered. It was not her original surname. And that, it transpired, was the last part simplicity was to play in Taylor's story. The golden upbringing that Darac had imagined she had enjoyed proved to be precisely that: a product of the imagination.

Piecing her life together from police files and social welfare records was like reading a scenario for a particularly depressing road movie; Darac could almost see the drifting dust, hear the haunting slide guitar soundtrack. Born Taylor Ann Riggs, she had spent her early years being dragged around the trailer parks of the desert states by her unstable, unmarried mother. A former small-town beauty queen, Charlene Riggs was seventeen when she'd had Taylor. Four years of debt and drug dependency later, the loved but neglected little girl was taken away from her. Three months after that, Charlene died, her body bagged up with the rest of the trailer-park trash and destroyed.

The record showed that four-year-old Taylor had been snapped up for adoption within hours of becoming 'available'. 'On the market', it more or less implied. The lucky family were the Mechovs of Monterey, California. Jonathan Mechov, owner of a small lumber business, and wife Luanne were described as a model couple. Taylor's future seemed set fair, at last.

After an hour's reading, Darac still hadn't discovered how Taylor had come up with the Walters-Halberg surname. But examining the Monterey Police Department's records explained why she had changed it from Mechov. From the age of twelve, she had been sexually abused by her adoptive father on a regular basis. The offences hadn't come to light until Taylor managed to extricate herself from the family home at the age of sixteen. At that point, Jonathan Mechov himself went on the run, committing a series of offences including the attempted murder of a police officer who was trying to arrest him. Caught and sent for trial, he was found guilty and sentenced to life in the state penitentiary. Luanne Mechov was sentenced to five years for turning a blind eye to the horrors to which she knew her adoptive daughter had been routinely subjected. Three months after her release, the woman committed suicide. *Fin.*

Feeling exhausted suddenly, Darac decided to shut everything down and call it a day. But he couldn't just throw a switch to turn off all the *what if?* questions running through his head. As he did most nights, he picked up his lounge guitar and began strumming through as many chord changes as it would take.

Chang, chang, chang, chang, da-da-da-da... chang, chang... Neglected, acquired and then abused: that was the beautiful one's early life and perhaps, Darac conjectured, it threw a different light on her relationship with the Lamberts. Perhaps the drive to 'worm her way in' wasn't the sly attempt to advance herself that Ivo Selmek had suggested. Perhaps she was seeking to expunge the pain of the past by adopting the Lamberts as surrogate parents. Indeed, she had said that Maggie was like a mother to her. Perhaps Taylor had seen Jeanne Mesnel in a similar light.

Chang, chang, chang, chang...

Taylor's history perhaps also accounted for something Selmek had alluded to in passing: the apparent lack of lovers in her life. Darac had sensed in her a certain antipathy to sex. If that were true, and not just a reflection of his own lack of sexual interest in her, it would hardly be a surprising legacy of what had happened.

Chang, chang, chang, chang...

Darac felt desperately sorry for Taylor Walters-Halberg, fka Taylor Ann Mechov, fka Taylor Ann Riggs. But his compassion was moderated by wariness. 'Damaged people damage others' was one of Agnès Dantier's starkest, truest axioms. Just how damaged was Taylor? He thought back to their lunch. She'd been more than merely evasive about her relationship with the Mechovs; she'd lied about their visiting her at Villa Rose. Yes, she was hardly likely to have come clean about them but she hadn't just given a false impression, she'd really sold the fiction, smiling happily about events that had never happened. Smiling happily and tugging her pearl earring. Tugging her earring...

Chang, chang, chang, chang...

It was something she often did, he realised, an unconscious mannerism. Was it a tell, something she did when she lied? He thought back through their conversations. He could picture her performing the gesture on several occasions but marrying it to what was being said at the time was difficult. Two instances, though, came back to him. One was when she insisted she had no prior knowledge of the Chemin Leuze house before putting in the offer. The other was over Lambert's refusal to acquire the Musée Matisse's *Woman at Asilah* for the forthcoming exhibition.

Chang, chang, chang, chang...

Countless choruses later, Darac finally ran out of theories that might explain these things. It took more choruses still to dispel thoughts of Gilles Voska.

31

'Morning, Lieutenant.'

Malraux clamped the phone under his chin as he squirted deodorant into his almost hairless armpits. 'Albert.' He already knew why the snitch was calling. 'What's new?'

'Old Brigitte moved back into Battail's last night.'

'If the slag gets up to anything, you let me know.'

'I will. I had *him* round asking questions – that Darac. Nasty piece of work. And he hasn't got a clue, like you say. Anyway, I've got to go. Over.'

'If we had more like you we could double the cleared-case figures, Albert. Over and out.'

Darac was playing over the outro to Miles Davis's 'Solea' when his landline rang.

'Not interrupting your morning detox, am I?'

'Just finished, Didier. What's up?'

'Favour to ask. I'd do it myself but time, tide and maths students wait for no man.'

'I'm listening.'

'I've been trying to email "Lil' Darlin'" to Sticks so he has a heads-up for tonight's practice but his mobile must be kaput. I've got no way of getting a physical disc to him now. You've got the album, I imagine?'

'Sure and I'm out and about today.'

'He'll probably be at the Hotel Grande Scarabée on Promenade des Anglais. Does shifts there with his brother in the kitchen.'

Darac looked at his watch. It was two hours before the evidence from the vault was due at Joinel. He'd planned on visiting Chemin Leuze after breakfast but it could wait. 'No problem. I'll take the CD in to him.'

'Thanks, man. See you tonight.'

Few people could have been easier to spot in a crowd than Sticks N'Pata but on a preliminary scout around the Hotel Grande Scarabée's huge kitchen area, Darac saw no sign of him. Nor could he find anyone who admitted to knowing him or his brother. Darac began to feel uneasy.

'You're late. And where's the other one?'

A griddle the size of a sunbed clamped under his arm, Darac's inquisitor was a large, rudimentary-looking soul.

'Sorry.' Darac peered at his ID. '*Gino*. What other one?'

'The other replacement. Second shift in a row those two fucking brothers have missed. No word. Nothing.'

Darac gave him a conspiratorial look. 'Shameful.'

'Too right.' Gino ran a closer eye over the visitor. 'Just a minute. *You* don't look… Who are you?'

'Lamanne, room 496. I'm looking for the spa.'

Gino's expression didn't change while he thought it through. 'This is the kitchen.'

'You should really do something about your reception staff.'

Using the griddle as a pointer, Gino indicated the ceiling. 'First floor. At the back.'

'Thanks.'

Darac exhaled deeply as he walked back to his car. The pattern was all too familiar. A man of African origin was suddenly incommunicado; he and his brother had failed to turn up for work without explanation; co-workers were scared to talk. Darac wasted no time in firing up his laptop. Erica was always telling him that no computer file could be trusted 100% but on checking the relevant sites, his growing suspicion that the brothers were illegal immigrants dissipated. To all intents and purposes, Rama N'Pata was what he said he was: a fully fledged French citizen who until last summer had been living in a low-rent apartment block in the *banlieues* of Nantes with his brother, Modibo. Darac checked the criminal database. No known offences. He checked current arrest listings. Neither N'Pata was on it.

His mobile rang.

'Didi?'

'Manage to hook up with Sticks?'

'He still hasn't replied to your email, then?'

'No.'

'I'm at the hotel. He's not here either. Bunking off with his brother, by the look of it. I've got a L'Ariane address for them. I'll nip up there later.'

Darac ended the call and set off to Joinel. He'd been ensconced at his desk for no more than a minute when Granot mooched in, carrying a box of assorted *viennoiseries*.

'That's kind of you,' Darac said, knowing none of it was for him.

'I need these. Hypoglycaemia's no fun, you know. Coffee?'

'Got one. And you're about as hypoglycaemic as fondant.'

Banter was displacement, the lull before the storm of what promised to be a difficult squad meeting.

'Briefing room ready?'

'Everything's set.'

Darac's desk phone rang. 'What?' His eyes rolled. 'OK Charvet, thanks.' He jabbed a button to end the call but kept the phone to his ear. 'The stuff from the vault's going to be late.' He keyed in another number. 'Frankie, sorry if this screws up your day but we can't do the squad meeting until two o'clock this afternoon. Is that alright?'

Granot muttered all the way back to his seat with the nearest thing the Koffeemat had to a *noisette*: a '*makiato*'.

'OK, see you then.' He hung up. 'Hurry up and wait. That's our lives, Granot.'

'Have you only just realised that?'

'So how did your digging go on the Mesnels?'

'I'm eating. Tell me about Miss America, first.'

Darac recounted everything he had on Taylor.

'Difficult life,' Granot said, at length. 'In terms of establishing some pre-existing connection with the Mesnels or the villa, it's nothing though, is it?'

'Not in itself but I have some ideas. And you? Any interesting past owners of the Mesnel villa? Any hidden goldmines?'

'Doesn't look like it. And the Mesnels seem the most interesting owners of the house in its history. Mainly because Alain had more jobs than the rest of Beaulieu put together.'

'That gels with what Madame Corot told me.'

'But he kept one longer than the others. A Monsieur Dubroqua of the Mairie confirms that Alain worked as an electrician for the maintenance department for four years. He did jobs in half the public buildings in Nice, he says. That's all I've got so far.'

Darac shook his head. 'Alain Mesnel… That man could have exhibited his photographs in any of the city's modern galleries. Instead, his work survives not *on* walls but behind them. And then he gets killed in a car crash.'

'That's life.'

Darac stared at the floor. 'I wonder if he ever did any electrical work at Villa Rose? He painted it, you know.'

'I doubt an electrician would—'

'No, I mean he did a painting *of* Villa Rose. It's at the Chemin Leuze house.'

'So? It's a picturesque spot, isn't it? Thousands of people paint it.'

'And he did paint other local spots, to be fair.'

'There you are.' Granot stuffed in another pastry. 'I'm almost frightened to say this, but you had some ideas?'

'Plenty. Not so many connections, though.' Darac glanced at his watch. 'But as we've got a breathing space, I'm going to follow up a couple now.' He swiped his mobile. 'Lartou? Just checking the Mesnel bequests haven't been crated up yet?'

'They're ready to go, chief, but we won't be doing it until the morning.'

'Good. That's it.'

Granot flicked a crumb-clearing finger through his moustache. 'What are you after?'

'I've realised I saw something remarkable at the Mesnel villa the morning after the body was discovered. Saw it but didn't see its significance.' He got to his feet. 'I need to look again. Want to come?'

'No chance. I've got a tonne of paperwork to get through. Bonbon's up in Drap on that knifing. Perand is probably free. Or take Malraux.'

'I'll take Perand.'

32

The living room felt more desolate than ever.

'What are we looking for?' Perand said, yawning.

'You feel it, Perand? That dead quality?'

'Well, it's an old lady's place, isn't it?'

Darac gave him a look. 'She had life, this lady. A full and vibrant life.'

'OK.'

Darac began flicking through the CD racks. No luck. He turned to the LPs. There it was: Sonny Rollins *At the Village Vanguard*. He slipped it onto the turntable and lowered the cartridge on to the in-groove. After a spoken introduction, 'A Night In Tunisia' lit up the space like bougainvillea tumbling over a wall. It was presumptuous, but once again Darac felt sure Jeanne would have approved.

'What we are going to do is look through these LPs and cassettes. I'm interested in any that were purchased in the USA.' He glanced at the Rollins sleeve. A yellowing label read: MELLOW TONE RECORD STORE, E 52ND STREET, NYC. 'Like this, for example.'

'Why are we doing this?'

'All will become clear. I'll make a start on the LPs. You take the tapes.'

Perand shrugged but got on with it.

Lester Young's *Blue Lester* LP bringing the total to seventy-one, it took just over an hour to complete the task.

Seventy-one albums, Darac reflected. One for every year of Jeanne Mesnel's life. All of them had been purchased in New York and three were sprinkled with gold dust: they still had their original hand-written receipts trapped in the sleeves. Made out to a *Madame Jan Manelle*, a *Mrs J Mesnel* and a *Mister Al Menel* care of the Bennington Plaza Hotel, they were date-stamped between 9 and 26 September 1964, only a matter of months before Alain died.

Darac swiped his mobile. 'Granot? I'm over at the Mesnel villa. I'd like you to drop what you're doing and...' He jerked the phone away from his ear. 'Alright, but this could be important. Remember I said I saw something remarkable here that first morning?'

'Ye-es?'

'It was a jazz LP—'

'Good Lord almighty—'

'I was too interested in the thing itself to pay proper attention to where it came from. But then I remembered it was New York City and it turns out there are about seventy more like it in the collection.'

'Mademoiselle Walters-Halberg is American. There are American records in the Mesnel villa. What an incredible connection! No wonder she bought the place on spec!'

'It's not the fact that they are American, Granot. It's the fact that America is a long, long way from Beaulieu-sur-Mer. And it was further away still in 1964. I've got receipts to prove the Mesnels themselves bought the LPs there. She was a seamstress. He was a jobbing electrician. Where did they get the money to pay for a trip like that? Imagine how much transatlantic flights cost back then. And they were there for at least two and a half weeks.' Darac gave Granot the dates of the trip and the hotel address. 'It doesn't add up.'

'OK, it's an anomaly. There's probably an innocent explanation, though. Ask Madame Corot: she might know.'

'I will but it's unlikely. The trip happened twenty or so years before she met Jeanne and she never knew Alain at all.'

'What about the friend who lives in Paris now, Cartin? He knew Alain well.'

'I'll speak to him. But listen, it's facts we want, not anecdotes. There's a lot of unexplained money behind that trip. I want you to find it and follow it to its source.'

'Why me? I'm not the only—'

'Don't be coy. You're the best officer for the job and you know it.'

'Alright, alright.'

'In the meantime, I'll ring Cartin. Got his number there?'

'Give me a second.'

While he waited, Darac watched Perand idly flicking through Alain Mesnel's paintings. 'What do you think?'

'Unoriginal crap. Weird how some people spend their spare time, isn't it?'

'So how do you spend yours?'

'Sleeping.' Perand looked almost sheepish, suddenly. 'Although, as it happens, I have taken up something, lately.'

'Ah, yes?'

'Uh… It's not interesting.' Giving a snort, he showed the next canvas to Darac. 'I love the fact that he signed them. It's the only authentic touch.'

The work was an oil study of the steep, wooded *massif* that rose between the old port and the Rade de Villefranche as seen from the beach at Passable. Topped by the squat stone slabs of Fort du Mont Alban, the landscape was realised in a sort of grid of interlocking dabs of colour, the same method Alain had used in the work Bonbon had admired earlier. Perand went to put it back with the others.

'Hold it still a second.' Darac aimed his mobile and clicked. 'Thanks.'

'Why do you want a photo of this dreck?'

Granot came back on the line and gave him Cartin's number.

'Thanks. I owe you one.'

'*Another* one,' Granot said, ringing off.

Darac keyed in the number.

Perand clicked his fingers. 'Ah, I get the photo bit.'

'Do you?'

'You want to meme it. If you get stuck for a funny tag, ask me.'

'*So* generous… Monsieur Cartin? It's Captain Darac, Police Judiciaire de Nice.'

'Police? Haven't you lot persecuted me enough! I've been cleared completely of—'

'I know you have, monsieur.'

'And I told that other officer everything that might help your investigation. Don't you realise how upsetting this is for someone of my age? Jeanne Mesnel was the dearest friend to my late wife and to me.'

'I know and I'm sorry to trouble you but I want to pick your brains.'

'You've got time for socialising? I think you should be out

looking for the murderer.'

'Everything is being done, I assure you.'

'Well, alright. You're not interrupting anything here, I must say.'

'I don't know if you'll be able to help, actually, but I wanted to ask about the Mesnels' trip to New York in '64. Six months or so before Monsieur Mesnel died.'

'What about it?'

Expecting to have to coax the memory out of the man, Darac couldn't resist a smile. 'Speedy response, monsieur?'

'I remember it well. For one thing, the wife and I looked after little Sarah while they were away. We never had kids and we were glad we hadn't by the time they returned, I can tell you. What do you want to know?'

'I'll jump right in. How could they afford such a trip?'

'Easy. Alain had a quintet, a fantastic one, and that's what paid for it.'

Darac almost dropped the phone. Just as he was putting together a new scenario about Alain Mesnel, another bolt flies out of the blue. What a man! He'd won the heart of the glorious Jeanne. He'd taken the jazz photograph of the century. Now it turns out he was a superb musician as well? In terms of what Darac was trying to establish though, the news was at best confusing, at worst damaging. 'Sorry, he had a fantastic quintet, you say?'

'Certainly did.'

'He must have used a pseudonym. No one called Alain Mesnel had a quintet in this area in the sixties or I would have heard of him. What name did he go by?'

'What're you talking about?'

'You said he had a quintet.'

'Yes. Le Fabuleux won. I can't recall the placers off the top of my head.'

'You're talking about... a horse race?'

'Not *a* horse race. *The* horse race. The Prix du Jockey Club, 1964.'

Darac's heart sank. He had hoped for an entirely different provenance for the cash. 'So a quintet is…?'

'The one Alain had was to pick the first five horses home in the right order.'

'How much did he win?'

'Dunno, but it must have been a packet.'

'How did he make the bet? A bookie?'

'No, bookies cheat you. It was a legit bet. Through Pari Mutuel Urbain.'

'Do you know if records are kept for that?'

'We're still living in France, aren't we Captain? Although lately, who knows? Back in 1986, I had…'

Having to listen to a couple of Monsieur Cartin's own betting coups was a small price to pay for what seemed useful information. Darac resolved to delay giving Granot the information. Another interruption and the big man might explode.

'Let's go.' At the door, Darac took what would probably be his final look at the non-living room of Jeanne Mesnel. He was glad he wouldn't be around for the crating up of her belongings. He glanced at his watch. There was an hour still to go before Frankie's briefing.

The Musée Matisse stood in a corner of the Parc des Arènes, a stone's throw from Agnès Dantier's apartment in Cimiez. But there was no point in Darac calling in to see his boss. Her most recent postcard had been from Thailand. China was up next.

A simply framed oil painting on canvas, Musée Matisse's *Woman at Asilah* proved to be an interior scene no more than ninety centimetres high by seventy wide. Not quite abstract enough for Darac's taste, it was a gorgeous work, nevertheless. Inhabiting a shallow, frieze-like space, the eponymous woman was an odalisque half-dressed in vivid blues, purples and greens. She was depicted dancing out of a dark diagonal shadow toward a divan drenched in sunlight from an open window. It wasn't just the figure, the whole surface of the picture seemed to dance.

Further reflections were cut short. Drawing withering stares from his fellow art buffs, Darac's mobile rang. As a warden from an adjoining room rushed in to read the riot act, the detective was already on his way out.

'Chief? Charvet. Two things have just come in. Geneva have got back to us on Monsieur Adam Lepic's whereabouts on January 2nd, the day Madame Mesnel was murdered. It confirms he was there all weekend.'

Darac had already discounted Lepic in his mind but it was good to have the corroboration. 'And the other thing?'

'The consignment from the police evidence vault? It's arrived.'

'I'll be right there.'

33

'Erica? Frankie. Have you got a W-VHS player in your store of wonders?'

'I've got every audio-visual toy ever made.'

'Could you come and set it up in the briefing room?'

Darac was already addressing the squad as Erica wheeled in the machine. On the screen behind her, a slide of Voska's vacuum-packed skull stared out over the proceedings like a giant icon of the antichrist.

'The cleaner, Madame Loret, saw Voska at Madame Mesnel's a couple of weeks before the murder. He was posing, in disguise, as one Max Bernard, a representative of the hot tub company. He was from their publicity department, he said.'

Perand essayed a maniacal grimace. '"Hello, I'm from Happy Bubbles." Some rep.'

'We asked Monaco to check the company's payroll,' Darac went on. 'There was no Bernard and everyone else was accounted for. No one recognised the photo.'

'Did Loret speak to Voska, herself, chief?' Bonbon said.

'She was upstairs but she heard most of Voska's spiel. His company was making a show reel of recent installations. Could he come back in a few days to shoot some tests and then return a couple of weeks later to film the segment itself?' Darac had to steel himself to keep going seamlessly. 'Madame Mesnel consented. I'd noticed two kinds of scuff marks on her patio, right? Erica and I discovered that one set was caused by her mules. We were wondering if tripod feet had been responsible for the others even before Loret told me about Monsieur "Bernard" and his promo film. I remembered Voska's conviction for shooting and publishing obscene materials and as soon as I read in the file that he used a heavy, broadcast-quality TV camera, I knew what had made that second set of marks on the patio.' He turned almost apologetically to Erica. 'All set?'

Forgoing the usual flourish, she made the final connection into the rear of the TV. 'All set.'

His eyes stayed on her. 'I know you've sat through all sorts of crap but this promises to be distressing. You don't have to stay.'

'I know.'

'OK.' He stood and went to join the others. 'Frankie's going to take us through it.'

She stepped forward, handing Erica the tape, spine out. The film was entitled *Marie's First Communion*.

'Sure?'

Erica nodded.

Frankie faced the group. 'The first thing to note is the format. Tell us about it, Erica.'

'It's W-VHS, which is a high-def analogue tape format dating from just before the advent of DVD. The mid-nineties, in other words.'

'DVD killed it off,' Perand said, as ever trying to impress Erica. As ever, failing.

'The significant point', Frankie continued, 'is the high-quality image it provided.'

Malraux grinned. 'More bang for your buck, eh?'

'Maybe yours, Malraux.' Frankie shared a look with Darac. 'Roll the thing, Erica.'

In razor-sharp detail, a scenario as pitifully unfleshed as the limbs of its central character began to unfold.

Granot spoke first, his words emerging in a growl. 'How old was this poor kid?'

Frankie referred to the accompanying conviction sheet. 'Sixteen years, two days.'

Flaco had been watching the floor since the opening shot. 'She looks about twelve.'

'Apart from the track marks,' Malraux said.

Bonbon blanched at the girl's reaction to the entry of a second 'actor' into the action.

Flaco got to her feet. 'I don't want to even *hear* any more of this.'

'We'll tell you how it turns out.' Malraux looked around for a smirk to match his own. He didn't find one.

'Pause it, Erica, and blank the screen.' Frankie trained her large, green eyes on Flaco. The movie froze and then faded to black. 'I understand your reaction, Yvonne, and I think we've all seen enough to understand the degree of obsessive control and violence we're dealing with in Voska. But I don't think we, as police officers, can just walk away from it, can we? If only for the victim's sake, don't we *have* to look and keep looking?'

Flaco stood for a moment, her internal debate etched sharply in her face. 'Yes,' she said at length. She resumed her seat. 'We do.'

'Carry on, Erica.'

As the scenario rolled to its climax, Voska himself joined in the action. Out of the corner of his eye, Darac clocked Malraux's reaction. Making crass jokes was one thing; but the young man seemed unmoved by the sight of three men ejaculating over the face of a sick, frightened, girl. Meanwhile, Bonbon et al. had all but thrown up. As the TV image whited out, Frankie waited to clear her head before continuing.

'Note that the girl wasn't technically under age. And she survived the experience. And she survived making *ten* subsequent *Marie's First...* videos over the next three days, all of them shot by Voska and featuring the other two men. That was July 1994, Paris.' She swept the group, holding her gaze on Malraux. His small pink-lidded eyes returned the look. 'She died shortly afterwards.'

'She was a junkie, right? I've got no sympathy. At all.'

'Of course you haven't.' Somehow, Frankie managed to leave it there. 'Voska didn't focus solely on young girls. The obese, the freakishly endowed: it's extremes in general that seem to fascinate him. He didn't always take part himself but he did always shoot the videos. And he was proud of their high visual quality, he said in court.'

'So with Madame Mesnel, he was adding granny porn to his portfolio?' Perand said. 'And by accident or design, it turned into a snuff movie?'

'Granny porn.' Darac exhaled deeply. 'Jesus. When everything is taken into account, it seems likely.'

'Right.' Bonbon caught Malraux's reaction. 'Something funny?'

'Just thinking it should have been great-granny porn, then. Great-great-granny, even.'

'How would you like it if someone filmed your granny being fucked to death? Sicko.'

Darac eyeballed Malraux. 'Let's continue.'

Frankie took a sip of water. 'Any questions, comments?'

Granot shifted in his seat. 'Voska knew the likely penalty for a further offence. And filming a rape, even if it didn't cause a fatality, is a much bigger deal than what he went down for previously.'

Bonbon threw up his hands. 'What do you call what we have just seen?'

'You know what I mean.'

Frankie turned to face the projector screen. 'I can't say why he took that risk.' She stared into Voska's huge, hollow eyes. 'He got greedy or careless or he couldn't help himself. I don't know. But I do know we want him.'

Malraux finally seemed to take an interest in the policing aspect of the case. 'The two other guys in the video could be a way to Voska.'

'Dead. The older one from AIDS; the younger from a crack OD.'

'So that's two vacancies for you to aim at,' Bonbon said. 'You might get lucky.'

Without warning, Malraux went for him, pulling him off his seat by his jacket lapels. 'I am not a fucking—'

'Stop them,' Frankie said, taking a pace back.

While Perand limited his intervention to striking an impressively pugilistic pose, Bonbon wriggled out of Malraux's grasp and butted him in the face, splitting his nose. Before he could retaliate, Darac and Flaco got in between them, forcing them apart. Clamping her arms around Bonbon's wiry frame, Flaco steered him safely to one side. Darac gave Malraux a hard shove, sending him stumbling into the projector screen. Buckling with the impact, Voska's face rippled as if underwater.

'Alright. Flak, let go,' Bonbon said. 'I'm fine. It's over.' Malraux was a different animal. He came up again.

Giving off testosterone like a heat haze, he and Darac faced off. Darac held the younger man fast as he writhed and flexed. The others looked on as Malraux's resolve gradually ebbed.

'Had enough?'

But then Darac's expression darkened. Feeling a hard shape pressing against his chest, he reached into Malraux's jacket. 'A cosh? What are you doing with this?'

Lungs heaving, Malraux could hardly speak. 'It's an old... riot baton... cut-down... The lads gave it to me... for luck. A souvenir.'

Darac slung it away, bouncing it like a ricocheting ten-pin into the corner of the room. 'If I see that rattle again, I'll throw you out of the pram with it. For good. Clear?'

'Uniforms... carry batons. Why can't I?'

'Because you're not a uniform any more, you idiot. You're a detective.'

'God help us,' Granot said.

'OK. Let's put the place back together.'

Chairs were righted, the projector screen straightened, and in an uncharacteristic show of unity, Perand offered his handkerchief to Malraux. 'Pinch your nose with this. It'll soon stop.' He may as well have offered the man a tutu. 'Alright, let it bleed.'

Darac shared a little eyebrow semaphore with Bonbon. He nodded that he was fine.

'Frankie, I think the air's clear now so let's move on.'

The briefing continued for another half-hour. As it broke up, Darac called after Granot and Bonbon to ask them to wait in his office. 'Maybe it's not surprising that tensions ran high,' he said to Frankie, once they were alone.

Her eyes slid to the far corner of the room. 'A cosh. And I used to think Max Perand was a worry.'

'Malraux has his uses.'

She drew down the corners of her mouth. 'I'd hate to think what they are.'

'He's still on probation, remember. If it doesn't work out, I can move him on.'

Voska was still staring at them. Darac shook his head. '*Marie's First*, Frankie...'

'I know.'

He turned to her. 'Are *you* always able to keep looking?'

'I think it's important to try.' She gave a sad little smile. 'My Jewish heritage coming through, perhaps.'

'Perhaps.' Other events flooded back into Darac's head but now wasn't the time. 'Erica handled it pretty well, didn't she?'

'I'm beginning to realise she's not the youngster she sometimes seems.'

'We're both guilty of babying her, I think. How old is she, anyway?'

'Twenty... five.'

'See, we're only eight years older than she is.'

'I'm nine years older, sonny. A little respect.'

They exchanged parting kisses. Respecting Frankie was no problem for Darac. He adored the woman. Platonically speaking. As he went back to his office, he considered the little rutting session he'd had with Malraux. The boy had been put in his place and he knew it. Maybe that was all he needed to settle down.

'That got frisky,' Granot said.

'It's that kind of case. Decent head-butt you got in there, Bonbon.'

He raised both hands palms outwards. 'I shouldn't have done it.'

Granot downed his espresso in one. 'We haven't had this for a while, have we?'

'Had what?' Darac said, checking his emails. 'A cuckoo in the nest?'

Granot binned his cup. 'I was thinking more a runt in the litter.'

'Excellent. The DNA report is finally in.' Darac pressed the print button. 'Malraux can't help the way he looks, can he?'

'He can help everything else. A Category Six, if ever I saw one. Even a Seven.'

Darac took the pages and began reading. Unable to believe the first, he turned to the second. Disbelief turned to dismay. Exhaling deeply, he tossed the report to Granot.

'The motile sperm? It wasn't Voska's.'

'What?' The big man read out the salient points. 'The semen is likely from a man of African origin... No matches as yet... No HIV... And no DNA matching Voska's was found at the scene at all.' He looked up. 'Shit.'

Nothing was said for some moments and it was Bonbon

who finally broke the silence. 'Alright, it seems Voska may have confined his activity to setting up and filming the rape but we still need him. We're not completely back to square one.'

'Not completely,' Darac said. 'But it's clear there are squares on this board we don't know anything about. Yet.' He picked up his desk phone, setting it to speaker.

'Frankie?' He summarised the report. 'Black porn actors. Many known, locally?'

'Of course and I can question them but the most likely culprit's an amateur. Pros who don't use a condom usually have HIV and the semen sample findings show that wasn't the case.'

'Yeah, that makes sense. Thanks again, Frankie.'

Darac rang off and called the cell block.

'Another dig at Battail?' Granot said.

'He's the best link to Voska we have. And we'll be losing him later today.'

'He's going to know he's been in an interrogation after this one.'

For once, Darac felt like letting Granot use the brass knuckles for real.

34

Lined by double rows of plane trees, Cours Mirabeau in Aix-en-Provence was an elegant thoroughfare. The terrace at Restaurant Lervit was the place to be, and be seen.

Stuffing a carrier bag into his pocket, a large red-faced man plodded wearily in, selected the nearest empty table and plonked himself down with his back to the view. As if on castors, an aged waiter appeared and with no more than a raised eyebrow, invited the man, Lieutenant Henri Clerc of the Police Nationale, to place his order.

'Over a hundred of those bloody things I've put up!' With

a back header, he indicated the poster he'd fastened to the tree shading the entrance. 'I'll have the *daube de bœuf*. Two hours I've been walking around!' The waiter raised the other eyebrow. 'And a bottle of the Mercier.' Sighing, Clerc turned off his mobile, folded his arms and closed his eyes.

At an adjoining table, Gilles Voska glanced at the poster, and although he clocked his own face depicted under the word WANTED, he saw no reason to hurry his steak tartare and mineral water. Who else, he wondered, would recognise that bullet-headed man as him? Not the fat *flic*, and he'd looked right at him.

Feeling the satisfaction that came with living successfully on his wits, Voska went over the steps that had got him thus far. A lesser man, he believed, especially one trained in wilderness survival techniques, would have driven north out of Nice and set about losing himself in the Mercantour. But the eyes of country folk were such that not even an unfamiliar cat passed unnoticed. It was the kind of error Battail would have made. Battail, the pathetic excuse for a man Voska held responsible for his current predicament.

Voska understood that the best place to hide was in plain sight among people. In plain sight while wearing an effective disguise. His wig choice, he felt, was a masterstroke. Bald men tended to go for luxuriance. Best practice was to wear a thinning piece. The same strategy applied to eyewear. Shades and thick frames only drew attention.

The poster carried photos of Voska's tattoos: on his right forearm, the dagger insignia from his Legion outfit; and rearing up between his shoulder blades, a spitting king cobra. Hiding the tattoos in winter was easy. Come summer, he would have them removed.

As he sipped his mineral water, Voska appeared to be watching the world go by but with each new pass, he read another line on the poster. It referred to the clothes he had last been seen wearing: navy-blue T-shirt, combat trousers and boots – his 'regular apparel'. Not any more, it wasn't. Slacks, shirt and blazer were the new order of the day.

Despite being hastily arranged, Voska's departure from Nice had gone without a hitch. Selling the RV to a dealer who owed him several favours, he'd traded vehicles twice en route to his first stopover, an old bolt hole of his in Draguignan. As home to a major unit of the French army, he knew it was the last place they would think of looking for him. Following some serious physical exertion, he'd then traded vehicles again on his way to Aix. All he needed to do now was finish his lunch and take the A51 south. The huge melting pot that was Marseille was an excellent place in which to disappear.

The poster concluded with an instruction to the public not to approach him. *He may be dangerous*, it said. 'May'? He was reminded of the arsehole who'd dismissed a recent video as 'tame'. Voska twitched suddenly, tensing the muscles sheathed in the blue cloth of his blazer.

The instruction didn't specify the reason for the police's interest in him. He wondered about that. Surely, they couldn't have discovered anything?

Lieutenant Clerc was on his second glass of wine when his *daube de bœuf* arrived. As the waiter set down the bowl, Voska leaned across and confidently asked for the bill. The request silently acknowledged, he returned his attention to the avenue.

A girl strolled by, rapt in her mobile. Skinny. Bare-legged. Vulnerable. Following her with his eyes, Voska began picturing her in a favourite sequence from *Marie's First*...

A fat forearm tightening around his windpipe dropped a scrim of red pulsating stars over the scene. Voska felt a scrape on the back of his left hand. Handcuffs – the *flic* was fighting to close them around his wrist. One notch nearer. Two. A third would do it. Voska spread his legs, flexing forward from the waist. The *flic* flew over his shoulder and slammed on to his back, collapsing the table.

Before anyone reacted, Voska snatched up his rucksack and ran toward the nearest exit off the Cours Mirabeau, a pedestrianised passage. Anonymity was best preserved by walking but there was no time. He needed a ride and his own vehicle was out. He'd left it way over the other side of town. Voska would never admit it, but that had been an error. He darted into the passage. A sign advertised parking in a hundred metres.

He dodged between shoppers and kept going. He saw it. A street-level lot. That meant a quicker getaway but it was overlooked by everyone and everything – including an official building to his left. Now he needed a woman to return to her car. With a toddler, ideally. Better still, a baby. No one was more biddable than a frightened mother.

He clocked a young, petite woman carrying a couple of shopping bags. She turned into the lot and headed for the far corner. She would have to do. Two uniformed officers were coming his way. He needed a Plan B. He looked to cross the street but there were three more there. They couldn't have heard about the restaurant incident yet. Why all the uniforms? Then he saw the sign. The official building was Aix's Palais de Justice. He reinstated Plan A; the young woman still hadn't reached her vehicle. The two uniforms continued toward him. As they drew level, lapel radios cackled into life. It didn't sound urgent. Voska walked casually past the pair and turned into the car park.

He followed the young woman toward the corner space. At first, he couldn't see her vehicle, a grey Peugeot 307 with a child seat fitted in the back: the panel van parked in the adjacent space hid it from the rest of the lot. Using it as cover, he waited until she opened the driver's door. As he hoiked her off her feet, she kicked out, losing a high heel. He bundled her on to the passenger seat and threw the heel in after her. Clamping a hand over her mouth, he produced a thin-bladed knife and held the point against her jugular. He spoke to her calmly. 'I will release you unharmed shortly if you do as I say. If you don't, I will slit your throat and

235

your child will be motherless for ever after. Understand?'

He looked into her eyes. The knife point drew blood as she nodded frantically. He glanced into the foot well. It was empty except for a pair of flat shoes.

'When I tell you, roll the passenger seat back, squeeze yourself into a ball and crouch down. As I drive away, I'll have this knife against your spine. If you make a sound, or try to move, I will stab you repeatedly. Roll your seat back.'

It took her several attempts.

'Get down on the floor in front of the seat.'

He started the engine. The young woman's shuddering body scrunched forward. As soon as her head had ducked below the level of the window, Voska brought the side of his hand down on her neck. Her whimpering ceased and she collapsed into the space. Covering her body with his jacket, he rummaged through her handbag. Moments later, his eyes taking in the scene like a radar scanner, he backed the car out of the space and pulled out into the street.

Ahead, a trio of officers was standing at the kerb waiting to cross. He drove past them with no more anxiety than if they had constituted an honour guard. A smile played on his lips as he considered the likely reaction of the *flics* back in Nice: the idiots who had suggested he *may* be dangerous. He felt like ripping the girl's spine out there and then to prove it. But there was plenty of time. They wanted a manhunt? They'd got one.

35

Public Prosecutor Frènes's diminutive frame looked scarcely capable of containing all the righteous energy that drove him. His desk, the biggest and most cluttered in the whole of Nice's Palais de Justice, was, he believed, testament enough to the Herculean efforts he was making on the public's behalf. But in case visitors failed to notice, he endeavoured to be sitting behind it, eyes lowered over a stack of papers, whenever they were admitted.

Darac sat down opposite Frènes, concluding precisely the opposite: the desk shtick made the small man look even smaller.

Frènes kept his eyes on the file as he spoke. 'You were slow off the mark with Voska.'

Darac recalled that Frènes had barely seen the point of authorising the search for him in the first place. 'Not so.'

'Lieutenant Henri Clerc from Aix might dispute that.' Frènes turned the page. 'Not that he could do so standing up.' Finally taking off his reading glasses, he fixed Darac with a stare. 'He may be paralysed from the waist down for the rest of his life.'

Darac had already sent Clerc a get-well message. 'He should have called for back-up before tackling a man he knew was an ex-commando.'

'And Madame Simon might have doubts about your efficacy, also. *If* she is still alive.'

Darac got to his feet. 'I've got work to do.'

'Where are you…? Captain, I insist…'

Leaving the door open, Darac strode through into the outer office. 'Bye, Carole.' Flustered by the conflicting demands of the situation, Frènes's secretary wavered between casting Darac a reproving look, trilling out her usual bland valedictories, and rushing to Frènes's side. Going for the percentage shot, she chose the last as Darac took the stairs, unconcerned that another black mark would appear on his record. It wouldn't merit a suspension and that was all that mattered.

Emerging through the Palais's neo-classical façade, he swiped his mobile and called his opposite number in Aix, Captain Solange Chevalier. 'Hey, it's Darac.'

'Don't give me any more grief than I'm already getting, OK? Yes, he pulled the hijack right in front of the Palais and no, we've no idea what he did next. But I doubt he went far. We had roadblocks on all the major arteries and patrols out on the others within twenty minutes of his getaway.'

'But you didn't know about young Madame Simon at that point.'

'True.'

'When did her husband realise she was missing?'

'When she didn't return home with the shopping. It was his day off. Listen, Voska has got a daughter living in Nice, hasn't he?'

'Name of Adèle, yes. She hates her father but she's scared of him. I can't get a thing out of her.'

'Ah. Well, when we have something concrete, I'll call.'

'If you find the bastard, don't shoot him. Not dead, anyway.'

36

At the N'Patas' apartment block, Darac called the lift more in hope than expectation. But he had been too quick to judge. Releasing just a hint of disinfectant, the doors opened immediately. A sign declared that its aluminium surfaces were treated with a special anti-graffiti coating. *Paint Will Not Adhere To These Walls*, it said. *Another Lie* someone had daubed underneath.

Bass-heavy beats collided with one another as Darac rode the lift to the top floor. He wondered if the sound world of Rama's low-rent block in Nantes had been similarly chaotic, and whether it had helped to develop the young man's precise ear for rhythm. Perhaps as a reaction, a way of articulating the confusion.

As the doors opened, his stomach turned over. On the wall opposite, a spray-painted message suggested he *Eat Shit!* Realised in clashing Day-Glo colours, the work precisely aped the style of the infamous *Roast Pig Here!* sprayed on a wall in one of the Paris *banlieues*; a wall against which a police officer had burned himself to death.

An argument Darac had had with Angeline came unbidden into his head.

'Do you know that fifty officers committed suicide in this country last year? Fifty.'

'That's tragic, of course,' she'd said. 'But how many of the *racaille* they were policing took that same route? Many, many more.'

Impasse. There was another essential French term for Ridge's collection.

The soundtrack of the twelfth floor added TV football commentary to the aural mix. It made for a bizarre-sounding rap as Darac walked along the landing to Rama's apartment.

A short, shiny-looking man wearing blue overalls had beaten Darac to it. 'If you're looking for a Monsieur Modibo N'Pata, he's not in.' He pushed a piece of paper through the letterbox. 'These kids take on commitments. I feel sorry for them. I do.'

'You're here to…?'

The man smiled. 'Repo Monsieur Modibo N'Pata's car. More's the pity.'

So the boys were skint. Maybe that's why they were flying under the radar. Darac wondered if he could rectify at least part of the problem. 'How much is owed?'

'No idea. I just tow the vehicles.'

Darac felt the door give a little as he pushed the letterbox open. 'Rama? Sticks? It's me, Darac from the club. Are you there? Modibo, are *you* there?' He looked through the fissure between the curtains. There was nothing to indicate the boys had left for good.

'Well, nice talking to you, monsieur. Bye.'

'I'll ride down with you.'

In the car park, the repo man had already backed his truck into position.

'That's it: the little Fiat.'

Rama cramming his limbs into the thing must have made quite a spectacle, Darac reflected. He showed the man his ID. 'I'm going to clear the glove box. OK?'

'Well, I don't know.' The man scratched his bald head. 'I haven't got a key, anyway.'

'I have, fortunately. I'll give you a receipt.'

Darac took less than a minute to get into the car, collect the contents and bid the repo man farewell. He was making his way back to his own car when his mobile rang.

'Go ahead, Solange.'

'We've found the vehicle.'

'The 307?'

'Not Madame Simon's; the vehicle Voska had to abandon when he made his escape. It's a Berlingo van, obtained in Pertuis nearby. Just one print but we found it.'

'Quick work.' His eyebrows rose as if propelled by his rising hopes. 'Find anything?'

'There was a case with some DVDs in the glove box. Six of them.'

Darac had reached his car. Lost in the conversation, he turned and set his weight back against the driver's door. 'Has anyone looked at them yet?'

'No time. They've gone over to the lab.'

'Yours or Marseille?'

'Ours, naturally.'

Darac grimaced. Forensic staff in Marseille worked all night; the small Aix lab would be closed already. 'When does it open in the morning?'

'Eight o'clock. Right, I've got you up to speed—'

Had Darac turned and looked up at that moment, he would have seen a gift from the heavens dropping straight toward him. 'Favour time, Solange. I'd like to send one of my team over to you tomorrow morning – Granot.'

'Look, I was calling as a courtesy more than anything. I haven't time to—'

Boom!

Darac flinched as something thumped into the roof of his car.

'You alright, Darac?'

A couple of ten-year-olds came screaming up. 'Sorry, monsieur!'

'Yes, sorry, sorry, sorry!'

'Just a stray football, Solange... Messieurs! Go and kick that around somewhere else!'

The apologies kept coming as the youngsters gathered it and scurried off. 'Listen, what I'm proposing will *save* you time.'

Chevalier eventually agreed to Granot's visit, but made it clear she would be unlikely to interpret such interference as co-operation in the future. Darac got into the car and rang Granot.

'Can you get over to the lab in Aix first thing tomorrow morning?'

'I've just picked up something for the examining magistrate.'

'What's Reboux want?'

'Yours truly to review the Saint-Maurice business.'

'The most tedious blackmail case in history?'

'I'm looking forward to it, actually.'

'Bonbon there?'

'He's sitting right next to me.'

'Put him on... Bonbon?' It didn't take Darac long to pique his interest.

'There may be evidence of the crime itself on those discs, chief.'

'Exactly. If so it will be a really hard watch, clearly.'

'What did Frankie say to us, though? We've got to do these things? I'll get over there first thing.'

Listening to *Giant Steps*, Darac drove home to pick up his guitar for the band practice. It wasn't until he was almost ready to set off to the club, and the hoped-for reunion with Rama, that he looked more closely at the items he'd taken from Modibo's car. Receipts, user's manual, an IGN map of the area: the usual stuff. But then he unfolded the map. 'Shit.' He thought about it a moment and then swiped his mobile. 'Pascal?' Darac asked the doorman to cast his mind back a couple of evenings.

'Yeh, Sticks was up top when I went out for a smoke. He was waiting for his brother but the guy was late.'

'How did he react?'

'He's a mellow fellow, right? But he was pissed off. "Now I must call a cab," he said.'

Pascal had arrangements with several taxi firms.

'Did you give him a steer?'

'Sure, but I went back downstairs before he called any of them. *If* he did.'

'Where was he going, did he say?'

'Home, I guess. What's this about, Darac?'

'I'm just curious.'

'Right. So you coming to the Sven Nordin gig tomorrow?'

'Planning to. Failing that I'll see you on Thursday for our gig.'

Darac rang the cab companies Pascal had cited.

Five fares had been picked up from the club that night. None of them matched Rama's description.

Darac's growing suspicions didn't change his plans for the evening. He felt he needed the band practice more than ever. But for once, his motives in going to the club had as much to do with the *policier* in him as the *poète*.

37

Closing her eyes, Cristelle rotated her pelvis and began sighing, 'Yes!'

'Sweetheart... there's no need for the... theatrics quite yet... I'm not intending to... come for at least five more minutes.'

It took ten. Afterwards, the man found his other ride waiting for him. The driver's brand new convertible had made short work of the drive from Cap Ferrat.

'Successful meeting?'

Philippe straightened his tie and smiled. 'Thank you so much for the lift, my dear.'

'Thank *you* for my beautiful new Mercedes, Philippe. I love it.'

'Your Golf was such an old wreck. I don't know why we didn't think of it before.'

Taylor knew exactly why. 'And have you had the opportunity to look into the other issue we discussed?'

Philippe's mien darkened a shade. 'The question of Ivo is not so straightforward.'

'The man has never been on message. Now, there's a danger he could become a reputational risk.'

'That is putting it very strongly.'

'He was far too loose-tongued in talking with Captain Darac.'

'I have scheduled a meeting with Ivo next week. I intend issuing him a stiff warning. One he won't forget.'

'I'm sure he won't but that may not be sufficient.'

'Dismissing a member of the senior management team is a process fraught with complications. The scope for appeal being just one.'

'It's a step that may have to be taken, nevertheless. I can't bear the thought that a rat like him might cause you or Maggie even a moment's distress. Or ruin our work.'

'My dear, I value your concern, but leave it with me.'

Taylor retreated into herself for the remainder of a journey she could have driven blindfold. In any other circumstances, she would have attempted to discourage Philippe from attending his clandestine 'meetings'. But whereas lively sex might have propelled most men of his age into an earlier grave, Taylor understood that it was a part of what kept him going. And his keeping going was important to her.

She recognised that Maggie would have been furious about his whoring if she had known about it, even though, over one margarita too many, she had once confided that the only good thing about her 'wheezy old bellows' was that they gave her a perfect excuse for avoiding that side of things with her 'horny old centaur' of a husband.

Taylor understood Maggie's position. Philippe, for all his stratospheric levels of refinement, had revealed the wanton side of his nature on her very first evening at Villa Rose. He had tried everything to get his new protégée into bed, only desisting when he realised Taylor's 'silliness' was genuine distress. Mortified, he had begged her forgiveness and swore it would never happen again.

When Taylor had finally fallen asleep that night, she had dreamed about one of her many childhood homes, an A-frame house high in the hills above Monterey Bay. After rain, huge yellow slugs used to appear in the yard. For a joke, her adoptive father Jonathan had once picked up a choice example and dropped it into her hand. The feel of the thing disgusted her. How he'd laughed. Taking pleasure in a child's revulsion, that was how it had all begun. Soon afterwards, the slugs gave way to something even more repulsive. Each time it happened, Jonathan swore it would be the last. Years later, Philippe had made the same promise to her but he had been true to his word.

Maggie was in high dudgeon on their return to Villa Rose. 'You scoundrels, I've been looking for you all over the place. What did we say? When off the premises, mobiles on?'

Taylor mimed shooting herself in the temple.

Philippe spread his arms wide. 'What can we do to make it up to you?'

'I'll think of something for you later. In the meantime Taylor, you and I have a date.'

'Alright, but I do have work to do around here, you know.'

When it eventually came time to buckle down, Taylor found it hard to concentrate. It wasn't the effect of two slowly sipped mojitos down in Saint-Jean, nor the nature of the task itself: running over arrangements for the following Sunday's press preview. It was something far less routine. Her musings were interrupted by a knock at her door.

'May I come in?' Ivo said.

'Is it urgent? I have a lot to get through, still.'

'What a pity. No, I can wait. Or is "*it* can wait" better?'

'Ivo, I would rather you didn't turn up at my door unannounced.'

He looked her up and down. 'I'll ring next time.'

'Goodnight.'

Hoping Ivo wouldn't be around long enough for there to be a next time, she returned to her desk. On the notepad in front of her were written just two words: *Paul Darac?*

38

Jazz club owners lived for the special nights; the rare gigs in which performers found something extra in a sound, a solo or even a whole set, and blew away the paying public as a result. On the occasions it had happened at the Blue Devil, Ridge had felt as proud as a new father. You couldn't buy that feeling.

Monday night practice seemed to offer far less. Yet although it brought in not a single cent, Ridge had a special fondness for the institution. Practice night would be one of the things he would miss if, after so many years of toil, the club closed its doors for good.

In the curtained-off cubby hole that passed for his office, he put his glasses back on and added up the quarterly figures for a third time. Maybe he'd missed something. After a couple of minutes of concentrated tapping, his trusty old Commodore calculator came up with precisely the same bottom-line figure as before.

For the seventh quarter in a row, a more creative approach was called for. At least Ridge would be reprising his role as the Harry Houdini of the balance sheet to the accompaniment of one of his favourite soundtracks in the world: jazz musicians loosening up to play. There were silvery tinkles, arpeggios and block chords from Didier's piano; thick-toned slams and woody flurries from Luc's bass; honking clarions and butter-soft harmonies from the alto and tenor saxes of Charlie Pachelberg and Dave Blackstock; glittering fanfares from Jacques Quille's trumpet; feather-light runs and four-to-the-bar *changs* from Darac's guitar. But as other instruments added their voices to the melange, there were no flams, rolls or paradiddles from Rama N'Pata's drums.

Downstairs, Didier concluded his warm-up and began handing out manuscript paper. 'OK everyone: "Lil' Darlin'". Just the opening bars.' He threw up a hand toward the drum kit. 'Where *has* young Sticks got to?' He checked his mobile again. 'Anyone?'

Trombonist Pierre Leconte's ears pricked up. 'Who the hell is Sticks?'

'Yes, some of you horns haven't encountered him yet, have you? Rama is his real name. *Very* special. Providing he turns up.'

Englishman Dave Blackstock had a characteristic take on it. 'Jazzers: unreliable bastards. Is the kid coming from work or what?'

'I suspect he's not going to make it at all,' Darac said, unable to elaborate on his suspicions, nor let anyone in on the sleight of hand he now knew he would have to pull off later in the session. 'Let's get on.'

'Alright.' Didier gave up on the call. 'Without drums is there any point doing this?'

'I've got an electronic metronome thing on my guitar tuner,' Darac said. 'I can put it through my amp. It'll sound hideous but it will give us the tempo.'

'Let's do it. Set it at seventy beats per minute, to start.' Darac rigged up the device and adjusted the volume to a level the band would be able to hear when they were all playing together.

'Nice tempo,' Luc said. 'Seventy thuds per minute.'

'I told you it wouldn't sound good.'

Didier had a better idea. 'What say we get Ridge down here? He's not the worst drummer in the world – close maybe – but it might just give us more feel.'

'If Ridge can keep time to "Lil' Darlin'", I'll finally admit French cheese is better than English,' Dave said.

Charlie took a pair of headphones out of her sax case. 'Darac?'

His mind was elsewhere – Argentina, in fact, where for the next couple of weeks Marco was on a research trip and unreachable. But what light could he have shed on Rama's life away from the music scene, anyway?

'This is Earth calling.'

'Pardon, Charlie?'

'Plug these cans into your time machine and give them to Ridge.'

'Good idea.'

Having taken little coaxing, Ridge settled on the stool and proceeded to smash, splash and slam-dunk his way around the kit.

'Close enough for you know what,' Dave said.

'Just warming up, brother.' Ridge swapped his sticks for brushes. Wearing Charlie's headphones, he at least looked the part. 'Ready.'

His head buzzing with questions, Darac was staring into his guitar case as Didier counted the band in. It was a moment or two before he realised all eyes were on him.

'The intro?' Didier said.

'Yes?'

'Feel like playing it?'

Three hours later, the rehearsal concluded with a competent 'Milestones' but, overall, it had been a mediocre session. Even with the beat pulsing in his ears, Ridge had proved incapable of handling the super-slow tempo of the Basie tune. For his part, Darac's work had been uninspired and plans to perform the number were shelved. The knives were out for Rama. The kid may have been a genius, but an absent genius was no use to anyone. Didier ended the evening by calling another mate of Marco's to sub his sub for the gig.

On his way out, Darac paused at Jeanne Mesnel's feet.

Ridge's voice rumbled up from below. 'Garfield, what was that about?'

Darac cursed himself. The simplest bit of sleight of hand imaginable and he'd bungled it. 'So you saw, huh?'

'Saw what?'

It seemed he had got away with it after all. And now he had to lie about it. 'Well, I played like a drain in there.'

'That's not what I meant. You OK?'

He felt far from OK but there was nothing he could say about it at the moment. 'Ridge, you know I never talk about the cases I work on. When the current one is over, I'll tell you all about it. See you later, man.'

As sombre as black marble, Ridge watched him go. 'Take good care now.'

Darac stepped quickly across Avenue des Diables Bleus, his mind alive with ideas, counter ideas and conclusions. The trigger had been the IGN sheet map he'd removed from Modibo's glove box: someone had drawn a cross in red ink over the campsite at L'Ancienne Bastide, the last known address of Gilles Voska.

What business did the N'Patas have there? Darac remembered that one of the offences for which Voska had done time was providing quality documents for illegals. He hadn't been their original source but the middleman in a series of deals that netted him some serious money and in the process, a serious hold over the illegals concerned. Rama and Modibo N'Pata, though, were bona-fide French citizens. Could Voska have some other hold over them? The boys were certainly broke: Modibo's repossessed car proved that. Wondering if drugs, as so often, were at the bottom of it, Darac had earlier rung Narco chief Armani Tardelli. But Armani had absolutely nothing on the brothers. Squads in the boys' home city of Nantes had nothing on them, either.

Darac decided to abandon the question of their connection and concentrate on what had actually happened to Rama. He went over every moment he'd spent with him. Contextualised, what had seemed innocent took on a new complexion. During the Joao Pinsa gig, a casual remark – 'She's too old for you' – had discomfited the young man. So much so, it temporarily short-circuited his preternaturally precise sense of rhythm. That's why Darac noticed it.

Now, with the accumulation of other details, a possible explanation was emerging.

DNA evidence from the hot tub had implicated a man of African origin. *In a murder case*, Agnès always said, *there is no such thing as an unthinkable possibility*. Darac had proved this many times. Modibo, he didn't know. But Sticks? He was as sweet as could be imagined. A kid in thrall to an all-purpose criminal like Voska, however, was more capable of the unthinkable than most. But *this* crime? *This* kid?

Reluctantly following his train of thought past every green signal, Darac had almost reached Place Garibaldi when three frisky teenagers derailed it. He moved to step around them but the pin-pupilled youngsters weren't having any. There would be no 'Sorry, sorry, monsieur!' this time.

The younger boy eyed Darac's case. 'The dude's got a guitar. Bet I can play it better.'

'Fuck off, you're crap.'

It appeared to be the funniest remark ever made. As they doubled up, Darac jinked out of the way but once again, his new best friends couldn't get enough of him.

'Come on, guitar man,' the girl said, breathing weirdness all over him. 'Play us a tune.'

The younger boy made a grab for the case. 'I'll fucking play it if you won't.'

'Look, I've given you two chances. Two is all you're going to get.'

The younger boy got in Darac's face. He looked no older than seventeen but he was burly enough to be a handful and wired enough to try proving it. Before he made a move, the older one pulled him back.

'Leave it! He's a pig. I've seen his picture in the paper.'

'You don't read the paper. And he can't be a pig, he's got a fucking guitar.'

'He's a pig. I know he is. Let's get out of here!'

'Fucking *flic*!' the girl shouted as they ran off.

Darac had reached the tram stop when the sound of roller shutters clattering down across the Place masked the sound of stones pinging the pavement around his feet. And then, to cries of 'Yes!' and 'Run!' what felt like a fair-sized pebble caught him just above the ear, stunning him. Although Darac was a devout atheist, his first reaction was a good Catholic one: guilt. The clout was punishment for having gone out to play when he should have been working exclusively on the case. The fact that he'd come away from the club with what might prove significant evidence did little to stem the feeling.

Applying pressure to the wound with the hem of his scarf, he continued past the tram stop. Etched on to the platform screen were the aphorisms: NO ART WITHOUT TRUTH and SEEK AND YE SHALL FIND. Irritated and improved in equal measure, he crossed the Place and turned into the Babazouk. A familiar voice called from the doorway of Cave Martini.

'Darac? Or is it Saint Stephen?'

'Just kids, Denis.'

'I saw them running away. Come in, my friend. We'll have a drink.'

It was another hour before Darac finally went home.

39

Darac's morning detox wasn't working. Nothing lifted his spirits; not even Armstrong's 'Potato Head Blues', the best argument he knew for the existence of the human race.

He set down the guitar, picked up his mobile and stepped out on to the roof terrace. Gazing up toward the viewpoint on

Château Park, he called the lab. 'Patricia, has Barrau gone home yet?'

'Yes, about half an hour ago.'

'So who's in this morning?'

'Professor Bianchi's here now. And Dr Mpensa will be in at ten.'

'Will you tell Deanna I'll be over with some evidence in about half an hour?'

Skipping breakfast, he emerged on to a Boulevard Jean Jaurès washed clean by overnight rain. Expiation, renewal and growth were in the air but Darac didn't believe it. It was going to be a hell of a day. He swiped his mobile.

'Granot? I won't be in for a while. Off to the lab and then back to L'Ariane. If Frènes wants to know anything, we're making good progress.'

'We are? That's nice.'

Misjudging the speed of an oncoming tram, Darac hopped into the path of a motor scooter, causing the rider to swerve. 'Has anything… Yeah? And you're another one, arsehole!' Darac shouted, off mouthpiece. 'Anything come in on Voska?'

'The Aix lab isn't open yet, is it?'

'I meant from Chevalier.'

'Nothing.'

At the commissariat over in Aix, Bonbon had picked up his clearance for the lab and was wrapping things up with the duty officer when the desk phone rang.

'*More* reinforcements?' He rolled his eyes at Bonbon. 'I'll patch you through.'

'You've got a lot out looking for Voska, then?'

The duty officer re-routed the call. 'We'll have no bugger left here, soon. You've heard about the phone business?'

So much for Chevalier keeping them informed. 'Not as such.'

'Eight o'clock last night, they traced young Madame Simon's mobile to a half-kilometre square just south of Mauran. An hour later, they found the phone. Old model. The last thing on it was a text to her husband saying she was scared but OK.'

'Good news? I'd forgotten what that was.'

'Don't get excited. The phone was switched on but the message hadn't been sent. And then, they found a pair of women's shoes nearby.'

'Ah.'

'They reckon she was trying to type the message while Voska's back was turned and dropped the phone in panic. She couldn't pick it up without alerting him, so she left it. Or maybe he caught her, she threw it away, and Voska was in too big a hurry to go looking.'

'Got a copy of the message?'

'Don't go anywhere.' The duty officer put in a call.

'Where were the phone and the shoes found?'

'The phone and one of the shoes were picked up on the bank of a water-filled ditch off the Étang de Berre. The other shoe was in the ditch itself. They dragged it for the poor woman. Nothing. Now they're dragging the whole Étang.'

'What? Be like dragging the Atlantic.'

'Naturally, they were hoping to find her in the ditch. If you see what I mean.'

Bonbon saw it all too clearly. 'Where is Mauran, exactly?'

'On the eastern side of the Étang. About ten kilometres north-west of Marseille airport.'

'With all the added security, Voska couldn't have flown out of there, could he?'

'No way. He didn't even fool poor old Clerc at the restaurant, did he?'

'A boat, maybe?'

'Not unless he's got a private submarine.'

A uniform came in with a transcript of young Madame Simon's

text message. Bonbon signed the appropriate form and ran his eye over the message. 'Is this exactly how it appeared?'

'Yes.'

'Uh-huh.' He stared off for a moment, then feigning panic, cast a spurious glance at his watch. 'Look at the time! They won't thank me at your crime lab if I'm late.'

'Only take you ten minutes. You'll get there easily.' Bonbon thanked the duty officer and took his leave, anyway. He may have had time to spare. But there was something he needed to do first.

* * *

Darac was arriving for his meeting with Deanna when his mobile rang.

'Bonbon? Wasn't expecting anything from you for a while yet.'

Bonbon updated him.

'What was the exact wording of the message?'

'I just emailed it to you.'

'It hasn't come through. Read it to me.'

'Here goes: *darling i am kidnapped. he is treating me ok but i cannot see where I am and i'm scared he does not know i send this tell the police! I love—* And then it stops. I have to say, it looks completely bogus to me.'

The message finally pinged into Darac's inbox. 'Hang on, Bonbon, it's just come in.' He read it. 'Yes, I've got a lot of time for Chevalier but she's got this one round her neck, hasn't she? A message typed in panic would be barely readable. All this has is a few missing capitals.'

'It has an apostrophe and an exclamation mark, as well. And look at the length of it. Most people in young Madame Simon's position would have keyed in one or two words, not twenty or thirty or however many it is.'

'And one quick key stab and she could have actually sent the message. She didn't do anything in panic. What fits better is that Voska keyed in the message, himself. And there's a second significance in the fact that it wasn't sent. He wanted to be well clear of the area by the time the phone was found.'

'And think of the location, chief: a ditch next to a huge lagoon. OK, it's a water-filled ditch but the phone was above ground. Voska *wanted* to draw the police to the area. I bet you Madame Simon is either still alive, and let's hope so, or she was killed elsewhere.'

'Agreed. Voska is making us play Russian dolls in reverse. First we have to search the ditch, then the Étang, then its boundaries which include another vast area, the airport.'

'Which, as a bonus, has a huge workforce for us to question. This whole Étang thing is a decoy designed to drain as many officers as possible away from wherever Voska is.'

'Absolutely.'

'Madame Simon's shoes were found near the phone, incidentally. Stilettos.'

'Anyone looked at footprints?'

'No stud marks from heels were found. Here, they're thinking Voska either made her take them off so as not to leave prints, or he'd already killed her and was carrying her over his shoulder.'

But equally, she might never have been there at all. He planted them.'

'I'd like to be a fly on the wall when you tell Chevalier all this,' said Bonbon.

'She'll see our point. Listen, ring me as soon as you've watched the DVDs, OK?'

'I'll be at the lab in about twenty minutes.'

Initially, Darac's call to Chevalier went better than he'd imagined. But although she saw the sense in his argument, officers had already been deployed so sticking to Plan A was the only option. Darac ended the call with a reminder to keep him abreast of *all* developments in future. That went down less well. *Tant pis.*

Chief pathologist Deanna Bianchi took the offering in her small, rubber-gloved hands. 'So what have we got here?'

'It's a towel.'

Behind her exam glasses, Deanna's keen black eyes flared with amusement. 'A *towel* is it? I've often wondered what one looked like.'

'Yeah, yeah. It's a towel that lives with a drum kit set up at the Blue Devil. You'll find at least four individuals' sweat soaked into it. And maybe some hairs, et cetera.'

Deanna took off the glasses and slipped them into the breast pocket of her lab coat. 'The individuals being?'

'One Marco Portami, whose towel it actually is; club owner Eldridge Clay who used it last night; and there may be something of mine on it. I wasn't able to put gloves on.'

'The fourth?'

'A young man named Rama N'Pata. For elimination, my sequence is on the DNA database, obviously. Marco had a drink-driving charge last year so his might be. Ridge Clay's I assume isn't. But I have a horrible feeling that Rama N'Pata's may be and it's him I'm interested in.'

'A horrible feeling?'

'I'll tell you about the kid if it checks out.'

Her eyes slid to her prized La Marzocco espresso machine. 'Time for a coffee?'

'Always. But make it a quick one.'

As they talked, she carried out the rituals of knocking out the grounds, grinding the beans and then tamping the powder into the holder with clinical precision.

'You haven't been over to our temporary home yet, have you?'

'Haven't had that particular pleasure.' Deanna's tobacco-rasped voice lent a deliciously earthy edge to words like 'pleasure'.

'Enjoying it?'

'Working in a sealed glass box with nothing but koffee with a k to drink? Oh, yes, it's great.'

'You'll soon be back at the Caserne.'

'Let's hope so.'

'This Rama N'Pata. You think he's the one who took a dip with Madame Mesnel?'

'That's not an especially nice way of putting it.'

Deanna nodded. 'So it's true what some are saying.'

She coughed; not such a deliciously earthy sound. 'Captain Irreverent has lost his sense of humour.'

'I haven't.'

'Of course not. It's everyone else.'

He dragged a hand through his hair. 'Well if I have, maybe it's no bad thing.'

'Yes it is. Humour is insulation, isn't it? A much-needed commodity in our business.'

'Maybe.'

'You know it is.'

The espressos were soon ready. As Deanna handed over the cup, she took a close look at Darac's right temple. 'Who's been throwing stones at you?'

Darac gave her a wry look. 'You ever considered pathology as a career, Deanna?'

'No. Far too difficult.'

His signature smile made a brief comeback. 'It was just kids.'

'Lucky the "just kids" missed your just eye.'

'I suppose it was.' Darac downed his espresso in one. 'Perfect.' He got to his feet. 'Will you get back to me on the towel as soon as you can?'

'I will.'

He gave her arm a squeeze.

Darac headed back to his car. This time, he would gain entry to the N'Pata apartment whether the brothers were at home or not.

40

'I know you've asked me to ring before calling in person but this is urgent.'

Taylor's pulse quickened. Perhaps Philippe had delivered at last. 'Come in.'

Opting for the intimacy of the small sofa, Ivo headed to the far corner of the room. Taylor went no further than her desk.

'What do you want?'

Retracing his steps with exaggerated graciousness, he sat down opposite her. 'I must say everything looks magnificent for Sunday.' He grinned. '*Never* has a preview here been so well organised.'

'Save your backhanded compliments, Ivo.'

'As so often, you misunderstand.'

'I understand only too well. Why do you want to see me?'

'Any man with blood in his loins would want to see you if he could.'

Taylor exhaled deeply. The situation, it was clear, had not yet changed. 'Get to your point.'

'Alright. I've come to offer you my help. In advance.'

'In advance of what?'

'Of our beloved leader – what's the term? – passing away. I want you to understand that when "that day dawns", as you put it, I shall be here to help you.'

'If I need a shoulder to cry on, I shall look elsewhere.'

'You might need more than a shoulder.'

'What do you mean?'

'Let us just say that after Philippe dies, I stand every chance of being appointed the curator of this museum piece – sorry, *museum*. There are people at the Academy, you see, who think –'

'The sun shines out of your ass?'

'If you like.'

'I do not like.' She stood. 'I think we've said all we need to say.'

He stayed put. 'We haven't even begun, Taylor.'

Ivo clearly had a card to play. She decided to let him play it. 'You have one minute.'

'I know you're concerned about the future so I have an offer. How would you like to be my assistant in the new Villa Rose?'

'*Your* assistant?'

'I can make it happen. And, to be blunt, it is the only chance you have of securing such a post here or anywhere else. You are beautiful, Taylor. But I'm sure you realise that as a scholar and as a gallery executive, you're so far below average, it is laughable. However, I would overlook that. I would still appoint you. And all you would have to do for it is *one* thing.'

Taylor's eyes were a blazing blue fire. 'Get out.'

'Think! When Philippe is gone, I will be here and you will not unless you agree to my suggestion. And if you do, Taylor, you will not regret it.' Ivo's wolfish grin returned. 'Like our current exhibition, I, too, am very well hung.'

'I would rather lick shit off a spoon.'

'You don't have to decide now,' he said, rising. 'It's not as if Philippe is likely to drop dead just like that, is it? Although, of course, he might. I think you'll change your mind.'

'Get out!'

Ivo looked more wolf-like than ever as he loped away. If Taylor had had a pistol to hand, his making it to the door would have been an evens call. As it was, she had to quell an urge to hurl something heavy at his back. She picked up the phone instead.

41

Sound systems yet to be powered up, Rama's apartment block was pulsing to a different rhythm this morning: the sound of bodies on the move. As Darac entered the lobby, the lift disgorged a gang of school-bound kids of diverse ages. Flying out of the stairwell with a loud *clack! clack!* a daredevil on a skateboard came surfing up behind them. The kid put Darac in mind of Madame Mesnel's errand boy, Henri Lepic, the young man with the fractured leg and the self-righteous mother. How was he getting on? he wondered.

The price for taking the lift up to the top floor was another encounter with *Eat Shit!* As he stepped out, the doors closed behind him. A couple of young dreads came running up. Multiple button-punching and cursing did not bring the lift back. The boy gave Darac the once-over.

'I apologise for the language, Monsieur *Flic*.'

He spoke in the same delicately articulated French as Rama. An octave lower, Darac reflected, and their voices wouldn't have been easy to tell apart.

The girl smiled cheekily. 'Don't arrest him.'

Darac hadn't expected chattiness.

'That obvious, eh?' The pair gave him a pitying look.

Darac indicated the graffiti. 'What do you think of that?'

'Eat shit? Personally, I think it's puerile.'

'Me too,' the girl said. 'On the seventh floor landing is something super brilliant. *Death Of The Vertical Neighbourhood*, it's called. Check it out.'

'I might. Did you paint it? Is that why?'

'No. It wasn't us.'

'It wasn't Rama N'Pata's work was it, by any chance? I'm a great fan of his drumming. Wouldn't have surprised me if he could paint brilliantly as well.'

'I don't know anyone of that name.'

'Me neither,' the boy said.

'I call him Sticks. Others Bones or Stretch? You get the idea. Lives with his brother Modibo. Apartment 1207 just along there.'

'We never go that way.'

He showed them Voska's photograph. 'Know him?'

'No.'

More kids arrived. A few eyed the dreads suspiciously. And then something was said in the backwards argot known as verlan.

Something sharp and threatening. For some of these youngsters, Darac realised, co-operating with a *flic* was a serious offence.

'Anybody ever see this man?' He held up the photo. 'No? Alright, anybody here know Rama N'Pata or his brother, Modibo? Apartment 1207.'

A couple of head-shakes was as close as Darac came to a response. He picked up his bags and weighed his options vis-à-vis the dreads. He could either preserve their cred with the others or promote a gentler image of the police. Not both. He eyeballed them.

'Any more like that out of you two and I'll arrest you. Got that?'

The pair playing up to the act, Darac pushed through the crowd and set off along the landing. From the outside, the curtains at 1207 appeared not to have been touched since his last visit. Checking the safety on his automatic was off, he knocked, rattling the door in its frame. No one answering, he took out his lock picks and slipped inside.

'Sticks? Darac from the DMQ.' Looking only for signs of life – particularly the armed and dangerous kind – he moved smartly through the apartment. 'Modibo, you here?' No one. Holstering his gun, Darac slipped on a pair of bootees and gloves. The reason for the give in the door soon became clear. The room-side edge of the strike plate was depressed deep into its slot; its leading edge, anchored by partially ripped-out screws, was standing proud. Conclusion: the door had been forced from the outside. Where the impact had cracked the paint layer, the colour and smell of the bare wood and paint flecks suggested it had happened recently.

Evidence of forced entry wasn't necessarily sinister. Many people had locked themselves out and broken in. But more disturbing possibilities began to occur to Darac as he picked up the car repossession notice from the mat.

The small lobby opened into a living room off which doors led to a kitchen and a bathroom. Two further doors led to the bedrooms. Darac sniffed. The place evidently hadn't been aired for a day or two and there was a staleness to the spice notes emanating from the kitchen. His father would no doubt have identified all of them but Darac Junior compiled a reasonable inventory. Of one thing he was certain: weed was not regularly smoked in the living room.

Sparsely furnished, the place was clean and aside from a slew of magazines and newspapers on the sofa, it was tidy. Darac checked the dates. The previous Saturday's *Nice-Matin* was the most recent. That was the day of the Joao Pinsa gig – the day Voska had absconded; and the last time anything had been seen or heard of Sticks.

Darac walked through into the kitchen and checked the fridge. No drugs or other surprises. The bathroom proved clean, also. The two bedrooms were next.

A Spartan with OCD would have felt at home in the first. Just about the only personal item on view was a Hotel Grande Scarabée ID sitting on a bedside cabinet. Bearing the name Modibo N'Pata, the photo showed a young man with a thick neck and a strong, broad-boned head. A certain humour about the eyes relieved what was a tough-looking face. Reflecting that Modibo looked like a black version of him, Darac opened the cabinet and laid the contents out on the bed. A photo of Rama and Modibo posing outside the Hotel Negresco caught his eye. With their beaming smiles and arms raised in a sort of victory wave, they seemed to be saying: *We made it!* Whether it celebrated arrival or reunion or just captured a randomly happy moment, it was a touching shot.

He examined the remaining items: a gold chain; a broken, fake Rolex, by the look of it, the same one Modibo was wearing in the Negresco photo; a copy of Kahlil Gibran's *Sand and Foam*; a motorcycle magazine. That was it. Darac turned to the wardrobe. A different story here: everything was neatly hung but there was scarcely space for one more item. The boys evidently shared it, Modibo's bulkier garments taking up just over half the rail. If they had skipped for good, they had left a lot of clothing behind.

A TV with a built-in DVD player sat on a shelving unit in the corner. A hint of a dust pattern around the rear and side edges of the shelves suggested they had been well stocked with discs until recently. Now, they were empty. Darac turned on the set, opened the disc drawer and found a DVD-RW in it. He picked up the remote. There were two files on the disc. He selected the first.

Tagged 10 December at 14.21, the silent, unedited footage began with razor-sharp shots of a deserted living room; one that was all too familiar. Darac's heart sank. A title came up, something containing the words *Grandma* and *Jungle*. And then, action. Prodded forward by spears, a figure clad in a house coat and slacks stumbled protesting into the frame. Although the two spear carriers were got up as African tribal chiefs complete with face masks, the tall stick-thin one was unmistakably Rama; the other, thick-set one, probably Modibo. The woman was Brigitte Andreani.

In other circumstances, Darac might have laughed. A housewife going about her cleaning surprised by African tribesmen? Complete with spears? And for a woman who had proved herself a gifted actress during questioning, Brigitte's portrayal of pleading for mercy was risible in the extreme. But there was nothing fake about how she had performed subsequently. As the DVD rolled to its inevitable climax, she seemed to relish every moment of the encounter. He was happy for her. Their masks holding good throughout, he couldn't tell how the men felt about it.

After the final shot, Darac paused the image and stared at the wall. Never had he felt so unhappy at having a suspicion proved. But far, far worse, he suspected, lay ahead. However sick he felt, he knew he would have to watch the second film on the disc. Trying to forget what Jeanne Mesnel meant to him, his finger hovered over the play button. Finally, he pressed it. The screen blanked out. Nothing. The remote control shot out of his palm like a squeezed bar of soap. His head dropping, he exhaled deeply.

Get on with it, he said to himself. *Call Ormans.*

'I need forensics over here, R.O.' He gave the details. 'Anyone free?'

'I've got a couple you can have.'

'Soonest, please.' Next, he called Frènes. 'We need to find the N'Pata brothers.'

'*Another* search? Think of the cost of—'

'*You* think of it. No arrest; no tick in the right-hand column.'

Frènes's protest went on longer than usual but having achieved the result he wanted, Darac next rang the duty officer's desk at La Trinité. As he waited, the first stereo of the day struck up somewhere along the landing. A bright-toned guitar playing repeated clarions over a happily bouncing bass, it was one of the signature sounds of African music. For once, Darac didn't feel like tapping along.

'Dutoit.'

'This is Acting Commissaire Darac of the Brigade Criminelle.' He gave his ID pin and his location. 'Forensics are on their way but I need an officer to secure apartment 1207 in the meantime. Soon as, please.'

Darac then called Granot and updated him. He concluded with a thought on the damaged door lock. 'I think that before he escaped, Voska came here perhaps to tip off the N'Patas, brief them on what to do next – whatever. But the boys weren't in or had already skipped. Voska shoulders the door open and goes to work, checking for anything incriminating. He clears the DVD shelves but doesn't think of looking in the player itself. Or maybe he was disturbed by someone before he could. Anyway, he winds up leaving key evidence behind.'

'The evil genius that he is.'

'Indeed.'

'I was just going to ring you, actually. I've dug up some interesting things on the Mesnels' trip to New York.'

'Ah.' Realising he'd forgotten to relay the information about

Alain's betting coup, Darac gave his knee a slap. 'Granot—'

'It'll only take a second. In the time the Mesnels were together, their taxed earnings were enough to keep them no more than ticking over. And I can't see a home seamstress earning huge sums on the black, can you? I don't know what Alain got up to in his spare time but it's difficult to see how they could have afforded such a trip. Especially considering the quality of hotel they stayed in for a whole month.'

'A month? Anyway look, I'm really sorry, Granot. With all the… excitement, I forgot to tell you what I learned from Monsieur Cartin.'

He belatedly gave Granot the information.

'A quintet on the Prix? That's a one in a million shot.'

'Quite.'

'And it was a pari-mutuel bet, you say – through PMU? A win of that magnitude is checkable.'

Granot's enthusiasm shone a ray of light into Darac's gloom. 'It seems this thing's finally getting your nose twitching.'

'Just a bit.'

The call ended, Darac ventured back into Rama's bedroom. It was clear where the young man's priorities lay. A mattress rolled up in one corner, a drum set of mixed parentage took up most of the floor space. A poster of drummer Elvin Jones presided over the room. Darac nodded, hearing the connection between Rama's playing and the rhythmic complexities of the master. On the stool was a score for 'Milestones' annotated in Marco's handwriting. Darac let out a long breath. What was his old friend going to make of Rama's story on his return?

'Captain?'

Darac handed the place over to the uniform and went on his way. Stepping into the lift, he didn't turn around until the doors had closed behind him. He didn't need another dose of *Eat Shit!* He'd eaten quite enough shit for one day, already.

Darac's mobile rang as he pulled up outside Battail's place. 'Go ahead, Bonbon.'

In the middle distance, a Ventimiglia-bound train whirred on to the viaduct. Drawn to its movement, Darac kept his eyes on it as Bonbon began his report.

'There were six DVDs recovered from Voska's van, each in a clear plastic sleeve. The first three I examined were unused. The fourth had *Heroes of Telemark Documentary* written on both the sleeve and the disc. I scanned it just to check. Judging by the state of the sleeve, Voska seems to have watched it a lot.'

'Why, do you think?'

'Inspiration? The Heroes were a Norwegian commando unit. World War II. Just a few guys but they wrecked Hitler's plans to build atom bombs, then outwitted an entire German division sent to catch them.'

Darac's gaze was still on the train. 'Probably how Voska sees himself. A hero.'

'Maybe. The fifth DVD was video footage of Voska performing martial arts moves. Made karate look tame. And then, finally, the sixth one: it was blank except for one or two jagged frames at the start. I didn't notice them to begin with. It's less than a second of footage. But if you freeze the image you can just make out it's Jeanne Mesnel's lower patio. Complete with hot tub. And, chief, she is standing right there.'

Darac didn't notice the last carriage of the train disappear from view. 'Clothed?'

'Yes.'

He thought back to the items he'd found in her airing cupboard. 'Wearing?'

'An everyday sort of outfit. Sweater and a skirt, it looks like.'

'How does she seem?'

'Difficult to tell but not obviously nervous or scared.'

'Is she alone in the frame?'

'Yes. And get this: the shot is dated and timed. The figures are too jagged to read but they're working on straightening them. I'll bet it will come out January 2nd at about four o'clock. I'm on my way back now with a copy of the original. They're going to ring me when they're sure of what the figures are.'

'So what you've got there is a wiped disc of the whole episode, isn't it? There's no way the lab boys could recover the pre-deleted original, is there?'

'Like a computer hard drive? No. It would be useful to find *that* though, wouldn't it?'

'Voska's erratic but I'm sure he would've put a hammer through it, or whatever.'

'Or just his hand. The man's a real hard case, I'm telling you.'

'We'll see how hard he is. Anyway, listen, Bonbon: top work as always.'

Darac pushed through Battail's gate feeling so energised he almost took it off its hinges. He knew it wasn't helpful to feel blind hatred; it skewed judgement. Under Granot's classification, hate could turn a Category Two into a Category Six on the spot. But Darac couldn't help it. No number could be put on what he wanted to do to Voska.

The side door was ajar so Darac continued into the back garden. 'Brigitte?' No sign of her or the dog. He went back to the door, knocked, waited and then went in. 'Brigitte?'

Stepping into the living room brought Voska's DVD back to him. *Spears*, for God's sake. He went into the hall and mounted the stairs. 'Brigitte?' He looked up. The loft hatch in the landing ceiling was open. 'Brig—'

He heard a yell. A dark shape appeared, filling in his field of vision as it plummeted toward him. He flinched, flattening himself into the angle of the stairs. Too late. He felt booted feet scrape the nape of his neck and then the jumper's whole bodyweight crashing onto his back. Darac's lungs lost air like a stomped balloon as the pair jagged down, down, down. Hitting the bottom step, Darac the sled became Darac the doormat as the jumper scrambled to his feet. The final footfall was a brutal blessing, kicking Darac's lungs open to a scorching inrush of air. Through a blurred curtain of pain, he caught a glimpse of his assailant as the man launched himself through the door and ran. It was Marcel Battail.

Darac was breathing but the pain ripping up his spine was the only thing keeping him from being sucked toward the pulsating light beckoning him from the centre of his vision. Beyond the light was a world made of soft, grey feathers. He heard himself saying: *Don't give in!* from a long way away. It didn't work.

His hands were the first part of him to move after he came round. Then his legs. The world somersaulted a few times as he staggered to his feet. A pneumatic drill was breaking up his skull; he was bruised and sore but he was in one piece.

The staircase kept still long enough for him to mount it one tread at a time. He made the landing. Now the loft ladder. Coordinating his limbs proved difficult at first but he managed it. Grabbing for a hold at the top, he slowly raised his head over the parapet.

Her blood streaking the polythene sheet under her, Brigitte lay with her head jammed up against the water tank. She was naked and her throat had been ripped open. Thierry, her pet, lay dead a few paces away. There was blood on his muzzle.

'You won't let anything bad happen to me, will you darling?' Brigitte had said to him. Darac climbed back down the ladder. And then the stairs. When he could descend no further, he sank on to the doorstep and wept.

Pathology and Forensics managed to carry a surprising amount of gear up into the loft. Darac left them to it, opting to sit on the doorstep. It was an uncomfortable perch and he was obstructing the sole entrance to the house but he needed air. Besides, the concrete between his feet looked interesting. A hand touched his shoulder.

'How are you feeling?'

'Better, thanks, Patricia.'

Better except for pain and guilt. That Brigitte had known more about Voska than she'd revealed didn't staunch it. In persuading her to return to the house, Darac had sent her to her death.

'Incoming.'

Darac looked to the street. Granot and Flaco were making their way through the rubberneckers toward them. Proffering her clipboard, Patricia intercepted them before they reached the threshold.

'You in one piece, mate?'

'Yes, yes.'

Granot's chops flushed as he bent to slip on a bootee.

'You don't look it.'

'Bit sore. Headache. That's all.'

'News. We've already got Battail. Well, I say "we". Malraux got him. Single-handed.'

'Good.'

Above them, a white-clad figure appeared in the cone of blue-white light blazing through the loft hatch and climbed carefully down the ladder.

'One small step for man,' Granot said, missing the mood of the moment.

Dropping to her haunches, Flaco looked into Darac's eyes. Her concerned face was a thing of such deep seriousness, he could barely return her gaze.

'What happened, Captain?'

Darac massaged his temples as if manual stimulation were required to retrieve the words he needed. 'Her... throat was ripped out. The dog is up there. Dead, also.'

Granot nodded. 'Battail sets the dog on Brigitte. It kills her and then he kills the dog. I knew that trigger-word theory was correct from the beginning. So what was he doing up in the loft? Hiding the bodies until he could move them later?'

As the white-clad figure joined them, Flaco helped Darac to his feet.

'What have you got, Deanna?'

'What was that about a trigger word, Granot?' she said, coughing.

Granot hadn't quite caught the question. 'Sorry, Professor?'

'Trigger word?'

'Yes, you know: the word Battail used to get the dog to attack on command.'

Deanna looked unimpressed and amused in equal measure. 'It must have been quite a word to inspire a dog to handle a knife with such skill.'

'Knife?'

'My preliminary analysis is this: while Madame Andreani was taking a hot, steamy shower, the killer stole unseen into the bathroom and laid a polythene sheet on its tiled floor. After slitting her throat, he wrapped her body in the sheet and carried the parcel up into the loft, a remarkable feat of strength. There, using a second sheet in the manner of the first, he united the pet dog he'd killed on entering the house with its owner. But first, he manually worked the dog's jaws around the wound, trying to disguise what had actually happened. Unsuccessfully.'

Darac nodded, sending an eddy of pain around his skull. 'The murder was committed in the shower, Deanna?'

'I know it looks clean. But there's clean and there's luminol clean, isn't there? It's where it happened.'

Granot wasn't giving up on his trigger-word theory. 'Because of the sheet, the victim left no bloodstains between the bathroom and the loft. But how did the killer manage to not drop or smear any of her blood anywhere?'

'That's not too difficult,' Deanna said. 'Flaco?'

The young woman's concentration scowl didn't last long. 'Perhaps the killer took his clothes off before he entered the bathroom. He stabbed her, laid her out on the sheet, then used the shower to wash off the blood before he went on.'

'That alright for you, Granot?'

He gave a conceding grunt.

'A knife attack in a shower,' Darac said, staring into space. 'Remember Battail's tattoos, Granot? One of them was "Psycho".'

'So it was. It doesn't give us anything, though. Except to confirm Battail's a shithead.'

'Agreed. But here's a question: why would he bother disguising the attack?' He thought about it for a moment. 'What's your estimate of the time of death, Deanna?'

'At this stage, I'd say somewhere between 8 pm Sunday and 4 am Monday. If you held a gun at my head, I'd say a couple of hours either side of midnight.'

Darac looked up. 'What?'

Granot was equally nonplussed. 'You're saying the small hours of Monday morning? Are you sure, Professor?'

Deanna's features were of a sparrow-like delicacy. Her withering stare was not.

'Yes,' Granot said. 'Of course you are.'

Darac exhaled deeply. 'This is the second murder Battail's been brought in for he hasn't committed.'

Granot turned to Deanna. 'It's a matter of record that Battail's custody was extended until Monday afternoon.'

'I see.'

Darac saw a second implication. 'Which shows that whoever killed Brigitte and tried to frame Battail for it didn't know that.' He ran through a list of candidates in his head. 'No, it doesn't really help us.'

Flaco moved things on. 'Do you know what kind of knife was used, Professor?'

'Usually, one can deduce little about the weapon used in a throat slitting. Drawing the long edge of a blade across flesh...' she mimed the action '...produces an incised wound and not a stab wound as such. Consequently, it's not usually possible to determine either the width or length of the blade. Another factor is that slicing through the flesh around the throat tends not to break bits off, unlike thrusting a blade into, say, the ribcage; so there's almost never a piece left behind that we can later match with the weapon.'

'If the blade edge was serrated or damaged, might that show in an incised wound?'

The question made Deanna smile. 'It might.'

Modibo N'Pata looked capable of slitting someone's throat, Darac thought to himself. But Brigitte's? A woman he'd had sex with? And why kill her, anyway?

'What can you tell us about the perpetrator, Deanna?' he said, feeling more on track.

'First, there's a wide bruise between the T7 and T8 vertebrae on the woman's spine. Made by the killer's knee, I'd say, to assist in forcing the head back. That, coupled with the precision of both the start and finish points of the incision, and the clean continuity of the cut itself, convinces me that the killer is a professional. Someone used to slitting throats, at least. And from the topography of the wound, it's clear they are left-handed.'

Darac recalled the N'Patas' Negresco photo. In it, Modibo was wearing his knock-off Rolex on the left wrist; not conclusive but it was an indication that like Rama, the man was probably right-handed. But Darac knew who wasn't. Anger began to well up in him.

'It's Voska,' he said. 'One: he's an ex-commando, highly trained in the use of combat knives and such. Two: Brigitte told us Battail had taught the dog to attack on command and shown the trick to Voska. Three: he's left-handed.'

Doubt doubled the creases around Granot's eyes. 'Voska trying to implicate Battail with the dog trick – that I can believe. But with all the forces we've got looking for him, how did he get here? He was 180 kilometres away in Aix, yesterday, remember. And what makes you think he's left-handed?'

'If we'd had decent surveillance, we would've got the bastard before he got the chance to perform this butchery.'

To those who'd been around Darac for a while, the warning signs were there: a hardening of the eyes, a tightening of the mouth, a gathering flex of the torso.

'Don't go punching another brick wall,' Deanna said. 'This is still a crime scene.'

'I'll tell you where there will be a crime scene. Wherever I get hold of—'

She had heard enough. 'I have to finish off in the loft.'

Deanna was already halfway up the stairs before Darac realised she'd gone. Turning, he found Flaco staring at him, wariness vying with disappointment. He stared back.

'Alright, the case is getting to me. Your mentor isn't practising what he preaches. Give me a break, will you?'

Her expression didn't change. 'Like the Lieutenant, I was just wondering how you know Voska is left-handed, Captain. That's all.'

Realising he'd heaped misjudgement on misjudgement didn't help. 'Voska's daughter Adèle told me about it,' he said, looking away. 'It's in the file, also.'

'I see.'

'Uh… Any thoughts, either of you?'

'I have,' Flaco said. 'It's on record that Voska is left-handed and an ex-commando?'

'Yes.'

'If I were him, I would've held the knife in my right hand. The wound would've looked neither left-handed nor as clean, so less like a pro's work.'

'Difficult to switch in a situation like that,' Granot said. 'It's a good thought, though.'

Once again, Darac nodded and wished he hadn't. But he took comfort in Deanna's assurance that the pain would soon subside and that there was nothing seriously amiss. 'I agree that even a bodged job would have killed the victim. But maybe this fits in with the picture we're forming of Voska. His thinking seems to go so far and no further.'

Lab assistant Lami Toto called through the loft hatch, 'The Professor wants to know if anyone would like to take a look up here?'

'I would,' Flaco called back. 'Captain?'

'I've got all I need. Go, by all means.'

'Lieutenant?'

'Me and a loft ladder?' Granot's look suggested that the combination set new standards for incompatibility. 'You're on your own.' He turned to Darac. 'Voska's motive in killing Brigitte was to stop her spilling about the porn video business, thereby leading us to him, right?'

'He should've had more faith in her. She never looked like letting anything slip.'

'At what stage do you think she knew about Voska's involvement at the hot tub?'

Darac pursed his lips as he thought back through their various meetings. 'Not until I told her about it in the Irish pub, I think.'

'Because she cried? Let's not kid ourselves, she could act her way out of anything.'

'Except her vanity, perhaps. I'd assumed she was crying for Madame Mesnel, but maybe she wasn't. Maybe she was crying for herself.'

'How do you mean?'

'Having filmed the movie with the N'Patas, I think what upset her was learning that Voska had then turned to a woman over twenty years older to... feature, albeit unwittingly, in the next episode in the series. "Old lady," Brigitte kept repeating, outraged. That Voska could have thought of *her* like that, too?'

'Yes, I don't suppose he'd told Brigitte he'd earmarked her masterpiece for fans of so-called granny porn?'

As if attracted by the term, Malraux appeared cheerily in the doorway. 'Battail's in custody already. How about that for service, chief?'

It was the grin that pushed Darac nearer the edge.

Granot took a step closer to him.

'Voska did it,' Darac said, getting into Malraux's face. 'Despite all the uniforms and your army of fucking little snitches, Voska came here—'

Granot interposed an arm. 'Hey, hey!'

As sore as he was, Darac brushed Granot's ham of a forearm aside.

Granot tried once more. 'Mate, come on. This isn't the way.'

Whether it was Granot's words or the look in his eyes that made the difference, Darac saw the need for calm. 'Voska came to this house undetected, Malraux. He killed Madame Andreani and got away undetected. As of now, you're off surveillance.'

'You can't do that to me,' Malraux said. 'Ever since I joined—'

'There's nothing I can't do, Malraux, understand? Nothing. When Bonbon gets back from Aix, give your list of informants to him. Now fuck off out of my sight.'

Malraux's body was shaking like a clenched fist and he didn't walk away immediately. When he did, it was as if he'd been fired from a catapult.

'No, wait a minute,' Darac said.

Malraux paused but didn't look back.

'You can head up the slog squad. Make sure everyone has photos. *Now* fuck off.'

Another moment to think about it. Another high-speed getaway.

'Chief...' Granot's eyes slid toward the trolley dollies waiting to take Brigitte. 'No one gets it right all the time.'

Darac was punishing himself enough for both of them.

He let the remark go.

'So back to the commissariat?'

'Yes.' Moving stiffly, Darac climbed halfway up the stairs and called to Deanna. She appeared in the hatchway, light flooding around her like a halo. 'Any news on the towel?'

'Nothing yet, and this takes precedence now. But Map's gone over to L'Ariane so he might be able to collect samples from the brothers' belongings, as well.'

'Thanks. You keeping Flaco?'

'She'll be right down. And Darac? Go carefully now.'

'Of course,' he said, reflecting that Ridge had said something similar the day before.

Granot gave him a look as he headed back down the stairs. 'Towel?'

'I wasn't going to bother you with that just yet. I took it from the club. It's got Rama N'Pata's DNA on it.' He felt nauseous, suddenly. 'Let's go and wait by the car.'

Their appearance causing a stir in a gathering crowd of onlookers, Darac turned his back on it as he leaned back against the driver's door. Granot seemed to know what he was thinking.

'So do you reckon the brothers escaped? Or has Voska got to them, as well?'

'I don't know.' Darac essayed a slow frontal bend. 'But I have a feeling it won't be long before we find out.'

Granot looked back up the path. There was no sign of Flaco. 'Come on, young lady. Not exactly "she'll be right down", is it?'

Darac looked for something positive to latch on to.

'You know, on Day One, I had Flak down as diligent, principled, strong-minded.'

'She's a strong one, alright.'

'But there's a lot more to her, isn't there?'

Granot grunted. 'God, yes. Worth two of Perand and ten of Malraux. If she gets the breaks, she'll go far.'

They fell silent once more and then Granot slapped his forehead in irritation. 'Completely forgot with all this. I've heard from Pari Mutuel Urbain. Alain Mesnel's bet on the big race never happened. Wherever the money came from, it wasn't there.'

Darac turned to him. 'Go on.'

'Alain lied to Cartin. And you know you mentioned the cost

of transatlantic flights back then? They did indeed fly back from New York but they sailed there on the liner *France*. Not in first class but not in steerage either. Cost them a bomb. As did the hotel.'

The news was all Darac needed to rekindle his favourite theory on Taylor's purchase of the Mesnel house. And it reminded him that the experts of the Musée Granet in Aix hadn't yet got back to him on an email he'd sent. Aix again, he mused. What was it about this case and the city?

Flaco joined them. 'Sorry but that was fascinating.'

'No apology necessary. You should grab every opportunity to listen to Deanna. There's no one to touch her in her field.'

'And that's why it puzzles me...' Flaco seemed wary of continuing. 'Nothing.'

'Not speaking your mind? It must be one hell of a puzzle.'

'Alright, why does someone with such incredible knowledge and experience of the human body... smoke cigarettes?'

'Because she *is* human,' Granot said. 'Like some other people.'

Darac gave Granot a look as he eased his frame into the car. 'Alright, let's go and talk to Marcel Battail. This time, he might just tell us the truth.'

42

Battail seemed smaller.

'When Brigitte didn't appear to be home the day you got out,' Granot said, for the first time using the polite *vous* form, 'didn't you wonder where she was?'

'I thought she was hacked off or playing hard to get.' Battail's whole body juddered. 'But she *was* there.' He lowered his head into his hands. 'She was there all the time.'

'When did you suspect something was wrong?'

Battail seemed not to have heard the question. 'Monsieur?'

'Uh... when she didn't come home last night. I rang the salon today and they said she hadn't been in. Not yesterday either. She never did that.' Staring straight ahead, Battail began to relive the moment that would always be with him. 'There was no noise or anything from the loft but something told me to go up there.'

Darac gave it a beat. 'I'm truly sorry about what happened to Brigitte.'

Battail said nothing. His grief was his own. He wasn't sharing it with anyone.

'Thierry's attack word?' Granot said. 'Just for the record.'

The Brigade's records being of no concern to Battail, he said nothing. Darac saw a different way in. 'The dog wouldn't have gone for Brigitte, anyway, would he? However many times you said it.'

Battail shook his head. 'No. He'd *never* have done it.' He steadied himself. 'Psycho. Psycho was the word.'

Granot nodded. 'On to the other matter. Saturday, 2nd of January. Do you know what happened at the hot tub?'

'No.' Battail's head dropped, his voice going with it. 'I wasn't there and that areshole never told me anything about it. Never saw him again, afterwards.'

Darac sensed that Battail was too exhausted to lie. 'Rewinding a few weeks, did you ever mention to Voska that there was this dotty old woman who lived across the way? A woman who played loud music in her hot tub?'

'Yeah but I didn't think he was even listening. It was weird what he wound up doing. It's young girls that turn him on, not old bags like Mesnel.'

'Why do you think Voska went on to kill Brigitte? And then tried to frame you for it?'

Battail's shoulders heaved. 'I don't know. I've never done anything to him.'

'You hindered our efforts to get to Voska before,' Darac went on, 'but things have changed, haven't they? I know it goes against the grain but you can help us.'

Granot essayed his most sympathetic look. 'For Brigitte's sake.'

'Where does Voska go? Who does he spend time with?'

'Adèle's his only family but she hates him. And he doesn't think much of her. There is one bloke: Pazzo.'

'Who is he? The source of the fake ID documents Voska deals in from time to time?'

'Dunno. Dag—' Battail couldn't bring himself to use either of Voska's names a second time. 'He keeps the people he knows apart. All I know is, Pazzo drives a truck.'

'How do you know that?'

'The RV broke down when he moved into L'Ancienne Bastide. He got a trucker he knew to give him a tow. Supposed to be a nutter. That's all I know.'

'What sort of truck?' Granot said.

'Dunno.'

Darac handed him the photos of Modibo and Rama N'Pata. 'They're brothers. Ever seen them?'

Battail shook his head.

Reasoning that the man would be able to live more easily with anger than grief, Darac decided to tell him the truth. 'They shot a video with Brigitte, too, I'm afraid.'

'You're lying.' Tears misted the hard man's eyes. 'Lying!'

Darac produced the DVD. 'I can arrange for you to see it but I wouldn't if I were you.'

'The fucking slag!' Showing such raw emotion in front of his interrogators seemed to make Battail hate himself all the more. 'I want to go.'

'You can go but not home, just yet. If you need anything from there, you'll have to go through Officer Lartigue, the crime-scene coordinator. Got that?'

'I'll stay at the tattoo parlour.'

Darac called in a uniform from the floor. 'Take this gentleman to the Babazouk.'

Darac offered his hand. Battail ignored it. As he made his exit, the desk phone rang.

'Charvet here, chief. I've got a Captain Marc Galtier on the line from Paris. He's got something on the Alicia Simon abduction for you.'

'Put him on.' A knot forming in his stomach, Darac's eyes stayed on as Granot as he hit the speaker button.

'Go ahead, Galtier.'

'Madame Simon has washed up here in Paris. She'll be staying in hospital for a day or two but apart from concussion, a stiff neck and a burgeoning head cold, she's in good shape.'

Darac exhaled deeply. 'Excellent news, Galtier.' He shared smiles of relief with Granot. 'Anything on Voska?'

'Afraid not. No sign of him. Nor any lead.'

'So what's Madame Simon saying happened?'

'After Voska jumped her, he drove her to Aix TGV station, gave her sufficient cash to buy a ticket to Paris and told her to take the next train. Which she did.'

'What's she been up to in the meantime?'

'Keeping quiet.'

'Keeping quiet barefoot?'

'I'm not with you.'

'Voska dumped her shoes and her phone at the Étang de Berre as a diversion. Meanwhile, we now learn, she was on a train to Paris.'

'She was wearing shoes when we picked her up.'

Darac recalled that Angeline kept a pair especially for driving in her car. 'The shoes that were found at the Étang were high heels. These were flats, were they?'

'It should be in the report… Yes, they were.'

'OK. Any thoughts on why she carried out Voska's instructions so assiduously after he'd let her go?'

He phoned "some people in Aix" telling them to burn her husband and their two-year-old son if she was picked up within 24 hours. It was a staged call, of course.'

'But she believed it.'

'Well she *had* been kidnapped while out shopping and what were the odds on that? Besides, Voska is one mean-looking guy. *I* wouldn't have taken the risk.'

'Neither would I,' Granot said, under his breath.

'Why the 24-hour moratorium?'

Once again, Galtier's tone supplied the quotation marks. 'Some "other people" were going to be flying Voska out of the country in that time. We don't buy that, either, obviously.'

'Quite. What did Madame Simon do when she got to Paris?'

'She thought it too risky to check into a hotel so she walked around and then slept rough.'

'She was more likely to get picked up doing that.'

'Nevertheless, she managed to evade us. For slightly *more* than 24 hours.'

Darac ran a hand through his hair. 'You're right. She did well, especially when you think how terrified she must've been. Very well, in fact. So have you managed to keep a lid on the story?'

'Media don't know a thing.'

'It won't last. Thanks for the update, Galtier.'

The call ended but Charvet rang immediately.

'Captain, I've got a young American woman on the line who insists on talking to you.'

'Put her through… Taylor, hello.'

The woman said something indecipherable.

'I'm glad you rang, Taylor, because—'

'Hello? I say to Captain Darac?'

It wasn't Taylor. The voice had a deeper timbre and her French was execrable.

Who's speaking?'

'My name is LaManda Coteel.'

She spelled the name and asked if she could continue in English.

'English? Yes, English is OK.'

Granot sat back *hors de combat*. He knew only a few words of

English and most of them related to sport.

'My friend Davis Chadburn and I were staying at the campsite over near Eze until a couple of days ago. L'Ancienne Bastide?'

'Yes?'

'To cut to the chase, we saw the wanted man. Voska? We're camping up in the Mercantour now and we've only just seen the poster.'

'Thank you. We also know he stays there – stayed – pardon, there.'

'Yes but here's the thing. We saw him hours *after* he'd driven away. He returned on foot after dark. No RV.'

'Could you...' what was English for *élaborer*..? 'Say more?'

'We were camping with some other people and needed to be alone for our special time so we went off to the woods beyond the site.'

"Special time"? If Darac understood what had been said, the January night air must have made it very special. 'Continue, please.'

'We saw him on the edge of the woods, starting to walk across the scrub... walk across the clearing.'

'Which night did it happen?'

'It was about quarter after midnight last Saturday night. Sunday morning, really.'

That was Joao Pinsa night at the club. The night Rama missed his ride with Modibo. 'You and Mister Chadburn are certain the man was Gilles Voska? It was dark, no?'

'There was a moon and we'd seen this man around the campsite. He made a real impression, believe me.' Darac heard a voice prompting her. 'Oh yes, this is important, Captain. As he walked away, we could just make out something glinting... There was something in his hand that caught the light? It was a tool of some sort.'

LaManda said what they thought the object was but Darac didn't recognise the word. 'Just a minute, Captain, we have a dictionary.'

Darac heard her mumble, 'Soap... space... spacious... Here it is: it's *bêche* in French.'

Darac's stomach turned over as he repeated the word. 'Yes, that's it.'

Darac was already picturing the scene at L'Ancienne Bastide. 'Mademoiselle Coteel, exactly where are you now?'

* * *

The car containing the American backpackers bounced to a stop outside the site office. A couple of days into his one and only camping trip, Darac had looked and smelled like a mountain goat. LaManda and her special-time boyfriend Davis stepped out of the car like nominees arriving for *Ebony* magazine's Young Couple of the Year Award.

'I am Darac. Thank you very much for coming here,' he said in the sort of Francophone tones English speakers always seemed to adore. He offered his hand.

'You're welcome.' The young man had a steam-hammer grip. 'Davis Chadburn.'

LaManda shook Darac's hand only slightly less powerfully. He indicated the woman standing next to him. 'This is Officer Monique Bayet and she will translate anything I do not understand.' Darac and Bayet had never worked well together and had the matter not been so important, he would have preferred to have busked it. 'Monique?'

'So where are you guys from?' she said in English.

'Oh cool!' LaManda shook her hand. 'Washington DC. Davis and me both.'

'I know DC very well...'

At the head of a dozen-strong entourage that included a dog-handling team, the quartet set off toward the woods that screened off most of the site from the road. By the time they reached the outermost curtain of trees, Monique had elicited answers to a wide range of background questions, not once treading on Darac's toes.

'Captain Darac,' LaManda said. 'We can guess something heavy has gone down in there. We'd rather not see it.'

Darac knew the idiomatic usage of 'heavy' but Monique insisted on translating the entire sentence before he could reply. He gave her a look and continued. 'We have looked only between the trees—'

Monique broke in, explaining that the investigation had not got properly underway and there would be nothing grisly to see. They just needed the visitors to pinpoint the exact spot they had seen Voska.

Davis nodded. 'Surely. Although it was around midnight, there was one particular tree I would recognise again.'

Monique looked astonished. 'How?'

'It had a plate fungus formation we've never seen before.'

'I see,' Monique said, readily understanding the term. 'We got photos of it the following day.' Davis displayed the images on his camera screen. 'The guy... Voska? He came out of the trees right next to it.'

Darac nodded. 'Let's go there.'

They found the tree with only minor difficulty.

Darac turned to the couple. 'Thank you. This is so far as you go. What we will do now is use our dogs to—'

'Backtrack into the woods,' Monique continued, cutting him off. 'We have articles belonging to Voska the dogs have scented. We will examine the ground carefully. The fact that the guy was carrying a spade is obviously suggestive.'

Feeling physically sick at what might lie ahead, Darac turned to Monique. 'After you have seen our American friends back to the car, take full statements and all relevant details, then tell the driver to take them wherever they want to go. Within reason.'

He shook hands with the pair again as Monique relayed the information, and then the trio began to make their way back through the woods. Darac turned to the officer leading the dog-handling team.

'Let's do it, Roulet.'

The dogs found the trail and followed it through a mixed area: clearings alternating with tangles of dense undergrowth. It was a terrain that matched Darac's mental state. He didn't want to find Rama dead and buried but from the moment he'd known what fate had had in store for Jeanne Mesnel, he had wanted to do more than catch her tormentors, he had wanted to make them suffer. Now he didn't know what he wanted.

After no more than five minutes, the dogs were excited to come on what seemed an impenetrable patch of gorse. They found a way in immediately.

Roulet turned to Darac. 'This is it, Captain.'

Darac stood them down, sent in the diggers and then rang pathologist Djibril Mpensa, who was awaiting further orders back at the site office. 'I'm afraid you're needed.'

'We'll be with you in ten minutes.'

Darac ended the call and turned to Lartigue. 'Lartou, get the tape and start cordoning off the area.'

'The men haven't found anything yet, Captain.'

'Get the tape.'

As preparations were made, Darac's mobile rang.

'The dogs are still interested, Captain. Looks like there's a second site around here.'

'Get them on it and keep me posted. Thanks, Roulet.' Darac started as a hand clasped his shoulder.

'Holding up?'

'Just about, Granot.'

'Why don't you wait in the car?'

Darac shook his head. The pair stood shoulder to shoulder as the first spade went in. Neither spoke for some moments.

'Any further thoughts about the Mesnel house purchase?'

'Some.'

'Want to share them?'

'Not just now, Granot.'

Darac could think only of what might be about to emerge from the cold, hard ground. Minutes went by. As Mpensa and his team arrived, one of the diggers gave a shout.

'Something here!'

The team leader stepped forward. 'Spades down!' At the bottom of the pit, he parted the earth with his hands. 'Captain? Polythene sheeting. Several layers thick.'

'Right.' Picturing the scene in Battail's loft, Darac steadied himself. 'Carry on.'

Smaller hand tools were produced and the process continued as an archaeological dig. It was some minutes before the whole shroud was freed from the earth.

'Cut through it one winding at a time,' the team leader said. 'Carefully, now.'

As each layer was removed, the colour of the victim's skin and clothing became more visible, the smell of death more pungent. At the final reveal, it was clear that no textbook incision wound would be found this time. Wearing a vibrant, palm-print agbada, the corpse had the look of a tropical island that had been ravaged by hurricanes.

Granot stared at the mess. 'Rama N'Pata?'

Darac exhaled deeply. 'Modibo.'

No other remains were found in the grave.

'But for the polythene routine, you wouldn't think it was the same killer, would you?' Granot gave Darac a sideways glance. 'He wasn't expecting anyone to find this body.'

'No.' Darac turned to Mpensa. 'Preliminary thoughts?' The young man gave as full an account as he could.

He believed Modibo had not been overcome immediately. Multiple knife cuts to the hands and arms indicated he'd attempted to fend off his attacker's strikes several times. A box cutter, its blade retracted, was found in his pocket.

'Unused.' Mpensa showed it to Darac. 'Probably didn't have time to get it out.'

Lab tests would confirm it but Mpensa believed that the kill strike itself was a thrust through the neck that had severed the jugular. The nature of the blow meant it might be possible to determine the type, size and condition of the knife used. He also suspected that the body had sustained a range of bone-breaking injuries post-mortem.

'The time?'

'Can't pinpoint it until we get him back to the lab, obviously, but it was no earlier than last Saturday morning and no later than Sunday afternoon.'

'That puts it before Brigitte Andreani's murder. And it was probably the catalyst for it. Thanks, Map.' He looked around. 'Granot?'

'Before you go on, Captain, I have something else for you.'

Darac turned back. 'The towel evidence findings?'

'That will come later. Step into my office a moment.'

They took a couple of paces away from the action. Mpensa looked around, checking no one was in earshot. 'What I have for you is advice. I've known you for three years and I have never seen you so overwrought. And if that doesn't mean anything, Deanna has known you for twelve and neither has she. It is our professional opinion that you need a rest. Two or three days at least.'

Darac didn't have a defence prepared. 'Uh… Could *you* take two or three days off in the middle of a case? Besides, I'm fine.'

'Poète Policier Paul Darac is a doctor as well now, is he? We say you're not fine.'

'There's a gig at the club tonight. And I'm playing there with my band on Thursday. Depending on how things go, I'm intending to do both. That's all the rest I'll need.'

'Not enough.'

Forestalling further debate, Darac's mobile rang.

Excusing himself with a shrug, he took the call. 'Paul. It's Taylor. Don't hang up.'

As if shielding her, Darac turned his back on the bloodied corpse of Modibo N'Pata and looked through the trees toward Cap Ferrat.

'I have no intention of hanging up, Taylor, but I can't talk now.' Granot's news from Pari Mutuel Urbain came back to him. 'May I ring you later?'

'Surely – on this number, please. I'll look forward to speaking to you then.'

In the time it took Darac to ring off, the dogs appeared to have scented further buried treasure. He and Granot looked on as the process began again. The big man couldn't help voicing what he was thinking.

'Butchered, rolled up, chucked into a hole. What an end to a life.'

The tension built with every strike of the spade but then the dogs began to lose interest and nothing was found. Twenty minutes later, a second false alarm shredded Darac's nerves still further. Throwing out a wider net, he called Officer Serge Paulin who was coordinating the squad detailed to interview anyone within a six-kilometre radius of the campsite. Another blank. What had become of Rama N'Pata?

'We're not doing any good here, chief. Let's leave the diggers to it.'

The no-news theme continued as Darac and Granot arrived back at the commissariat. There was nothing from Aix on the DVD time stamp or from the Musée Granet. The men were drinking cardboard espresso when a burly uniform wearing a sheepish expression appeared at the office door.

'Captain? Compliments of Monsieur Frènes, sir, but as acting commissaire your presence is required in the press-conference suite. I am to escort you.'

'The media has finally realised we've been finessing them,' Granot said. 'Good luck.'

Darac let out a long breath and got to his feet. 'How *did* Agnès keep this up?' A full hour later, he returned to find Bonbon waiting for him in his office.

'The time stamp, chief. It's not what we'd been hoping for.'

'Shit... Coffee?'

'Never touch either.'

At the machine, Darac opted, *faute de mieux*, for an *Amerikano*. 'They couldn't straighten out the figures, then?'

'They did but they came out as 23 December at 2.41 in the afternoon. Ten days before the murder.'

'Sod it.'

'Granot's updated me on everything here. Rough.'

'We've had better times. Let's see those few frames, Bonbon.'

They watched what was effectively just a still of Jeanne Mesnel standing next to her hot tub. It affected Darac deeply, nevertheless.

'At the briefing, you said Voska asked Madame Mesnel if he could come back later to shoot a test sequence? That's what this DVD is, isn't it? The beginning of it.'

'Almost certainly. But the evidence against Voska is building all the time. If we can catch the bastard, he's going down a hundred different ways.'

'We've got DNA from Modibo and Rama N'Pata to be matched up now, haven't we?'

'The lab's on it.' Tasting the *Amerikano*, Darac binned it immediately.

'So how did the press conference go?'

'Frènes did most of the talking so we came out of it brilliantly. He's still there now, feeding off-the-record scraps to the newshounds.'

'Arsehole.' Bonbon got to his feet. 'One last thing. This surveillance and stealth role you want me to take on. I can't stand Malraux but I think he deserves another chance. I'm not certain

I'd have fared any better in preventing Brigitte's murder. And I doubt if we would've got any closer to reeling in Voska if I'd been the one casting the line.'

Darac could see where Bonbon was going. 'You don't know that.'

'With the sole exception of Agnès, we all make mistakes, chief.'

Darac knew he'd been hard on Malraux. 'I know, I know. It wasn't that he'd stuffed up. It was that he didn't give a shit.' Darac was starting to feel riled up all over again. 'A woman he'd had sex with a couple of days before was lying there like a slaughtered animal and all he could do was crow about bringing Battail in.'

'He's a shithead. But that doesn't make him—'

'Alright. Give him back his contacts list. I'll look the other way if you make a copy of it, first.'

Bonbon chuckled as he took his leave. 'Already have.'

Darac went to sit behind his desk and it was only then he spotted the answer phone light was blinking. He played back the message. The caller was a Madame Lecamier of the Musée Granet in Aix. She reported that she and her team had studied the image he'd emailed and all had endorsed the comments he'd made about it.

'Well, well…'

With the rider that a definitive judgement would have to be deferred until the object itself could be examined, she signed off assuring him of the museum's assistance at all times. Darac needed no further assistance: it was the principle he was trying to establish and now that he had, he could test the next link in the chain. He called the Mairie and spoke to Granot's contact in the estates department, Monsieur Dubroqua. As city officials tended to respond, 'No, that's quite impossible!' to any direct request, Darac opened by stressing the difficulty of the challenge he was setting. Dubroqua wouldn't be able to help with such a ludicrously taxing query, would he?

'Of course I can find out for you, Captain. No problem at all.'

Thanking him profusely, Darac rang off and finally called Taylor. As before, he soon found himself on the back foot.

'Paul, I wanted to say that I'm sorry we got – *I* got – kind of derailed when we last met. Not for the first time and probably not the last, I got things wrong. I know you're just doing your job. My only excuse is I'm feeling very vulnerable at the moment.'

At the moment? He thought it something of a miracle that anyone with Taylor's past managed to fare as well as she did. On the surface, at least. 'I'm sorry to hear that.'

'But anyway, I was wondering if you were free to come over to Villa Rose soon. I have a treat for you. At least I hope you'll think it's a treat. I'm sure you will, actually.'

Offering treats? So much for believing he'd got their relationship on to a proper footing. Still, the request played nicely into his hands. 'Mademoiselle—'

'Taylor.'

'Taylor, would you mind telling me what you have in mind?'

'That would spoil the surprise.'

'Alright. How about tomorrow morning?'

'Oh, I hadn't expected you to be available quite so soon. I'm afraid tomorrow morning is our weekly progress meeting.'

"Our" presumably included Philippe de Lambert.

'I'm afraid of progress meetings also. Although I imagine Monsieur de Lambert creates a cordial atmosphere for such things?'

'Yes, he does, but this one promises to be stormy.'

'Oh?'

'Just an internal thing. I'll be free from two o'clock.'

'I'll give you a ring beforehand.'

Taylor's call had set Darac's options for the following morning. Plan A was to respond to anything that came up relating to Voska; Plan B involved a trip to Villa Rose. While Taylor and the management team were busy, Darac intended to break the law.

43

Ensconced in a pair of shabby rooms in the Belsunce quarter of Marseille, Gilles Voska was preparing dinner when he heard his own name emanating from the TV behind him. He turned and there, for the first time, he saw the face of the officer charged with the responsibility of catching him. A caption put a name to him and the man in overall charge of the investigation. Voska turned off the stove.

As Public Prosecutor Frènes outlined the case, Voska's eyes stayed on the officer. He saw immediately that the oily and voluble Monsieur Frènes didn't impress Captain Paul Darac. But Voska was reasonably satisfied with Frènes's account of the abduction of Madame Alicia Simon that followed. As he knew she would, she had done exactly as she had been instructed.

A photo of Modibo N'Pata flashed up on the screen. The expected missing caption failing to materialise, Voska began to feel uneasy. Footage of the burial site rolled. They had found his body. Voska's eyes bulged. 'How?' he shouted.

And then, Brigitte Andreani looked back at him. The programme's anchor turned to Frènes. 'Monsieur, how was the second victim killed?'

The prosecutor's head filled the screen.

'The dog, arsehole! Tell them it was the dog!'

'It was a stabbing,' Frènes said. 'A stabbing in which the perpetrator made a botched attempt to disguise the knife wound. The victim's dog was found nearby.'

'Botched?' Voska spat out the word. 'Where's the skinny drummer boy? Where is he? He was the one you were supposed to find!' In an adjoining room, someone banged on the wall. Voska's eyes bored into the screen. 'Show *him*!'

As the broadcast ended, Voska knew he was ahead in one battle only. Frènes had stated the need to locate 'Voska's associate, the lorry driver, Pazzo'. But it would be difficult, he'd said, because the police had no photofit nor any detailed information.

It wasn't surprising: Pazzo didn't exist. Deriving, as did many of Voska's tactics, from an old Legion ploy, Pazzo was a fiction designed to divert and delay the enemy.

When Darac finally spoke, it was in answer to: 'How would you describe Voska?'

'Dangerous and resourceful.'

'Yes I am,' Voska said, feeling an even greater connection to the officer. A moment's thought told him he had no alternative but to reprise his heroic efforts of the past weekend. Reprise them but more so. He had to stop the man at the centre of the investigation. The real man, not the mouthpiece. He had to stop Captain Paul Darac.

That, he swore there and then, he would not botch.

44

On Jean Jaurès, tail lights streaming like red vapour trails led Darac back to the car park. His eyes felt heavy. His head felt heavy. His heart felt heavy. Maybe Map and the others were right. Maybe he was overdoing it.

The chill early evening air brought him round a little as he crossed the boulevard and headed into the Babazouk. In the teeming Rue Pairolière, his mobile rang.

'Captain Darac? This is Dubroqua from city maintenance.'

Darac stood still. 'Listen, it was an unfair challenge I set, monsieur. I'm sure you haven't been able to rise to it.'

'On the contrary.'

'You still have Monsieur Mesnel's job sheets from fifty years ago?'

'All of them, yes. I've collated them into a dossier.'

Darac gave an involuntary laugh. Even if the outcome proved inconclusive, he knew this could have happened only in France.

'May I come and examine it?'

'It's too late for that today but I could have Cécile fax it to you, tomorrow?'

'I don't suppose she would have time to look for one docket in particular?'

'Cécile is my secretary, not my wife, Captain. She will look.'

Darac gave the details. 'Monsieur, I am indebted to you both.'

★ ★ ★

As Darac rang off, encouragement gave way to unease. Out of nowhere, he had the strongest impression that someone was watching him. He walked on, waiting until he'd covered ten metres or so before jetting a glance behind him. No one dodged into a doorway or held up a newspaper. A little further along, he repeated the manoeuvre. Still no one. Yet he could have sworn... No, he was overwrought. And tired. Tonight's gig would restore him.

Reaching the last of the kinks in Ruelle Fente, he took out his keys and, as automatically as a Pavlov dog, closed his eyes and yawned. The keys weren't needed. Not for the first time, someone had left unlocked the iron gate that gave into Place Saint-Sépulcre. Checking no stray tourists were still inside – the Place's sundial-topped well-head had found its way into a couple of guidebooks – he returned to the gate. As he locked it, he thought he saw something run back down the ruelle. 'Hey!'

Quickly unlocking the gate, he ran back the way he'd come. At each new turn in the alley, Darac expected to catch a glimpse of a fleeing back. It wasn't until the junction with Rue Neuve that he finally did see someone. 'Suzanne. I...' Breathing hard, he looked around. 'Did you see anybody... come running out of the ruelle just now?'

'Only you.' She took his hand. 'You alright?'

'I'm not sure. According to... one medical opinion I've had today, I'm overtired.'

'Want a second opinion?'

'You're going to give it whether I want it or not.'

'I am.' She looked into his eyes. 'Keeping busy can help someone who's going through a bereavement or a break-up. But overdoing it can cause a complete crash.'

She glanced at her watch. It was only then that Darac realised she was taking his pulse. 'Have you been downing double espressos all afternoon?'

'Me?'

'You're getting out of shape. And have you had your blood pressure checked lately?'

They walked back to the Place, locking the gate behind them. Before they separated, Darac promised to go on a health jag 'once the case is over'. Suzanne said the last part in unison with him; another woman who knew him only too well.

It was a cool evening and it was about to get cooler. Darac didn't much care for the cerebral approach of the Sven Nordin trio but maybe tonight was the perfect time to see them. First, he had to pass under the poster. For a moment, it held him like a force field.

Ridge's voice rumbled through the open lobby door. 'That you, Garfield?'

'Have you seen TV or *Nice-Matin* yet, Ridge?'

'Haven't had time.' He lowered his voice. 'Those Swedish meatballs have had me running round like a blue-assed fly. I'm thinking of changing my name to Rochester.'

'Come outside a second.'

He joined him. 'Any news on Sticks?'

'No and when there is, it won't be good.'

'How come?'

'I'm going to break a ground rule. I'm going to tell you something about the case I'm working on.' He kept quiet as a young couple bounced past them and continued into the club. 'Madame Mesnel, the lady who bequeathed you her LP collection?'

Ridge's brow took on an extra couple of furrows. 'Yes?'

Darac reached up and touched the poster. 'That's her.'

Ridge didn't reply immediately. 'Are you sure?'

'Yes. It's her and it was her husband who took the original photo back in the early sixties.'

'Olga, the woman I bought the place off in '84? She was the one who came up with *Blown Away by the Brass Section*, you know. She never knew anything about where the photo came from or anything.'

'I told you Madame Jeanne Mesnel had drowned accidentally.' Darac paused at the sound of light, quick footfalls from above. They belonged to Jacky, a local artist and one of the club regulars. The three of them shook hands.

'We're in the middle of something, man,' Ridge said.

'Looks serious. The quintet want more money?'

'Pas is on the door.'

'OK.' Jacky continued down the steps. 'Three's a crowd, I guess. For this place, especially.'

They were alone again.

'Ridge, Jeanne Mesnel did not die accidentally. We believe she was raped in her hot tub while a psycho named Gilles Voska filmed it. As a result, she suffered a heart attack and drowned. Raped to death, in effect.'

Ridge's mouth moved but no words came out. He staggered slightly. Darac put his arm around his shoulders, trying to steady him.

'I... I'm alright.'

'It gets worse, Ridge. It could be that Rama and/or his brother Modibo were responsible for the rape itself. I saw them performing in a video with a woman who was later murdered, we suspect, by the same Gilles Voska. Then this morning, we found Modibo's body, also we suspect, murdered by Voska. We're still looking for Rama.'

Ridge shouldered his support aside and staggered past him up the steps. Darac followed him onto the street. They stood together for some time before words came.

'How do you know what they did to Jeanne… Jeanne Mesnel?'

'I can't go into details but we know Voska had been setting it up for some time.'

'No, no. Rama is as sweet as sugar and he has everything going for him. I can't believe he would be mixed up in shit like that.'

'I don't know what the story is but I'm sure Voska had them in some sort of bind.'

A car drew up at the kerb. The driver's door opened.

Darac looked up. It was Frankie.

'Listen, man.' Ridge's words emerged as if quarried from a pit of sorrow. 'It can't be.'

Reading Frankie's expression sent a chill down Darac's spine. 'Just a second, Ridge.'

'Paul,' she said, softly. 'It's Rama N'Pata. He's been found.'

45

Witnessing the diggers' skein-by-skein exhumation of Modibo's corpse had been slow torture for Darac. Rama revealed all at once was another thing again. 'Extreme trauma' was written on the form but it didn't convey the scale of the damage. 'Smashed' said it better. Swollen monstrously, his face looked like a morphed caricature, a blue-black mass stained in strangely gorgeous whorls of wine-red.

Darac wondered what Rama would have made of the ventilator's rhythm: a *beep* on the one; a *phhht* on the three. At the measured tempo of 'Lil' Darlin'', it was as basic a four-beat as could be imagined.

Dr Sibile was a short, round man, long on smiles and helpfulness. 'He was lucky.'

'And will he stay that way, Doctor?' Darac said.

'Too early to say. Excepting the possibility of aneurysms… Sorry. Excepting dangerous rupture-prone arterial bulges, the multiple corporeal fractures pose no great threat. The punctured lung, spleen damage and so on, should not prove an insuperable problem. The critical issue is the fracture to the skull and associated injuries to the brain.'

Frankie turned to him. 'And that's why the patient is in a coma?'

'Yes. A coma can act as a healing state, a sort of time-out, if you will. But it is essential that we monitor as many factors as possible during it. We can't allow large subdural haematomas to develop, for example.' He made a clicking sound with his tongue. 'We don't want the brain to bleed a lot is what I mean.'

'I see.' Frankie had understood him perfectly the first time. 'Prior to the eyewitness coming forward, you had already deduced that the victim had been hit by a vehicle that was bigger than a car?'

Sibile held up his hands, palms facing, then made a fist with one of them. 'When a car hits a pedestrian frontally, there is typically a forward jack-knifing of the body.' He ran his fist into his palm, demonstrating the effect. 'Our patient's injuries are not consistent with that.' He unclenched his fist. 'This is the vehicle now, high and flat-fronted. This, the pedestrian as before.' He clapped one palm against the other. 'That's the difference. It was as if our patient ran into a wall, not fell over a fence, if you will.'

'Thank you.'

Darac had been taking in the array of equipment wired, piped or clamped to Rama's broken body. Or to the body of Barthelmy Sokora, according to the tag on his cot. It was as good a name as any.

'How long might he be in the coma, Doctor?'

'A day, a year, indefinitely. We cannot say.'

'If he does regain consciousness, is it possible he could make a complete recovery?'

Sibile smiled. 'Let's take it one step at a time.'

Noises off indicated that one of those steps was about to be taken.

'Time to leave now, please. My colleague Dr Tan and I are going to set up a line so we can keep an eye on the pressure in his skull.'

'You'll let us know if… of any major change, Doctor?'

Without thinking, Darac extended his hand but Sibile took it and shook Frankie's, also. 'I needed to scrub, anyway. Yes, we will, of course.'

Darac gave Rama a final look.

Beep… phhht. Beep… phhht. Beep… phhht.

'Once again, apologies to you both for not identifying him sooner but with all the oedema and without a *carte d'identité…* And we had, let's say, other priorities.'

'Of course. We'll list Rama N'Pata as having been killed in an RTA but we'll leave his in situ ID as Sokora. It might prove safer for everyone. We'll be in touch.'

Once outside, Darac turned to the burly uniform guarding the room. 'Officer…?'

'Marque, sir.'

'You know what Gilles Voska looks like, Officer Marque?'

'Yes sir.'

'He's already tried to kill the patient once. In fact, he thinks he has killed him, probably. But just in case he has second thoughts, turns up here and sees through the name switch, be ready, OK? You won't be flying solo. I'll arrange appropriate back-up as soon as I get to the lobby.'

Darac was expecting to receive a call, also. Bonbon had been dispatched to interview the van driver Alain Gasquet, who had witnessed the hit and run that had all but killed Rama N'Pata.

Darac said nothing further as he and Frankie made their way out of the intensive-care suite. She threaded her arm through his.

'You know, people are worried about you. And with good reason.'

'I'll be fine.'

'Not if you keep breaking Agnès's number-one rule, you

won't.'

'*Engage with facts; keep your distance from people?* I'm doing that.'

'Of course you are.'

Darac was suddenly aware that, in Frankie, he'd found the eye of the storm. 'I'm glad you're here.'

'I was in with the dispatchers when the call came in. I knew where you would be.'

They walked in silence for a moment. And then without giving it proper thought, Darac said, 'We probably shouldn't be walking like this. I could get very used to it.'

A half-reproving look; a nervous little laugh; the remark seemed to unsettle Frankie. 'Don't be silly.' For a moment, it seemed she might withdraw her arm but she kept it where it was. 'What do you think happened, Paul?'

He was back out in the storm. 'We know some things.' They got into the lift and pressed the button for the ground floor. 'Modibo was meant to pick up Rama outside the club. They'd obviously arranged to go up to the campsite together but Modibo doesn't show and drives out there by himself. Voska kills Modibo in the subsequent fight...'

A couple of nurses joined them, stilling the conversation until they got out on the ground floor and headed for the lobby.

'Following the fight, Voska buries the body. Then, perhaps driving Modibo's car back to L'Ariane, he goes up to the apartment expecting to find Rama. No answer. He shoulders the door, takes all the DVDs, or so he believes, and makes his way back to L'Ancienne Bastide. There, he picks up the RV he left down the road from the site. Now he spots Rama who's been looking high and low for Modibo. Voska floors the pedal and we know what happened next.'

'Bit of a coincidence, running into him like that.' Frankie rolled her eyes. 'Sorry. Isn't it more likely that Voska called Rama? To lure him to the scene.'

'Lured him to the roadside? Why not the woods where he

could have made absolutely certain of killing him?'

Frankie drew down the corners of her mouth. 'And then hidden the body, true. The boy's phone has gone over to Forensics, by the way. The SIM card might still be in one piece. And Télécom might be able to come up with a trace on the call.'

'Whether Voska rang Rama or not, once he'd hit him, he must have thought he'd killed him. Nevertheless, I think he would have gone back to make sure but for Monsieur Gasquet following in his van.'

Reaching the lobby, Darac made the call to strengthen the guard detail on Rama's room. Then he played a message Bonbon had left summarising his interview with Gasquet. On seeing Rama, Voska had speeded up and 'ploughed straight through the guy', he reported. And he would testify to it. 'Especially if there was a reward.'

Darac next rang Frènes and explained the need to go with the fiction that Rama N'Pata had died of injuries sustained in a hit and run perpetrated by Voska. For once, Frènes agreed without argument.

'Now let's get out of here, Frankie. Hospitals... I dislike them, don't you?'

'Only the bad ones.'

Darac gave her a look. Did she always have to be so sensible? Rama stayed with him every step of the way to Frankie's car. Had they started monitoring the pressure in his skull yet? How did they do that? Drilling a hole and inserting some instrument through it? No, 'introducing' was the word they always used, wasn't it? Harmless-sounding. They did brilliant work, these people. But Jesus.

'Shall I drop you back at the Blue Devil?'

Bonbon had interviewed Gasquet. There was really nothing Darac could do until the morning. And he had unfinished business at the club.

'I need jazz. And people. And below-average food at above-average prices.'

Frankie's contralto chuckle was an infectious sound. For once, Darac didn't catch it: Armstrong's '(What Did I Do to Be So) Black and Blue?' had started up in his head. He needed to go to a different thought.

'Uh… The pianist Sven Nordin and his trio are at the club this evening.'

As Frankie turned into Boulevard Carabacel, a drift of night-blooming girls edged off the kerb in front of her. 'Sven Nordin?' she said, without missing a beat. A couple of dabs on the horn sent the girls fluttering back to safety. 'Never heard of him. Good?'

'Bit cerebral for my taste but you might go for it. I don't suppose you…' He turned to her. 'And Christophe, naturally.'

'He's out of town and I'm on duty, anyway.'

'Yes, of course.'

They hit slow traffic along Boulevard Risso. Drawn by the yellowish glow from its windows, Darac looked across at his favourite lunch spot, Café Avanti. The evening crowd consisted of six diners. All were sitting apart, all were seemingly lost in their own thoughts. Nighthawks Niçoises.

The traffic cleared, they were off and running again.

'I know what I was going to ask you, Paul. Any closer to understanding what the Walters-Halberg woman was up to in buying the house?'

'Thanks partly to a Monsieur Dubroqua from the Mairie, I think I could be, yes.'

She turned to him. 'Really?'

'Hey, eyes on the road! You've nearly totalled one lot of pedestrians tonight already.'

Frankie's full mouth widened into a smile. 'Women drivers.' She waited for a tram to clear the junction before peeling off into Avenue des Diables Bleus. 'But you *are* closer?'

'With everyone drowning in paper, I need a little more before I throw it open, though.'

'Well, you know where I live if you think I can help.'

'You always help.'

They pulled up outside the club.

'Why do people say, "Here we are," whenever they arrive somewhere? I nearly did it myself, then.'

Darac smiled. 'You've got me.' He gave her knee a parting pat. 'Well... See you, Frankie.' He remained seated.

'Take care.'

Darac opened the passenger door, hesitated, then got out and walked away. After a couple of paces, he turned on his heel and walked back. Frankie rolled her window.

'You know that Rama should have been playing with us the day after tomorrow?'

'Yes?'

'A kid we were all knocked out by is mixed up in something terrible and now he's half-dead. His brother is about as dead as it's possible for a person to be. Brigitte Andreani, a woman I persuaded to return home, wound up being butchered there a few hours later. Jeanne Mesnel... Well, I don't need to say any more about her, do I? So, OK, you saw I wasn't faring all that well earlier but what am I doing now? I'm enjoying myself. Putting it behind me. Moving on.'

'To retrieve that essential distance.' She smiled. 'I'm relieved. See you tomorrow.'

As her window whirred back up, Darac took the steps down into the club, reflecting he'd made a good fist of reassuring Frankie. But he knew it hadn't fooled her.

As a number faded out and the crowd began to applaud, Darac joined Ridge, Didier, Luc and Charlie. Disbelief hung over the table like mountain fog.

'Having to view his body,' Charlie said, her heavily mascaraed eyelashes looking blacker than ever. 'Terrible for you.'

'I've had happier moments.' Darac didn't correct the assumption that Rama was dead. It was only half a lie.

With no words of introduction, Sven Nordin's group set out on another icily precise original. At the end of it, Darac turned to Ridge. 'Before I left for the hospital, you were going to tell me something?'

'Was I? I can't remember what it was, now.'

'It seemed important.'

A voice as subtle as a market trader's thudded between them. 'Fusion food, everyone.'

A platter of pork, prunes and couscous was set down before them. 'Fused-together food, anyway.' Roger, the Blue Devil's long-serving chef, was already on his way back to the kitchen. 'Eat and be happy.'

'Guys, shall we tie one on after the gig?' Didier helped himself to a meagre portion. 'Although I don't suppose Sticks would have approved.'

'No, I guess not,' Ridge said, showing even less interest in the food. 'But we should.'

Whatever the mood, Charlie was always up for a party. 'Of course we should. Darac?'

'Not tonight.'

He left immediately after the final number. Just missing a city-bound tram, he set off down République feeling as if he were wading through deep water. What a day. What a week. What a world.

A stuffed wild boar stood in the window of a hunting store halfway down the avenue. Darac had reached it when, once again, he had the impression he was being followed. He turned. No one stopped suddenly or pulled any other suspicious moves. It was his imagination. Wild boar, guns, stalking; it was the power of suggestion working on an overwrought mind. Wasn't it?

Knees high, arms pumping, Darac launched himself down the avenue. After twenty metres or so, he slammed on the brakes, sling-shotting around a lamppost with a hooked arm. Chest heaving, he looked back down the avenue. No one was behaving suspiciously.

No one, he realised, except himself. It was the majority view: a young couple avoided eye contact; a black kid gave him a wide berth. 'It's alright,' he called out, 'I was just running.' Pulling up his collar against the breeze, he continued at a walk.

In his head, he was still running.

46

After a night of polythene-shrouded dreams, Darac needed the beat, life and energy of jazz more than ever. But on this of all mornings, he knew his detox wouldn't work as usual. Besides, there was someone who needed it more.

'Any change, Dr Sibile?'

'Pressure is down in the skull. The... let's just say other signs are favourable. I'm hopeful. What have you got there?'

'It's a portable CD player and some discs. I think the patient is more likely to respond to them than the sound of those machines.'

'It's very thoughtful but there's no real evidence—'

'Rama is a brilliant musician. Each of these discs features a drummer named Elvin Jones. He's the boy's hero. If he can't bring him back to life, nobody can.'

Dr Sibile chewed his lip while he thought about it. 'There's nothing raucous here?' He ran an eye over a couple of the discs. 'Headphones are out of the question and I have to think of my staff, also.'

'I've selected them carefully.' He picked one out at random. 'This, for instance.'

Dr Sibile examined the jewel case as if it were written in a foreign language. '*Ballads... The John Coltrane Quartet*. I see.'

'Elvin Jones is the drummer. I think you'll like it.'

'I don't think so.'

But Sibile agreed to it and Darac set off to breakfast with a slightly lighter heart. After Bar Cantron, Darac walked to the Théâtre Esplanade car park, still feeling the need to jet occasional glances behind him. Crossing Boulevard Jean Jaurès, he called Granot for an update. It ended with the usual Plan-A question: 'Any word on Voska?'

Cue Plan B. With Sonny Rollins's 'G-Man' acting like an aural amphetamine, Darac set off for Cap Ferrat. On a normal day, he would have enjoyed the drive. Rounding Mont Boron, the sun blazing over the hip of the Grande Corniche opened up the Rade de Villefranche like a peacock displaying its tail feathers. But his head was elsewhere and the entire journey to the Villa Rose passed as if on auto-pilot.

How to play it? He hadn't bothered applying for a search warrant – he knew Frènes would never have granted it however the case for it was made. Risk humiliating the celebrated Philippe de Lambert? That really was an impossibility.

From his previous visit, he knew how to take the secret route to Lambert's terrace. Once there, there would be no problem with burglar alarms or CCTV, which was just as well because Darac intended to pick the study's lock. If he were challenged en route, he'd play the card of his open invitation from Taylor. 'Sorry, isn't this the way to her rooms? She's in a meeting all morning? I must have got my wires crossed.'

An unfamiliar face on the desk suiting Darac's low-profile strategy, he bought a ticket and filed into the atrium with the rest of the early morning visitors. His eyes glued on the conference room door, he stepped smartly up the stairs to the first floor. Here, the various items of an eighteenth-century boudoir fascinated him until the coast was sufficiently clear to slip unseen into the cleaners' room.

He encountered no one in the service corridor and his arrival on Lambert's terrace was witnessed only by its stone statuary. So far, so good. But then, a coach reversing into a parking space off the lane below backfired and a plume of black smoke rose into the air. As it dispersed around the gods and emperors, Darac hurried to the porch, entered the lobby and listened.

Hearing the measured clack of a woman's heels descending the stairs, he considered retreating. But the woman may have been heading to the terrace, perhaps to remonstrate with the coach driver. The clacks grew louder. Darac inserted a pair of picks into the study-door lock and set to work. They failed to engage. He cast a glance at the landing. A shadow appeared on the wall. A couple more steps and he would be face to face with the woman herself. The lock clicked. He opened the door and, closing it quickly behind him, peered through the keyhole. On the staircase, Maggie de Lambert passed by, lost in thought.

Darac wasted no time in taking a smaller pair of picks to the mystery cabinet's outer doors. The inner box was the next obstacle. Reaching into its top corners, he released the catches and removed it in one quick action. A further set of doors was revealed. The picks were inserted again. The locks gave. Feeling a frisson of transgressive pleasure, Darac raised both hands and slowly swung the doors open.

There it was in all its sinuous beauty. He had seen *The Woman at Asilah* at the Musée Matisse and now here was the same work again. The two paintings looked identical but Darac understood there was an important difference. Only Philippe de Lambert's version had been painted by Henri Matisse; the Musée's *Woman* was an original Alain Mesnel. Savouring the moment, Darac lifted it out and looked closely at the surface of the paint. Alain's copy had looked just as vibrant to him. More importantly, it must have looked just as vibrant to the experts at the Musée. He couldn't resist a smile. In nearly fifty years, no one had spotted it was a fake.

Darac's mobile groaned in his pocket. It wasn't the moment to talk but he checked the caller's number. It was Granot. He'd call him later.

Darac turned the work over and examined its back. Alain had made a neat job of reframing the original but there was a narrow indentation, about twenty centimetres long, between the upper stretcher bar and the frame. Alain was human after all.

The phone vibrated once more. Granot had sent him a text, an almost unprecedented occurrence. Darac read it.

News. Call me soonest.

Darac's heart jumped. News of Rama? Voska? After so many years, there seemed no harm in leaving the stolen Matisse in situ for a little longer. Darac returned it and left the room exactly as he'd found it. Once outside, he swiped his mobile.

'Granot?'

'Deanna Bianchi has come back with the DNA analysis of the towel.'

'There's a match with the semen sample?'

'Yes, chief. There is.'

47

The ghost of Jeanne Mesnel followed Darac to the door and stayed with him as he banged hard on it. He didn't have to wait long.

'What are you doing here at this hour? I've only just finished breakfast.'

Darac looked Ridge in the eyes, saying nothing. As if it were suddenly too heavy to bear, the big man lowered his head and stood aside. Darac walked past him and saying nothing, headed for their usual table. On the bandstand in front of them, Marco's drums were already set up for the quintet's gig the following day – the kit that Rama N'Pata had been due to play.

'So you know.'

'Tell me what happened, Ridge.'

'I never meant for anything to happen.'

'Tell me what happened!'

Holding on to the table edge, Ridge avoided Darac's eyes as he started to speak. 'Yes. Well... Jeanne and I got to know each other years ago.' It was a husk talking. 'Just after I took over the club. '84. Maybe '85. We had a thing going for a while but it didn't work out. After that, she never came here again. Then just a few weeks ago, she writes to me out of the blue. Wants to see me about something. Could I go over? I went.'

As if disavowing memories of the day, a tremor was shaking Ridge's head slightly. 'It was good seeing her again. She always had life. And beauty. It was rare. And she still had it. She called because she wanted to tell me about her will and leaving me her jazz library.'

'Get to the hot tub.'

The tremor intensified. 'It was a last waltz kind of thing, I guess. Sweet, really... But immediately afterwards, Jeanne started to breathe heavily and then she grabbed her left shoulder. I knew what was happening but I panicked, not knowing what to do for the best. She was thinking for both of us. "Get an ambulance," she said. I got out of the tub and hurried back to the house. I couldn't get a signal on my cell phone so I looked for her landline. I couldn't see it in the kitchen or the hall. But then I found the docking station in the living room. The handset wasn't in it.'

'Go on.'

'I went upstairs to the bedrooms. I found it later. It was on a shelf by her bedside but at the time, I didn't see it. So I went back down to the living room, picked up my cell phone and ran back outside to see if I could get a signal there. But with every step I got nearer to the hot tub, I could see I was too late. Jeanne... had slipped under the water. I tried reviving her but it was no use. She was dead. I'd left her alone for... a minute? Two at the outside. But I shouldn't have. I should have stayed with her. I should have tried giving her CPR right away.'

'So you're saying that sex was consensual and that she died afterwards?'

Ridge gave Darac a look that went right through him. 'You're questioning whether I raped her? You think me capable of that?'

Darac brought his hand hard down on the table. 'I think you capable of acting as if you'd never heard of Jeanne Mesnel. I think you capable of covering up the fact that you were ever at the scene. And of leaving her body in the water believing it would wash away your semen. But it didn't, Ridge. The body ballooned and festered and turned into dog food but it *did* leave a trace of you.'

Clasping his hand to his mouth, Ridge got up and crashed across to the bar. He dropped the first whisky glass he picked up. He filled the second and downed it in one.

After he had stopped shaking, he held up the bottle to Darac.

'No.'

Ridge poured another.

'Why, Ridge? Why didn't you report what had happened? Why didn't you tell *me* about it, for Christ's sake!?'

'Why?' Ridge walked slowly back to the table. 'Because... I'd already been arrested for rape. Back in '82 when I was living in Paris. A white woman was the victim. I was innocent but I spent four days having my ass kicked by cops who didn't believe me. It was only when the rapist struck again while I was still in custody that they let me go. I didn't think I'd get that lucky twice.'

'You can't believe anything like that would have happened this time? We've been friends for fourteen years. Or I thought we were.'

'Yes. We've been friends for fourteen years.' Ridge's eyes were heavy with the suffering of ages. 'But I have been a black man for seventy.'

Darac winced.

'Besides, what could you do, Garfield? Huh? What can any man do against the system?'

'I... wouldn't have been allowed to question you. That much is true.'

Nothing was said for some moments.

'When you told me about how that low-life Voska was exploiting Rama and his brother, I knew he'd never shot the...' Ridge took a breath. '...video with Jeanne you mentioned. That was what I was going to tell you when your friend arrived in her car.'

Darac didn't need Ridge's confirmation that Voska's rape

video, the focus of so much police activity, had never actually happened. The realisation Jeanne had not suffered that fate had been the first thing to hit Darac during Granot's call. 'I gave you the opportunity to tell me that again when I came back to the club, Ridge. I asked you outright.'

'But by then you'd found Rama's body. I couldn't see the point.' Ridge's eyes locked on Darac's. 'I never intended to harm anyone. And I'll have to live with what happened to Jeanne for the rest of my life. But I've got to know, understand? I've got to know whether what I did after made the other deaths happen. I've got to know!'

Ridge put his hands over his head and wept. It was all Darac could do not to comfort him. He waited for the juddering to cease before going on. 'I think the brothers had been on a collision course with Voska from the first moment he got them into his clutches. Jeanne's death in the hot tub made that collision happen sooner, that's all.'

'How?'

'Once Battail had whetted Voska's appetite with stories of his elderly neighbour and her bathing habits, he formed a plan to shoot a video that would put his most recent work to shame. The rape of an old lady. Only a small percentage of rapes are reported but as Voska couldn't take the chance that his victim wouldn't be part of that silent majority, I imagine he planned to leave immediately afterwards, properly prepared. But then something happened. Didn't it?'

Ridge lowered his eyes.

'Voska hears that his victim-to-be has drowned in her hot tub just days after he reconnoitred the scene in person. Police are called. Given his connection to Battail and the nature of his record, he has to get out quickly.' He kept his voice on an even keel as he got to the crux of Ridge's question. 'But first, there was the problem of what to do about the three actors he'd used in the earlier video: Rama, Modibo and Brigitte Andreani. Could they be trusted to keep quiet if questioned? He was suspected of murder now – the stakes were higher. It seems unlikely that he decided to ensure their silence by killing them: it was a strategy likely to bring even more heat from us. More probable is that Modibo forced Voska's hand by intercepting him at the campsite before he skipped. Having murdered Modibo in the fight, Voska then *had* to kill Rama, who most certainly would have come forward at that point, and also Brigitte, who just might have.'

Ridge nodded, took a moment to gather himself, then laid a hand on Darac's shoulder. 'Thanks, man.'

'Ridge, in trying to avoid trouble, you've created a lot more for yourself. The autopsy on Madame Mesnel concluded she'd been raped.' He looked Ridge in the eyes. 'I'm going to have to bring you in.'

'I know.'

'As I said, I won't be allowed to question you. I suspect it will be a man named Jules Frènes, the public prosecutor.

At first, he'll listen quietly to your story. If there's a lie anywhere, or an inconsistency, he'll find it and tie you in knots with it later. Whatever is said, pressure will still be put on you to confess to rape. Don't, Ridge. Just tell the truth, confessing only to the various post-facto offences you committed. There'll be no violence. But at times you may be goaded, shouted at, ridiculed. Now, however angry and humiliated you may feel, you must not lash out in any way. Understand? Whatever happens, you must be co-operative and contrite at all times.'

'If he gives me shit, I'll eat it.' Ridge stared into space. 'I can do that.'

Darac began tapping the table with the side of a loosely clenched fist as he considered what to do next. He wouldn't be able to question Ridge but there were some things he could do behind the scenes.

'If, despite everything, you're charged with rape, I sincerely hope it would be dropped before trial. In terms of the other offences: with your guilty plea, your age and other mitigating factors, you'll almost certainly avoid a custodial sentence.'

The utter strangeness of the encounter was taking a toll on both of them. But just for a moment, something like normality returned as Ridge went to a different thought.

'The night the fat cop came for you – Granot, is it? – we were talking about how things were changing, remember? About how life at the club and in the whole country would never be the same again? I want you to know this. What I did in covering things up that afternoon, I wasn't doing it only for myself. I was doing it for the Blue Devil. Without me, this place would die.'

It struck Darac that for the first time he could remember, no music was playing in the room. It was a lonely sound. It might be lonelier still when the sizeable financial penalties Ridge faced started hitting him. Fighting closure was a daily reality for most jazz club owners. The Blue Devil, the only club like it left on the Côte d'Azur, had itself been dark at various times in its sixty-year history, sometimes for months. In the almost thirty years Ridge had been at the helm, though, it hadn't missed a week. What now?

'Get your jacket. Has Pascal got keys to the place?'

'Yes he has but… I was hoping to be back later.'

'Possible but unlikely.'

Ridge looked steadily into Darac's eyes. 'And tomorrow? I don't want to miss your opening number.'

Darac didn't know how he felt about it. Did he even want to play for Ridge again? Hadn't their bond of trust been shattered? But then he thought of Rama. Darac hadn't trusted Ridge with news of the boy's true fate or trusted any of the members of the quintet, come to that. There was just too much going on to make any definitive judgements. 'I won't be joining the band tomorrow; that's certain. I'm playing like shit, anyway. Get your jacket.'

On their way out, they hesitated as they passed under the poster but neither could face confronting Jeanne. Gaining the pavement, Ridge closed a hand around Darac's forearm.

'There's one mercy. It was better she died with me than with that butcher Voska.'

The raft of emotions taking a white-water ride through Darac's head took another jolt. 'Yes. It was.' They got into Darac's Peugeot but he didn't drive away immediately. 'I wasn't planning on telling you this yet, but our our friend Rama? He's still alive.'

'He is?' Ridge closed his eyes. 'Thank the Lord'.

Turning the ignition fired the Ellington orchestra into orbit. Ridge lowered his head into his hands and wept once more.

48

It promised to be a different style of squad meeting but, first, Darac needed to get an unlikely ally on board.

'Barrau? Darac.'

'*Dr* Barrau speaking.'

Good start. Across the desk, Granot rolled his eyes.

'Doctor, of course. I'd be grateful for your assistance with something. It's about your autopsy report on Madame Jeanne Mesnel. The question of the sexual encounter.'

'Ye-es?'

'Finding slight tearing in the vagina, you concluded that sex had been non-consensual. But might consensual sex have caused similar effects in a woman of her age?'

'Lovers, Captain, do not tend to kill their partners, fail to report the death and then remove all signs of their presence at the scene. A rapist might well do that, mightn't he?'

'Doctor, Madame Mesnel was seventy-one years of age, yes? And so, might—'

'Yes, she was seventy-one and had not, in my estimation, experienced penetration in some years. In perilous health latterly, it seems unlikely that she would have chosen a cold January day to rekindle a long-dormant interest in sex *and* do so outdoors. Weighing all the evidence, is it not reasonable to conclude that she was raped?'

A misogynist and a prude, Barrau couldn't imagine any older woman engaging freely in sex, Darac believed, and it had skewed his judgement. 'Reasonable, perhaps.' Knowing he didn't entirely have Granot's backing in what he was doing, Darac kept his eyes on the big man. 'But based solely on the condition of Madame Mesnel's body, is it forensically *possible* that sex was consensual?'

'Forensically *possible*, of course. But the point of this is what?'

'Just wrapping up the case, Doctor.'

Darac hung up, pressed stop on his digital recorder and played back the conversation.

'Working for the defence now.' Granot's forehead buckled like a car's crumple zone. 'It takes *Paul Darac, Maverick Flic* to a whole new level.'

Darac copied the file to his mobile. 'Our job is to gather evidence. We gathered it.'

'Considering all the trouble that Monsieur Eldridge Clay has caused us, you're very forgiving. Not to say indulgent. Not to say—'

'Well don't say it. Ridge is a good man, Granot. He was completely misguided in what he did but he's paying for it, believe me.'

Granot shrugged. 'How did Frènes respond to your glowing testimonial for him?'

'He said he'd take it on board.' Darac glanced at his watch. 'The interrogation should be over. I had a word with the custodial at the break. Frènes seemed to be leaning in Ridge's favour, he thought.'

'Could've been a tactic. We do it all the time.'

'Maybe, but he hasn't heard Barrau's inadvertent testimony yet.' Feeling slightly better about things, Darac slipped his mobile into his pocket and stood. 'Shall we?'

Like a derrick lifting a roped cargo, Granot gathered his bulk and hoisted himself on to his feet. Before he got underway, a printer in the corner of the office began spitting out a document.

A panel light indicated it was an incoming fax.

'Hold it, Granot, I've been waiting for this. It's from your mate Dubroqua.' Darac's voice trailed off as he scanned the document. 'Or rather from Cécile, his secretary…' Feeling a surge of energy release up his spine, he gave the air a stiff uppercut. 'This is it! The last link in the chain.' He handed it over. 'One of the chains, anyway.'

A sort of proud certainty lit up Granot's eyes as he read. 'Don't you just love our country? Eh? *Vive le dossier!*'

'For once, I agree.' Darac put his arm around Granot's shoulder as they left the office. 'I'm not going to refer to this in front of Frènes, though, alright? Immediately after the briefing, round up the inner circle. We'll reconvene here.'

The briefing had been scheduled for Joinel's conference room B. Trying to look more confident than he felt, Darac filed in behind Erica and Officer Serge Paulin. There was quite a turnout for the performance. Apart from the place reserved for Frènes, there was scarcely a spare seat in the house. He glanced at his watch.

'Ready, everyone? I've called this meeting partly to clear the air. By now, you should all be *au fait* with the situation with Monsieur Eldridge Clay. Public Prosecutor Frènes will be joining us shortly but, in the meantime, any questions or comments?'

In the centre of the front row, Malraux seemed perplexed. 'Yes, Captain, I want to make sure I've got it.'

His tight little mouth smiled. 'So it wasn't your friend Rama N'Pata who raped the famous Madame Mesnel. It was your friend Monsieur Clay, right?'

Darac could handle criticism. He could handle insubordination. He couldn't handle small-mindedness. But now wasn't the time to lose it with Malraux. He dug deep.

'If you'd read the statement, you would know we now have grounds to question the rape verdict on Madame Mesnel. Dr Barrau himself has just confirmed that possibility. When Monsieur Frènes is apprised of this, I think his inclination toward Monsieur Clay's position will only be strengthened. But I welcome your question. Yes, Ridge Clay is a friend of mine. And I hope Rama N'Pata might in time become one.'

'A friend?' Erica's forehead was scrunched in disbelief.

'Sorry, but he—'

Darac looked into her earnest blue eyes. 'Took part in the Brigitte Andreani sex video? I know. None of us would have done that but none of us knows what it's like to be in the clutches of someone like Voska.'

Malraux squirmed in his seat. 'Here we go.'

Flaco raised her hand. 'Do you think they argued with Voska over his proposed video? Is that why Modibo and Voska fought to the death?'

Darac ran a hand through his hair. 'Now that there's better word on the condition of Rama N'Pata, we may yet learn a definitive version, or at least his account of it, but I doubt if they knew anything about Voska's plan. Romping around with a willing partner like Brigitte is a very different scenario from raping an old lady – however great the coercion on them. I suspect Voska intended to film himself committing the act.'

'People are capable of anything, though,' Malraux said. 'Isn't that what you believe, Captain? In fact, you *did* believe your drummer mate might have done it.'

'Now we know how Madame Mesnel died, we no longer have to consider that.'

Frènes entered the room. With the air of a priest heading to the pulpit, he processed to his place next to Darac and sat down. But not without first touching his pen against the frame of the chair. Conference room B was a highly charged environment.

'Before we go on, monsieur, I think you should hear this recording of a conversation I had earlier with Dr Barrau.'

As he listened, Frènes absently fingered his cufflinks, a design of chisels set in gold.

'Thank you for that, Captain. In fact, I had already arrived at the conclusion that sex between Clay and Madame Mesnel might have been consensual.'

'Excellent. So I take it…' It was worth a shot. '…you're releasing him?'

Frènes's forbearance was not an infinite resource. 'In not coming forward as he should, Clay has cost this department thousands. He will be in custody for two full days. Possibly, a further two.'

As the group dispersed at the conclusion to the meeting, Frènes called Darac aside. 'While you were following your nose, struggling with your conscience and then following your nose again this morning, I was receiving a reprimand from the Chief Examining Magistrate for the way in which the case has been conducted. A reprimand!'

'That was uncalled for. I hope you gave him short shrift.'

'Everything is a source of amusement to you, isn't it, Captain?'

'Oh, absolutely everything. Yes indeed.'

Suddenly, Frènes had the look of a general who was about to dispatch a troublesome subordinate to the Front. 'You won't find this so amusing. Counterfeit currency is flooding the area. Now the Mesnel case is effectively over—'

'Forged bills? That's not for us. Foch can handle it.'

Frènes smiled. 'I know but I'm assigning the Brigade.'

It was punishment and Darac knew it. He also knew Frènes had the right to assign cases to any unit he saw fit. 'Alright, monsieur, but it will have to wait. The Mesnel case is far from over. There's a whole other dimension to it.'

Turning an alarming shade of puce, Frènes jabbed his pen into Darac's arm. 'I work on nine, ten cases at once! Has it ever occurred to you that I…?' As if a circuit had blown in his head, Frènes's eyes stared and his mouth fell open. When the power came back on, his mood had defaulted to a different setting. 'I beg your pardon, Monsieur Acting Commissaire. That was indefensible.'

Darac realised he'd been given a break. 'Forget it, even though what just happened technically constituted an assault.' He indicated Granot, looking on. 'An assault in front of witnesses.'

He massaged his arm.

Mugging that he had indeed witnessed the attack, Granot gave a rueful nod.

'I don't *think* I'll bring charges,' Darac said. 'On this occasion.'

Frènes opened his mouth but, recognising that his subordinate was well and truly back from the Front, whatever he was intending to say remained unsaid.'Especially,' Darac went on, 'if you give me a further twenty-four hours on the Mesnel case. At the end of it, I guarantee we will have something remarkable. The Chief Examining Magistrate, the Head of the Police Commission, the Most Worshipful Club Hammer in the Sacred Order of Masons – everyone will love us for it.'

Frènes chose to ignore the rib. 'One more day?'

'And then I'll get to it.'

'Alright, but I need to make a start now. Let me have Granot.'

At last, Darac reflected, Frènes was learning; he hadn't bothered asking him to elaborate on the 'whole other dimension' to the case. 'I need Granot. I could spare Malraux. And perhaps Flaco and Perand eventually. They're well up to the task.'

Frènes adjusted his tie while he considered it. 'Very well.'

Darac thanked him and left the briefing room, resolving to go and see Ridge later if there was time. The thought prompted another consideration. He swiped his mobile. 'Didier? I won't be able to make the gig but you're used to doing without me so let's not worry about it.'

'You sound stressed.'

'There'll be another absentee and this one's a first.'

Darac led the bandleader through as much of the story as he could squeeze into the trip back to his office. The conversation concluded in the way he knew it would.

'Will the Blue Devil still exist after all this, Darac?'

'I sincerely hope so.'

Finding Granot, Bonbon, Flaco and Perand waiting for him in his office, Darac got straight to it.

'What we've got here is not one case but three joined together.

Apologies for not realising that sooner. To recap, case one: the death of Jeanne Mesnel. Despite compelling evidence to the contrary, we now know that Voska wasn't responsible. Case two combines Voska's murder of Modibo N'Pata; the attempted murder of his brother, Rama; the murder of Brigitte Andreani; and numerous other serious offences including abduction. Case three: the Villa Rose connection. As you know, I was always dubious about Taylor Walters-Halberg's purchase of the Mesnel property and at various times, we've looked into different aspects of it. We're now within a gnat's eyelash of solving what is quite a complex case in its own right.'

Bonbon offered his sweet packet to Granot. 'We're so good. Sherbet lemon?'

Darac continued. 'As so often, the breakthrough began with an isolated clue – in fact, not even a clue, just an observation. And you provided it, Bonbon.'

'Not about the clock? That was a dead end.'

'No, not the clock. It was you who first noticed that one of Alain's paintings was 'Cézanne-like'. Remember?'

'Yes?'

'Combined with other details, that observation eventually acquired new significance. I'll talk you through the sequence.' He opened his notebook. 'First, we have an object of fascination locked away in a secret cabinet owned by art historian Philippe de Lambert; we have a Cézanne-like work painted by Alain Mesnel, an electrician who had also painted Lambert's home patch; we have Lambert vehemently opposing the inclusion of a key work, *Woman at Asilah*, in an exhibition dedicated to his favourite artist, Matisse; we have Alain and his seamstress wife Jeanne Mesnel buying jazz LPs on a luxury trip to New York in the sixties, the first indication they had come into a lot of unexplained money; we have confirmation from the Musée Granet in Aix that in his faux Cézannes, Alain had successfully imitated the techniques of the master. And finally, we have this.' He held up the fax.

319

'Just received it. It's a copy of a fifty-year-old job sheet from the Mairie. It reveals that Alain, an electrician, you remember, had rewired the very floor of the Musée Matisse in which *Woman at Asilah* was hanging.'

'*Vive la France!*' Granot proclaimed, not altogether tongue-in-cheek.

'And so we arrive back at the object of fascination locked in the secret cabinet. No prizes for guessing that it's that same work. Lambert commissioned Alain to paint a fake version of *Woman at Asilah* which, because of his job at the Musée Matisse, Alain was able to substitute for the real thing. Lambert paid Alain for his handiwork and took possession of the masterpiece, which has been living in his secret cabinet ever since. After a quick session with my lock picks, I saw it there today.'

Once the hubbub had eased, Granot teed-up the 'What next?' question. 'We've got a problem now, haven't we?'

'Better have another sherbet lemon,' Bonbon said.

The big man took one. 'Considering the status of Philippe de Lambert, the only way Frènes would grant a warrant to search that cabinet would be if we had incontrovertible, not circumstantial, evidence. The only incontrovertible evidence we have is sitting in the cabinet for which we need the search warrant.'

Perand extended a hand to Bonbon. 'Two of what he had.'

'Better take three.'

'In fact,' Granot continued, 'you can't even mention it to Frènes. The only reason we *know* the painting is there is because you broke into the place. Once that was established, the case would be thrown out.'

'You're right.' Darac glanced at his watch and then picked up the phone. 'Fortunately, I have another way into the thing.' He keyed in a number. 'Taylor? Just ringing to check you're on schedule?'

'For your treat? I certainly am.'

'I'll be with you in half an hour.'

49

Philippe de Lambert capped his pen, straightened his cravat and without so much as glancing at his secret cabinet, walked resolutely out of the room. Once out on the terrace, he passed between the ranks of statuary as deliberately as a general inspecting his troops. There was even time to stand and look at the view, but after a moment he understood why he so rarely did that any more. His eyes were not as they once were and nothing looked clear. Returning to what seemed *very* clear to him, he took a deep breath and continued on his way.

Trusting his team to leave no stone unturned, Darac had assigned a range of tasks to Granot and the others before he had taken his leave.

He had another great team player along for the ride. Hank Jones began to open out on 'Bluebird' just as Darac swung on to Avenue Denis Seméria and began following its sweeping curves up on to the lush crest of Cap Ferrat. Above the green-tiled roof of one of the Cap's most spectacular mansions, he turned and took the narrow leafy lane that wound up to the main entrance of Villa Rose.

Nearing the top, a beige Citroën seemed to speed up as Darac's Peugeot came around the bend toward it. He made eye contact with the Citroën's driver. It wasn't, was it? Yes, it was Cristelle. He lost control, slamming on the brakes. The Peugeot skidded on the loose surface, its nearside offering itself broadside to the inevitable collision. Somehow, the Citröen slipped past. Darac watched as it slid, wheels locked, toward the retaining wall flanking the villa's gardens. Closer. Closer still. He held his breath. And then let it out: the Citroën had stopped, juddering to a halt just shy of the stonework. For a moment, the two drivers did nothing, then Cristelle restarted her engine, reversed a few metres and got out. She was wearing a caramel-coloured trouser suit, the sort of outfit Taylor might have worn for a meeting. Darac wondered what business she had at Villa Rose as he got out of his car. Giving Taylor grief over buying her grandmother's house? But unless the solicitor had spoken out of turn, she couldn't have known the identity of the buyer.

'You alright, Cristelle?'

She dropped on to her haunches and scanned the vehicle for damage. 'No thanks to you. You drove straight toward me. Fucking idiot.'

'I'm sorry. And the car?'

She stood. 'Don't worry.' She held him with a look. 'You didn't touch me.'

'Right.'

She swept an escaped skein of hair from her face, exposing her strong jawline. It made her look more than ever like a young Jeanne. 'So why are you following me?'

'Following? You're leaving and I've only just got here.'

'So? You lot have phones and radios, don't you?'

'No one is following you.'

'Good.'

Getting back into her car, she reached immediately for her handbag. Darac held on to the driver's door as she took out a cigarette. 'What's going on, Cristelle?'

'You almost ran into me. Now I'm in need of a smoke. Is that alright?'

Her lips puckered into a glossy, cherry-red pout.

'I meant what are you doing here?'

She lit up, savouring the in-breath before blowing out a long column of smoke. 'I like to visit museums and galleries. It's quite legal, I believe.'

'So what took your fancy today?'

More pouting. More smoke. 'I liked the Watteaus in Room Three. The Fragonards. The Bouchers. I loved some of the eighteenth- and nineteenth-century jewellery.'

As far as Darac knew, those artists all had works on display in the villa. 'And that's the only reason you came here today?'

'Yes.'

Perhaps Taylor would have a different story to tell.

'May I go now?'

'One second. You might like to know that we're closing out your grandmother's case.'

'You've found her killer?'

He couldn't give her the details yet. 'You could say that, yes.'

'Uh-huh.' Cristelle went to take in another lungful of comfort but something stopped her. She seemed to be in a different place, suddenly. Staring at the cigarette in a sort of curious reverie, she began to twirl it slowly between her fingers. ' "A cigarette that bears a lipstick's traces…" What song is that?'

Darac felt his skin pock with goose pimples. 'It's… "These Foolish Things".'

'Of course.' Her sloe-black eyes slid to his. 'Would you like *this* foolish thing, Darac?' As its smoke spiralled thinly away in the breeze, she offered him the cigarette. 'It's yours to keep. A souvenir of a real, live Mesnel girl.'

Goose pimples and guilt. She understood, he realised. Understood where his head had been from the beginning.

'No. Thank you.'

She shrugged and tossed the cigarette aside. Coming to rest in a miniature shower of sparks, it flattened under her wheels as she drove away. Darac waited until Cristelle was out of sight before he walked slowly back to his car.

At the desk, the man with the ironed face waved Darac through and he headed off to the tea room. Hovering in the doorway, he saw Taylor sitting with a colleague at a corner table. It was clear she hadn't gone through any sort of confrontation with Cristelle. Wearing a figure-accentuating dress in cerise silk, she seemed aglow with well-being.

He looked on, seeing through the lustre into the darkness of her past. For Darac, whose parents had first met in this very room, the moment was doubly resonant. He appreciated the need some people had to rewrite their lives; to remake the past into a golden age that never existed. But he wasn't looking through Villa Rose-coloured glasses when, allowing for the usual ups and downs, he assessed his own early childhood as a time of sweetness and light. It was a few days after his twelfth birthday that everything changed. His mother's sudden death from an undiagnosed brain tumour had ushered in a desperately dark time. With his father's arms around him, young Paul somehow managed to get through it.

Taylor's experience could hardly have offered a greater contrast. The fatherly arms that engulfed her were working to a very different agenda.

With Agnès's dictum *Engage with facts; keep your distance from people* once again struggling against the tide, Darac made for Taylor's table.

'So Marianne, we're all set— Oh hello!' The smile widened. 'Paul Darac, may I introduce Marianne Ondarts, our catering manager?'

Darac shook her hand.

'We're finished here, so shall we go, Paul?' A final word with Marianne and they were on their way. 'I'm so glad you came.'

Walking in the sweet slipstream of her perfume, he followed her out of the room and into the atrium. She indicated the staircase. 'And so to my treat.'

'Don't tell me. Chefs from the Chantecler are preparing something fabulous for us on your terrace.'

She smiled her radiant smile. 'It's better than that.'

'Impossible!' Unless she'd invited the Kenny Barron Trio along, as well. 'Can't wait.'

A guard exchanged nods with Taylor as she and Darac emerged at the top of the stairs.

'To the left, Paul.'

'Not to your rooms?' Needing to be alone with Taylor, Darac hoped he'd kept the disappointment out of his voice. 'Intriguing.'

No, we're joining the masses. En route, at least.'

'And then we'll be by ourselves? I'm not fond of crowds.'

'Quite alone. You know, you're a dark horse, Acting Commissaire Darac.'

'I am?'

' "The Blue Devil Club presents the Didier Musso Quintet." I saw the ad in *Nice-Matin*. Your name along with eight others. You do know quintet means five?'

'Does it? I must tell the others.'

'A *poète policier*. I knew you were different.'

'You're into jazz?' He doubted she was or she would have mentioned it in relation to Jeanne Mesnel. 'I had no idea.'

'Actually, I usually listen to classical music but I do own three jazz CDs.'

'Just three?' He bet he knew which. 'What, out of interest?'

'*At the Blue Devil*, *More At the Blue Devil*, and *At the Blue Devil Again*.'

'I'm flattered.'

'We go along here.' They had arrived at the entrance to the elegant, silk-lined walkway known as the Ponte delle Belezze. A sign indicated it led to the temporary exhibition wing. 'You know, listening to your CDs made me realise I'd never paid proper attention to jazz before. It's beautiful.'

'Jazz is a lot of things.'

'I especially loved the guitar playing.'

'Yes?'

Gilding the lily, she smiled at him with a slightly different emphasis. 'Truly.'

The sooner they got to where they were going, the better, Darac reflected. 'You're into classical music?'

'Mozart, especially. Chopin. Some Debussy I love. But back to jazz. Who do you like listening to? Who's your favourite guitarist, for example?'

What harm could there be in answering truthfully?

'All-time favourite? Django Reinhardt.'

'What about a contemporary player?'

'There are so many... Among the very best is someone from your part of the world: Bruce Forman. A genius.' As if Angeline were still on the scene, he felt the shadow of her disapproval fall on him, suddenly. 'That is, if you give any credence to the notion.'

'Of genius? Of course I do. And that brings me very neatly to my treat.'

A couple of moments later, they arrived at the closed-off entrance to Matisse: Figure, Face and Form. Seeing Taylor, the security guard reacted as if the sun had just come out. With the exception of Ivo Selmek, Darac reflected, all her staff seemed to adore her.

'Paul, may I introduce Anatole Feilleu? He's been keeping Villa Rose secure for almost thirty years.'

'Monsieur.'

Smiling warmly, Anatole unhooked one end of a pink cordon rope and allowed them to pass. For Darac, it was like entering a crime scene in which a particularly genteel murder had taken place. The doors into the gallery itself were locked.

'We talked a little about the exhibition before. You do like Matisse's work?'

'You may as well ask, "Do you like wine?"'

'Then I have fifty-three glasses of the finest *grands crus* for you.'

Taylor keyed in the door entry code. Numbers on the lock's display began to tumble over one another in a random dance.

Darac looked into her cornflower-blue eyes. 'And we *will* be alone in there, Taylor?'

She returned the look. 'I said we would be.'

'Good, because there's something we need to discuss.'

The doors buzzed open and they walked through into the gallery.

'You know, I'd come to think—'

Taylor threw up her hands and screamed. They were not alone after all. In front of them, Philippe de Lambert was gazing with rapt attention at one of Matisse's masterworks. Gazing through eyes that were wide open but unseeing.

50

Public Prosecutor Frènes and Examining Magistrate Reboux only just beat the media to the scene. As they expressed their sadness at the tragedy, Darac was already driving away from Villa Rose. Ten minutes later, he found Cristelle in Mirrazi, a trattoria at the foot of the Escalier del Pountin in Villefranche. In summer, the place was packed. Today, she was the sole diner.

'If you're not following me, what do you call it?'

He slid in next to her. 'I'm sorry, Cristelle, but it can't be helped. You said you went to Villa Rose because you love the Watteaus and the eighteenth-century jewellery?'

'I said I liked the Watteaus. I *loved* the jewellery.'

'I think you went there because you had an appointment with Philippe de Lambert.'

She took a sip of San Pellegrino. 'Never heard of him.'

'I bullied Léonie Salle into telling me where I would find you.'

'Léo bullied? Never.'

'I threatened to close her down if she didn't.'

Cristelle considered it, then shrugged. 'Well done. Hope you're proud of yourself.'

Darac pointed a finger toward the quayside. 'See that van? In it are Madame Patricia Lebrun and Monsieur Lami Toto from our forensic laboratory. They have every facility on board to test—'

'Alright. I've just had sex with the man. For money. I'm a prostitute, remember?'

'Where?'

'In the traditional place. I'm not particularly into anal.' Darac was tiring of Cristelle's routines but maybe that was all he could expect from her now. Maybe all he had a right to expect. 'I meant where in Villa Rose, obviously.'

'Oh. In his private office. On a chaise longue. Mainly.'

She looked concerned, suddenly. 'Why are you here? His heart hasn't given out or something, has it?'

'Or something.'

'He's dead? I'm sorry. He was nice.' She regained her cool. 'There, I've said something positive.'

'Was he a regular?'

'Of our little stable, yes. Me, just the second time.'

'How regular is regular?'

'Couple of times a week. He was a remarkable man for his age. For any age.'

'Always at the villa?'

'It was the first time there, I think. But what does it matter now, anyway?'

Darac's mobile rang. 'Go ahead, Deanna.'

'For God's sake, get back here. I can't move with the twin monster that is Frè-Boux, R.O.'s forensic team and half the world's media under my feet. And your friend Mademoiselle Walters-Halberg's tears are making the floors slippery.'

'I'll be back as soon as I can. What have you got?'

'First, you were right about the hanging rope. R.O. found it was cut from a reel they use for cordoning off exhibitions. Lambert's wife – doughty soul – has identified the handwriting in the suicide notes as definitely his.'

'We have only her word for that but let's leave it for now. Is it a definite suicide?'

'Almost certainly, yes.'

'Bear with me a second. *Could* Taylor have strung Lambert up and showed up with me later as her alibi?'

'No.'

'Could the girl Lambert had sex with be involved? An erotic

game that went wrong?'

Her eyes flaring, Cristelle shaped to give Darac a slap.

He threw an arm across her.

'Again, no. The neck broke with the fall so I can pinpoint the time of death. It happened just a couple of minutes before you and Walters-Halberg entered the gallery together and that clears her. You met the prostitute as she drove away, I gather, earlier still. Ditto.'

Darac released Cristelle, taking a sharp dig on the shoulder for his trouble. 'Could *anybody* else have been involved? Perhaps to assist him?'

'Just on the pathology, I can't say yet but other evidence appears to preclude it. The guard swears only Lambert entered the gallery before you arrived.'

'Security guards are always bunking off.'

Possibly so.' She coughed, the eruption lasting longer than usual. 'There are entry codes, CCTV and other factors to be considered but that's not my concern.'

Quite. Let's put the suicide notes back on the table. Lambert referred to his cancer as incurable, right? But could his health have been that bad? His penis obviously worked.'

'Means nothing. You can give a corpse an erection with the appropriate chemicals. I couldn't get through to his oncologist just now but I'll find the extent of the cancer in the lab, anyway.'

'Anything more?'

'Only that I shouldn't have let the morgue trolley go. I could've used it as a battering ram to get through this lot.'

'It'll calm down. Thanks for the call, Deanna. I'll be back shortly.'

Cristelle shoved her plate to one side. 'You manhandle me like that again—'

'And I'll have to pay?'

'Fuck off.'

Darac raised his hands palms outwards. 'Cheap shot. Forgive me.' He took a breath. 'Alright, it *looks* like this. After you left,

Lambert washed his tackle in a naive attempt to mask what he'd been up to, penned three brief but rather wonderful letters to his wife, to his staff, and, Saint Paul-style, "to the French people", went to the exhibition room, stood on a bench, suspended a rope from the chandelier above, fixed his gaze on his favourite painting and stepped off into oblivion.'

'God… He had cancer you said?'

'Apparently.'

'In that case, I don't blame him.' A shutter came down. 'Just a moment. You actually thought that during sex, I could have left him hanging from the ceiling and walked away? Quite calmly and without saying anything even to you, moments later?'

Ridge crashed back into Darac's head. 'People *have* been known to walk away from such things, Cristelle. Believe me.'

'Have they?' She looked drained, suddenly. 'I suppose they have.'

A beaming waiter breezed up to clear the table. He was either deaf and blind or one of the finest actors of his generation. 'The usual, mademoiselle?'

Cristelle nodded.

'Monsieur?'

'Double espresso.'

'Two double espressos. Right away.'

The waiter cleared away her plate and disappeared as jauntily as he had come.

'I need a word with the guys outside, Cristelle. Please don't run off in the meantime.'

'Before coffee?'

The driver's door window rolled down as Darac approached the van.

'Dead end, Patricia. You and Lami can go back to the villa. See you shortly.'

As she drove away, Darac called Bonbon, updated him and then went back inside.

Another beam from the waiter. 'Your coffees are on the table, sir.'

Cristelle gave him a look as he slotted in opposite her. 'Was I the last person to see Lambert alive? If so, I'll have to give evidence, won't I?'

'The guard seems to have that distinction but you will have to appear, anyway.'

'Great.' She felt blindly for her handbag. The cigarette was halfway to her mouth before she realised she couldn't smoke. 'Ah, shit.' Sighing deeply, she slid it back into the packet. 'It's only been two whole years, after all.'

He downed his espresso. 'Look, Cristelle, if it turns out your being with Lambert just before he topped himself was coincidental, as I fully expect, I'm going to lose your ID on this thing. OK?'

Lowering her gaze, she returned her cup to the recess in its saucer with the care of an astronaut docking a spacecraft.

'And in return for that you would want?'

He leaned across and kissed her on both cheeks. 'I would want you to be careful.'

A broad cross-section of the media was waiting at the scene.

'*Nice-Matin*, Captain. Just thirty seconds. Why did—?'

'*Télé Sud*. It's me, Annie Provin. Come on Darac, we've worked together. Is it true Philippe de Lambert... Hey, wait! Arsehole!'

Darac fought his way through and caught up with Granot.

'Forensics have shut up shop, chief.'

'I know, just passed them in the lane, followed by the other half of the world's press. Have you seen Madame de Lambert?'

'She's in her private apartment with Frènes. And possibly Reboux.'

'What about Taylor?'

'What about her?' With unexpected ardour, Granot kissed his fingertips and muttered a stream of verbiage on the theme of divine beauty. 'Ai, ai, ai!'

'So you've seen her. She's still in her rooms?'

'I assume so, you sly bastard. No wonder you've flown solo when you've come here.'

'Is anybody with her?'

'Flaco *was*. No reason to keep her confined, is there?'

'Get across there and, if she hasn't wandered off, keep her talking until I turn up. Fascinate her with stories of *Le Gym's* greatest matches or whatever.'

'Gladly. But what will you be doing in the meantime?'

'I want to have a look around the exhibition room. There wasn't time earlier. Deanna and R.O. cleared it?'

'All done and dusted.' Granot adjusted an imaginary tie. 'Right, Mademoiselle Walters-Halberg, here I come. If you lose her to me, you'll have only yourself to blame.'

'You're married, remember.'

'To *Le Gym*, to the Brigade and to Odile.' He left at the double. 'In that order.'

Lartou saluted Darac – a sure sign top brass was about – as he ducked under the red tape cordoning off the exhibition room.

Inside, Anatole the security guard was recounting his story to Bonbon. 'When I hear the scream, I go running in. "Help him down!" the mademoiselle was shouting at your boss. Seems she thought Monsieur de Lambert might be still alive.'

'She had reason. Swingers sometimes do survive.'

'Do they? Anyway, they get halfway to the body and she faints away in his arms, the poor girl. He carries her out and he puts me in charge. "Lock the place up," he barks. "Don't let anyone in unless they're police or forensics." "Yes sir," I says. "And no nipping off for a pee, fag break or anything else." Let me tell you something, I've never done that in… Hang on, here he is.' He gave Darac a concerned look. 'The mademoiselle alright now, sir?'

'I think so.' He indicated the open door. 'That's all for the moment.'

'Oh. Right.'

As Anatole walked away, Darac scanned the room.

And then he saw it.

'Come on, Bonbon. Let's improve our minds. There's something I think will catch your eye, particularly.' They examined each work in turn. 'Thanks to Deanna, we can rule out Taylor and Cristelle Daviot, but could anyone else have been involved in Lambert's death? What do you think?'

Bonbon shook his head. 'No one directly. First, there's the door entry code. It was known to only three people: Lambert himself, Walters-Halberg and her assistant, Dr Selmek. Did you know that after a meeting they had this morning, he left for Paris? The Académie des Beaux-Arts. Not due back until tomorrow.'

'I've requested the Paris Palais de Justice get hold of him soonest for an interview. You know, we believe only three people have the codes because that's what we've been told.'

'In theory, any number could; that's true.'

'CCTV? There are no cameras covering the floor of the gallery itself, are there?'

'The paintings are protected in all sorts of ways but the area outside the doorway is the only one fully—'

Darac's mobile rang. 'It's Granot. Hang on, Bonbon.'

'I can't find Mademoiselle Walters-Halberg.'

'She's not here in the exhibition room. Keep looking.' Darac rang off. 'CCTV, Bonbon?'

'I've only been able to run the discs on forward scan so far but assuming they haven't been tampered with – and I can't see how they could have been – I'm almost certain that nobody came in here between Lambert, and you and the mademoiselle.'

'How about before Lambert?'

'If there was somebody hiding in say, the storeroom where Lambert got the rope, where are they now?'

'There's no other exit except through the main door and Anatole swears he never leaves his post. And there's nothing on the disc.'

'There are no opening windows, skylight or air shaft in the storeroom?'

'None. It's unassisted suicide. Has to be.'

Darac's hands went to his hips as he stared at the floor. 'OK. Unless we learn something to the contrary, I'm not contesting that any further.' They moved off, after a moment arriving at a pair of small Moroccan scenes, one hung not quite evenly above the other. Darac gave Bonbon a look. 'What do you make of this?'

'This is what you wanted me to see? Lovely. Although the upper one looks to have been just thrown up on the—' He performed a double take. 'Is it what I think it is?'

'It's *Woman at Asilah*, yes. The other one is its sibling, *Souk at Asilah*.'

'What's it doing here?'

'The fifty-fourth of the catalogued fifty-three paintings in the exhibition? Exactly, Bonbon.'

A commotion at the entrance made them turn. Taylor and Maggie de Lambert had arrived.

'I'm sorry, no one is allowed beyond this point just now, mesdames,' Lartou was saying. 'If you wouldn't mind just—'

'Be with you in a second, Lartou,' Darac called out. He turned to Bonbon. 'Lock up the exhibition room. No one is allowed to enter until further notice.'

'Right.'

Wheezy yet imperious, Maggie de Lambert's voice rose above the cordoned area like a torn flag. 'This is my house, in case you've forgotten.' She indicated the tape. 'And what do you think I am? A damned limbo dancer?'

'Of course not, madame.'

'We don't want to go any further, anyway, you idiot.'

'I understand, but—'

'I'll take over, Lartou.' Darac ducked under the tape. 'Allow me to offer my personal condolences, Madame de Lambert.' He offered his hand. 'I'm Captain—'

'I know who you are.'

Conveying that it was solely a matter of form, she extended

her hand in return. From her flawless hair to her handmade shoes, Madame de Lambert seemed to Darac the very model of the elegant chatelaine. But shaking her feisty little fist confirmed what her level, unblinking gaze and indomitably set jaw also suggested to him. Behind the appliqué was the heart and soul of a fighter. 'Have you seen a doctor, madame?'

'I have, and a fat lot of good it did. Another one's arriving soon. Isn't he, sweetheart?'

At her side, Taylor gave the slightest of nods and then her gaze met Darac's. In that moment, she looked to him as pale and perfect as an angel in a Renaissance altarpiece. In the silent space between them, he read the message 'I need you' as if it were a stream of gilded letters.

'Are you feeling better now, Taylor?'

'A little.' She touched Darac's forearm. 'But can we get away from here?' She continued to Maggie in English. 'If that's alright with you, darling?'

'You don't think I want to hang around...' Her whole body shuddered. 'Yes, for goodness' sake, let's get out of here.'

The older woman turned to Darac as they processed back across the Ponte delle Belezze toward the main body of the building. 'When are you and your men going to be finished... swarming all over the place, Captain? We're laying on the biggest preview in the history of Villa Rose on Sunday.'

'You still intend to—'

'Of course we intend to go ahead.'

Darac couldn't resist the thought that if the exhibition were not sold out for its run before, it would be now.

'The Matisse show is the summation of Philippe's whole life in art. Thank God we've got our Taylor.' She took a breath. And another. 'Selmek can stay in Paris for all I care.'

Taylor wiped away a tear. 'Maggie, those sedatives will be starting to work soon so we must get you to bed.'

' "We?" ' She jerked a thumb at Darac. 'Leave *him* out of it!'

Her words lobbed like gobbets of spittle into the silk-lined space. 'I'm sorry. I'm overwrought. Forgive me.'

'Of course. Let's go.'

'Yes, because…' Looking Taylor in the eye, Maggie seemed on the verge of collapse, suddenly. 'Because you and I must have a… must have a conversation now.'

'Later.' A figure was striding purposefully across the Ponte toward them. 'Thank goodness, here's the nurse. We'll be there in a trice, darling.'

'Taylor,' Darac said. 'You need to be with Madame de Lambert now, but may I meet you shortly?'

'Please.'

'The English Tea Room. In an hour?'

Darac spent part of the interim with Valentin Bichat, the villa's chief security officer. Considering the status of the works on show, Bichat conceded that the villa's CCTV set-up was a fairly crude affair.

'It's always the cheap things that don't get replaced, isn't it? We've got this dual pressure pad and photo-electric system guarding the exhibits themselves and they are state of the art. No one could take an object off a wall, off a cabinet, off the floor, off anything without everyone in the place knowing. There's a direct link to you lot and apart from the room attendants, we have two armed guards patrolling at all times.' Without a pause, he continued, 'Cancer led him to it, they're saying.'

'Yes.'

'Shame. Wonderful man.'

'You say no one could take anything. What about you and your staff?'

'It's still not possible. Supposing I wanted to steal… the Pia Lancia necklace, for example. I have only half the code necessary to deactivate the pad, half to deactivate the invisi-cell. Every day a new code is generated.'

'And the other half goes to the curator and assistant curator?'

'That's right.'

'So if they wanted to take something off a wall?'

'They have to go through us. You're talking as if something *has* been taken.'

'Taken? No, no. Thanks for that, Bichat.'

Darac was on his second espresso when Taylor walked into the Tea Room and joined him at a table next to the *porte-fenêtre*. The public cleared from the site, they had the place to themselves. More or less. She ordered a pot of Earl Grey and on Darac's insistence, some food. Toast was all she thought she could manage.

'How are you feeling now, Taylor?'

'Somewhere between numb and terribly sad. With a stopover in denial en route. I didn't even know Philippe was ill.'

'Is Madame de Lambert resting?'

'Didn't you see the ambulance? The doctors insisted she be admitted to hospital.'

Darac grinned, keeping it light. 'I bet she didn't go willingly.'

'She doesn't know she *has* gone: she was sound asleep.' Taylor smiled, weakly. 'When she wakes up, she will be furious.'

'And the conversation she wanted to have with you?'

'The sedatives kicked in before we even got her into bed. It'll keep.' Another smile, fuller this time. 'She'll probably be back here in an hour or two, knowing Maggie.'

'Indeed. So what happens now? To Villa Rose, I mean?'

The change of tack seemed to throw Taylor. 'Oh. Uh… well, it will take several months, I suppose, and then the Académie des Beaux-Arts will take over the place. But let's not go there.'

'And will you retain your post, do you think?'

'I… would hope so.'

'What about the Lambert apartment? Although Philippe had cancer, I don't suppose anyone expected him to pre-decease his more obviously ailing wife. Can she stay on?'

'Uh… I don't know.' The thought really didn't seem to have occurred to her. 'Paul, please.' Distress was etched on her face.

'Let's change the subject, for goodness' sake.'

'I'm sorry. Of course.'

For the first time, Taylor noticed Granot sitting all on his own by the door. And another officer standing on the terrace outside.

'*That's* good.' She indicated them. 'Any media stowaways won't disturb us.'

'Quite. Taylor, I'm going to have to leave for Marseille now and I won't be back for a day or two. But I *will* be back.'

Scrunching her forehead, she took his hand. 'Don't go.'

'I have to.'

He was only partly lying.

51

'Madame Salle? Darac.'

'We go no further unless you call me Léo.'

'*Léo*. Listen, I need your help.'

'Changed your tune with me since lunchtime.'

'Sorry about that. I was in a hurry. Still am, actually.'

'Well, you were sweet to Cristelle eventually so let's hear it.'

'She mentioned that Philippe de Lambert was a regular client.'

'I wish I had a euro for every time he'd screwed one of my girls. That's a joke.'

'Yes. Listen…'

Darac gave her the times of Lambert and Taylor's mutual alibis on the day Jeanne Mesnel had died.

'I understand. I'll get back to you as soon as I can.'

As Darac rang off, Bonbon appeared in the doorway of his office. He looked even more happy with life than usual.

'Any second now, you should be receiving an email. I had to pretend to be you to get them to agree.'

Right on cue, a message came in.

'From the Crédit Bal-Med bank?'

'That's the one.'

Bonbon moved in behind Darac. 'The date is the key.'

'Ah, yes.' As Bonbon straightened, Darac turned to him. 'Mate, you've got something here.'

'Authorising the warrant will take some swinging, mind you. And I don't think your usual wrecking-ball approach will work.'

Darac stared at him.

'In a good way, I mean,' Bonbon said.

Darac picked up the phone and keyed in a number. 'You're right, of course. If you can't stand to see a grown man grovel, I'd leave now.'

'You kidding?' Bonbon sat down. 'I'm looking forward to this.'

'Monsieur Frènes? Just to let you know we're making progress on the case but we can't go any further without a written search authorisation.' He shared a look with Bonbon. 'Just a bank. If you could fax it over straight away, I would be grateful.'

As Frènes began to outline his reasons for declining, Bonbon clicked his fingers at Darac. He mouthed something. Darac couldn't read it. Bonbon went into a mime, puffing up his chest à la Frènes and jabbing a finger into his arm, then pointing at Darac. The penny dropped.

'I take your argument, monsieur. On another matter, I've been asked to reassess the assault that took place in the briefing room. As you know, I was minded to take no action against you but we must consider the unions…'

While Darac made his pitch, out on the floor, Granot and Perand were continuing their cross-check on every piece of evidence from the Mesnel case. After well over an hour, nothing had leapt off the page at either of them. But then Perand, who had already nodded off twice, suddenly sat up straight. In an almost surreal act of revelation, he was experiencing, just for a fleeting moment, what it must feel like to be Granot. In an avalanche of information, he had spotted one stray pebble. A detail concerning the happenings of Friday, 1 January, the day before Madame Mesnel's death, didn't fit. With a copy of the report in question in front of him, he rang Hôpital Saint-Roch. After obtaining the necessary clearance, he secured the services of Michelle, a clerical assistant in records.

'I'm interested in A and E admissions, Michelle. For Friday, January 1st.'

'I'll bring up that screen.'

'You should have an entry for one Henri Lepic. Age thirteen. Leg fracture.'

'Just a moment.'

As he waited, Perand experienced what for him was a rare emotion: he felt anxious. What might be about to happen could change everything and it would be all his doing.

'Got it, Michelle?'

'A second... yes, I have it. 16.47 he was admitted.'

'That's what I have, too.' On the report in front of him, the name of the doctor attending the boy was cited as one J. M. Kenteh. 'Who set the leg?' He unconsciously rubbed his right thigh while he awaited the answer. *Say it was Jacob*, he said to himself.

'It was... Dr Kenteh.'

'Dr Jacob Kenteh?'

'That's right.'

Perand rapped his desk. 'Listen, is there any way of determining who filed that entry?'

'Sure... B.R.L. initialled it. That's Berthe. Berthe Lepic.'

'Thank you.'

Perand ended the call and immediately rang Darac's number.

Bonbon arrived back on the scene. 'If that's the chief you're calling, he's trying to get a search warrant out of Frènes.'

Perand smothered the mouthpiece. 'What for? The painting is out in the open now.'

'Not for the painting.' Bonbon's tawny eyes twinkled. 'For treasure of a slightly different kind.'

'Well, Lieutenant, I have just come up with some treasure of my own.'

'Those sherbet lemons must really be the business, mustn't they?'

Shortly afterwards, not one member of the Brigade was still occupying a desk. Darac, Bonbon and Flaco had departed for the Crédit Bal-Med bank; Granot and Perand had set off to Beaulieu-sur-Mer. Only Malraux, requisitioned by Frènes, had not been invited to the party. He didn't care. For some days, he'd been planning a party of his own.

Darac took a call from Paris as they arrived at the bank. Ivo Selmek had not shown for his meeting at the Académie.

'What do you make of it?' Bonbon said.

Darac ran a hand through his hair. 'I don't like it. Let's put an APB out for him.'

In the vault, the safety deposit box supervisor, a slight, tight-faced man in his mid-fifties, had evidently known better days.

'I know this is irregular,' Darac said. 'So is murder. The box?'

'Wait there.'

A back-handed swat directed the trio to an alcove. They formed a line outside it.

'Now we're here,' Bonbon whispered, 'I'm not feeling as confident.'

Flaco's eyes slid sideways. 'What will we do if there's nothing in the box? Nothing incriminating, I mean.'

Darac canted his head discreetly toward her. 'We've got pen and paper, haven't we? Any good at sleight of hand, Flak?'

Just for a second, Flaco wasn't sure Darac was kidding.

Carrying the box with funereal ceremony, the supervisor passed in front of them and set it down on the inspection table.

'Bravo.' Darac smiled. 'The key?'

The man went through a final agony of conscience before handing it over. Then he took five backward paces and, with his hands clasped in front of him, stared neutrally into space. The box was open before he had completed the manoeuvre. It contained a card-backed A4 envelope and a folded sheet of paper. As Bonbon opened the envelope, Darac unfolded the paper and began reading its handwritten message.

'Does it support your theory, Captain?' Flaco asked. 'So far, so…' And then, letting out an involuntary breath, he shook his head in disbelief. 'My God.'

52

'Subject approaching, Captain. Be with you in about four minutes. Over.'

'Copy. Over and out, Lartou.'

Darac took out his earpiece and turned the radio off. 'OK, Anatole. You know what to do.'

He didn't look happy about it. 'Yes, sir.'

As the security guard hurried back to his post, Darac slipped into the storeroom, aligned his feet on the chalk marks he'd made earlier and pulled the door almost shut. Only two pictures were visible on the sliver of wall Darac could see. It was all he needed.

After a moment, the lights went out and the heavy gallery door closed. Anatole had carried out the first part of his brief, at least. Standing still, Darac was enveloped in darkness, which seemed to deepen with every second. And with it, so did his doubts. A number of things could go wrong, Anatole failing to play his part being just one.

Four minutes went by. And then possibly another four until a loud buzz signalled that someone had keyed in the entry code. Out of his line of sight, the gallery door opened. A wash of light broke thinly up the sliver of wall, incrementally revealing the two *Asilah* pictures. The light fell back and the door closed with a loud, reverberant thump. It was dark once more. Silence. Had the subject merely glanced into the gallery and gone away? Had

Anatole issued a last-second warning? Had…?

Darac heard footsteps. A sharp *tock*. Bright light splintered through the fissure in front of him. Resisting the temptation to open the storeroom door any wider, he could do no more than keep his gaze locked on *Woman at Asilah* and wait. And wait. 'Come on,' he whispered. 'The painting has done its job: Philippe de Lambert is out of the way for good. Take the damn thing.'

Hands appeared and reached up to the frame. A woman's hands. Darac pushed the door open.

The woman gasped and spun around, dropping the work. 'You? I… It's not what you think.' She began moving toward him in slow, deliberate steps. 'I wasn't—'

'I know what you were doing, Taylor.'

'No, you don't, Paul. I was taking it—'

'You were taking it back to where it belongs: a cabinet in Philippe de Lambert's office. True?'

She reached out and ran a hand over his shoulder. 'Paul, I suppose I have to come clean.' She nestled into his chest and, pressing her fingers into his flesh like a treading kitten, she continued in a low, breathy whisper. 'You're right, of course. You're an artist yourself. I should have known that as soon as you saw it, you would recognise the impostor; the Moroccan cuckoo in the nest. I didn't put that painting in this room, Paul. I want you to believe that.'

'I do believe it.'

The corners of her mouth twitched slightly. 'Good.'

'Ivo Selmek put it here.'

'Ivo?'

'He saw it as the perfect way of speeding up his accession to the throne of this palace. I doubt he anticipated Philippe would kill himself at the disgrace, but he knew that whatever happened, it would spell end-of-story for the old man's tenure at Villa Rose.'

'But he didn't know—. How did he know about the painting?'

'Until a couple of days ago, I don't think he did know. But

we'll find out. Our Paris people have caught up with him.'

She shook her head. 'But how did he get in here carrying a painting undetected?'

'You were going to *leave* with one undetected. Two tame security guards are all you need. One on the door, the other on the CCTV console.'

Wariness covered her face like a veil. 'I don't know what you mean.'

'Taylor, you turn people with your charm and your beauty. He used money. And it didn't seem terribly wrong to Anatole and Bichat. Selmek was adding a work to the exhibition, not taking one. Wiping the disc for that? What harm was there?'

'You're amazing, darling.' She essayed a smile. 'You've got it all worked it out.'

'Yes, Taylor, I have.'

Her lips stuck to her teeth as her smile faded, leaving them bared for a moment.

'We're here, chief.'

Granot and Flaco had arrived.

'Take the cuckoo, guys. The one lying on the floor.'

'Why are the officers here? You said you knew I wasn't trying to steal it?'

'Just to look after the painting.'

'I'm sorry. It's been a hell of a day. Literally. And for a minute, I thought you were going to— Oh, I don't know what I thought.'

'There's still a lot to talk through, so let's go, shall we?' He offered his arm.

'Go?' she said, taking it. 'Where to?'

Feeling about as noble as a Judas goat, Darac led her away.

53

By the time Perand led Taylor into Darac's office, her mood had darkened considerably. With five pairs of eyes upon her, she sat, crossed her legs and began kicking the air with her free foot.

'The interview is not being recorded nor is anyone taking notes,' Bonbon said, trying to make it sound as if the encounter were no more than a chat.

'I am not answering any questions without a lawyer *and* the American Consul...' Taylor froze as she noticed *Woman at Asilah* leaning against the wall. 'I... want them here now.'

Darac was sitting on, rather than at, his desk. It seemed more informal but it also gave him the higher ground. 'In the situation you find yourself in, you are not entitled to have a lawyer present nor even consult with one just yet. However, appreciating your unfamiliarity with our system, I have sent for a Monsieur Hector Duclaux, anyway. He will be here presently. As will the Consul.'

'Duclaux?' Bonbon smiled. 'Good man.'

Granot nodded. 'Get you off anything, he will, mademoiselle. Would you like coffee? It's revolting but it's all we have.'

Taylor ignored the offer.

'Water?' Flaco said, indicating the cooler.

'Yes.' Taylor re-crossed her legs. 'Thank you.'

Darac turned to her. 'So, Taylor—'

'Taylor!' Her voice keened through the air like a razor-edged Frisbee. 'You have forfeited the right to use my forename, Captain.'

'*Mademoiselle*, let's go back to the painting you were returning to Philippe de Lambert's study.'

'I am not saying anything without—'

'Surely you have nothing to hide?'

'No, of course not.'

'A word of advice?' Bonbon's avuncular-concern face was the envy of many a con man. 'Nothing looks more suspicious than silence.'

'Don't give away all our secrets,' Granot said.

Taylor thought about it as she took a sip of water. 'I… was taking the painting back for Philippe's sake. To protect his memory. He was a wonderful man—'

Darac shook his head. 'I believe you did hold Lambert in some esteem but that's not why you did it.'

'I am not saying anything further without the lawyer and the Consul being present.'

'Sure?'

'Yes.'

'Very well, we could wrap this up quickly but if you won't talk, mademoiselle, I will. I'll tell you a story. The narrative may falter occasionally and we've had to use our imaginations here and there but, in all essential regards, it's a true story.' Nevertheless, Darac could have begun it: *Once upon a time there was a beautiful princess, but she was a very sad princess.* You're sure you don't want to say anything?'

Taylor sat back in her chair, apparently uninterested.

'Alright, I'll begin. It was a red-letter day for you when, against all the odds, you landed the assistant curator's job at Villa Rose. You proved to be diligent and reliable in the role rather than brilliant, but on the personal level, you shone. Gradually, your many acts of devotion got you closer to the centre of Monsieur and Madame de Lambert's lives and eventually, you became indispensable. That was helpful because you knew that under the terms of Rose de Sainte-Caranville's agreement with the Académie des Beaux-Arts, there was no guaranteed future for you at Villa Rose once Monsieur de Lambert was dead.'

Bonbon essayed a clueless look. 'You've lost me, chief. Why was it good?'

'Because the Lamberts were childless.'

'Ah. The mademoiselle was setting herself up as the daughter they never had?'

Taylor's closed-down expression didn't change.

'I think it was more of a two-way street than that, wasn't it, mademoiselle?' Darac gave Taylor space to answer and although she remained silent, he could see she was weighing her options. Once that happened, suspects almost always talked sooner or later. 'No? I'll continue. I think it understandable that someone with the childhood of a Taylor Ann Riggs might later cultivate surrogate parents; people to whom she could give and receive the love denied her in her earlier life.'

Taylor looked exposed, suddenly. 'Spare me your amateur psychology, Captain.'

Bonbon had a point of his own. 'People have also been known to cultivate surrogate parents, surrogate children, surrogate *anything* not to... "give and receive love" but to express hate. Some victims of abuse seek to punish the innocent for what the guilty did to them. That's not amateur psychology, mademoiselle. That's twenty years in this job.'

Granot folded his arms. 'And some people are simply out for Number One. Isn't that true, mademoiselle?'

Staring resolutely ahead, Taylor ignored both comments.

'As the child the Lamberts never had,' Darac began again, 'you were in a good position to inherit when they died. And they were already in, as you put it, the December of their lives when you started at Villa Rose.'

Granot nodded. 'It was almost New Year's Eve for Madame de Lambert.'

Bonbon turned to him. '*Madame?* He had terminal cancer, though, didn't he?'

'No. He had a mild form of prostate cancer, which he could have lived with for years. And according to his oncologist, he knew that, interestingly.'

'So what was the wife's problem?'

'Heart. One more attack and they won't be able to do anything for her.' He turned to Taylor. 'You thought she was certain to pre-decease the monsieur, didn't you?'

She eyeballed him. 'I thought no such thing.'

'Dragging her around all those shops. One more trip might have done it.'

No indifference now. Taylor was as angry as a cornered cat. 'That is outrageous!'

'I too believe you thought Monsieur de Lambert would outlive Madame,' Darac said. 'But back to the question of your inheriting the Lambert fortune. The thought excited you because you assumed the monsieur, alone, was unimaginably rich. In reality, the couple's resources were less impressive than that, as you began to suspect when they came to rely on you for their day-to-day financial dealings as well as so much else. Nevertheless, you stood to gain handsomely and that was important because as we've said, once Lambert was dead, the likelihood was that you would lose both your post and your apartment.'

She took another sip of water. 'I was devoted to Philippe.'

'But then doubts crept in. It occurred to you that despite all that tireless devotion, there might be nothing for you in the will.'

Flaco spoke up. 'She didn't have access to it, Captain?'

'The sole copy was lodged with the Lamberts' solicitor, an old friend of the monsieur. There was no way of examining it without arousing suspicion.'

'This is all nonsense. Nonsense!'

'But then everything changed. You discovered that Lambert had a stolen object secreted in his office. Something of great value. You probably had no idea what the work was—'

'Of course I…' she began, then bit her lip.

'Thank you. I can imagine your thoughts on seeing the monsieur's very own Matisse. Somehow, you realised, he had engineered one of the great art swindles. He'd commissioned the painting of a replica of *Woman at Asilah* and had that replica installed in place of the original by someone with access to the Musée. And so with no one but himself, the forger and the thief in the know, Lambert was able to consummate, so to speak, his relationship with a work he'd loved at one remove all his life. Now, *Woman* was his to enjoy whenever he wanted.'

Taylor glanced at her watch. 'When will that lawyer—'

'Shortly. It was then you understood why Lambert had flatly refused to approach the Musée for their version of *Woman* for your Matisse show; refused when sound aesthetic judgement demanded its inclusion. With its pendant picture *Souk at Asilah* arriving from America, the Musée work would clearly have been a significant addition to the show.'

'I explained that. It was too parochial a choice for an exhibition with such global scope and ambition.'

'I know that's how Lambert justified it but his explanation doesn't ring true and neither did his uncharacteristically ill-tempered refusal. Selmek has told officers in Paris that those anomalies began gnawing away at him, there and then. Yesterday, he was able to understand the reason. He discovered the secreted masterpiece. As did we.'

Bonbon shook his coppery head. 'Sorry, can we rewind, chief? Why didn't Lambert want to send for the fake from the Musée Matisse? Don't galleries secretly mark the works they lend? As long as the Musée got the same one back, what's the problem?'

'I gather that encrypted tagging is standard practice nowadays but the Musée's *Woman* hadn't been loaned out in years. I guess Lambert didn't want to initiate any procedure that would lead to the fake being examined more closely.'

'Got you.'

Interested parties were starting to gather at the office door. Concerned they might start wandering in, Darac gave Bonbon a nod. Grinning foxily, he got to his feet.

'Come on. There's nothing to see here. Break it up. Come on…'

None too happily, the group dispersed. Although the hiatus lasted only a few seconds, by the time Bonbon returned to his seat, Taylor seemed to have composed herself.

'Alright, I'm guilty. You're right about *Woman*. I know I should have taken it to the police but whatever you may think of me, I am a very loyal person and I couldn't bear the thought of Philippe, and Maggie, suffering the consequences. So I decided to just forget about it. After all, what harm had been done? No one at the Musée had missed the original painting in almost half a century.'

Granot studied the work. 'Not surprised. My niece does stuff like this all the time. She's eleven.'

Darac decided to pick up the pace. 'Opting to "just forget about" the painting is an interesting thought, Taylor – sorry, mademoiselle. But it's not true.'

There was blue fire in Taylor's eyes as she stared up at him.

'What you actually did was work out how you could profit from the knowledge that a rare and valuable stolen painting was sitting out of sight in your boss's study. Unlike the will, this wasn't a maybe, it was definite. A potential goldmine. But how could you best exploit it?' Darac got to his feet. 'Take over a second, would you, Granot?'

'You decided to put the bite on Monsieur de Lambert,' he said. 'He may not have had untold assets, but his current account, the one you so kindly helped him with, wasn't exactly a pauper's. Enjoying your brand new Merc, by the way? And that was just going to be the start, wasn't it?'

Taylor said nothing but as Darac went to pick up the Matisse, he noticed her kicking foot had sped up a couple of beats. 'Before you took that step,' he went on, 'you decided to open Lambert's cabinet and take another look at this.' He held up the painting in the manner of an auction-house porter. 'In handling it, you noticed something you hadn't seen before. A sliver of wood had been removed from one of the stretcher bars where it meets the frame at the back.' He turned it. 'See?'

She glanced at it and shrugged.

'Here.' He ran his finger along it. 'Forms a sort of slot. You looked closer and saw something else. Just visible to your keen young eyes was a thin white line. No?' She shook her head. 'Lambert, you were sure, would never have noticed it. He would be too rapt in the painted side of the work, the image of *Woman* herself. Whatever that white line was, it was paper thin. And *that*, you discovered on dismantling the frame, is just what it was: the edge of a sheet of paper sandwiched between the bar and the frame. The paper turned out to be a letter.'

'Rubbish,' she said, tugging her earring.

'It was *this* letter.' He reached into the inside pocket of his jacket and took out a sheet of A5. 'Dated 5 July 1964, it was written by one Alain Mesnel.'

Wiring Taylor to one of the electrician's wall sockets would scarcely have given her a greater shock. 'How... How did you—'

'Acquire this? It's not the actual letter, of course. Just a transcript.'

The detail seemed to offer her some sort of comfort. 'I'll read it to you: *Dear Philippe, First, well done on finding this letter. I didn't think you had it in you. There's no knowing what life will bring, is there? Who could have predicted what you seeing me painting at Villa Rose that day would lead to? So are you enjoying owning your very own Matisse, then? It's lovely, isn't it? I hope you'll still enjoy it when I tell you that what you've been looking at all this time is not a Matisse at all. It's a Mesnel!* Exclamation mark.'

'Brilliant.' Bonbon grinned, just as amused as when they had read the original at Crédit Bal-Med. 'Cheeky bugger.'

'The letter continues: *You see, I never did take the original off the wall at the Musée and swap it for what you've got there. I know we shook on the deal but I could never do such a thing. It's against the law and besides, I would never have got away with it. You can't just short-circuit the alarm wiring like I told you.*'

Taylor had stopped kicking the air altogether.

'There's more: *Lucky the original had just been cleaned or I wouldn't have got away with doing a new one for you, would I? You might have smelled the rat that was the new paint and varnish. Now Phil, if you're thinking of getting back at me or my wife over this, I've got something to tell you. Just as my job at the Musée gave me the chance to take photos of every square centimetre of the original painting, so you coming over to my place gave me the opportunity to take photos of every stage of our business deal. I had a remote camera hidden in the window. I've got shots of you handing over the money, the lot.*'

Darac tried to read the next sentence without any special emphasis. '*I'm pretty good at photography and the shots came out very well, by the way. Don't worry that I'll put the squeeze on you, Phil. I've got a heart. But don't try anything funny or I'll expose you to the whole world for what you are: a thieving art expert who's been fooled by a complete beginner. All the best, Alain. PS, if you fancy any Cézannes, I think I could manage one of them as well.*'

'That bit really kills me,' Bonbon spluttered, slapping his thigh. 'Priceless.'

Darac folded Alain's letter and returned it to his pocket. 'Obviously, mademoiselle, when you'd recovered from the shock, you did not put the letter back in the frame.'

Taylor's perfect face looked as if it were slowly being put through a shrink-wrapper.

Bonbon was still grinning. 'To think that for all those years, the old boy had been sneaking into his room, opening his secret cabinet and getting off on a complete fake. And he paid Alain Mesnel God knows how much for the privilege.'

It was a phenomenon that interested Darac but this was no time for intellectual debate. He set the painting down and resumed his perch on the desk. 'Your plan depended on Lambert never finding out that the *Woman at Asilah* on show at the Musée Matisse was the genuine, un-swapped original. If he ever realised he'd been duped, he might have destroyed his Mesnel replica and then you would have nothing with which to bargain. True, you had an incriminating letter but it was the flimsiest possible lever. Anybody could have written it; *you* could have. That was when you thought about the photographs Alain Mesnel had taken. If you could somehow lay your hands on those, you'd have documentary evidence of the crime being commissioned, the money handed over, everything. It would be excellent insurance.'

'No.' Her voice drying, she gave a little cough. 'Not true.'

'Would you like more water, Taylor?'

Unconcerned at Darac's use of her forename, she nodded and he went to the cooler.

'I'll go on. If you could obtain the photographs, it didn't matter whether Lambert destroyed his painting or not, you had a lever to prise open his wallet at will.'

'I'm not saying anything further until the lawyer and the US Consul get here.'

As he handed over the cup, their hands touched momentarily.

'Carry on, Granot, will you?'

'With pleasure. Your quest to find and secure the photos began as any enquiry does. Checking things, speculating, footslogging. You were like a one-woman police force—'

The angry cat had returned. 'Do *not* patronise me!'

'If you insist. You decided to find out what you could about Alain Mesnel, hoping some opening might present itself. Your skill at ingratiating yourself is well attested. Who knows what you might be able to pull off if you could find the man himself? I reckon you started with the local phone book and didn't have to check out too many Mesnels before you hit the bull's-eye. And, what a bonus! The address was just around the corner. It turned out Alain had died shortly after his involvement with Lambert but his widow might still have the photos. All you needed was to get her out of the way long enough to find them, and you could start blackmailing the man you were so devoted to.'

A little eyebrow semaphore and Darac was back in. 'There's

no need to go into great detail about what happened next is there, mademoiselle?' he said. 'Engineering the meeting with Jeanne Mesnel, putting in the house purchase offer, et cetera? It suited you both. Buying her the hot tub you knew would be yours one day was a shrewd move. You took to taking baths together. Every now and then, you would offer to run errands. "No, you stay here. I'll go." As always, nothing was too much trouble. And of course, you would occasionally have to go up to the house on your own account. For calls of nature, and so on.'

The reference made Taylor squirm.

'So while she was luxuriating in the hot tub, you were mounting a search for the envelope of photos. You didn't find them. Your plan to blackmail Lambert started to look more uncertain but you had killed two birds with one stone in your purchase of the villa. You thought Madame Mesnel was unlikely to live much longer so you wouldn't have to wait long to become its legal owner. That meant you would be freer to search the place. And of more immediate benefit, having spent every last euro of your savings to set up the house purchase, you would be spared any further monthly payments. But then you read about the Marcelline Boule *en viager* house sale case, and that got you thinking again.'

'More nonsense. I've never even heard of... whatever her name was.'

'Bonbon, refresh the mademoiselle's memory?'

'It began when one Jean-Jacques Philibert bought Madame Boule's house in Le Havre in 1989. It was all above board: fair price, fair bouquet payment, fair monthly rent. Madame Boule was eighty at the time and very ill. He was forty-one. But nineteen years later, he's still paying her rent when *he* pre-deceases *her*. Madame Boule, now almost a century old, is thinking of putting the place on the market again! Supposing Madame Mesnel hung on similarly? You might have found yourself losing your job, having nowhere to live as a result, and yet still be paying her for living in *your* house.'

'I've told you. I knew nothing about—'

Granot slapped the arm of his chair. 'You read the original article and follow-up pieces on the internet. You deleted your search history, of course, but our lab people found it on your hard drive.'

'So I read an article. What does that prove?'

Darac ran his hand through his hair, thought about it for a moment, then reached into his briefcase and took out a manila envelope. He tossed it on to the desk.

'Timing. Timing is everything. You had never taken out a safety deposit box in your life. Then just two days after Madame Mesnel died, three days before the body was discovered, you did precisely that. In the box we found the photographs and Alain's original letter—'

'You had it all along? So what you read out wasn't a transcript, it was a photocopy. You liar!' Taylor bit her lip so hard, beads of blood began to seep through the coral gloss. 'And you're lying about the lawyer and the Consul. They're not coming, are they?'

'I give you my word that they are, Taylor.'

For the first time, their eyes met and retained the connection. The amplitude on the range of Darac's emotions was wider than ever.

'Paul?' she said softly, leaning forward, keeping her eyes on his. 'I can explain why I had the photos and the letter under lock and key. It was to protect Philippe should Madame Mesnel ever decide to start blackmailing him.' Her voice dropped still further. 'May we continue alone?'

Bonbon and Granot shared a look. After a moment, Granot coughed, stagily. 'Uh… chief?'

Darac unlocked his gaze. 'Let's continue, shall we?' Taylor stiffened and sat back.

'Yesterday, mademoiselle, I re-interviewed Henri Lepic, a nice kid as you know, who had broken his leg, skateboarding. He hadn't initially told us the truth about the unseemly circumstances surrounding the accident because his fine, upstanding parents had drummed into him that he mustn't. At all costs, we the police must never find out what Henri had been up to because once we knew, the world at large would know and the family's reputation would be sullied forever. Or that's how they saw it. But help was at hand. The Lepics saw it as a sign of divine providence that the mother, a clerical assistant at Hôpital Saint-Roch, had access to the computer file detailing Henri's visit to A and E. All the humiliation that the boy was about to heap on the family could be averted, she realised, by simply altering the date of the visit on the file. Reckoning that if the police checked at all, we would look no further than the date, she did just that.'

Sitting behind Bonbon, Perand had the look of a dog who knew he was finally about to be let off the leash.

'But two things conspired against her,' Darac continued. 'The eagle eyes of that young man.' He indicated Perand. 'And the dead hand of fate. Enlighten the mademoiselle.'

'Henri's mother put the treatment date back a day from the 2nd to the 1st of January but it was too complicated to alter the other details. But that didn't matter. The time and date of Henri's admission on the file matching the Lepics' version of events, she was right that we wouldn't have looked any further. But then I noticed the name of the doctor cited as setting the leg. There was just one problem. At 16.47 on the 1st he wasn't at work. He was teaching a class, a special event for New Year's Day. I know because I'm one of his students.'

Taylor seemed undisturbed by the development.

'So the world is full of liars. What bearing does this have on anything?'

'Plenty,' Darac said. 'It was from about two o'clock on the afternoon of Saturday, January 2nd that young Henri was out stunting on his skateboard. He was trying to emulate people like your countryman, Troy Pinto. They don't just scoot along roads and pavements, these daredevils. They get up high. They defy gravity.'

Blood began to drain from Taylor's face.

'Aping the approach of his heroes, Henri somehow succeeded in getting on to the wall that forms part of the barrier between Chemin Leuze and Rue Balmette. That was his first misdemeanour – trespass. He was working out what sort of stunt to perform when something distracted him. Away to his left, he saw Madame Mesnel taking a soak in the hot tub, as was sometimes her custom, in the nude. His interest waned after no more than a few moments but as he was about to return to what he was doing, he saw an elderly black man walk out of the house and join her.'

Taylor was sitting so absolutely still, she looked like a waxwork figure of herself.

'More out of curiosity than anything, he watched as they made love. He knows he shouldn't have but he did. Misdemeanour number two – voyeurism. He was still watching as Madame Mesnel suddenly became distressed and clutched her left arm. The man panicked, not knowing what to do for the best. She managed to say something and he got out of the tub and hurried back to the house. Less than two minutes later, he emerged with his mobile but he aborted the call when he saw he was too late. Madame Mesnel was dead. He got back into the water and held her in his arms for a moment. Then taking his champagne glass, he returned to the house, dressed, and made his exit.'

'And what does this tragic drama have to do with me?'

'Everything. You arrived right in the middle of it.'

'I... did not.'

'The boy saw you dodge behind the wall where the waste bins are kept. As Madame Mesnel became distressed, you watched the man get out of the tub to call an ambulance. The moment he was out of sight, you stepped forward.' His hands balling into fists, Darac looked Taylor in the eyes. 'The boy assumed you were going to comfort the lady.'

'Lady? Letting that fat old ape screw her!' She looked startled

357

at her own words. 'No. I meant—'

'I think I understand why what you saw upset you.'

'Oh spare me that... garbage!'

'As you approached her, you had a shock. She held out a hand to you. You realised she was recovering. Whatever had happened to her heart had been more of a warning shot than a potentially fatal attack. All that uncertainty came back into your mind. She might live for years, mightn't she, this vile old woman? In your heightened state, you decided to make sure she didn't. Here was a golden opportunity to advance all of your plans with one simple action. And considering the circumstances, you knew nobody would suspect you of anything. There would be an investigation, of course. But once you had charmed your way through that, you would be home free, as you Americans say.

'But was there time to murder Madame Mesnel? In her condition, holding her under the water for a few seconds was all it would take. If the man caught you, you would simply have said you were trying to save her. It would have looked more or less the same. But you didn't need to. You took her hand, pulled her under the water—'

'This is all lies,' she said, shaking. 'Lies.'

'You murdered her and got back to your hiding place just before her lover reappeared. Then things got even better for you. The man, weeping, started erasing traces that he'd been at the scene. He felt guilty, you see.'

Her lips stretching over her teeth like a tourniquet, Taylor essayed a smile. 'How should I know?' She took a further sip of water. 'I wasn't there.'

'After he'd gone, you went back into the house to search for the precious envelope of photographs knowing you would not be disturbed. You found them. At long last, you believed everything was set fair.'

Taylor appeared to gain strength. 'You and the boy are wrong.' She tugged an earring. 'You're forgetting my alibi. At the time all this is supposed to have happened, I was with Philippe de Lambert.' She uttered the man's name as if it were a trophy. 'Remember?'

'At the time you both swore you were together, Philippe was actually having paid sex with a schoolteacher by the name of… we'll call her Violette. You have no alibi, Taylor, and we have an eyewitness to what you did at the hot tub.'

'No!'

A knock on the open door heralded the unbidden entry of lawyer Hector Duclaux.

'Execrable!' He was by Taylor's side in the blinking of an eye. 'The American Consul has just arrived, my dear.' He fixed Darac with a look. 'I absolutely insist you release my client. Immediately. Release her or charge her.'

'Alright,' Darac said. 'Taylor Walters-Halberg, I charge you with the murder of Jeanne Honorine Mesnel…'

54

The first move Darac made after Taylor had been charged was to arrange for Ridge's release. He was still culpable of the post-facto offences he'd committed at the scene but the word from the Palais was that the matter would be dropped. 'I know it's hugely hard to take, Ridge, but learning how Jeanne really died must be some sort of comfort to you.'

Pain was etched deeply into the man's face. 'If I had done what I should have, it would never have happened at all. Jeanne would still be grooving around, sipping champagne and listening to the Duke.'

What could Darac say? 'I called Didier. He's *au fait* with everything. Relieved you'll be back for tomorrow night. Delighted, in fact.'

Ridge nodded, accepting the compliment with his usual

gravity. 'You going to play?'

'Too much to do. Especially with Gilles Voska still at large. But I may be able to drop in last thing just for a listen.'

Another senatorial nod. 'Thanks, Garfield.' He held out his hand. 'I'm sorry, man.'

The two men embraced and Ridge walked free.

It was 5 pm before Darac and Granot threw in the towel. Neither of them had had any sleep the night before and the call they had just concluded with Maggie de Lambert's solicitor seemed to draw a line under the day.

'Koffee, chief?'

'Why not?'

The big man hauled himself up on to his feet but, for the moment, just stood, staring.

'Forgotten the way?'

There was no cause for concern. Indented into the carpet was a trail of Granot-shaped footprints leading unerringly to the machine. Giving himself a slap on the chops, he set out on the pilgrimage once more. 'Poor old Madame de Lambert, eh?'

Within the past hour, confirmation had come from the medics that the woman had withstood the first crisis that could have killed her, but she hadn't withstood the second.

'Learning that Taylor had betrayed their bond of trust was just one blow too many, wasn't it? Especially after she had made such huge provision for the girl in her will.'

'Not that Miss America knew that, of course.' Granot handed over the espresso. 'Or she would never have embarked on the journey that ended at the hot tub.' He shook his grizzled head. 'Taking an old lady's hand and holding her under the water. Ai, ai, ai.'

'And it was all for nothing.' Darac drained his espresso. 'What will happen to the Mesnel villa now? Might Cristelle still inherit?'

'If she has the stomach and the wherewithal to contest it, she probably will, yes.'

Trying to assimilate all that had happened, Darac clasped his hands behind his head, sat back in his chair and stared at the ceiling. Nothing was said for a couple of minutes.

It was Granot who finally spoke. 'It's no wonder Henri wound up falling off the wall, is it? Witnessing sex and murder.'

'Henri, the global teenager…' Darac felt as if he were back where it all began. 'You know, in a way, there's been a theme running through this case. The changes toward what Ridge Clay calls "France Lite; the Coca-Colonisation of the planet", and so on.'

'*Theme?*' Granot grunted. 'We've been investigating a murder, not throwing a party.'

'I'm quite serious. And the irony is that but for a thirteen-year-old French boy mad for all things American, "Miss America" would have got away with the murder.'

As rare as an endangered species, Granot's concession face was there in plain sight. 'Henri wouldn't have caught her in the act if he'd been playing football, I'll grant you.'

His mind on themes, Darac saw others. Cristelle, Taylor and Adèle were all motherless girls who, in one form or another, had suffered at the hands of their fathers. He decided to keep it to himself. He'd tried Granot's patience enough for one day.

The big man downed his coffee. 'One thing I will take from this case is Perand finally turning up trumps. I'd wondered if I'd ever say that, believe me.'

'Perand winning File Ferret of the Month is a first, alright. Although he did get lucky over Dr Whatshisname teaching the class he's started.'

Granot spluttered, wonderment giving way to what looked suspiciously like mirth. 'You'll never guess what the class is.'

Darac was already grinning. 'Tell me.'

'Kickboxing! He's only doing it because Flak does, I'll bet.

Can you believe it?'

'I thought he was looking a bit more…'

'Awake?'

'And a bit less…'

'Weedy? You must have good eyesight!'

Fuelled by their exhaustion, the two of them laughed far too much about it.

'Let's get out of here, Granot.'

'No stamina, you acting commissaires.' Granot consulted his agenda as they rode one of the building's whisper-quiet lifts down to the basement. 'Is Malraux off this evening?'

'No, on. Why?'

'Some of the lads were talking about taking him to a bar and getting him legless. Only thing we haven't tried.'

'It'll have to wait. He's following funny money around the Babazouk.'

'With Flak?'

'I hope so. They're both rostered.'

Granot rattled the phlegm in his throat. 'How the hell do those two work together?'

'If he had any sense, he'd take his lead from her. But he hasn't got any sense.'

'When are you going to eat your guitars, by the way?'

'What?'

' "If Taylor Walters-Halberg turns out to be the killer, I'll eat my guitars," you said.'

'All I can say in my defence is that she was a brilliant actress from the start. The way she kept a check on our progress by engineering meetings with me in which just a little more was promised each time? It was brilliantly done.' Ridge's performance, Darac couldn't help thinking, had been more impressive still. Yes, he understood his old friend's reasons. But it wasn't the greatest moment they had shared.

'So Taylor was "a brilliant actress". And so was Brigitte

Andreani. Maybe Cristelle was. You know something? You're not very good at women just now, are you?'

'See you later, Granot.'

Perhaps, Darac reflected, he had *never* been 'good' at women. Conversely, women seemed to be able to read him. He was still exercised, though, by Angeline's assessment that *hit someone, make love, play the guitar* were his first-call solutions to any crisis.

As he walked to his car, he couldn't shift the image of Taylor being led away to the cells. Other images piled in on top: Jeanne's bloated corpse; Brigitte's slit throat; Rama pulsing rhythm and Rama broken; cigarette smoke blown away.

So one goddess had drowned another. Drowned her for gain and because she thought that, given the circumstances, she was certain to get away with it. It was as clear a proof of Agnès's axiom 'damaged people damage others' as he could think of.

After a couple of hours' shuteye, Darac rang Dr Tan.

'We are very pleased with Rama. Perhaps it's your CD.'

'He's surfacing?'

'We're hopeful he'll be rejoining us quite soon.'

'And what are his chances now of making—?'

'We don't know yet about the degree of recovery.'

At that moment, a hope, an idea – something – flared brightly in Darac's consciousness. With it came the absolute conviction that Rama was going to be fine.

He could have used similar extra-sensory help on two other questions that concerned him. First: Voska. The various agencies still looking seemed no closer to finding him. In the morning, Darac intended to instigate a squad review into the manhunt. Every move had to be gone over and it was clear that the Brigade needed to be more active in the search, less dependent on Aix and the others.

The second question concerned a detail Darac had spotted in one of the safety deposit box photos, a stray from the Mesnels'

New York trip. With the Manhattan skyline as a backdrop, it featured Alain and Jeanne sipping champagne from entwined glasses. The shot was an exact replica of an LP cover known to jazz fans everywhere: *Cin-Cin!* by legendary singer Jessica O'Kane. Darac alone had spotted the detail. Indeed, he was the only officer in the Brigade who *could* have spotted it. Suspecting it might have a further role to play in the story, he drove to the Caserne Auvare, where the packing cases containing Jeanne Mesnel's property were being stored for the moment.

A familiar face greeted him. 'Captain? Haven't seen you since the move.'

'*Temporary* move, Georges. Still got your Gaggia coffee machine?'

'This is the Caserne. We can do what we like over here. Fancy one?'

Two espressos later, Darac went to the store and removed Jeanne Mesnel's poster from its crate. After everything he had come to know about its subject and its creator, what did he feel about it now?

The question made him think first about Philippe de Lambert's fake Matisse. He had taken as much from the work as if it had been the real thing. Suppose he had discovered the work hadn't been genuine; would those same brushstrokes that had amazed and delighted him all those years suddenly have lost their power?

Darac called to mind the lithographs he'd enjoyed while he was waiting to meet Taylor for the first time. He thought he recognised them as the work of Jean Cocteau and he'd looked at the wall label to check. Would he have taken less pleasure in them if they had proved to be the work of a 'lesser' artist?

He turned back to the poster. Inevitably, the drummer in the shot would always put him in mind of Rama N'Pata. Rama who had battles still to fight but who might yet realise his true potential. And the poster would always conjure up memories of Taylor and to a lesser extent, Adèle Voska. They too had been damaged by the accidental circumstances of their lives. Damaged beyond repair, it seemed, in Taylor's case. And then there was Ridge, a black man plunged into a nightmare of conflicting allegiances, delivered from part of his anguish by the belated intercession of a young white kid.

So despite everything, was Darac still blown away by *Blown Away by the Brass Section*? Yes. In fact, it had taken on an infinitely greater resonance for him.

The time had come. He turned the work over. As in Lambert's 'Matisse', a thin white line was just visible between the top of the frame and the print backing. Anyone seeking to hang the poster might see the line, but to one person in particular, the five-word song title written in black ink just above it was an instruction. The words were *Look for the Silver Lining*, the song Cristelle remembered Jeanne singing to her as a child.

Carefully, Darac dismantled the frame. The white paper sliver proved to be the top edge of a small envelope. On it was a message written in Jeanne Mesnel's hand, dated 22 July 2009 – around the time of Cristelle's surprise visit:

My dear Cristelle,

Do you remember our song? I hope so. As you are reading this, it means that you decided not to reject this gift but to keep it as a memento of your once beautiful grandmother; almost as beautiful as you, in fact. Because you accepted this knowing there was nothing of any value in it for you, you will find something of interest in the envelope. Perhaps you will remember me wearing it when you were little. Perhaps you will remember playing with it, yourself. Perhaps it's how you acquired your love of jewellery. It may not appear particularly special to you but it once belonged to someone who was very special indeed and therein lies its value. Should you wish to sell it, you will find eager buyers. But I hope you will keep it. Don't grab for things, Cristelle, and they will come your way. Keep your heart full of joy and gladness.

With all my love,
Grande-mère Jeanne

Darac opened the envelope. There it was: the detail that had caught his eye in the Manhattan photograph. Half-hidden by her bubbling champagne glass, Jeanne's ring finger had borne more than just her wedding band. Where Alain had obtained the garish concoction of base metal and paste that Jessica O'Kane had sported on the *Cin-Cin!* album cover, Darac had no idea. And he could only hazard a guess at how much such a ring might be worth to a collector. Maybe he'd ask Bonbon about it, sometime.

Rolling the ring around his fingers, he was entertained by the thought that Alain might have faked it. Perhaps he'd even created the original. Whatever its provenance, Darac realised he was in a position to play God over what happened next. He could ensure Cristelle received it whether she had decided to keep the poster or not. The question didn't detain him long. He took a last look at the ring, returned it to the envelope and sealed it back into the frame. In due time, the solicitor would contact Cristelle about the poster and then it was up to her. It was what Jeanne had wanted. And Darac had to be true to his Muse. He'd promised her that.

55

As things panned out, exchanging texts and calls with Ridge and Didier was as close as Darac got to the DMQ's big band gig at the Blue Devil. The consensus was that it had gone only reasonably well. It was hardly surprising under the circumstances.

He crossed Place Garibaldi, casting a long shadow across its empty colonnades. After the day he'd had, his brain felt like tenderised meat but one thought occurred to him: for the first time in some days, he felt sure no one was following him.

He stepped into Rue Neuve and turned into Ruelle Fente with no sense that beyond its dogleg, a malevolent presence was waiting. A presence to whom he unconsciously signalled his increasing vulnerability by closing his eyes and yawning as he reached for his keys. He dropped them as a shock of pain wired his head to his feet and then numbed his left side. Feeling a hand closing around his windpipe, he knew he had to react immediately. He felt his attacker buckle slightly as he landed a hard elbow into his ribs but the hold around his throat intensified, threatening unconsciousness. He tried to jack-knife but explosive movement was impossible. Then, somehow, he managed to twist slightly and gain sufficient purchase on the ground to drag his attacker forward. They banged through the opened gate into Place Saint-Sépulcre. The man was still crushing Darac's windpipe and thudding punches into the side of his head. He retaliated with everything he had: back-heels to the shins; elbows to the ribs; all the time trying to break free. Nothing working, Darac understood a terrible truth. He was overmatched. The suffocating hold tightened and blood began to spill from his mouth.

Refusing to give up, he made one last effort. *Come on!* Instead, his world turned upside down, cobblestones flying under and over him as his attacker executed a body-slamming throw. Something hard and sharp dug into his back. With every rasping breath, Darac felt his spine splinter and separate. As helpless as a stunned calf, he saw the bullet-hard skull of his attacker looming above him. Darac tried desperately to move but he couldn't. He was done for. His last image of this world was not going to be of Angeline's face, nor of the Blue Devil's bandstand, nor of the Babazouk from Château Park. It was going to be of a psycho named Gilles Voska savouring his kill. Darac closed his eyes, trying to conjure an image of his parents. He couldn't picture them.

'I'm disappointed in you, *Acting Commissaire* Darac.'

The red sea gave way to fog. The fog gave way to nothingness. By the time the gunshots cracked out, Darac was dead to the world already. The shooter emerged through the exhaust smoke from his revolver, his eyes glued not on the man he'd shot but on the twisted, blood-flecked figure of his victim.

'Are you still alive?'

Darac moved slightly. Malraux knew that one kick under the chin would deliver the coup de grâce he'd stolen from Voska. He'd say the dead man had done it. Malraux had been tailing Darac for days looking for an opportunity to take him out. And now Voska had laid it on a plate for him. He looked up at the shuttered windows. No lights had come on. No one appeared to be looking out. It gave him no comfort that he would probably be doing Darac a favour. If he lived, he was sure to be paralysed.

'My God!'

He looked around to see Flaco running toward him. 'Is he alright?'

'I... don't know.'

'Call an ambulance!' She knelt to take Darac's pulse. 'He's still alive.'

Malraux stayed put. 'Let's move him,' he said, apparently concerned. 'Take his legs.'

'No!' Flaco took off her coat and used it as a blanket as Malraux dialled 112.

A dressing-gown-clad woman came running out of the shadows. 'Forget the call. I already made it.' Suzanne lowered her cheek to Darac's mouth, simultaneously feeling his carotid pulse. 'Was the rate speeding or slowing?'

Suzanne's focus and professionalism instantly apparent, Flaco ceded control. 'Slowing.'

'It's weak and thready...' She jetted a glance at Malraux. 'You wanted to move him! What do they teach you?'

'How to shoot straight is one thing. Or he'd be dead already.'

Another was never, under any circumstances, to give up.

56

A white screen. A skull rippling as if underwater. Pain… Stick… Sticks… 'Voska!'

'It's alright. It's alright. You're quite safe here.'

The angel looked kind. She looked the kindest angel in the…

'He's gone again.'

It was another three days before Darac emerged fully into consciousness.

'My spine hurts like hell.'

'You were thrown onto your back, landing on the pointer of the sundial in your courtyard. The force of the impact was such that your spinal cord…'

As the nurse spoke, the Aixois Police Nationale officer almost paralysed by Voska came into Darac's head. He recalled his words to Frènes. Critical words about how slow the officer had been to cuff the man. 'I can be a bastard sometimes.'

'Pardon?'

'I'm not paralysed, am I?'

'You should be fine in time. Move your hands as a tester.'

Darac tried.

'Feet…? Good. Toes…? Excellent! That will do for the time being.'

'Am I allowed visitors yet?'

'You've had half of France in, already. Your parents have been virtually living here.'

There seemed little point in correcting the assumption that Barbara, his father's current squeeze, was his mother.

'And you've had several musicians and other colleagues. That

Monsieur Frènes is a lovely man, isn't he?'

'Beautiful.'

'You play in the police band then, I take it?'

'Yes I do. I want to sleep now.'

'Garfield. You kick anybody's ass today?'

'Oh yes. Lost count.'

'You sound strong. That's good, man.'

'I'm feeling strong enough. Khara here?'

'She'll be back.'

'She's been here? I don't remember.'

'She's been here. So what's new?'

Darac drifted off occasionally in the conversation that followed. When it finally came time for Ridge to leave, he had the look of someone who had saved the best until last.

'I'm putting plans together for something. Every July, we're going to have a week of special gigs and events at the club to honour Jeanne. The Blown Away by the Jazz Festival, I'm going to call it. How's that sound?'

Darac patted the man's knee. 'It's a great idea.'

'It's no idea. It's happening. Made my first signing already.'

'Wonderful. Who?'

'Oh, nobody much. Just Mister Sonny Rollins.' Ridge produced a bed-shaking laugh. 'He's got a day free before he plays Juan Les Pins.'

'Yeah, of course.'

Ridge couldn't possibly have signed The Great Man. Could he?

'Round up those who couldn't be bothered visiting and put them on a charge.'

'They all came,' Granot said. 'Agnès was looking well, I must say.'

'Whoa, whoa. Agnès broke her round-the-world trip? Just to—'

'You don't remember? Me, Bonbon and Frankie had a great chat with her. She's all ready to come back, she says. How's that for news?'

Darac would have punched the air if he could. 'Brilliant.' He exhaled as if he'd been holding in that breath for the past six months. 'Agnès back? Wow!'

'So we'll all be together again. With the addition of Malraux. Aka your saviour.'

'Did he have to shoot Voska? Couldn't he have just subdued him?'

'*You* couldn't. And where's your gratitude? The arsehole had been trotting around after you for days, he said. Hiding here, dodging there, convinced Voska was going to show up to ice you. Malraux could have gone home after his shift with Flaco. Instead, he decided to take a quick look around first. Good job he did.'

'It doesn't sound like the Malraux I know. I *am* grateful. Of course. But now Voska's dead, we'll never know how he managed to come and go unseen.'

'Actually, we do.' Granot went no further.

'You're waiting for your lawyer to be present? Tell me.'

'He… cycled.'

Darac laughed. It hurt. 'Cycled, of course. Why didn't we think of that before?'

Granot's expression didn't change.

'For God's sake, tell me you're not serious.'

'I wish I could.'

'He cycled all the way from Marseille?'

'In two day-long stages. On the Thursday, when he jumped you, he'd ridden in from Draguignan where he kept a couple of rooms. And it looks as if it was there that he spent the night after his bloody encounter with the N'Pata brothers. It was also from

371

there that he rode incognito to Beaulieu and back, in order to murder Brigitte Andreani. And then he drove to Aix where things got more complicated for him, for Lieutenant Henri Clerc, and for a young mother called Alicia Simon.'

'Just a minute. Draguignan must be eighty-odd kilometres from here. Marseille further still. How did he complete all those journeys unseen? He wore an invisibility cape?'

'Just the opposite. Under that black skin suit he had on, he was wearing a complete pro-cycling outfit. Garish pink and blue. You could see it for kilometres.'

'Jesus Christ. What is it with this country and bloody bicycles?'

'He was so ludicrously visible and he so looked the part, nobody thought to—'

' "Nobody thought to." There's been far too much of that in this case.' Granot gave him a look. 'I'm including myself in that. If I'd picked up Berthe Lepic's use of the word "ambulant", obviously a medical term, we might have got to the stunt she pulled at the hospital sooner.'

'Rubbish. Alright, we never asked her what kind of work she did but she could have picked the word up watching hospital dramas on TV.'

'Let's move on. What's been the outcome for Malraux?'

'He's going to be decorated.'

'Good.'

Nothing was said for a moment, then Granot decided he'd waited long enough.

'Haven't I always predicted this would happen? Eh? I've told you time and time again that it's too dangerous for a *flic* to live in the Babazouk. Haven't I? And so has Bonbon.'

'Yes, yes.'

'Move out! And here's a final thought for you. Take that Suzanne with you. She's sexy, caring, bright. Everybody thinks she'd be perfect for you. Why look any further?'

Granot the matchmaker. If it didn't hurt to laugh, Darac

would have been in pieces.

'She's a friend. And I'm very fond of her. But that's all.'

'At the moment.'

'She was a mate of Angeline's, anyway.'

'And that disqualifies her?'

'I think it disqualifies me.'

'Don't get up.'

'Suzanne. Great to see you.'

The woman's cheery disposition was therapy in itself. 'Just a flying visit, I'm on my way to Endoscopy. You're doing very well, I hear.'

'I hear that too. And a lot of that is due to you. If the ambulance had turned up a couple of minutes later, I could've been spending the rest of my life in a wheelchair, peeing into a bag and generally feeling sorry for myself.'

'You can thank the fact that I was changing shifts from nights to days. I couldn't sleep so I got up to read. About ten minutes later, I heard this big rumpus. The rest you know.'

'I won't forget it, Suzanne. And are *you* alright? I don't suppose you've ever seen anyone shot dead before.'

'I'm fine. It was a shock, though. It even shocked the officer who fired, I think.'

'Ah, yes?'

'He froze. Just stood there, looking around, not knowing what to do. Then he wanted to move you, for crying out loud.'

'You can train all you like for these things but it's different when it happens for real.'

Suzanne didn't buy it. 'That young female officer knew what to do. He panicked. She didn't. And it made all the difference.'

'Yvonne Flaco is her name. A top girl.'

'Listen, I've got to run.'

'Suzanne, would you do me a favour? On my bedside cabinet

at home there's a book, *Another Country* by James Baldwin. Could you bring it in for me?'

'Sure.' She indicated his locker. 'Keys in here?'

'There's a fob in the drawer at the back.'

Suzanne found them. 'Right, I'm on my way. Oh, I nearly forgot. I so enjoyed seeing Angeline again.'

Darac's pulse quickened. 'Angeline? She came?'

'Don't you remember?'

'No. Was she—?'

'She was just the same,' Suzanne said, smiling.

'Did she give any...? Did she say—?'

Suzanne squeezed his arm. 'Paul. She was just the same.'

Three days later, Darac was sufficiently recovered to take a slow spin around the hospital in a wheelchair. His first port of call was Intensive Care. As a favour to Suzanne, a nurse allowed him access to Rama's room. There was no longer any *beep... phhht, beep... phhht* measuring out the boy's existence: the ventilator had been turned off the day before. The heart-rate monitor had been set to silent. Rama still looked broken, swollen and bruised and he was still connected up to metres of tubing but he was awake and breathing normally.

Their eyes met but Rama's reaction was way behind the beat. When it came, the slightest of smiles, it moved Darac to tears. Before he could say anything, Dr Sibile craned his head around the door.

'You're allowed visitors now? I don't remember authorising that.'

'Sorry. You get used to going where you're not supposed to in my line.'

'One minute then, Captain.' Sibile glanced at his watch. 'Just one, I mean it.'

After all that had happened, what could be said in sixty

seconds? The clock ticked on.

'So… not listening to the Elvin?'

Rama's words came out in a blurred, slow-motion monotone. 'Aren't I? I can still hear it in my head. They told me you brought it. Thanks.'

Darac wondered if he should mention Modibo. Or Voska. No, it could wait.

'Why are you wearing… that?' Rama said.

'I had an accident, also. Be out in a day or two.'

'Visiting over!'

Darac's spine felt a tremor of pain as he looked to the door. 'I'm leaving now, nurse.'

He turned back to Rama. 'Take care of yourself, Sticks. I'll be in again.'

With each day that passed, Darac witnessed Rama regain more and more sovereignty over his body and mind. Finally, he felt able to broach most of the questions for which he needed answers. Frènes had agreed to postpone formal interviews.

Darac's reading of the N'Patas' relationship with Voska proved correct and he accepted Rama's statement that he had never heard of Madame Jeanne Mesnel nor knew of any plan to shoot a video involving her. The revelation that Voska had murdered Modibo on that dark night came as no surprise to the young man. It devastated him, nevertheless. News of Brigitte's fate only deepened his grief.

'What's the story with Voska, Sticks? What did he have over you?'

'My name *is* Rama N'Pata and I am a French citizen. Modibo wasn't.'

'He wasn't your brother, then?'

'Not by blood. My real brother died back in Mali. The man you knew as Modibo was his best friend, Moctar. They were so alike, everyone used to call them "the twins". Moctar always looked out for him. And then he looked out for me. I loved them both.'

'So that's how Moctar could pass as Modibo. But how did Voska come to know that?'

'With the tightening up on immigration, the quotas and everything else, Moctar got cold feet about being here. He needed better papers than a borrowed passport. He talked to a man. That man talked to someone else. Talk, talk, talk until finally, he talked to Voska. It was the biggest mistake of his life.' He closed his eyes. 'Of both of our lives.'

There was a rhythmic knock on the door.

Rama opened his eyes. Darac turned his wheelchair. A man with a beer belly and a ponytail was standing there.

'Fancy a jam?' Marco said.

57

The club was packed, the evening was spring-like, and Pascal the doorman had been looking forward to his break for the past half-hour. He was firing up a second cigarette when across the avenue, a woman got out of a car, walked around to the passenger door and began escorting a hobbling figure toward him. Pascal grinned.

'Darac! Good to see you.'

'Same here, man.'

Pascal turned to Darac's escort, running his eye over her with scarcely disguised approval. Full-figured women with luxuriant black hair and green eyes had that effect on him.

'I've never seen a couple with heads of hair like yours! You two ever have kids, they're going to be the super locks babies! The hair world champions, man!' Producing his toothiest grin, he extended his hand. 'You must be Suzanne.'

'Sorry.' She shook Pascal's hand. 'But thanks for the thought.'

'Ah. I thought you must be his nurse friend. Nurse neighbour. Just nurse, I mean.'

'Pas?' Darac put his hand on the man's shoulder. 'It's alright. This is Captain Francine Lejeune of the Brigade Criminelle. We're colleagues. OK?'

Frankie confirmed it with a smile.

'Got you.' Pascal grinned at her once more. 'But you still have great hair. And also, may I say —'

'Many in?' Darac said.

'For Gilad Atzmon? You can't move. And, for once, not just on the bandstand.'

'Great. See you later.'

They walked toward the light and the sounds spilling up from below. Frankie paused at the top of the steps.

'These risers are very deep. With your back, it won't be easy.'

Blown Away by the Brass Section wouldn't make it easy, either. Darac stood for some moments before he accepted Frankie's arm and took the plunge. 'This guy Atzmon's great but he can be pretty full on. Hope you'll be able to stand it.'

'So do I.'

They came to a dead halt under the poster.

'What are you thinking, Paul?'

There was so much to say, he didn't know where to begin. But he knew where not to.

'I'm thinking it's a pity Christophe couldn't make it tonight.'

Their eyes met in a way they never quite had before.

'Me too,' she said, at length.

A slow-burning smile morphing into an effortful clench, Darac reached up and touched the poster as they passed underneath it and continued into the club.

ACKNOWLEDGEMENTS

My wife Liz has been there for me during every stage of the creation of the Captain Darac Mysteries. Without the benison of her discerning eye, good humour and encouragement, the experience of writing this second novel in the series would have been a very different one. Our immediate family, Rob, Clare, Katey and Bryan, has also been a huge source of inspiration and help. First call players, all.

Others, too, have played a significant role. For her invaluable insights on the text, my thanks to Susan Woodall. For their many and various kindnesses, thanks to Lisa Hitch, Boris Blouin, Jacky Ananou, Fabien Caillaud and Richard Reynolds.

A particular debt of gratitude is owed to Commandant Jean-Baptiste Zuccarelli of Nice's Commissariat Foch. And as ever, for her all-round support and for her translation work both from texts and during in-situ interviews with officers of the Police Nationale, my special thanks to Katherine Roddwell

ABOUT THE AUTHOR

Peter Morfoot has written plays and sketch shows for BBC radio and TV and is the author of the "cult classic" (*Time Out*) satirical novel, *Burksey*. He has lectured in film, holds a PhD in Art History, and has spent over thirty years exploring the life of the boulevards and back streets of the French Riviera, the setting for his acclaimed series of crime novels featuring Captain Paul Darac of Nice's Brigade Criminelle. He lives in Cambridge with his wife Liz.

TRACK PLAYLIST OF ARTISTS AND NUMBERS
REFERENCED IN *FATAL MUSIC*

Django Reinhardt: To loosen up, Darac always plays through
a chorus of 'Limehouse Blues' before taking the stand with his
band, the Didier Musso Quintet.

Charlie Mingus: 'Better Git It In Your Soul'. The gospel-infused
gallop that opens the celebrated *Ah Um* album.

Thelonious Monk: The notoriously difficult-to-play 'Brilliant
Corners' is part of the soundscape of the novel.

Duke Ellington Orchestra: 'Flirtibird' from *Anatomy of a Murder,
part of character Jeanne Mesnel's record collection in the novel*.

Charles Trenet: Legendary singer loved by France's older
generation. 'Douce France'.

Jean Sablon: France's answer to Bing Crosby, 'J'attendrai' one of
many huge hits.

Thelonious Monk: 'Ba-Lue Bolivar Ba-Lues-Are'. Off-kilter
blues à la Monk.

Woody Shaw: 'Bemsha Swing'. The Monk tune here played by
trumpeter Shaw and his group which features one of Darac's
favourite pianists, Geri Allen.

Martin Taylor: 'Nuages' Darac greatly admires British guitarist
Martin Taylor. Hear why in this version of the classic Django
tune.

Shelley Manne and his Men: 'Whisper Not' from - *At The Black Hawk Vol 3*, a favourite tune from one of Darac's favourite series of albums.

Miles Davis: 'Milestones' from the landmark album of the same name.

Louis Armstrong and his Hot 5: 'Heebie Jeebies', a classic from 1926.

Louis Armstrong's All Stars: Swinging 1955 version of 'When You're Smiling'.

Bill Evans: a great out-of-hours tune, 'You Must Believe In Spring', title track from from the album.

Bill Evans: 'Sometime Ago'. Same mood; same album.

Sonny Rollins: 'St Thomas', iconic opening track of the *Saxophone Colossus* album.

Sonny Rollins: Darac loves the beat change in 'Asiatic Raes' from *Newk's Time*.

Count Basie Orchetra : "Slow as molasses on Mogadon yet still swings," is Darac's verdict on 'L'il Darlin' ' a new number in the DMQ's eclectic repertoire.

Miles Davis: 'Solea' a track from *Sketches of Spain*, Davis's third collaboration with composer/arranger Gil Evans.

Sonny Rollins: 'A Night In Tunisia', a searching performance by the reeds man from *A Night At The Village Vanguard*.

Lester Young: Mellow tones from "Pres" in 'Crazy Over Jazz' from *Blue Lester* .

John Coltrane: Mellower still. 'I Wish I Knew' from *Ballads*.

Cecil Taylor: avant-garde pianist of uncompromising complexity. 'Question.'

Ornette Coleman: free-playing reeds man. One of Darac's favourites – 'Eventually.'

Sun Ra: Professed cosmic connections and traditional big band stylings – an eccentric combination that appeals to Darac. 'Horoscope' from *Jazz In Silhouette*.

Sonny Rollins: Darac loves the muscular work-out for tenor sax that is 'G-Man.'

Orchestra Baobab: Exponents of many of the signature sounds of African music, this brilliant outfit from Senegal is one of Darac's favourites, especially live.
'On Verra Ça' from *Specialists In All Styles*.

Bruce Forman: The U.S guitarist is one of many contemporary players revered by Darac. 'Chasin' The Blues' from *Coast To Coast*.

Martha Tilton: 'These Foolish Things'. "A cigarette that bears a lipstick's traces..." By the end of the novel, the lyric will never mean the same to Darac.

Chet Baker: 'Look For The Silver Lining'. Ditto.

Kenny Barron: In Darac's assessment, the pianist has no equal. 'How Deep Is The Ocean' from *Minor Blues*.

Gilad Atzmon: 'Lust For Sale' from his Orient House Ensemble's *Nostalgico* album.